Mortal Fear

Mortal Fear

Scott and
Denise Ciencin

**An original novel based on the hit television series
by Joss Whedon**

SIMON PULSE

NEW YORK LONDON TORONTO SYDNEY SINGAPORE

Historian's Note: This story takes place in the
sixth season of *Buffy the Vampire Slayer.*

First Simon Pulse edition September 2003

™ and © 2003 Twentieth Century Fox Film Corporation.
All rights reserved.

SIMON PULSE
An imprint of Simon & Schuster
Children's Publishing Division
1230 Avenue of the Americas
New York, NY 10020

The text of this book was set in Times.
Printed in the United States of America.
2 4 6 8 10 9 7 5 3 1
Library of Congress Control Number 2003108402
ISBN 0-7434-2771-8

To Jim and Lauria Bush-Resko, Tom Hurxthal,
Martin and Michele Nicholas, and Renelle
Desjardin, with love

Acknowledgments

We would like to thank Lisa Clancy, Micol Ostow, and Lisa Gribbin at Simon & Schuster, and Debbie Olshan at Fox, Goth Wiccan Lauryn Panaccio, and Jeff Mariotte, Jamie Rich, and Paul Storrie for their friendship, inspiration, and support.

Prologue

The skulking vampire shifted his gaze from the bright, bulbous moon, which lazily drifted up over the gently swaying, leaf-filled treetops of Weatherly Park, to size up this evening's dinner. His soon-to-be victim sat alone and vulnerable on a bench a dozen feet away, the collar of her white silk blouse open, the inviting and sumptuous length of her neck practically aglow with moonlight as she stared up at the stars. A light breeze toyed with her long, honey-blond hair, sweeping her tresses playfully to one side with the confident touch of a longtime lover's hand. Her hair fell back as the wind died down, then danced with it again as it rose. The effect was practically hypnotic on the vampire.

He wasn't in the mood for an interview, or so he

would have said if you'd asked him. *Then* he would have gone on to tell you his entire life story. It was after eleven, late to begin the hunt, but he'd found it hard to tear himself away from "Must-See TV," even when his belly was bothering him, even when the need for blood boiled up inside him, so this was the earliest he'd come out to hunt. That put him firmly up against much of his competition among the undead, but what could he do? When his shows were all in repeats, he would manage a much earlier start.

Hugo Courtney, bloodsucker at large, fell instantly in love. He was hungry, so *very* hungry, but the romantic in him sensed that this night, this woman, this *kill,* would be special, and thus he wanted to make it last. No rushing in awkwardly, no violent fumbling struggle, no accidentally snapping the neck or spine before he could get the victim's adrenaline surging to spice up the blood, because even after two years as a card-carrying member of the undead, he couldn't get used to his own strength.

No. None of that.

Tonight would be about seduction.

"Okay, explain it to me again," Billy Bob said hours earlier during a commercial break. "How does a putz like you manage to survive in Sunnydale for two years without being staked by the Slayer or her kid sister or even their dog?"

"I don't think they have a dog," Hugo said defensively.

"Yeah, well, if they did, and I were you, I'd be

worried." Billy Bob was a recent addition to the ranks of the undead, yet he always talked as if he was certain he knew everything. Beyond that, his cowboy fixation was just plain sad.

Mullets were a bad, bad thing, but no one could get that across to Billy Bob. Not now, not ever.

But they liked the same shows, and Billy Bob knew how to tap illegally into the cable feed so they could get the best channels, so Hugo let an awful lot go. A challenge like this, however . . . he had to defend his honor.

"I've only been back in Sunnydale a couple of weeks," Hugo said. "I did the smart thing. After I got turned, I split. The last two glorious years I've been going up and down the coast, pigging out at one all-night buffet after another. The blood out there, it's like twenty-four hour liquor stores, I'm telling you. And the thing is, when I've run into other people like us, just sat down and chatted up other vamps at all-night diners, clubs, planetariums, y'know, the usual haunts for vamps with a wild streak but still a brain in their heads, when we'd get to talking about it, we'd end up laughing our heads off at all the absolute dumb asses who'd been turned in Sunnydale, managed not to be staked after rising from the dead, and *stuck around*."

"Yeah, but . . ." Billy Bob scratched his head. "This is Sunnydale. Here. Now. You get that, right?"

Hugo ignored him. He'd get to that part. "What I'm saying is, look at the odds. Here's you, here's the Slayer, here's the entire world. Stay where she is, the odds of getting dusted go up. Get the hell out of

Dodge, the odds of sticking around a couple of centuries get much better."

"Yeah, if you don't get so wasted on blood that you let yourself fall asleep on a park bench and nearly get fried when the sun comes up."

"I didn't know that girl had so much to drink!"

"You were getting plastered right in there with her."

Hugo frowned. This was beside the point. "Look, you go out there, into the big bad world, and sure, you'll find a couple of amateurs who've picked up the calling, devoting all their leisure hours to turning otherwise inoffensive, if murderous, fangsters like ourselves into dust." He shuddered. "Dust that could be vacuumed up with a Hoover."

"Hugo, the commercial break's almost over."

"What you can do is check things out on the Net, or just rely on old-fashioned word of mouth to find out where it's safe and where it wasn't. And those humans who've seen *Blade* one too many times, they're usually too cocky to realize that a pack of vampires never attacks one at a time, like in the movies."

"Yuh-huh."

"Ten or twenty, soulless, demonic killers with speed, strength, and agility beyond anything a human could aspire to. And then there's this *one,* decked out, overconfident, kung fu–fightin' mortal. 'Oh yeah, how's that working out for you?' 'Probably not good.'"

"The show's back on, and I don't like having it on mute."

Hugo was on a roll. "Or gee, hire a bodyguard. Or

get a couple of wanna-bes. Give 'em some knife training, a .45, whatever. Guns seemed to work best. Bullets travel faster and farther than any crossbow bolt a
hunter might use. And bam, you're covered. It's
just . . . the vamps who stay in Sunnydale, I don't get
that. The one place in the world where you've got an
official, supernaturally charged Slayer. Why hang
around?"

"Better question," Billy Bob said, raising the
remote to turn their show back on. "Why in tarnation
did you come *back*?"

Hugo didn't have an answer for that one. Not then. But
it was possible that he was getting a little insight on
that score, now.

Much as he hated to admit it, he was homesick.
And he wanted to know whether his sire was still
around.

Stupid as it sounded, he missed Sunnydale.

*There's no place like home. There's no place like
home. . . .*

Hunger roiled in Hugo's belly, and fire raced
through his brain as he stared at the blonde, who was
just the picture of ultimate hotness. Short skirt, long
legs, a nice rack . . . damn. It had been more than three
nights since he'd last fed, because he *was* scared, a little, of the Slayer. If only he had come out last night,
like he'd originally planned, he wouldn't be feeling
this impatience now. But that would have meant missing a Jennifer Connelly appearance on *Letterman*. If
only he had TiVo. . . .

Hugo really enjoyed being a vampire—except for this part. He loved wearing black all the time and not having to get up until after the sun went down (prime time is the right time, always). Tonight, he was wearing his "dressed to kill" costume: a black silk shirt, tight black pants and his black Gucci loafers. Ever since he had been turned—more a result of his sire's carelessness than of any glimmer he might have displayed of great potential, he had *no* illusions about that—Hugo had been having the time of his life.

His, um, unlife.

Whatever.

Clinging to the shadows, he gazed longingly at the stunning blonde who was practically calling out to him with her vulnerability. Hugo employed all of his enhanced senses to ensure that he and his prey were alone, that this girl wasn't just the really, *really* hot bait left behind by the Slayer to lure in schmuck newbees for a quick and painless—for her—see ya, wouldn't wanna be ya, bit of slayage.

The coast was clear. Nobody was around.

Another concern stopped him in his tracks. What if the girl on the park bench *was* the Slayer? He couldn't really see her face from this angle. And if she was going out posing as bait, she'd need some kind of disguise, right? Some way to ensure that she wouldn't be instantly recognized by her prey.

Indecision. Indecision.

Worse than that, hunger.

In life, he had been hypoglycemic. After he'd been turned, it had taken him a long time to realize he no longer needed to feed every two hours to keep his blood sugar from crashing. That made things dicey in the beginning. A vamp could only leave so big a trail of mini-meals before he had the Slayer after him.

God, he was nervous!

The woman on the park bench shifted, quickly sliding one hand into her purse.

Okay, here it comes. This had been a mistake. He had been hungry, and that was making him careless, making him stupid. The girl on the bench was the Slayer. Had to be. She was going to have a stake tossed and buried in his heart before he could even get within five feet. He knew it.

Slipping out a paperback novel, she settled back and started reading by the streetlight.

Okay, that's it.

Hugo left the shrubbery. Rising to his full, impressive 6'2" height and striding right over to his prey, he decided then and there that he was *not* going to spend his days living, if that was the right word, in fear.

He strode into the golden pool of light from the lamppost high ahead and delivered his most heartfelt opening line: "I once signed a petition calling for a feature-length version of *B. J. and the Bear. B. J. and the Bear: The Movie.* I was for that. There. Now I've told you my most embarrassing moment. The worst part of getting to know someone is out of the way."

She looked at him and smiled. It struck him instantly that she was unafraid. A strange man had come out of nowhere and babbled at her, and it hadn't fazed her in the slightest. She was serene, her hands lightly folded over the cover of her book, her gaze bright and inquisitive, welcoming and warm. "I don't do banter," she said. "Never developed the gift. Banterless. Lacking, what is technically known, as the banter. Banterese? A foreign language. Can't banter. Babble, yes. Banter, no. Was that banter or babble?"

"Banter," he said defensively.

"See? I just don't have those skills."

A possible explanation for her calm slammed into his brain. His shoulders slumped, making him look more like Corey Feldman from *Surreal Life* than Jude Law in just about anything (the image of himself he carried in his head). The worst thing was, he knew it. He felt it.

He was going geek.

"Please tell me you're not a prostitute," he whined. The general atmosphere of enforced vampiric arrogance which drifted off him now dissipated with his words. The moment he spoke, he found himself terrified that he may have offended her.

Prey, dammit, prey. She's just meat! Eat up and get it over with! the demonic part of him that still had a shred of dignity screamed inwardly.

She laughed and didn't appear at all offended. "No, I'm not. Are you?"

His eyes widened. He thought about how much product he'd used. Cologne. Hair gel. Embarrassed, he could see where she might have the wrong impression. "No!" he protested.

"Just wondering."

I am in control here, he chanted in his head, just as

his self-help tape *How to Be a More Powerful You (Without Really Trying)* constantly urged. *I have the power. Me, me, me, me, me!*

I hope she realizes that.

To hell with this. He wasn't getting what he needed out of this encounter. No terror. No unease, even.

He changed. Fangs sprouting, forehead crinkling and morphing into demonic ridges, eyes going dark and predatory, he curled his hands into claws and hissed at his victim.

She only smiled pleasantly in return. "Now that's something you don't see every day."

He didn't know what to think. The blood thirst was upon him now, stronger than ever before . . . so were his doubts and his need for affirmation. "What?" he asked. "This isn't scary?"

"I'm quaking on the inside," she reassured him.

With a savage snarl he pounced on her, one hand clasping each shoulder with superhuman strength. Lifting her into the air, he could have sworn she allowed her head to fall to one side, serving up her neck for him like a tasty treat.

She didn't even have the courtesy to scream. *That* was just rude.

In his mind, he flailed about for an explanation. Grasping hold of one, he held on tight. *She knows about vampires. She wants to be turned. She wants me to sire her, that's it!*

He dug his fangs into her neck and drank deep. At first, she sighed and patted his back the way one might when giving a sympathy hug after a bad blind date, then, as death approached, she apparently thought to fight back. He gorged himself on her blood until her involuntary kicking and squirming subsided. Pulling back, he looked into her pale, gray, lifeless face, and thought he still saw a satisfied smirk.

Unsettled, though quenched, he tossed her aside and stormed off, working hard on the story he would tell his peeps about tonight's encounter.

After all, a man had to be left some dignity, right?

Especially in death.

Undeath.

Whatever.

After a precise, predetermined interval of time had passed, the dead woman willed her heart to start beating again. The world came into focus as her glassy eyes regained their usefulness, and her limbs registered pins and needle pricks as she flexed her hands, curled her arms, and twisted about in the bushes until all of her musculature became vibrant and responded to her mental commands.

She hopped to her feet and stretched as if she had just woken from a nap. Her blood was everywhere.

"No one likes a messy eater," she said, making a mental note to return and do a full cleanup of the area once her primary task had been achieved.

Her paperback, an older book by Fay Weldon, *The Cloning of Joanna May,* was ruined. The pages were red and soggy, just like her blouse and skirt. Picking up her purse, she walked to the shrubbery and removed a sealed bag she had planted there earlier. The science described in the novel was ridiculous, but that didn't matter; the story used cloning as a metaphor, it talked about people, and she could appreciate that. She'd long considered herself a people person. . . . Even now, directing a steady flood of endorphins through her body to level out the pain from the still stinging twin puncture wounds and the generally achy feeling that always came with death and resurrection, she still felt that way.

There were those who had argued with her claims to continued humanity after she had become—*enhanced.* Honestly, she hadn't thought treating their heads like screw-top lids was that much of an over-reaction, and the fact that she could do such a thing now, was, all told, quite the thrill.

Stripping off her blood-spattered blouse, she opened the plastic bag and withdrew enough Handi Wipes to mop up all the mess on her face and neck, though there was little she could do with the red streaks in her hair. She shrugged, slipping on a new silk blouse from the bag. It would look like a designer 'do, that's all. No one would get close enough to tell it was anything else. She could easily make sure of that.

She was G-1 class, though she preferred the abandoned term, Generation Alpha. She went by Gwen, even though that wasn't her true name. Gwen . . . G-1 . . . it was close enough.

Gwen's "technical specs" made it simple for her to catch the heat signatures of all living things in her immediate vicinity no matter what solid matter that person, animal, or otherwise classified being might be hiding behind.

Tracking the vampire would have been tougher . . . if he didn't have her blood, rich with microtransmitters, coursing through his body.

Buttoning up her blouse—then popping the top few buttons back open for effect—Gwen disposed of the major evidence of her nighttime encounter and briskly strolled off toward the swings, a clump of trees in the distance, and the warehouse three miles south, where she tracked him by scent with her enhanced senses. Even from this distance she could hear the tune the vampire hummed.

The theme song from *B. J. and the Bear* was on her lips as she bounced happily toward *her* target.

"It was better than sex, I'm telling you," babbled Hugo. "We had a moment."

"Which means it took *longer* than sex," Billy Bob chided, his spurs chinking as he walked to the minifridge and snagged a wine cooler. "For his sorry ass, that is."

Tressa, a brunette with creamy-cocoa skin and scarlet contacts she'd had specially made, sprawled over an old sofa the pack had snatched from the front yard of a house over the weekend. Her spiked boots tore at the already foam-frothing fabric of the sofa, and her belly ring looked like the next item to get caught on something the way she squirmed about, putting her arms around an invisible companion, grinding a little in her low-riders while thrusting out her tube-topped chest, and wriggled her tongue obscenely. Then she cackled, going vamp face, and pouted. "Aw, I'm sorry," Tressa said. "I shouldn't make fun. Hugo's in love!"

"Got that," Billy Bob said, pulling on his frizzy, auburn beard as if the act might somehow grant him wisdom. He'd said often enough he thought it was possible. If rubbing some fat dude's belly was meant to give you luck in certain religions, why not the stroking of the beard for him?

"She's special," Hugo said. "I can feel it. I've *never* tasted blood like hers before."

"Shoulda brought her home to share," Billy Bob said.

Tressa seconded the motion.

Sighing, Hugo went to the corner and curled up atop a huge leather press. This warehouse had belonged to a shoe manufacturer. When their plant had been closed down, all the gear they couldn't sell was moved here. And when the warehouse owners had gone missing, like so many did in Sunnydale, the property went to whoever was strong enough to take it and defend it. Battles had been fought over these presses and sewing machines, and throughout the spacious, smelly dump that now served as the pack's home.

Hugo loved it here. The smell of leather that hit him each time he entered the building was intoxicating . . . and the mountain of stacked-up shoes amounted to the closest thing to Mecca any style-conscious vamp could possibly desire.

His posse of fellow monsters were all in attendance tonight. Besides Billy Bob and Tressa, Phillipe was here, a bony, black-haired, dark-eyed guy down from Canada, along with Serge, Amanda, Mordo, and Fitz. They were all huddled around the high-definition television set they had stolen from one of the high houses on the hills outside Sunnydale. Lisa, Maive, and Jennifer, the killer pep squad, were by the shoes, arguing over who was thinner and what category of thin each of them might be classified under: anorexic, bulimic, plain, old desiccated.

"Your ankles are fat!" Lisa stated calmly.

"Are not," Jennifer smartly retorted.

Leaping to his feet, Hugo screamed at the tops of his lungs until at least three other vamps gave him their attention.

Billy Bob, Tressa, and Phillipe gathered round and let the vampire tell his tale. It was that or deal with his dramatics until sunrise . . . and beyond.

Truth to tell, Hugo always had a story when he came back from a hunt. None of the others bothered. It was all, "hi, how ya doin', score any blood?" "cool" with them. Restraint was not his watchword.

But he was fun to have around, and he *knew things* from having traveled so much and survived so long.

For that reason, they didn't stake him in his sleep, as had been suggested countless times. Also, for that reason, they always drew straws to see who would have to humor him when he came back from a hunt.

The short-straw trio of Billy Bob, Tressa, and Phillipe looked up at Hugo with sad, weary eyes, hoping the vampire would at least keep the story mildly interesting.

Hoping . . . but not really expecting much.

With dramatic gestures, the vampire recounted his conquest: how he stalked his prey, how even his fear of the Slayer didn't stop him, and how delicious the blood was when it poured down his throat. The creature of night laughed wildly as he talked about the ridiculous fear of the Slayer they all shared.

"Yeah, you're the man," Billy Bob said without inflection, taking another swig of his wine cooler to dull the pain of listening to Hugo's blather.

Then Hugo stopped his performance. His face went pale. Paler than usual.

"Hugo?" Billy Bob said, surprised by the note of true concern in his voice.

Panic overtook the darkly clad vampire. Stumbling down from his perch, he spasmed as if he was having some kind of fit, his powerful arms and legs smacking chins, shoulders, chests, forcing his friends to simply plop him down on the filthy concrete floor, where a rat squealed and scurried away in terror.

Clutching at his chest, his face, his throat, the vampire managed to stand for an instant, then dropped to his knees. He quaked with terror as strange patterns rose up on his flesh, starting on his face and quickly spreading over his entire body.

"Hugo, what the hell's gotten into you, boy?" Billy Bob asked, staring down helplessly while glowing golden marks sizzled their way through his flesh.

For the first time since Hugo had returned to Sunnydale, he captured the attention of every member of the pack. They formed a circle around his writhing, convulsing, burning form, watching as something tore at him from within. Hugo's steady torrent of screams faded as a second set of lines, brighter than the first, coalesced under the thin flesh of his throat, near his Adam's apple, and moved up to flow throw his carotid arteries and spiral over his cheeks.

"What are those marks?" Tressa asked in hushed tones.

"Tattoos," Phillipe said. "Writing of some kind. The language looks ancient."

"I used to repair computers," Billy Bob said. "It looks more like circuitry to me. Like some of that government stuff we were hearing about."

"Initiative's gone, buried," Tressa mumbled. "I was dating one of those guys before I got turned. Told me everything, then split."

Before them, Hugo beat the back of his skull against the floor, as if trying to cave it in to avoid the agony that roared through him.

No one even *thought* to stake him and put him out of his misery.

The band of creatures suddenly ran out of time to speculate further over his condition. Hugo's body sprang up, like a bow, resting on the top of his forehead, the tips of his shoes, his belt buckle aimed at the ceiling—and he burst into flame and ash—*from the inside out*.

For a moment, the group stood there and stared at the collection of ash on the concrete floor of the warehouse.

Tressa pointed at a nearby window. "Someone's out there!"

Billy Bob and the others caught a flash of golden hair, a figure darting away. He raced outside with the others to give chase, but whoever had been watching them was long gone.

"It was a blonde," Tressa snarled.

"The Slayer's a blonde," Billy Bob hissed, considering what he had just witnessed. "The woman Hugo *bit* was a blonde . . . she had something in her. Must have. Something in her blood that went right through Hugo and did him wrong."

"Pretty big leap," Phillipe ventured.

Billy Bob was on him fast, slamming the slimmer man against the warehouse's tinny, echoing outer wall. "You got a better idea? You know anything else out there that can move that fast, get away from us that easy?"

"I just wonder if we should think about doing what Hugo was saying, get out, get away from the Slayer. If she can do this—"

"The Slayer *did* this," Billy Bob snarled, hauling Phillipe inside and tossing him down to skid across the still sparking ashes of their former pack member. "I know Hugo was a pain, but he was one of us, and we cannot let this stand!"

"Vengeance," Phillipe said softly, in his wispy, Donnie Darko voice.

"Bet your backside," Tressa added. "The Slayer poisoned him somehow. She set him up to snag someone who was . . . I dunno . . . *infected* with that stuff."

The others, the ones who weren't cowering in fear after the horrifying display, nodded and cheered.

"Rip her damn head off!" Lisa squealed delightedly with her high, cheerleader voice.

The murmur of voices grew behind them, becoming a low, threatening hum.

The Slayer, it was the Slayer. . . .

The vampires had no way of knowing just how wrong they were.

Gwen sauntered into a dimly lit apartment downtown. Floorboards squeaked, and something rustled in the near darkness.

The Progenitor sat in his favorite chair, reading a newspaper by the light of a single, bottled firefly. He didn't need light, of course. But Gwen thought the firefly was a nice touch, anyway. "Reading the investment section?" she asked, shrugging off her blond wig. It brushed her shoulders, trying to get a grip during its descent, then opened like a parachute and cascaded to the floor.

"You know I've always been shrewd in that department."

"Of course." She sashayed to kitchen and slid open a small drawer. A hypodermic and a host of other emergency medical equipment were laid out before her, set neatly in gray foam containment units. Selecting what she needed, Gwen drifted to the refrigerator and found the supply of blood she would need to replenish what the vampire had taken. Her body could regenerate what was lost, given time, but why wait? She was at .02 percent diminished capacity, and it bothered her. Like, a lot.

"You're not saying much," the man in the shadows observed, setting down his newspaper.

Gwen prepared the blood, working with mechanical ease and efficiency with the equipment she'd selected. "You're just vexed because I haven't sat down in your lap and given you a cuddle."

"Possibly. Or I might be put off by your reluctance to give a simple progress report."

"It's like this," she said. "I sat around, got the weirdest come-on line I've ever heard from anyone living, dead, or otherwise, got myself killed—like in the plan—then followed the vampire back to his 'lair.' There, he met with his little friends, did a little dance, and went 'poof.'"

A sigh came from the darkness.

Gwen had already set the blood pumping into her veins. She was feeling more like her old self already.

No, scratch that. If she had been her *old* self, she would be weak, unable to punch through steel walls, unable to see the world with the eyes of eternity itself, a worldview belonging to a god. Not that she was a god. Or goddess, more appropriately. Sunnydale had dealt with its share of that business in the past.

I am something new.

"In summation, vampires, it appears, won't make suitable hosts," she stated.

The man nodded. "Let's try to pass on our gift to a few more subjects among the undead, just to be sure," he said.

"I agree. The vampires are strong and fast, they possess enhanced senses and sharp instincts. It's a shame to write them off completely as candidates. Plus, if it doesn't work the next time, watching 'em blow up is a real trip."

"Thank you, Gwen, for your impartial analysis."

"Anytime, boss."

"We'll test a few more vampires. However, I see no reason to delay the *human trials* any longer," the seated man said. "After all, there's so much work to be done. . . ."

In the near darkness, Gwen nodded and smiled, her eyes glowing with a tender, inhuman shade of gold.

Chapter One

"Not so tough with a sword in your chest, are ya?" asked the Slayer. Yanking the weapon back, Buffy kicked the wounded and wobbling demon from the stage. From the liquid *splorch* it made when it finished its Slayer-assisted stage dive, Buffy had a pretty good idea that it was now dead. Deceased. An ex-demon. Formerly of the living, now otherwise engaged.

She frowned. *Somehow, that worked better with parrots.*

All hell had broken loose at the Bronze tonight. Again. And, as usual, that phrase had to be taken quite literally. A normal fistfight, a scrap over whether a band sucked or a girlfriend was cheating or anything remotely normal like that . . . nah. That wouldn't fit the profile of this place.

Instead, the particular demons who had decided to go on a crunch-and-munch fest tonight in an effort to cut down on the average number of students per classroom at Sunnydale High—gotta give 'em props for at least trying to solve one of the community's problems—looked like something that might have only been dredged up from the lowest depths of that really bad, ultra-warm-and-toasty spot way below.

This small army of fiends looked like snakes grown to over six feet tall who'd had the good sense—since they were planning on attacking humans and needed opposable thumbs to help open doors and scaly little feetsies to make 'em more mobile—to sprout arms and legs, three of each, in this case. Their tall and thin bodies were covered with scales, their wide mouths hanging open to reveal forked tongues and six-inch-long venomous fangs.

The snake dudes were all over the place, multiplying like sea-monkeys, or so it seemed. For every one she cut down with her double ax or ran through with her short sword, two more popped up to take their places. They ran rampant through the crowd, hissing and clawing, causing more damage by frightening their victims than anything else. Teenagers were running everywhere, screaming, trampling one another as they tried to make it to an exit.

Buffy wasn't alone. She had Willow, Xander, Dawn, and Spike with her—though she hadn't exactly *brought* Spike, he had just kinda wandered into the whole thing and started fighting because one of the demons had called him a dirty name.

Spike hadn't been himself at all since returning from halfway around the world . . . but that was a whole different deal that she didn't have time to worry about right now.

A pair of scale-brothers bounded onto the stage and attacked.

"Thank you," Buffy said, dodging their sweeping claws. "I was hoping if I just made enough of a spectacle of myself, more of you would come rushing up here to take me on instead of messing with those kids."

Kids. She'd thought of the people who went to the Bronze as *kids*.

Now that was scary, though not quite as much the wig out as the hissing forked tongues of her enemies—which could, she just realized, extend about the length of someone's arm and spatter acid on an enemy. Her now *hissing* brown jacket had taken the brunt of that learning endeavor. Little whorls of smoke rose up from where droplets of snake spit had struck the fabric.

Better the jacket than my face, Buffy decided, but . . . her jacket!

Whipping the ax in a blinding arc of extreme prejudice, Buffy relieved both demons of their evil wagging tongues, which went flying over each of her shoulders, careened off cymbals on the abandoned drum set behind her, and landed on the floor, still wriggling a little.

Buffy felt vexed. There had to be some easy quip she could—and by rights should—deliver to make this moment more memorable, but she was quipless. Lacking in the quip department. Then—

"See what you made me do? Gives a whole new meaning to tongue-lashing!"

The demons shrieked, the Slayer decapitated. Headless bodies dropped.

Buffy curled up her lips in disgust as twin geysers of ink-black ickiness—was that blood? Yuck—fired up into the air and speckled down onto her newly shorn and tinted golden hair. The heads made the same splorch as the body of the last one, but these drooled something gooey onto her boots. Great. Now only her tight crème ribbed sweater and hip-hugger jeans hadn't been gooped or slimed.

"You people should get a bill for my cleaning expenses," Buffy said as four more snake guys sprang out of the shadows, coming at her all at once, and from every direction.

Yup. Just like sea-monkeys. Multiplying, multiplying.

Xander had given her the 411 on sea-monkeys, great intel he'd picked up from a combination of the ad pages in old smelly comics he'd picked up at a convention or garage sale or someplace and some recently written demonic tomes Anya had bought on eBay. (Hey, those books couldn't all be old and smelly, could they?) Sea-monkeys were a vicious little race, and all those ads had turned out to be a part of a worldwide demonic invasion attempt that only stalled out because kids kept doing really twisted things to the critters before they could reach maturity. Such was the lore one learned when called to be the Slayer.

Or when one was really bored enough to let Xander go on and on about such things.

Buffy leaped into the air just as the fearsome foursome landed and lunged. She snagged a support beam ten feet up with the curly part of her ax, whirled up, over, and around it like a champion gymnast who just happened to be well dressed and heavily armed, and angled her descent so that she could drop down behind the dazed and confused demons, who had just ripped and torn and acid-tongued one another. Hitting the stage hard, she jammed her sword, one-handed rapier-style, into the mid-back of the closest demon, then planted one boot in its mid-spine beneath the weapon, freeing her sword as she kicked the snake fellow into the startled midst of his pals, who were just beginning to recover from finding themselves sans Slayer in the middle of their clawing and acid-tonguing.

Suddenly, two figures appeared on the other side of the snake demons—Dawn and Xander. Each wielded swords, each used them without hesitation, leaving only one snake demon for Buffy to handle.

"Oh, this is too easy," Buffy said, advancing on the seemingly stunned last snake demon.

And so it was.

The demon came at her with a series of kicks that she hadn't been prepared to meet—she'd just plain never dealt with an attacker with three legs and three arms before. *At least not in the Bronze. Not that I can remember.*

Balancing on one leg, the snake demon feinted

with one scaly and fork-toed foot and whacked the other into the underside of Buffy's jaw. Her head snapped back, quickly followed by the rest of her, and he pounced on her chest, his arms going all rubbery as they coiled about her and threatened to squeeze her hard enough to rupture her lungs with her own ribs before she even hit the stage floor.

"Nuh-uh!" Dawn hollered, sweeping with her sword.

Buffy wanted to warn her little sister about the icky black spraying stuff, but she didn't have the air in her lungs. The head went flying, the demon blood shot into the air, and Dawn let out a few choice words Buffy was surprised to learn her sister would favor. Heard, yes, that was unavoidable these days, but use, and in a sentence, short as it was . . . that was surprising.

She was on the floor, Xander sawing the rubbery arms of the convulsing headless snake demon corpse from her, when her head turned to one side and she saw what was happening in the rest of the club.

There were more demons, and much more chaos. And still, most of the injury Buffy was spotting came from self-inflicted craziness. The hundred or so teens and twenty-somethings in the one cool club in town were hurting themselves and one another because of the blind panic the demons were inducing.

Willow was by the door, using a little magic to create a demon-free corridor of force leading to the rear exit of the Bronze, giving innocent club goers a way out. Buffy knew how badly Will had wanted to avoid using magic under any circumstance, and prayed, rightly along with her pal, she was certain, that nothing bad—particularly of the Big Bad Dark Willow variety—would come of this.

Giles's favorite researcher had been going through a hard time learning to control her magical powers while she was in England, and it was even more difficult now she was back home. Willow called to her: "You'd think with how often this kind of stuff happens in Sunnydale, these people would know how to cope with this kind of situation. Walk single file to the exits, no pushing or shoving."

Buffy got it. Not a whole lot of people were taking advantage of the exit strategy Willow had devised. The witch needed help, and Spike, who was kung fu fighting with the best of them, but probably wouldn't be enough. At least he was handling *some* of these replicating reptiles.

"Guys, I'll handle these," Buffy said, peeling off the last of the stinky, scaly, snake demon body, then bounding to her feet. She could sense even more of the demons surging from the crowd, heading for her. "Go help—"

No less than two dozen demons climbed onto the stage at once, blocking any and all avenues of retreat for those without Slayer reflexes and grasshopper-like leaping abilities. Buffy had no choice but to stay right here and fight from the center of this makeshift demonic maelstrom, or else Xander and Dawn would surely pay the price.

"Okay, Will's on her own for a little while longer," Buffy said, raising her weapons.

The fighting went into full swing. Demons here, demons there, tongues, claws, feet. Buffy warned her companions of the demons' demonic advantages in combat, then went straight for the hacking and slashing.

Soon they were all awash in gore, trying not to slip on the slick floor, desperate to keep calm above the steadily rising drone of panicked cries from the crowd.

"You know, we end up here onstage a lot," Dawn noted.

Xander nodded, whipping his sword at the neck of a snake demon. "Maybe we should start a band."

Running another through and barely avoiding its acid tongue, Dawn leaped back. Buffy surged forward, using a roundhouse kick to send one demon crashing back into several others behind it, giving her and the others a little more room to form a proper combat circle. Another demon attacked, his arm raking at Dawn. She took a slight cut to the arm and paid her assailant back by relieving him of the offending appendage.

They were right on the edge of tripping over all the dead demon bodies, but then again, so were the still-breathing critters, so Buffy thought that made them all just about even. *It was a good thing these guys didn't use weapons on top of everything else. . . .*

Spike careened onto the stage, tossed by a demon. The platinum-haired vampire tucked and rolled, sliding between a crack in the demon ring Buffy had made, and sprang to his feet.

A demon dropped down onto Buffy, knifelike hands flailing. Ducking all the flailage without missing a beat, Buffy stabbed it in the heart with her short sword, then kicked the guck-spewing, altogether too twitching soon-to-be corpse off the stage.

"I don't know these blokes," Spike said. "One thing's for sure, though. They're getting off on chaos and fear. That's what's makin' them stronger . . . that's what's makin' more of them, period!"

Chaos demons. Perfect. So how do you fight chaos? With order.

Control.

And that was something that was sorely lacking in Buffy's life right now. . . .

This was not how she'd wanted to spend her evening. The Slayer had been planning to "slay" some dust bunnies with her sister as they tackled the weekly cleaning of their home. Well, it was supposed to be weekly, but at this point, they were feeling good if it was monthly. Then the phone had rung and it sure as hell wasn't Avon calling.

"Let me see if I've got this straight," Spike said, continuing, with everyone else, to fight the good fight against the ever increasing odds. "You're now getting anonymous tips. Like the cops."

"Pretty much," Buffy confirmed.

Xander chimed in. "So instead of the Bat-Phone we've got the Buff-Phone?"

With a sigh and a parry, Buffy said, "You want to call it that. Just *don't.*"

But Xander wasn't through. "This guy Simon calls up and says—hey! *Simon says* . . . whoa!"

Buffy leaped before Xander, her arms aching as

she halved a snake demon and worried it might grow into two of the beasties right in front of her eyes. Regeneration might also explain the great numbers of these creatures.

Buffy wondered how long they'd be able to hold out. Even with Spike punching and kicking, going fang-faced and tearing these things apart, even more were on the horizon, and the crowd still wasn't going for the exit.

Chaos, chaos, chaos. Buffy had to keep it together, keep it under control. Their "chat" seemed to be the only thing preventing them from giving into the creeping terror these snake guys were projecting. It had taken her time to start feeling their magical effects, but it was there, she couldn't even begin to deny it.

"What did this Simon guy sound like?" Dawn asked.

"I dunno. Normal. Whatever normal sounds like. He could have been anyone. I didn't recognize the voice. The important thing is, he knew what he was talking about, and he must've wanted to help—why else would he have called?"

Xander had an opinion on that. He always did, bless him. "Maybe he has it in for these guys. They might have welshed on a bet. Not paid up in puppies or something."

Buffy hadn't thought about it.

"Kittens," Spike said testily. "We use kittens for cash."

Xander killed another demon. "Ah, but these guys

could be a whole different deal. Whole boxes of innocent, mewling puppies—"

"Puppies don't mewl," Dawn added helpfully.

"You get my drift."

Buffy saw poor Willow trying to hold open the magical corridor and *shove* the panicking public through it. The chaos demons must have suffused this entire place with their dark, fear-inducing magics. The Slayer said, "Drifting is something it would be good for you to do, right about now. As in, drifting over *there* and helping Will get these people out of here."

"Yeah, if I could get *through,*" Xander snarled.

"I could toss him," Spike offered. "The boy's a bit of a tosser as it is. That would only be fitting—"

"Shut it," Buffy snapped as she hacked away in the ever-maddening circle of death and chaos.

Xander sliced another demon tongue off and fell back, narrowly avoiding its acid venom.

A snake demon got too close for comfort. Buffy dealt.

Thunk-thunk-thunk.

Buffy killed another demon, kicked two more. "I'm amazed this place stays open. Don't you think it should have been closed down, I dunno, after the first couple of times this happened?"

"This meaning the brand-new, not sold in any stores 'Chaos Demons Gone Wild at Local Hangout' video series?" Xander asked.

"This meaning any of it. Demons, wereleopards, vampires, elder gods, you name it. I've sniffed the evil-rich air of the Bronze and I'm getting one big sock of doom smell."

"Your point being? Not that I'm against the 'distract everyone from imminent death with playful banter so they stay frosty' approach or anything, I'm just curious."

"The bad guys *must* have a piece of this place. How else could it stay open? You've got your wrongful deaths, zero precautions against unwarranted and *seemingly* unmotivated attacks by the forces of darkness, who knows how many kids last seen with a suspicious-looking character at—you guessed it—the Bronze . . . I think it adds up to something."

Spike frowned as he snapped the neck of another demon and hurled it off the stage. "Put it that way, pet, and I'll take it one step further for you. I want to know why all the knuckleheads keep coming back here when it's so bloody dangerous."

"Come on, Buff," Dawn put in. "Where else are you gonna see all the really cool bands?"

This had gone on long enough. These demons fed on chaos and terror and had a nearly endless appetite for destruction. When the Scoobs arrived, the demons were in the middle of a smorgasbord of pain and cruelty—which the ex-cheerleader *had* to interrupt. It was in the job description, after all.

But now, besieged by the endless legion of snake guys, she'd had enough. There was something else here. Had to be. These demons were just the grunts. The front line soldiers meant to soften up the enemy. That's how it had happened in countless demon battles before now, why should this one be any different?

"Why am I always the last to know when it's two-for-one demon night?" she quipped. Then she looked out beyond the wall of reptilian invaders and shouted, "Hey, Big Bad, ultimate scaly, whatever you are. Scared to take on one little *girly-girl*?"

It was a childish low blow, but as expected, it yielded results. The ring of demon fighters parted, the grunts falling back, and Buffy shooed all her companions, even Spike, off the stage. "Help Willow get these people *out* of here," she commanded.

Buffy used that tone that would brook no response other than a solid, "okay," a quick, sharp nod, or a "yes, ma'am."

She got the first two. The third she received only in spirit, thank goodness. One "ma'am" and she'd be in therapy, the first Slayer in history worried she was getting *old*.

As she suspected, there was a new Mr. Big Snake. He was nothing like the Mayor. This one was humanoid, like the others, albeit with the three arms and three legs that were just enough to wig someone out but good. The third leg, well, that was like a trip stand, okay, the third arm, though, that had manifested in a variety of locations on the bodies of the subordinate demons: The middle of the back, the chest, below the right arm or left, even grasping outward from the tummy.

This one was three times the size of the others, and his emerald and crimson speckled, scaly third arm rose from what should have been his nice flat noodle. Nope, no slopey skull for this one. It bent, its spine more serpentine than that of the lesser demons it ordered around, and its tongue reached farther, too, and annoyingly snapped back each and every time she had a chance to slice it.

Well, at least they haven't thought to start sending acid spitballs, Buffy thought . . . and was very happy she hadn't mentioned that one out loud, because she would have felt like a nit if she had handed them a fresh idea.

As it turned out, the new Mr. Big Snake didn't need any new ideas. He was just big, mean, and quick as lightning.

Perfect.

The petite blonde surged forward, leaping from the stage at the newcomer, her ax raised high over her head. In mid flight she twisted to avoid its grasping hand and brought the ax down in a diagonal motion to her left, quickly pulling it up so that the broad side of the ax hit the demon just under the jawbone. Buffy smiled as she heard the demon's teeth smash and crackle together. She'd hoped it might bite off its own tongue, but no such luck.

Landing gracefully, Buffy kicked it hard in the midsection, throwing it off-balance. Hoping she had the snake deity, or whatever this particular king of chaos was all about, on the ropes right off, she took a chance and hurled her ax at him, hoping to bury it in his scaly skull.

Mr. Big Snake recovered faster than Buffy would have liked, batting the ax away with one of its many clawed hands. Buffy somersaulted ahead, missing the sweeping claws of the master demon who radiated such chaos that it was becoming hard for her to think, and annoyingly making quippage out of the question. Springing up directly before the big guy, she kicked out, both heels making intimate contact with the creature's knees. There was a sickening *crack,* and it fell forward, grunting in pain, landing right on those ruined knees as Buffy hit the ground and rolled out of the way. The ex-cheerleader performed a cartwheel and came up with the battle-ax in her hands. With all her strength, she buried it squarely in the chest.

That was when Mr. Big Snake said his first word.

"Tickles." Then the weird arm atop his head sliced downward, making Buffy jump back—and right into the path of its oncoming left hand, which batted her a dozen feet into the air. She mashed against a bank of speakers and collapsed to the floor, the equipment falling on her in a rain of blocky, heavy, and scarifyingly sparking electronics.

She didn't get up as Mr. Big Snake stalked over to her, grimacing with pain as his knees crackled back into place, bone and muscle regenerating itself as it stalked its prey.

Throughout the club, chaos ruled. The demons who had been onstage had followed the Scoobs, determined to keep them from interfering.

Halfway to the rear exit, Spike flew at one of the demons and was backhanded away for his trouble. The demons, which had been so easy to kill just a few moments ago, seemed to have been recharged by the appearance of their lord and master.

Dazed, head lolling, he heard a hissing and saw little spots of acid rise up from the floor next to his head. The demon snarled and reared back to send its killer tongue straight through Spike's skull—and froze. With a choking sound, it dropped backward, twisting and falling to one side, dead as a demon should be when it had just had a drumstick jammed into its brain from behind.

"Their heads are all squooshy," Dawn said, trying to control her own reaction to the *ewww* factor.

Close to the door, Willow shouted at the crowd, "This way! Come on! Um—big concert outside? Hooters girls waiting? Free wine and cheese?"

Few appeared to be able to hear her over the screaming of the terrified teenagers, and those who did were too overwhelmed by the chaos-inducing rings of fear swirling throughout the club. A regular person wouldn't see them, of course, but they were clear to Willow, emerald and crimson bands, matching the color of the scales spotting each of the serpent demons.

Finally, someone came her way. Just . . . not the kind of someone she was hoping for. A snake demon slowly stalked toward her, clearly unaware of who—and what—it was going up against.

Willow could take it out with magic. She could end all of this with the use of the roiling power within her . . . but she knew how much power would be needed, and couldn't be sure she could control herself if she loosed the spell that was in her mind, couldn't know that she wouldn't replace one threat with another of the much bigger, world-threatening variety.

Willow's hand tightened on the grip of the sword she carried, her knuckles turning white, her vision blurring as her eyes threatened to change, turning pure obsidian.

"You really don't want to do this," Willow suggested.

Snake-Eyes had other ideas.

But before it could make its move, Xander was peeling out of the crowd, jumping onto the three-armed demon's back. They went down in a tangle of limbs and quickly separated.

The carpenter watched for an opening, let the demon stick its tongue out at him, and darted to one side to hack off one of its arms.

One was not enough. And the floor, suddenly slick with demon blood, was darned slippery. Xander went off-balance, and the demon used the arm springing out from its rib cage to claw at his back. It tore through his shirt and sliced into his bare flesh—holding him in place. Willow raced to help her fellow Scoob, lifting her sword up and lunging at the demon, trying to stab it in the throat. The creature sidestepped her thrust and slapped Willow away. But Willow's gesture gave Xander the distraction he needed to take the wretched thing's head off, though he winced as it scraped its claws down his back on its way to the floor—and oblivion.

Light-headed from blood loss, Xander bent down and helped Willow to her feet.

"Are you okay?" Xander asked.

"Yeah. How 'bout you?"

"Fine, but my shirt will never be the same again."

"Liar." She cast a quick healing spell, making him feel like a new man in seconds.

Not that there was anything wrong with the old one, that is.

Together, they rounded up the confused and frightened people who were still inside the Bronze and led them toward the safety of the exit.

Near the speakers, Buffy's head lolled as the serpent god hauled the speakers and other debris off her. He picked her up by the scruff of her jacket, hauling her limp form up so that he could stare straight into her eyes as he punched his tongue through her face.

That had been the plan, anyway.

"Don't you guys ever read the chapter on playing possum?" Buffy asked, driving her short sword through the monster's right eye. It fell back, dropping her, clutching at the weapon as it dropped to the floor. Landing catlike, Buffy hefted her ax. "Me, I don't even know if possums play all that much, or what games they might be partial to. But they have wisdom, by all accounts. You fellas should learn from that."

Swinging the ax once, Buffy separated Mr. Snake Guy from his big snake head.

A sudden flare of crimson and emerald energies appeared overhead, and struck at each of the snake demons. They shuddered, eyes rolling up into their heads, and dropped to the floor, dying as one.

"Finally, something nice and tidy," Buffy said.

With demons dispatched, Buffy leaned against a wall to rest and survey the damage. Several teenagers lay on the floor of the Bronze. Willow and Xander were helping to carry out those people who were too badly injured to walk out on their own. Dawn was calling for an ambulance. Spike had left, probably to crawl back into his hidey-hole in the high school's basement to have a long conversation with the voices in his head.

Buffy shook her head.

The owners of the Bronze—assuming they weren't partnered up with the forces of darkness, who always had a nice bankroll, or so it seemed—must have great insurance. It had to cover *every* kind of foreseeable and unforeseeable disaster that could strike a club in Sunnydale. Maybe she should get the owner's contact info from Xander and ask if the insurance company they used had homeowners' policies. It would sure help if she could get some cash from an insurance company every time her house was trashed by demons, zombies, or other undead nasties . . . as opposed to having Xander make her some new windows and shopping at Goodwill for table bargains.

Buffy suddenly felt something strange at her back, like invisible fingers shaking and shuddering as they brushed against her through the wall. Startled, she leaped back, turned, and saw a message being written on the wall by an invisible hand.

SIMON SAYS, the message read, *IT'S GOOD YOU LISTENED.*

Willow and Xander re-entered the Bronze and saw Buffy staring at the wall. They ran to her side.

"Simon," the witch absently noted. "Wasn't that the name of the guy who called warning you that there would be trouble at the Bronze?"

Buffy nodded. "Without Simon's warning, we would have arrived too late and everyone in this place would have died."

"So that makes Simon a good guy, right?" the carpenter asked.

Buffy had no answers. All she knew was that the creepy, almost smug writing on the wall had left her feeling chilled.

The writing began again: *I'LL BE IN TOUCH.*

Buffy thought of the unnerving feeling of the invisible fingers at her back only a few seconds ago—another example of Simon, whoever, whatever he was, being *in touch*—and didn't know if she should take Simon's last words as a promise . . . or a threat. Buffy wanted to know a lot more about Simon before deciding whether he was a good guy. Certainly, the fact that he didn't show his face and only helped out by making phone calls and sending cryptic mystical messages didn't impress her. But if he was a bad guy, then why tell her about this thing going down at the Bronze so that they could stop the carnage? What was in it for him?

Buffy hugged herself, all too certain she would soon find out.

Chapter Two

Buffy stared through the front windshield of her mom's car, frowning as she focused beyond the downtown stoplight at the pale blue and ocher sky. Dawn was beside her in the passenger seat, squirming so much, it made Buffy wonder if the teenager had a rash.

"Here's what I'm curious about," Buffy began, genuinely perplexed.

Dawn became frightfully still. The light turned, and Buffy eased through it, screeching to a sudden stop to avoid a crazed driver who'd run the red.

"Butthead!" Buffy hollered. Then she accelerated again, thankful for her Slayer reflexes.

"This really isn't necessary," Dawn said from the

passenger seat. "I could walk. Get a ride from a friend. You know . . ."

"What, you don't like my driving? I haven't hit anything all week."

Dawn delivered one of her patented half-smiles, half-laughs, all groaning discomfort thingees.

"Seriously, is something up?" Buffy asked. "You know you can talk to me."

"Oh, yeah. Guidance Counselor Buffy to the rescue."

"So something *is* up."

"No!"

They drove in silence, Buffy on high alert for nutcase drivers.

"All right. Fine. So what is it?" Dawn asked at last.

"It's just this phrase. 'Dawn is breaking.' I mean, the sun's coming up, fine. But what does Dawn's breaking mean exactly? How does dawn break? It either arrives, or—"

"Doesn't seem so weird to me," Dawn growled, looking away from her sister.

Okay, Buffy thought. *It's going to be another one of those fun mornings.*

The rising sun caused Buffy to squint, so she dug into her purse for her sunglasses. Another driver cut her off, this one zooming up the parking spaces in front of the main street stores as if it were another lane, then clipping in front of her with only inches to spare.

"That was *not* my fault," Buffy said, noticing Dawn's fingers digging into the dashboard.

"Yuh-huh."

The rest of the drive was uneventful—and quiet. Too quiet, as they always said in those cheapie horror flicks Xander was fond of bringing around. Buffy had no idea what was bothering Dawn until they came to the last light before the school.

"I'll get out here," Dawn said, reaching for the door handle.

"Whoa!" Buffy said, snapping her gaze to her little sister—and really seeing her for the first time that day. The brunette seemed to shrink inside her denim jacket and combat tee. Her paisley skirt–clad knees drew up a little, and worry lines creased her heart-shaped face. Her almond-shaped eyes crinkled, and her lips were downturned in disapproval. "The deal here is what, exactly?"

"Just want to stretch my legs."

The light changed, and four drivers immediately started honking. Buffy didn't move, and Dawn shrank down into her seat, covering her face in embarrassment as cars with other parents bringing their kids to school whipped around them.

"So that's it," Buffy said. "You don't want to be seen with me."

"It's complicated," Dawn said.

"Apparently." Buffy waited until it was clear, pulled to the side of the road, and let Dawn out. Not another word was spoken, but Dawn slammed the door as she made her dramatic exit.

Was I like this? Buffy wondered. *Tell me I wasn't like this.*

You weren't, the calm, sweet voice of her mother

said in her mind. *You were much, much worse, sweetie.*

She waited for the light, found an opening, and slipped back into traffic. Dawn didn't even look over as Buffy passed her, then drove the next block to the school's gates.

The new Sunnydale High was still under construction. Most of it was up and running, but Xander's company had a handful of jobs left to finish, so that meant there were areas blocked off, and bulky construction vehicles bubbled up here and there in the parking lot.

Desperate to take her mind off the weirdness with Dawn, which might have been caused by hormones, possession by ancient evil, or, most likely, a nasty case of adolescent angst, Buffy mentally prepped herself for battle. It was one thing to take on vamps and demons. However, each day she came here to work in her capacity as part-time guidance counselor and full-time snoop into whatever new weirdness the Hellmouth might be cooking up, she had to steel herself for a different kind of chaos than the magical one she faced last night: the swirling, impossible to quantify, unrelenting angst and unbelievable demands of the many-eyed monstrosity known as the student body.

Even though this was a completely new high school, Buffy still got the same "feeling" whenever she stepped inside. Evil was there, just waiting around the corner.

Or maybe that was just some student cutting class. Hard to tell the difference these days.

Looking around for a parking spot, ignoring the pockets of suspicious-looking kids who were probably up to nothing worse than sneaking a smoke, Buffy thought back to when *she* had graduated from Sunnydale High School. That had been all about the fun, now hadn't it?

Class, we're here to see the Mayor turn into a really big snake, eat your principal, and stop the destruction of the world. Is everybody in?

Amazingly, they had been. The entire senior class had fought together to oppose Mayor Wilkins, and not everyone had survived. The school itself certainly hadn't. Buffy and her pals blew it up *real good* to destroy the Mayor after he turned into Mr. Big Snake.

The first Mr. Big Snake. Not the knock-off guy from last night.

Probably what had her thinking about those days . . .

Unfortunately, some things hadn't changed. Strange and deadly happenings were still the rage on the high school campus. Sunnydale High—though it didn't cover all this on the brochures—had a completely mad vampire hiding in the basement, a Hellmouth beneath the principal's office (formerly below the library), an assortment of vengeful spirits, and all kinds of supernatural delights!

She sighed, flustered. If only she could figure out a way of suggesting that Principal Wood move his office somewhere else . . . but she couldn't risk revealing her true calling as the Slayer and detailing the danger he was in just working here every day.

Buffy was about to pull into a faculty parking space when two loud, predatory muscle cars exploded into view, their overheated motors growling as their tires squealed and they barreled at her from around a turn in the parking lane. The two cars, one bright red, the other black with a single white racing stripe, were speeding side by side.

They nearly ran right into her car, and would have, too, if not for her Slayer reflexes—and that last tune-up. She jammed her car into the space so hard, her front tires bounced against the cement block directly before it and sent her careening back. Jamming the breaks, Buffy felt her car rocked by the force of the two drag racers coming within inches of her rear bumper.

Then they were speeding out of sight, tons of students laughing and cheering at the display.

Buffy slammed her car in park, yanked out her keys, and burst out onto the parking lot in time to catch the speed racers screech to a stop just before hitting the fence bordering the athletic field. Three teenagers stepped out of the cars, two boys, the drivers, and a girl. The drivers were a skinny white hip-hopster and an overweight blob, while their admiring passenger was a dark-haired skinny goth. Buffy was pretty sure the guys were juniors, the girl a sophomore. She also guessed that they really wouldn't appreciate the firm serving of fist sandwich she *so* wanted to give them.

All three laughed their fool heads off as they were quickly swallowed up by a congratulatory crowd of their peers, and the racing figure of the closest campus security guard.

Not my problem, not my problem, Buffy reminded

herself. If she was called, she would answer any questions put to her, but she was already getting a migraine and feeling the little veins in her throat and forehead popping from the stress of dealing with the apparently soon-to-be breaking down into a hissy fit Dawn and a load of other messes that were weighing on her mind, like paying the bills and wondering what was really up with Spike.

The Slayer walked into the front office to pick up her mail before going over to her office.

She heard Joe Butler, remedial math, and Alicia Towne, advanced English, comparing notes.

"I thought I was going to see a fistfight right there in class," Joe whispered. "I don't know what's gotten into these kids lately." He hesitated. "Did I really just say that? I sounded like my dad. . . ."

"No, it's true," Alicia said. "It's like that movie, Triple X, with that big muscle bald guy, Vin Damage or whatever his name is, and all the crazy stunts. I swear to God, it's all about one-upping the last lunatic stunt. . . ."

Hmmm. Maybe that's what she was almost a part of this morning. *A little monkey-see, monkey-do action.*

So it wasn't just her noticing a problem. Well, that was comforting. Usually when it was supernatural stuff, the population of Sunnydale just ignored it.

Class, today's word is "denial. . . ."

Buffy picked up her mail and went to her office. She had only just sat down and turned on her computer when her door burst open. In walked the lanky security guard she had seen outside, along with Larry, Moe, and

Curly, the Stooges who had nearly rammed her car on the way in.

The guard hiked up the waistband of his crisp blue uniform and thrust out his chest. What, was he trying to impress her with his manliness or something?

Sheesh!

"These three were caught drag racing in the parking lot. They need to see you and then Principal Wood, when he's free. Don't let them out of your sight."

Buffy frowned. "Yes. I'm intimately acquainted with the sitch."

"'Intimate'?" the guard said, raising an eyebrow. "*Never* use that word when it has anything to do with students, okey-dokey?"

Buffy hadn't noticed how much the guard had looked and sounded like Reverend Jim from *Taxi* until he said that. "Right, hoss," she muttered, wondering if she had heard just a little too much talk about TV Land rebroadcasts at the breakfast table lately.

The guard plopped them all down in seats around her desk. There was a small sound of pain from the old wood chair as the big one sat down, but it survived the ordeal. Buffy had no interest in judging people for their looks, but this kid's girth truly was enormous. In fact, there was a good chance he was morbidly obese, a health issue she'd take up with him some other time.

Fixing her gaze on the closest one, she peered at the tall, slim, good-looking one. He had fair skin, long straggly black hair, and a goatee. His large gray T-shirt hung outside oversized blue jeans that were almost falling off his hips, revealing the waistband of his

Calvin Klein underwear. Eminem he was not . . . but he clearly *thought* he was.

"'Sup?" he asked. "It's all good . . ."

"Okay, so which one are you? Fast? Or Furious?"

Buffy waited. Slim Shady wasn't talking. Nor did he seem the least bit concerned over his situation. It was like he had no fear whatsoever of the possible repercussions of their actions.

She could scare vamps and demons, but this crew wasn't fazed. Buffy doubted that even Principal Wood had a chance of getting through to them.

Nope. These three were almost certainly heading for juvie. . . .

Still, she had a job to do. "Well, you three seemed to have a busy morning," said Buffy. "I can't help wondering how you were planning to *end* your day, considering you started it with drag racing on campus and almost hitting the car of the school counselor."

"Oh, was that you?" the bigger one asked. He was also fair, but shorter, and at least a hundred pounds overweight. But he was clean shaven, and his brown hair was worn in a crew cut. He looked like a career academic who had surrendered to the Dark Side of the Force in his long-sleeved black shirt, black pants, and black boots.

"Yeah. Me. Fine, not like, with a wrecked car or a cracked-open head or anything," Buffy said.

"Cool," big boy said with a cherubic smile.

"See?" Slim said. "Toldya it's all good . . ."

The girl finally spoke up. "He always says that. Don't mind him."

Buffy turned what she hoped was a brutal and penetrating gaze at the girl. She wasn't even looking. Instead, she appeared fascinated by something in the ceiling. Little miss no eye contact was tall, slender, with straight purple hair, way too much eyeliner, black lipstick, and nail polish. She wore a black tank top, a red push-up bra that could be seen underneath her top, a short black pleather miniskirt, black fishnet stockings, and black combat boots.

Buffy doubted if she was ever going to see any of them trying to run for Prom King or Queen.

The first boy had his head down like he was napping. The second boy was leaning back in his chair and staring at the ceiling. The girl had tired of that so-five-seconds-ago practice and was removing some dirt from underneath her nails.

"All right, let's start with something simple," Buffy said. "Names?"

Slim, whose head was still down, peered at Buffy through his long hair. "Tommy Jacobs."

The second boy, who centered all his focus on the ceiling, said, "John Roberts."

The girl, who didn't look up from her nail cleaning, said, "Tina Jameson."

"All right, while we wait for Principal Wood, why don't you tell me what made you think that drag racing in the school parking lot, *during* school hours, was a good idea?" asked Buffy.

Tommy started to snore, so the Slayer snatched a pencil off her desk and threw it at him. The eraser hit him on the top of his head and he jumped up, awake, at least for the moment. "Whuh—what?" he said.

"You were having a bad dream. Now tell me about this morning."

"I was driving to school this morning and met up with Tommy at the stop sign just before school," said John. "Tommy leaned out of his car and said he wanted to go drag racing tonight. I said, hey, why wait that long? And so we drag raced the rest of the way to school."

"So you didn't plan this?" asked the counselor.

"Nah, the idea just came into our heads, so we did it," said John as he continued to glance at the ceiling.

An adjoining door opened, and Principal Robin Wood came out of his office. Buffy had to admit that the man always put in a lot of effort into his look for the day. He was a tall, handsome, bald, African-American man, and a very snappy dresser. Living in Beverly Hills had definitely given him taste in clothes.

"Wait here," said the Slayer to the students as she walked over to speak with the principal.

"What's going on?" asked Wood quietly.

"These three were drag racing in the school parking lot this morning. They almost ran into my car," said Buffy.

"Uh-huh. So we call the police."

"The real problem I'm having is that they don't seem to care at all about the consequences of what they've done. And it wasn't like they planned it, either. It was just, poof, in their heads, so they went ahead and did it."

"The poof part. That's a direct quote?"

"Sorta. Not."

"Don't worry. I'll talk to them." He turned to the troublemakers. "You three, in my office, now."

The less than heroic trio sludged their way into the principal's office. The door shut firmly behind them.

The second Buffy was back at her desk, she heard a commotion coming from right outside her office. Bouncing out of her chair, she yanked open her door and darted into the corridor.

"Girl fight!" a student screamed, almost right in her ear.

And there they were. In this corner, one with long wavy red hair, a pink peasant blouse, and white yoga pants. Taking her on today, another with long straight brown hair, low-riding blue jeans and a red tank top. They were yanking on each other's hair and trying hard to scratch each other's faces with their long acrylic nails.

Buffy didn't recognize these girls and she knew *all* the troublemakers. Well, except for the stooges who were drag racing. And these. But she would worry about who they were and what their damage was once she pulled them apart. She put one hand on the red-head's shoulder, another on the brunette's, and applied only the teensiest bit of Slayer strength.

They moved as one, suddenly shoving *her* right into a bank of lockers.

"Waitaminute!" she hollered. But they were already back at each other's throats. Going for take two, Buffy didn't hold back nearly so much as she usually had to, which was pretty weird.

What are they feeding kids these days?

Then she thought of one of those boring reports she'd been forced to read in class when she was still going to college, the statistics on people finding untapped fountains of extra strength and kinda "Hulking out" when they got mad enough. Well, if that was the case, the real question was, what had cheesed these two off so badly?

Buffy grabbed the redhead by the waist and carried her, kicking and screaming, into the office where she occupied her very own cubicle. The brunette followed, hurling obscenities. Buffy shoved them into opposite corners and stood between them, hands palm out, ready to smack them into next week if they wouldn't settle down.

Somehow, they got the message. Both sank into chairs, chests heaving, faces flushed. A throng of students gathered outside the office.

"Don't any of you have class?" Buffy asked.

"Yeah," the closest said. He didn't budge.

Risking the battling Betties being left alone for two seconds, Buffy slammed the door shut. She heard Principal Wood's raised voice—an unusual thing—and didn't worry about him coming out to see what this new discipline problem was all about. He clearly had his hands full.

Both girls were back on their feet, eyeing each other like pro wrestlers, when Buffy turned around.

"Sit!" the counselor snapped. They did. "How did this fight start?"

Both launched into an explanation at exactly the

same moment, but their hollering registered only as shrill babbling to Buffy.

"Enough!" shouted Buffy. She pointed at the girl with red hair. "You, tell me what happened and who you are."

"I'm Glinda Mack."

The Slayer's forehead crinkled. "Glinda? Like the good witch?"

The student rolled her eyes. Like she had never heard that one before.

Buffy glared at the other one. "Tell me you're *not* Sabrina."

She shrugged. "I'm Penny Carlyle, and *she* started it. She said that Colin Farrell is cuter than Josh Hartnett. I couldn't let her get away with that, so I punched her."

The many-time savior of the world was amazed. "This fight started because you couldn't agree on which movie star is cuter?"

The two teenagers looked at Buffy as if she didn't have a clue about what was important to them and why. Adults never understand.

Buffy gave them the usual lecture about trying to resolve differences nonviolently and handed out a week's detention for each of them, then sent them on their way. Separately.

The craziness kept up all day.

The Slayer was heading back to her office after lunch and saw a boy and girl making out in the hallway. Not so unusual. Frowned upon, yes, but nothing earth-shattering—

Yow.

The boy was kissing the girl's neck, and his head was sliding downward *fast*. The girl, who fortunately was wearing jeans, had one leg wrapped around the guy's waist and was grinding into him.

Before Buffy could say or do anything, a new crowd of teens gathered, and started egging the others on. The boy grabbed at the hem of the girl's sweater blouse, and the girl lifted her arms high over her head. Buffy had the distinct impression that the blouse was about to come off and there wasn't going to be anything underneath except freckles.

"Good lord," Buffy spat, storming in, separating the pair and hauling them right to Principal Wood.

Don't pass Go, don't collect $200.

Once the principal was done with the two love-birds, Buffy decided it was time for the two of them to have a talk.

"Okay, what's the deal?" Buffy asked. "You can't tell me this is normal."

Robin Wood smiled gently. "Buffy, I know you're new to being a counselor, but you were in high school yourself only a few years ago, and you *do* have a teenage sister. . . . This may seem like a lot today, and it is, but, on the whole, this is nothing out of the ordinary for any school at this time of year. The students are facing a lot of major stressors all at once: big tests, athletic tryouts, one form of competition after another. That's why you're here, to help take the pressure off, and you're doing a good job."

Buffy wasn't sure she saw it that way. Slaying

demons and monsters was, in comparison, a nice, safe, sane world compared with her new role as student counselor. At least there she felt like she had some kind of control over her existence. And it was equally stressful, equally chaotic, at home, where she was doing her best to raise Dawn while also being a good sister and good friend to her.

And that, of course, was a dicey thing even on a good day.

Buffy sighed and settled back behind her desk. "Okay, Principal Wood. I'm doing good. If you say so."

"I do."

Something broke in the hall. Shattering glass, running footsteps.

"Shall we?" he asked.

"After you," Buffy said demurely.

Together, they went to check it out.

Dawn Summers had been outside with the rest of her class when Tommy Jacobs and his all-too-amused crew were led away by the police. She wasn't sure why she looked up as he walked past. Mild curiosity, maybe. Normally, she hated gawking.

Tommy was staring at her, a thin, sexy smile on his lips. He tilted his head a little, a tiny jerk to the left.

Dawn did the same thing.

His grin widened to a smile. Then he was gone, and the moment had passed. Except . . . it hadn't. Not really. Dawn couldn't get Tommy out of her mind the rest of the day. She asked questions about him of everyone she knew, and finally, cut class to see if she could visit him in juvie.

His dad, a lawyer, had pulled some strings and gotten him out. But the police officer on duty said he'd be sure to let Tommy know such a sweet little honey like Dawn had been asking about him.

Dawn nodded, said okay, and left.

By the end of the day she had found out where he lived, and had gone by there twice, never once having the courage to go up and knock on his front door.

If she had been asked to explain her actions, she couldn't have. All she knew was that, normally, she would have been scared to pursue a boy, especially a troublemaker like he was. But now . . . things felt different somehow. Like she was changing inside.

She went home, having no idea that Tommy had seen her from his bedroom window and was already making plans for their next "chance" encounter.

Chapter Three

"I don't get it," Buffy said as they approached the building. "Who goes to church on a weekday evening?"

"Oh, lots of people," Willow offered. "A church isn't just a Sunday morning ritual for people. It's a community center, a gathering place, a meeting hall."

"I came here once on a Wednesday night for a meeting," Anya added. "But then I decided that being a sex addict, air quotes, wasn't a problem for me, it was just a problem for anyone who had a problem with it." She looked at Buffy and Willow, who were both staring at her, mouths agape. "What? It was after Xander and I, you know, didn't get married. And some of the guys there were pretty cute, but strangely uninterested."

"Can't imagine why," Buffy said. Anya hadn't exactly been crazy about the idea of coming along tonight, the former demon preferring to keep out of the line of fire when bad guys were being hunted down, but Buffy had decided, based on the message from Simon, that Anya's particular life experiences, her knowledge as a former demon, would come in handy tonight. Anya had only agreed after Willow had promised to take care of Anya's laundry and cleaning for a week.

Buffy turned her attention away from Anya—*which, who could ever figure her out, anyway?*—and back toward the church. The building was so modern that it might as well have been a fire station or a post office as a church—the only concession to "churchiness" being, to Buffy's mind, the concrete block tower that stood in front of it that, sort of, if she closed her eyes most of the way and squinted at it from an oblique angle, put her in mind of a steeple. It sat on a hill near the edge of Sunnydale, and the sun had set a few minutes before—the skies behind the hill were still painted with dark roses and violets slipping into indigo at the horizon.

There were a handful of cars parked in the lot, and some of the narrow, rectangular slits of windows showed lights, so Simon had been right, at least, about the fact that there were innocents inside. And he'd definitely been right about the demon disturbance at the Bronze. So, whoever Simon was and however much he was beginning to creep her out—*which is a lot, come to think of it,* Buffy realized—she knew she had to give him the benefit of the doubt this time too. He had called her, at home, which was bad enough in itself, what with telephone solicitors and creditors already making her think the telephone was an invention of pure evil, and told her that she needed to get to the church right away, or innocents would die. That was how he'd phrased it. No "Simon says," which was good. But even so, he'd sounded so self-assured, so certain that she would jump to his bidding, that she found herself wishing she could have just ignored this call as easily as she had that woman trying to sell portrait packages.

"I don't see any sign of demonic activity," Anya said, her voice hushed. Buffy had insisted that she be armed, so the former demon carried a small hand ax. "Unless you count that horrible caterwauling."

Buffy heard it too—multiple voices raised in anguish, muffled somewhat by the church's block walls and heavy steel doors.

"That's not caterwauling," Willow said with a grin. "That's choir practice."

"You say 'tomato,'" Anya retorted.

"We'll just take a look," Buffy said. "Vegetables aside."

"I thought tomatoes were fruit."

"Some things are not meant to be known by mere humankind," Willow offered. "Stick with five servings a day. Then it doesn't matter which they are."

As she placed a hand on the door, ready to open it

and find who knew what, Buffy found herself a little annoyed at both of her companions. They knew better, after all this time, but they still seemed to be treating this as a lark, a fun little excursion during which there was only a slim possibility of violent, painful death. Maybe it was the whole Simon thing—his calls, and especially his ghostly writing on the walls at the Bronze, were just weird enough to throw anybody a little off-kilter. Buffy knew that some of their patter was just black humor, meant to distract them from the very real dangers. But she didn't want to be distracted right now, by black humor or an unreasonable sister or any of the other responsibilities that pressed in upon her. She wanted to be focused on the job at hand. To that end, she yanked the heavy door toward her.

"Oh, hello!" a woman said, surprise in her voice. She was in her seventies if she was a day, stoop-shouldered and frumpy in a pink dress, and she held in her hands something that looked less like a demonic sacrifice and more like apple pie. *Smells like it, too,* Buffy thought. "You're a little late for choir practice, but if you've brought something for tomorrow's rummage sale, you're right on time."

Buffy held the door open and felt Willow and Anya crowding her shoulders. "Umm . . . no, no rummage here." She glanced at her companions. "Rummage, anyone?"

Willow held out empty hands. "Completely rummageless."

"I had rummage once," Anya added. She held her ax behind her back, Buffy noted. "But it cleared up."

"Otherwise, though," Buffy asked the woman, "everything's okay in here?"

"Oh, just fine," the woman replied. "Mrs. Brubaker just dropped off a box of clothes—you know how fast those boys are growing—and this pie will set nicely in the fridge until tomorrow." From behind her someplace, the singing was louder now, and more closely resembled human voices, almost in the vicinity of a tune.

"I . . . umm, I guess we'll be on our way, then. If everything's okay," Buffy stammered.

"Oh, just fine," the woman repeated. She still had an expectant look on her face, as if waiting for Buffy to either fork over some rummage or burst into song. Instead, Buffy simply released the door and let it close.

"So this Simon character isn't infallible after all," Anya said cheerfully, smacking the flat of the ax against her palm. "And we can go home."

Buffy shook her head. "Let's check the grounds first. Simon was right before, and I'd hate to walk away if there's a choir-hating, rummage-stealing, pie-eating demon somewhere on the premises just waiting for us to leave."

"It did smell good, didn't it?" Willow asked. "The pie, I mean. Fruit still counts as one of your five servings if it's baked in a pie, right?"

Buffy led the way through the manicured grounds, which looked, in the half-light of dusk, almost as sterile as the building itself did. Out in back there was a small children's playground with a padded rubber floor, so—*in yet another bow,* she thought, *to the over-*

protected generation—kids falling from the swings or slide wouldn't scrape their knees or tear their clothes. The playground was encircled by a tall fence, with a hedge behind that, and on the other side of the hedge was a small cemetery, with just a couple of dozen tombstones in neat, orderly rows as if the building's designer had planned them, too.

And among the tombstones were the demons.

"Or, Simon might have been right after all," Willow breathed.

"They look like they could use some of that pie," Anya suggested.

She wasn't kidding. *Not,* Buffy thought, *that I'm going to offer them pie.* But as demons went, these were among the most underfed-looking she could remember meeting.

Except possibly for the one who was standing inside a freshly uncovered grave, gnawing on what looked like most of an arm and staring at them over the top of his snack like a dog worried that someone was going to try to snatch an especially yummy bone away.

A couple of others sat on their haunches pawing at graves, but the rest were near the cemetery's edge, definitely headed toward the church. Simon's tip had been accurate after all, which Buffy found oddly gratifying. She still wondered about him, but at least he seemed to be on her side. The demons were moving on the church, a dozen of them, and even if one or two stopped off at the underground mini-mart for a snack, the others, had Buffy not shown up, would have walked in on choir practice in just a couple of minutes.

She doubted they were going for the pie.

"Come on," she heard one of the scrawny demons urging the one in the grave, apparently still unaware of the presence of the plan-spoiling Slayer. "They're fresher inside!"

"But I thought—" the munching one began.

"Change of plans," the other insisted.

"Talking with your mouth full," Buffy tsked. "If I were an authoritative parental-type unit—which I'm not—I'd put you on time-out for that."

Now they all spotted her, turning almost in choreographed unison toward the hedge and the three women who stood between them and live dinner. The eating one threw down his hand sandwich and clambered up from the grave to join his fellows. They were all quite tall and gaunt, and their height was exaggerated by shocks of wild hair standing on end.

Willow seemed to notice their common build at the same time. "They're like a demonic basketball team," she said. "The Hellmouth Globetrotters."

"Or a casting call for Michael Richards stunt doubles," Anya put in.

"Michael who?"

"Kramer," Anya said. "*Seinfeld*? Never mind."

As the tall demons moved toward them, moving stiff-legged and awkward inside their ragged suit pants and sport coats, one of them said, "We were going to go inside to eat. But since you've done us the service of coming to us, we'll take advantage of your generosity."

"I think you misunderstand," Buffy countered. She

pointed to herself. "Slayer." Then to Anya and Willow. "Slayer's friends. You guys have had your last supper."

Her words had the intended effect, or so she thought at first. There was a momentary pause in their advance, some hushed, hissing consultation among themselves. In their almost businesslike attire they gave the impression of a mad conference room where all of the conferees were shabbily dressed, barefoot, and some of them still had bits of decayed human flesh hanging from their jaws. The demons looked like stick men, as if she could snap them into little bits without working up a sweat. She wasn't even sure why Simon had warned her about this attack—the old lady with the pie could have taken these guys.

But then their consultation ended and they came toward her, and as they did they began to change. Their arms grew visibly shorter, sinking back into sleeves they had seemed too long for, but at the same time their fingernails—*not quite fingernails,* Buffy realized now, but spurs of bone at the ends of their hands—sharpened to points, grew longer. It was as if their flesh was malleable enough to expand or contract at will but the bones were of a fixed length. Then she noticed that their height decreased a little as well. They were still tall, well over six feet, but they had jutting claws sticking from their feet as well.

As they contracted they even began to look more solid, not quite so gaunt, and less ungainly. That was when she decided that they might in fact have a fight on their hands. "Brace yourselves, you guys," she whispered to her friends. The words had barely passed her lips when the demons attacked.

Buffy caught the first one by the wrists when he drove his bone claws toward her throat, and spun, using his own momentum to carry him past her, over her hip, and down on the ground. He was surprisingly strong, though, and he yanked his arms from her grasp, rolled quickly, and began to lurch back to his feet. She loosed a snap kick into his chin that snapped his neck, and he let out a grunt of pain. But then, head lolling at an impossible angle, he continued getting up. She kicked again, this time at his midsection, and he folded around her boot. Not sure what else to do, Buffy grabbed his head and yanked, tearing the flesh of his neck. The head came off bloodlessly in her hands, and she tossed it aside. Finally, the demon dropped to the ground.

"The heads!" she shouted. "Take off their heads!" But by then two more were on her. She could barely see Anya swinging her ax, or Willow—well, Willow was far from powerless, but she hadn't brought any physical weapons—but then both her friends were blocked from view by the demons. The bone spurs of one tore through her cotton top and ripped the skin of her abdomen, and the other was slashing for her face.

Flesh would heal, but the top had cost big bucks, even on sale. She grabbed the arms of that demon and twisted, trying to tie them into a pretzel and at the same time slam him into his companion. The demons breathed heavily through their mouths as they fought, but were otherwise silent.

"You might as well give up now," Buffy said

through gritted teeth as she tried to outmuscle two powerful demons. "Twelve against three when one of the three is a Slayer? Those are suicide odds." She kicked at the ankle of the one whose arms she held and felt bone snap under her assault, which was good, because he'd been trying to kick at her with those daggerlike toe bones. Now he was off-balance on one leg and she was able to spin him faster, keeping him between her and the third demon's lunges. The other demon drew back for yet another try, and Buffy saw her chance. She hauled the demon she held in front of the onrushing claws and was rewarded by a squeal of pain and an expulsion of really foul breath when they sank into his back. The demon went slack in her hands and she released his arms, grabbing his head and twisting it like a screw-off bottle cap.

When it tore off, she hurled it into the face of the third demon, who batted it away. But in the split second he worked to free his claws from his comrade's body, Buffy doubled her fists together and swung them into the side of his head, trying to knock one out of the park. His neck snapped but, like the first one, that wasn't enough to put him down. He drove his freed hand at Buffy. She had to step back to dodge the murderous claws, and doing so put her within range of another one coming toward her from behind. Dancing to avoid his attack, her foot caught on the corpse of the demon she had just beheaded.

She was a Slayer, though, well trained, and she didn't really trip. But she allowed her opponents to think she had, and she crouched low, over the body.

Both demons thrust their claws forward into empty air above her head. Then she uncoiled, using their extended arms to help catapult her into the air between them, spinning as she did so. Head high, Buffy released two kicks and then lightly touched down again. Neither demon had been decapitated, but both reeled from the blows.

"Buffy?" It was Anya, and she sounded scared. "A hand, maybe?"

Buffy slammed the nearer of the two demons in the gut and, when he doubled over, she caught him in a headlock, wrenching his head from his body, and glanced over at Anya. One headless demon lay on the ground at her feet, victim of her hand ax, but three more surrounded her, advancing simultaneously. Willow was similarly surrounded. She'd have to wrap this up fast.

The fourth demon kicked at her, and she sidestepped its foot claws. But it kicked again and again, and it supplemented the kicks with hand jabs. She tried to find a way past the claws, but this one was fast. Though she could barely see its eyes in the gathering dark, there seemed to be a glint of pleasure in them, as if this demon, in particular, relished a good fight. Which, ordinarily, she'd have taken in the spirit in which it was meant. But she couldn't afford to get tied up with one while Willow and Anya were overwhelmed by numbers.

"Any other time . . . ," she said. Then, ignoring the slashing bone spurs, she closed with the demon. She felt it cutting her over and over again, but she blocked out the pain and clamped her hands onto its neck. The sensation of bone crushing and flesh ripping underneath her hands was a little disconcerting, but, on the bright side, it made the claws stop jabbing into her, and a moment later there was one less demon in the fight.

Momentarily without an opponent, Buffy looked to her friends again. Anya had slashed a second one, but there were still two uncomfortably close, clawing at her. And four still surrounded Willow, who stood, seemingly calm and collected, in the center of them. Her hands were out, palms up, at her sides, and Buffy could see her lips moving even if she couldn't hear what her friend said.

A spell, she realized. *Willow's protecting herself with a spell. That's why they haven't reached her yet.*

But as she watched, she realized it was more than that. The demons surrounding Willow suddenly shrieked in pain and backed away from her. Even the two by Anya felt whatever it was Willow was dishing out. Anya swung the ax at one of the retreating forms, and its head tumbled in the air several times before thumping to the ground. All the remaining demons began to claw at their own bodies, as if trying to scratch unreachable itches, and began to run away from the church, away from the cemetery, tearing great gouges in themselves as they did so.

"You guys okay?" Buffy asked.

"Fine," Anya said. "If you don't count being disgusted and really needing a shower to get demon bits out of my hair."

"Will? Whatever you did, it worked."

Willow gave her a fleeting smile. "That's the thing," she said. "I didn't exactly do anything. I mean, I started a spell, but as soon as I did, the demons stopped and wouldn't get anywhere near me. As I continued it they started to act like they were in genuine pain from it. But I never even finished it—it's like they were running just from the idea of it, from the act of casting it, not from any effect of the spell itself."

Anya hoisted her ax to her shoulder. "Should we chase them? Finish them off?"

"I'm thinking maybe," Buffy started to say. But then her attention was caught by three of the demons she had beheaded. Their bodies were all on the ground together, touching in at least one spot—an outflung arm lying across a thigh, the bone spurs of another resting against the bloodless, ragged edge of a neck. As she watched, though, the bodies began to stir, to transform. For a moment she thought they were going to get up again, but they didn't. Instead, they—"liquefied," was the best word she could think of. Almost like mercury, a liquid with many qualities of a solid, they seemed to go soft and to melt together. Within the space of a minute, the three bodies were one puddle of ooze, and the physical space they had taken up on the ground had been reduced by at least half.

And still, the transformation wasn't over. Buffy, Willow, and Anya watched wordlessly as it continued. The puddle grew smaller as ripples in the liquid mass ran toward one another, toward a central point. At that point the substance seemed to congeal, becoming harder, more substantial.

Now Willow spoke, her voice hushed with awe. "From solid to liquid and back to solid," she said. "But what's it making?"

"A smaller mess than it started out as," Anya offered. "If they're not going to go poof like vampires, at least it's good that they clean up after themselves."

"I'm not sure I'd define whatever's happening as *good*," Buffy replied. The process went on, the shape that the liquid was forming into becoming more and more distinct, until finally it was no longer a puddle but a thing, as solid and real as the creatures had been a moment before, but far smaller. *And,* Buffy thought, *much more frightening.*

The three demonic corpses had remade themselves into a sword—part of one, really, just a pommel and grip and half a cross guard, leading into a few inches of shiny metal blade that glowed with a strange, mystical light of its own. It looked sharp and unnatural and definitely dangerous, even though it was just a fragment of a weapon sitting on the lawn of the church.

"Maybe if you had put them all together you'd have gotten a whole sword out of it, Buffy," Anya suggested. "Too bad you weren't thinking ahead."

"It's definitely not a natural sword," Willow said. "I don't think we should touch it. Not with our bare hands, anyway. We should wrap it in something. Something thick. Like a steel wall."

"I don't intend to touch it," Buffy said. "It's probably a trick of some kind, anyway."

But as she stared at it, riveted by the magickal transformation and the glowing object, the grass near her feet began to rustle. *Snake?* she wondered briefly. But it wasn't that—it was words, writing themselves in the grass as they had on the wall at the Bronze.

Good old Simon.

"Buffy, do you . . . ," Anya began.

Buffy cut her off sharply. "I see it."

SIMON SAYS, the invisible hand wrote in the neatly cut grass, *YOU OWE ME, SLAYER. SO SAVE THAT FOR ME.*

"It looks like we've been Simon-ized again," Willow suggested. "What are you going to do?"

Buffy shrugged. "Not much else I can do," she replied matter-of-factly. "I guess I'll touch it after all." She bent down and scooped the sword up from the grass. It felt almost normal to her hand, just like any other sword, even though it continued to glow. And there was something else, something so faint, she almost didn't notice at all. The sword seemed to throb just the slightest little bit in her grip, as if suffused with some kind of internal energy.

Or, she realized, *as if it were somehow alive. . . .*

Chapter Four

"**W**hy is research always so violent?" Willow asked when they got back to Buffy's house.

"Violent?" Buffy echoed. "Seems like about the least violent thing we do."

"But we always have to 'hit the books,'" Willow countered. "Or 'break out' some of the ancient texts and 'crack them open.' I like books. Why can't we massage some spines, or caress some pages, for a change?"

Buffy eyed her oldest friend carefully. Willow had been through a lot—*okay, that's an understatement; since Tara died, Willow had been through hell and back almost as literally as some other people I could name. I hate to think it, but maybe she could use a date.*

"You can massage and caress all you want, Will," she said after a moment. "If it'll make the books happy, more power to you. I don't care how we do it. I just want us to get the information we need."

They were in the living room of the Summers house—the empty Summers house, Buffy noted with a flash of concern, since Dawn didn't seem to be home. Buffy was still on her feet, but Anya had sprawled on a chair as if exhausted by the battle, and Willow sat upright, hands in her lap, on the couch.

"Willow, why don't you dig up what you can on the demons," Anya suggested, "and I'll take the sword?" She laughed at her own pun. "Get it? 'Dig up' what you can on grave-robbing demons. That's good."

"Not that good," Buffy replied, straight-faced. "And I have a better idea, anyway."

"Better. Okay," Anya said, sounding a little disappointed. "I can live with better."

"Will, you take Simon. We need to figure out what his story is, who he is, how he's getting this information. And how he seems to know what goes on even when he's not around."

"I can explain the remote writing if you want," Willow offered with a smile. "It's a classic."

"If it's just a parlor trick, I don't care," Buffy answered her. "But I don't think the rest of it is, and I think it's important to find out. I'll take some of the old books—gently—and look up our hungry demons."

"So I still get to look up the sword?" Anya asked. She seemed enthusiastic about the sword. Since sarcasm, not enthusiasm, had been her strong point lately,

Buffy didn't mind tossing her that particular metaphorical bone.

"Sure, you take the sword," Buffy said. "Knock yourself out."

She started to go into the other room to find some demon histories when Willow stopped her with another question. "About Simon, Buffy? I don't know if it was just me, but did you get the sense, at that church, that the demons themselves had just then decided what they were going to do? It looked like they came just for the graveyard, to me, but then decided they'd go inside for the fresh catch of the day. And they were just making up their minds about it when we got there. Which means—"

"Which means," Buffy interrupted, "Simon knew what they were planning before they did."

"Simple Simon is getting less simple by the minute," Anya put in. "He now not only knows what's going on when he's not there but he knows it before it happens? Is anybody else feeling those little hairs on the back of your neck standing up?"

Willow absently brushed one hand across her neck. "Well, that's one explanation. Or else maybe he knew they would go to the church because he instigated it in some way."

"Instigated? How instigated?" Buffy demanded. She had a great deal of faith in Willow's intuition, so when her oldest friend came up with a mental leap like this one, she wanted to know everything she could.

"He told you to go to the church," Willow pointed out. "And you went. Maybe he told them, too. Maybe he drew them there somehow. They may not even eat live humans."

"Then why were they going all Pavlov's dog at the idea?" Anya queried.

Willow shrugged. "I'm just saying, we don't know much about them yet. Maybe they're just extremely suggestible. If this Simon planted the idea, maybe they just ran with it. Or maybe he planted something in the church that he knew they'd be attracted to. Until we know more, we just can't tell if he's prescient or manipulative. Or both."

"Which is yet another reason to get cracking on— I mean, to get *started* on—the research," Buffy pointed out, anxious to get some solid answers before Simon called again—which she had begun to feel sure he would do. "Speculation is great, but if we could back it up with some facts, we'd be even better off."

"Right. Okay," Willow agreed. "Maybe I'll start on the computer instead of, you know, books, for Simon. Wouldn't want to have to break any spines."

Buffy left them to their own devices and found a couple of massive tomes—the *Demonica Britannica,* effectively, in which she could usually find at least some reference to any beastie she encountered. The tricky part was always figuring out where to look, since there wasn't anything like a handy-dandy cross-referenced index in which she could find a listing for, say, scrawny flesh-eaters with bad hair. She spread the books out on the dining room table and began turning pages, scanning for anything that might leap out at her.

Flesh-eaters were, of course, quite numerous in the

books. There were plenty of human examples, from the ancient Aztecs and Anasazi right up to modern serial killers like Ed Gein and Jeffrey Dahmer. But once past the human varieties, which were more common than Buffy liked to think about but still rare enough to merit special notice, the practice became far more widespread, to the point that it ruled out fewer varieties of demonhood than it included.

Which left the other aspects of their recent foes to narrow down the search. They were tall and gaunt and poorly dressed, but the most unique thing about them, as far as Buffy could tell, was the way they had been able to compress their arms and legs to allow their bones to become cutting and stabbing weapons. And, of course, the way three of them had turned into goop and then a sword—but that had only been three, not all of them, so she wasn't confident that it was a universal trait among their kind.

"Do you know what?" Anya said, walking over to Buffy with a different book in her hands. She slammed the heavy volume down onto the table with a force that made Buffy glad Willow was in the next room, online. "There are a lot of swords out there! Did I say a lot? I meant a ton. A kazillion. Or some other made-up word that indicates whole bunches of the things."

"I take it," Buffy said soothingly, "you haven't been able to find this precise sword in the texts."

"Not yet," Anya replied. "Maybe if I have some more time. A year, say. I can tell you what it's not. It's not Excalibur, it's not a Sword of Charlemagne, which it turns out is a type of sword, and not one guy's sword like it sounds. It's not an ancient Palestinian sickle sword or a *kopis* or a hoplite sword. There's just enough of it, as it turns out, to rule out a lot of things, but not enough to pin it down."

"Sounds like the same trouble I'm having," Buffy admitted. "Not quite enough information."

"It'd be helpful if there was something more special about this one," Anya went on. "An inscription, some etching in the blade, a particularly unusual hilt design. Anything."

"Umm . . . it glows?"

Anya tossed her a sneer. "Glowing sword? When you get past basic construction into the mystical sword category, that's about at the top of the list. You've got your glowing swords, your singing swords, your soul-eating swords—"

"They really have those?"

"By the boatload, apparently." Anya gestured toward the book. "There's even one in there that, if you look at your reflection in the blade, you see your own ideal you. Which, if I found that sword, how would I ever know?"

"There must be something special about this one," Buffy said, desperately trying to keep Anya at least in the same neighborhood as the subject at hand.

"Well, it was made of three dead demons," Anya reminded her. "But I haven't found any references to anything like that. And you're supposed to be figuring out just who our demon friends are, so maybe that's really something that should come from you."

Which I was working on when you interrupted me,

Buffy thought. But she didn't verbalize it. Instead, hoping to lead by example, she returned to her book and started once again scanning the pages. "You're right," she said. "Still working on that one."

Willow usually loved the research part of the job. She thrived on learning, on absorbing information like some kind of data-sponge. It was, she believed, the same thing that so enthralled her about school. She'd probably be one of those perpetual students, still enrolled at UC Sunnydale into her fifties, ticking off the young kids because she kept skewing the grading curve.

But somehow today she was finding it hard to get into the groove, to push everything else away and focus on the task at hand. No, things were weird in Sunnydale—*Well,* she thought, *that's status quo; it would only be notable if things* weren't *weird in Sunnydale.* But that kind of weird was the kind that involved grave-robbing, churchgoing demons. This kind of weird was something else entirely, and she couldn't put it out of her mind sufficiently to give all her attention to the search for Simon.

And there was one thing about the demons that had struck her as exceedingly odd—one aspect she hadn't even discussed in any detail with Buffy, although she thought maybe she should. Their response to her spell-casting. They had, almost as soon as she'd started speaking, frozen in place, refusing to come any closer to her. Then they'd reacted like she had done something truly terrifying, or—and this was closer to the truth, she realized—as if they were allergic to it.

But she hadn't actually cast any spells, for which she was glad. Magic was something she was wary of these days, and tried to avoid whenever possible. The demons had reacted not to a magical spell but to the process of casting one. She'd been standing there, palms up, speaking words, but she might as easily have been saying a prayer or reciting a recipe for blueberry scones at that point. Until a spell began to take effect, it was just a bunch of words.

All these threads ran through her mind, not tying neatly together into any real ideas but instead getting in the way of any insight she might otherwise bring to the task at hand. Which was finding out who, or what, Simon was. She had tried a few key-word searches, pairing "Simon" with "spirit-writing" and "clairvoyant" and "remote viewing," but had come up with nothing that way. Drawing a complete blank, she decided rather to take a more prosaic approach to the problem, and after fiddling with firewalls and probing passwords for a few minutes, she had hacked into the telephone company's files.

Accessing Buffy's number was easy enough. But there were a lot of calls coming into and out of the house in any given week. *Dawn needs her own line,* she decided. *That would help.* But Simon had called this afternoon, so that narrowed the scope of her search considerably. Buffy had text-messaged her right before her last class of the day, which started at five. Willow doubted that Buffy would have waited around for long after Simon had called her. But there were no incoming calls registered around there. She found the out-going call Buffy had made to her cell at 4:57, and backtracked from there.

And the last in-coming call recorded had been at 3:14. Willow ran a search on that number and found that it belonged to a local telephone solicitation company. The call had been brief, anyway—Buffy wouldn't even have been home from Sunnydale High yet, and she had mentioned something earlier about getting a message on the answering machine about carpet cleaning services. She had also specifically said, though, that she had talked to Simon on the phone, that he had called her at home with his warnings, on both occasions.

Just in case, Willow went back to the records for the night before—the first time Simon had called, when he had sent Buffy to the Bronze. There were several calls in during the course of the evening, but when Willow traced the numbers back to their sources, they were all perfectly innocent, or else were Dawn's friends. Nothing that she could identify as Simon, though.

Which just made the whole mystery of who Simon was that much more mysterious. He was either high-tech enough to cloak his calls, hiding them even from the phone company, or he was magically proficient enough to accomplish the same thing.

If he had done it magically, Willow realized, there was something she could do about it. Phone calls left records on the phone company's computers, and by the same token, magic left traces of its own, which could be discerned through the use of other magic. Willow had felt nervous about using magic at the church, to fend off the demons, but she'd been willing to do so to save herself and her friends and the pie-lady. Now she found that she was nervous again. And it wasn't just about using magic. It was about Simon himself—he seemed to be on the right side of things, but then why was he so secretive? He definitely had an agenda of some kind, Willow knew. She just hoped that it didn't come into conflict with Buffy's.

She could hear Buffy and Anya discussing edged weapons in the dining room. That was fine—she didn't want to broadcast the fact that she was about to use magic, anyway. And this was an easy spell, one that would only take a few seconds to get results—she'd be in and out before anyone knew she was up to anything at all.

For a starting point, she went back to the time that Buffy had called her, 4:57. *Figure Simon called the house less than five minutes before,* she thought. *So between 4:52 and 4:57.* Buffy's phone records were still on the screen in front of her, which helped focus her powers. She visualized Buffy's phone, and then the wire that led from the phone jack and connected, after a series of switches and connections, to the phone company. Even cell phone calls were transmitted to Buffy's land line as a series of digital signals over phone company wires. As Willow concentrated her thoughts so intensely on those lines at that time, her consciousness fled her body and joined the billions of bits of data on the wires. She traveled them like they were tunnels and she an infinitesimally tiny motorist riding on a data stream freeway. When she found the magical trace of the call she was looking for, it would glow with a brilliant blue light, like neon in a bar window.

There! She saw it, ahead of her, just as blue and bright as she had expected. Simon had magically concealed it, then, but whoever he was, he didn't know he was dealing with Willow Rosenberg, witch *extraordinaire,* against whom almost all other spellcasters were the rankest of amateurs. She reached out, figuratively speaking, to grab the blue line. She would follow it to its source and they'd know Simon's identity in just a few short moments—

But as soon as her hands closed on the blue thread—and even though it was all internal, she knew she was still sitting in Buffy Summers's living room staring at a computer monitor; even so, her hands made a clenching motion as she grasped the line—she felt an unexpected shock, like the glowing blue line was a live electric cable. It burned and sent wave after wave of agonizing power through her body, but once she had her hand closed on it, she couldn't let go; her hand was paralyzed in place. It was a trap! Simon had set a mystical backlash on the line, just in case someone tried this exact thing, and she had walked right into it, so overconfident that it hadn't even occurred to her to be careful of it.

Part of Willow knew that she was still sitting in Buffy's house, but the rest of her also knew that didn't really matter. This could still kill her. *Would* kill her, if she couldn't do something about it, and fast. But her hand wouldn't respond to her command. She couldn't release the line. Where her consciousness was, the line was sparking and flashing and the blue glow grew and grew, enveloping her, and once it did that, once it consumed her altogether, she was a dead witch, *that* she knew for certain.

But Willow Rosenberg didn't go without a fight. Simon had just proved himself a very capable magician indeed, and one with no qualms about killing anyone who tried to find him. That was fine, to Willow; that just defined the problem a little more clearly.

It also meant, though, that he wasn't someone the regular Willow could defeat. Regular Willow was afraid of magic now; she knew too certainly what it could do to her. But there was another Willow, inside that one, and the other Willow could do many things that the regular Willow would no longer allow herself to.

She just had to let the other Willow out.

Nothing to it, really. She wanted to get out, anyway. Open the door, just the slightest bit . . .

Willow knew that, from the outside, looking at her, there were definite physical manifestations of what she had come to think of as Dark Willow. The black, empty eyes, the ferocious expression, even the pure power that swirled around her. From inside, though, she couldn't experience those things. She felt it more as a kind of freedom, a lowering of inhibitions, kicking open a floodgate of forces that she could barely control . . . if she could at all.

Dark Willow wasn't constrained by the fears that

Willow had, though, about keeping her powers in check. The moment she let Dark Willow out, the blue line in her hand reacted, trying to draw away from her. She directed that power at the blue glow that emanated from the line, that threatened to devour her, and she pushed it back, back into the line it had come from. As the glow retreated, the line stopped trying to buck itself from her grip. She felt a momentary burn, different from the electrical one she had experienced just seconds before. This one was a flash of heat, and when she looked at the wire, it had consumed itself. It turned to ash, and then a wind blew in that scattered the ash in every direction.

Simon had won after all. His trap hadn't killed Willow, but he had managed to destroy the only thing that might have guided her to him. With more than a little difficulty—it was always, always hard, once she had let Dark Willow out—she closed the door again on that terrifying aspect of herself.

A moment later, sitting in Buffy's living room, Willow blinked and looked around. She was herself again, plain old Willow. She looked at her hands, half-expecting them to be scorched, but they were fine, just marked where she had dug her own nails into her palms. Physically, then, she was fine. Emotionally, though—emotionally, she was a train wreck. Unleashing Dark Willow was better than dying, but only just. There might even come a time when it wasn't, she knew. She would have to face that time when it came, though—stressing about it now wouldn't help at all.

On shaky legs, she rose and went into the dining

room, where Buffy and Anya both sat poring over their books, oblivious to what she had just gone through. Buffy looked up at her and smiled. "Making any headway, Will?"

"Not much," Willow confessed. "All I know for sure is that we have a problem. Your friend Simon?"

Buffy waited, expectantly.

"He *really* doesn't want to be found. And he's pretty powerful. Not pretty powerful. I mean, he's . . . he's strong, Buffy. He's scary strong."

Chapter Five

Eyes slowly opening, Xander contentedly gazed up at the ceiling of his apartment. His *amazing* apartment . . .

This place was like a dream come true.

Golden sunlight shone through the windows, bathing the bedroom with a warm glow. Smiling, Xander lay there for a moment, luxuriating in the feel of the two-tone blue silk pajamas he wore and the cool, clean sheets he rested on. Stifling a yawn, he asked, "You want some breakfast, baby?"

Beside him, Anya was just awakening. She frowned, but only a touch. "Mmm. Don't you have to go to work?"

"Nah, I shut the crew down for the day. My guys

start singing and dancing around me, I don't know if I can deal. It's a flab thing. So, waffles?"

Smiling dreamily, Anya looked into his eyes and said, "Will you still make me waffles when we're married?"

Xander shook his head slightly. "No, I'll only make them for myself, but by California law, you will own half of them." Leaning over, he gave her a quick kiss. "Hey, how about omelettes? I could do an omelette. I've almost got that. . . ."

As he dropped back onto his side of the bed and kept rambling, Anya sat up, throwing off her covers. She was wearing a slinky, lacy, two-piece red silk thingee, and it made Xander's breath catch in his throat. She was so beautiful. So perfect. He couldn't believe how lucky he was to have her, even though a few doubts still plagued him about the wedding. He watched as she took a deep breath and opened her mouth. Oh, good—the singing! Sure, it was kind of an awkward song, but how cool was the whole wacky romance dance number thing? And he frowned, trying to figure out exactly how he knew what was coming. Sound erupted from Anya's lovely lips, but instead of dulcet tones, it was a loud, annoying, and insistent, "BZZZZZZZZZZZZZZZ."

Xander shot up in bed, heart thudding. He wore a sweat-drenched, smelly, gray T-shirt and Daffy Duck boxers he'd had on for three days straight. The sheets weren't exactly fresh out of the laundry, either. Instinctively, he looked beside him. The expansive bed was empty, of course. No Anya. No *anybody*. Just himself and a plush toy of Ace the Bat Hound that he quickly slid under the pillow. Then he reached out and silenced the alarm.

Sunlight still streamed through the windows, but it no longer seemed golden. Instead of warming the place, it just threw everything into a stark, cold clarity. He gazed around, taking in the space. What had seemed perfect for two now felt very empty for just one. . . .

Rubbing his face roughly, Xander shook himself and rolled out of bed. "Get a grip," he said, doing his best to fake chipper even though there was no one around to hear or to judge. He had no idea why that sort of thing made him worry so much, he only knew that it did. "Yep! Just another morning in stately Harris Manor. No singing, no dancing, and no embarrassing revelations."

Stumbling out of the bedroom, he made his way through the living room and past the dining room table over to the kitchen. Fumbling through the cupboards, he grabbed a box of fudge Pop-Tarts. "Chocolatey goodness. Just the thing to start your morning right. Who needs the hassle of waffles and omelettes?" Opening the refrigerator, he snagged a carton of milk, squeezed open the spout, gave a sniff, and took a swig. "Excellent. No lumps. Banner day."

Scooping up the Pop-Tarts and the milk, he shuffled to the table and dropped into a chair. Near his place mat were two piles of comic books—read, face-down; unread, faceup. He shuffled through the "unread" pile. "Let's see, Catwoman, Nightwing, Fantastic Four and . . . ah-ha! Way of the Rat! Can't go wrong with a talking monkey."

Tearing open the foil envelope, he shook out one of the Pop-Tarts. Taking a big bite, he flipped open the comic book's cover.

That's when the phone rang. With a roll of his eyes and a heavy sigh, he got up to answer it. Under his breath he was saying, "Be Buffy. Be Willow. Be a dark gruesome from beyond the stars." Closing his eyes, he picked up the phone, held it tentatively a couple inches from his ear, and said, "Hello?"

A blast of noise assaulted him from the receiver. His shoulders sagged.

Another telephone solicitor. Xander allowed the salesperson's call to go on all of fifteen seconds before, rolling his eyes, he decided that he couldn't take much more. He made a quiet "tik" noise with his tongue. "Oops, sorry. Did you hear that? Uh-huh. Call Waiting. Gotta go. Talk to you soon. Buh-bye."

He hung up the phone very gently, because he was fighting the impulse to slam it down. After a couple deep breaths, he promised himself that he would invest in Caller ID as soon as he got home from work.

Glancing at the wall clock, he realized he was running late. Dropping the half-eaten Pop-Tart into the trash under the kitchen counter, he headed for the bathroom.

After his shower, Xander wiped the fog off the mirror and stared at his reflection. Gingerly, he reached up, his fingers tracing the skin where Will had scarred him when a nasty combo of grief and magic addiction had sent her over the edge and she'd tried to end the world. His face was now perfectly smooth. There was no sign of the injury.

He gave a deep sigh as he squirted shaving gel into his left hand. There *should* still be marks. Unfortunately, he'd made the mistake of sacking out on the couch at the Summerses' house one Sunday afternoon. Dawnie, full of good intentions, had used a healing crystal from the Magic Box to take those nasty scars away.

She just didn't realize . . . those scars had *meant* something to him.

Sure, it wasn't the first time he'd been around when the world got saved, but it was the first time *he'd* saved the world. Him. Xander Harris. He might just be a geek/sidekick/carpenter, but he'd managed to pull it off this time on his own. In fact, he'd pulled it off precisely because he *was* Xander Harris. Anyway, there should be something left of that. Some tangible reminder. Not just for him, but for the rest of the gang. He didn't want them to forget. Then Dawnie erased the scars, never thinking to ask whether it was okay. Just one more thing over which he had no control whatsoever. Like his parents. Like his empty, echo-y apartment. Like pretty much every aspect of his life, except for work.

Work. The word hit him like a bucket of cold water. He finished shaving and threw on some clothes in record time. He heard the phone ringing and decided to let the machine get it this time. Soaring past the answering unit, he heard a woman's voice he didn't recognize say, "Mr. Antwerp, this is a once-in-a-lifetime sales opportunity, just for you!"

He frowned again. Getting solicitation calls was bad enough, but when they weren't even for you?

"Antwerp, Schmantwerp, never heard of the guy," Xander muttered, grabbing for the door. Suddenly, he felt a little woozy. Kind of light-headed. His body relaxed, the tension seeming to drain from it whether he wanted to or not.

Weird. He wondered if he was coming down with something, but it wasn't like him to be sick.

A ten-minute drive later and he was pulling onto the work site downtown, the dizziness by the door already forgotten. His company was putting in a new bank—and a big one too. Ten stories, with lots of room for office space. Right now, it was just a ten-story skeleton, gleaming metal beams overrun by bulky guys in hard hats who ran the girders with surprising grace. But one day, it would be a place where hundreds of people came to work, or cashed their paychecks, or maybe even met and fell in love. It was a thrill to be able to look at a building he had helped bring into existence and know that, for as long as that building stood, it bore his mark. He had done something worth doing.

Not that saving the world with the Scoobs wasn't a good thing, too. This was just different.

This was just about . . . him. And no one would take it away when he was napping.

As Xander exited his American-made four-door sedan, the shift leader, Dan Martin, strolled over. Martin was a big, friendly guy, 6'2", with broad shoulders, reddish hair, and an outdoorsy look. He'd been working construction for five years before Xander joined the outfit, but he didn't seem to mind that the younger man had been promoted over him. Xander reflected that Martin was a lot like a veteran sergeant coaching the green lieutenant through his first command. The thought made him shiver like someone had dumped ice down his back. It'd been a long time since a Halloween costume had transformed him, briefly, into a soldier, with all the experience that came along with the job. After the spell was broken, the skills and knowledge had slowly drained away. Still, every once in a while, some of that knowledge would pop back into his head. It was creepy, though occasionally useful.

Grinning, Dan clapped him on the back. "Mornin', boss. Cuttin' it kind of close today."

"Slow start this morning."

As they started walking toward the trailer that served as the site office, Dan said, "Hopefully the day will improve. What's on your agenda?"

"Couple hours here so we can go over the schedule for the next few days. Then I have to run over to the school. Some sort of hassle with the plumbing routing. After that, I've got that meeting with that return client, Rebekah Olschan. She really liked how we handled her last project and she's looking to develop some land just outside of town. Needless to say, I'm pretty pumped." Xander looked a little sheepish. "Could be a big boost for the company, I mean."

Dan smirked knowingly. "Uh-huh. Couldn't have

anything to do with the fact that Ms. Olschan isn't exactly hard on the eyes."

Xander made a face and waved off the remark. "Of course not. Purely professional. You know I don't mix work and—"

A sultry voice interrupted with, "Good morning, Mr. Harris."

The voice belonged to Mindy Wells. She was working her way through college as Xander's administrative assistant (he always had to remind himself that "secretary" was considered a no-no phrase). She stood in the doorway to the office trailer holding a black coffee mug with a yellow and black Batman emblem on it. Mindy was around twenty and slender, with short, glossy black hair and dark brown eyes. Below her killer smile she was wearing a red silk blouse, a short, black leather skirt, and black calf-high boots that showed off her exceptional legs. "You look like you could use a hot cup of java."

Xander gratefully accepted the mug from her as he climbed the two steps to the door.

"What did I tell you about calling me 'Mr. Harris'?"

Rather than ducking inside, she turned sideways to let him pass. "It makes you feel old."

As Xander eased by, they brushed slightly. She looked up at him, a playful smile on her lips, and said quietly, "Maybe I like older men."

Xander cleared his throat a little uncomfortably.

Once he was inside, Mindy followed him, leaving Dan the doorway all to himself.

She'd started flirting with Xander just a couple

weeks after she hired in. Not that he didn't flirt back. He always flirted with pretty girls. It was easier than making real conversation. Anyway, he didn't think she was really interested. Well, maybe, but if she was, she would probably turn out to be a minion of darkness or part demon on her grandmother's side or the harbinger of a new apocalypse or something. With his track record, anything was possible—so long as it was *bad*.

Mindy went to her desk and leaned over it to snag her purse, which was sitting on her chair. Xander tried not to stare at the view.

"I'm going to run to the little girls' room, *Mr. Harris.* Then I have to pick up some office supplies. I should be back before you leave for the school."

She offered a wicked little smile charged with endless possibilities—and a little wave—as she went out the door. "Don't forget me while I'm gone."

Xander stood up straight and replied, "No chance of that."

When the door closed, Dan grinned broadly. "What was that you were saying, 'Mr. Harris'?"

"Shut up, Dan."

Xander settled in behind his desk, and Dan sank down into the chair in front of it. "I do believe that girl has a thing for you."

"Shut up, Dan."

"Okay, sure, workplace romance can be complicated, but she seems nice enough. Cute, funny, just a little bit bad."

"Right. The last part. *Exactly* what I'm worried about."

"Huh?"

"Never you mind. You forget, Mr. Perfect Family Man, that things aren't so easy for the rest of us."

Dan chuckled. "Hey, I keep telling you it isn't a matter of easy, it's a matter of choice. Decide what you want, take steps to make it happen. You have to take charge of your life, my friend. That's what I did, and you know I'm a happy guy. You, on the other hand, are what some might call troubled."

"You have no idea."

"So tell me about it."

Despite himself, Xander couldn't help but think back to his wedding day. Or, rather, his non-wedding day. An older version of himself had showed up to talk him out of going through with it. He'd shown Xander what his life would have been like with Anya—maybe with anyone. He'd turned out old and frustrated and bitter and angry. Kind of like his dad. And his uncles. And his grandpa Harris. He saw himself lashing out at Anya. Hurting her, even though he loved her.

Sure, "old Xander" turned out to be some demony guy whom Anya had punished back in her days as a vengeance demon. Still, Xander felt he couldn't take the chance. It all seemed so real. Maybe it *was* the future. So, yeah, "troubled" might not be a bad word.

That odd feeling came over him again—a sense of relaxation and peace that sought to drive thoughts of the wedding, of anything he feared, out of his head.

Shifting confidently in his chair, Xander chose to divert the conversation, "Hey, don't pretend like everything is peachy-creamy for you, Danny boy. Sure, so you've got the perfect wife and the perfect house and the perfect kids, but you're still working for a mopey, broody guy like me instead of running the show."

Dan laughed as he got up to pour himself a cup of coffee from the coffeepot sitting on top of the filing cabinets over by Mindy's desk.

"Xander, my friend, that is entirely my choice. They offered me a job like yours a year or so before you came along. Not what I'm looking for out of life. I've got my family and I've got . . . hobbies . . . that take up my time. Don't need the extra headaches that go along with what you do. 'Sides, you've got a knack that I don't. You look at things from a different perspective than most. Helps you come up with all those time-saving, money-saving ideas the suits love so much."

"Maybe, but—"

A woman's shriek pierced the air outside.

Xander shot up out of his chair. He even managed to set down his coffee mug without spilling a drop. Years of responding to shrieks in crisis after crisis had yielded some useful skills. Dan, on the other hand, dropped his cup, spilling it all over the floor.

The two rushed out and down the steps. A crowd was beginning to gather outside. Mindy was in the center, pointing up toward some girder framework that was still under construction.

Xander looked up as she started running over to him. At the top of what was eventually supposed to be a set of penthouse suites, there was a man, his fists held in the air, kind of running in place. A naked man. A naked, hairy man. Well, almost naked. The only thing he was wearing looked like a sweat sock, and he wasn't wearing it in the usual way. Xander was grateful that the man had made some concession to modesty. The man seemed to be saying something, but it was hard to make out at that distance.

Dan squinted at the man above. "Crap. That's Davis. What the hell is he doing?"

Just then, Mindy crashed into Xander, hugging him tight and burying her face in his chest.

"Oh, Xander, it's so horrible! I was just getting in my car when I looked up and saw him. Is he . . . is he going to jump?"

Awkwardly, Xander patted her back. "Don't worry. It'll be okay. I think." Puzzled, he looked over to Dan. "What is he saying?"

Drifting down, they could only hear vague sounds. "Duh dun dada dun dada dun dada dun. Duh dun dadda dun dada dun dada da . . ."

Dan snapped his fingers a couple times, and his eyes went wide with recognition. "That's the theme from *Rocky*. He's doing the dance Stallone did on those steps."

Xander pulled roughly away from Mindy. The girl responded with a surprised, "Hey!"

Xander grabbed Dan. "The theme from *Rocky*?" The other man nodded. "Doesn't that go, 'Gonna Fly Now'?"

"Dammit!" they both said in unison, then turned and sprinted for the building.

Xander yelled back to Mindy, "Call the cops and the fire department! NOW!"

A minute and a half later, both men breathed a sigh of relief as they scrambled along the scaffolding toward their coworker. He was still there, dancing and singing triumphantly. Up close, he looked even sweatier—and hairier. He practically had a pelt.

At the sound of their approach, Davis turned and smiled broadly. The sweat sock had two green stripes at the top, and suddenly Xander was even more grateful for its presence. "Mr. Harris! Mr. Martin! How you guys doin'? Beautiful day!"

Xander and Dan exchanged a confused look.

"Yeah," said Xander. "Beautiful day. Warm. I guess you noticed that, though."

Still pumping his legs slightly, like a jogger at a stoplight, Davis glanced down briefly and then smiled. "Oh, yeah. Too warm for all those confining clothes. You guys should get rid of them. It's liberating. Had to keep the sock, though. It's a statement."

Xander nodded, edging out a little farther toward the man. "A statement. Sure." He gave Davis a nervous grin. "Big fan of the Red Hot Chili Peppers, right?"

Davis's smile broadened. "Yeah! Exactly! Still, I didn't want to restrict myself, y'know? No need to sing a Peppers' song just because I'm—whatcha call it— emeltating them."

Xander tried to keep his voice level. "Emulating. I think you mean emulating."

"Right! Exactly!"

Xander moved out a little closer. "So, why don't we head downstairs, where a broader audience can appreciate the statement close up?"

Davis scowled just a little, considering it as he kept up his shuffling. "Naw. I like it up here. There's a sense of freedom. The sky all around. The world so far below. Besides, it puts things in perspective. That's part of the statement. We all need to get a bigger picture. Up close, it's hard to see anything but the chaos. The big picture helps you see what needs fixing, how best to put things in order. Helps you realize that true freedom comes from being a part of the whole. Giving over control. We have to let go of our piddling little worries, y'know? Do what actually needs doing instead of what we think we're supposed to do."

Xander shook his head a little. "Sorry, I don't follow. Why don't you come over here and explain it a little more." Then he held out his hand and gestured for the man to come away from the edge. He wasn't up for debating a nutcase ten stories up. If he could just get close enough. . . .

"Sure, sure! Glad to. See, we think that there's all sorts of stupid things that we need to do to be a part of the big picture. To be accepted, right? To fit. Like wearing clothes and all that. But that's not what we need to do. What we need to do is pay attention to what our place is in the big picture, what cog we are in the big machine. All the rest doesn't matter. Accept your role and do what you're supposed to and you get all this." Davis began to spin around, his arms spread wide. The sock, pulled by centrifugal force, swung around him like a cheerleader's skirt. The thought made Xander flinch.

The man began to wobble a little. "Whoa. Head rush." Then he tripped.

Xander leaped forward, trying to grab him. He slammed down on his stomach on the catwalk planking, but he couldn't get a grip on the man's sweaty, hairy skin. Davis plummeted, and Xander's momentum carried him toward the edge.

A hand grabbed his ankle, jerking him to a stop.

Xander heard Dan Martin expel a breath the man probably hadn't even realized he'd been holding. He'd managed to keep Xander from following Davis, but just.

From below them came the joyous shout, "Wooo-hooooooooo! What a rush!"

Disbelieving, Xander peered over the edge. Davis was dangling a floor below, one hand grasping a scaffolding pole that jutted out from the structure.

Xander rolled onto his back. "I don't believe this. He's having a ball." As he lay there, catching his breath, he glimpsed a slight movement off to his left out of the corner of his eye.

Dan helped him to his feet. Xander punched his shoulder lightly. "Thanks for the save, buddy."

Martin shrugged. "I just don't want your job, remember?"

Xander replied, "Yeah, well, you may get it, anyway." He moved carefully toward the object that had grabbed his attention—a safety rope hanging nearby.

Grabbing the rope, he yanked it hard to make sure it was secure. Then he edged out toward the far end of the scaffold.

Dan gave him a panicked look. "Harris, are you insane?"

Xander tied the end of the rope to his belt, choking up on the slack and hoping he'd figured the arc correctly. From down below, Davis's voice rose in song, "Gonna fly now! Gonna flyyyyy *now*!"

Xander looked at Dan and replied, "Insane? Probably."

Yet, strangely, completely, unafraid.

Stepping off the scaffold, Xander dropped like a stone. The rope went taut, pulling him in an arc that swept toward Davis. Above him, he heard Dan Martin swearing.

Xander slammed into Davis just as the other man let go. He only had a second to wrap his free arm and legs around the man to stop his fall. From up above, he heard the groan of the scaffold as their combined weight dragged on the rope. They arced upward, Davis struggling and yelling at the top of his lungs, "Lemme go! You got no right!" Xander could barely keep his grip. The guy was strong. Too strong. Like, *Buffy* strong. As they reached the top of the swing and started back down, Xander could feel Davis slipping from his grasp.

Then a dozen hands reached out, grabbing them both, pulling them in. Xander collapsed to the planking, his back to a girder. Six guys from his work crew had climbed up to help while he was trying to talk Davis down. He stared in amazement as all of them struggled to keep Davis from pitching himself over the edge again.

Xander stood and wiped his hands on his pants before he started to untie the rope. "Ugh. Someone definitely needs to introduce that man to the concept of body waxing."

"Let me go! Set me free! I just—"

Davis's rant was cut short as one of the guys shoved a work glove into the man's mouth. Seconds later, Dan Martin worked his way past the others. "Harris, you are one brave, crazy, heroic madman!" As Xander stood up, Dan wrapped him in a big, rib-bruising bear hug. When he let go, Dan grinned and said, "Looks like you're gonna be famous."

"Huh?"

Pointing toward the ground, Martin laughed. "Take a look."

Turning and looking down, Xander saw the crowd staring up at him. A couple news vans had arrived as well, their cameras aimed squarely at where he was standing. Dan reached over and grabbed him by the wrist. He pulled Xander's arm upward, like a boxing referee declaring the winner. The crowd went wild.

After the paramedics had arrived and sedated Davis sufficiently to strap him to a gurney, Xander and Dan made their way to ground level. His coworkers surrounded him, cheering and slapping him on the back. Mindy pushed her way through the crowd and wrapped her arms around his neck. Surprised, Xander jerked back just a little, and her kiss landed on his cheek instead of his lips. He gave her another awkward hug as the news crews started to crowd him.

The reporters all started yelling, "Mr. Harris!" and

it took several minutes to get things calmed down enough so he could answer their questions. His coworkers had been pushed back to make room for the impromptu press conference.

A tall, pretty, African-American woman wearing a silk trench coat over an expensive suit—despite the warm weather—thrust a microphone in his face. "Mr. Harris, can you tell us what caused your coworker to endanger himself and you?"

Staring into the camera, Xander thought he would feel nothing but pure panic. With people, he could always gage how well his jokes were going over. The cold, glass eye of the camera lens just glared back, uncaring and unresponsive. Yet . . . it wasn't bothering him. For greater effect, he shifted his gaze to the reporter. "Well, I'm no psychologist, but I think it's safe to say he's got issues."

Another reporter, this one an older man in a rumpled suit, elbowed the woman out of his way. "Mr. Harris, how did you manage to pull off that stunt? Do you have some sort of special training?"

Xander gave a wide grin, his eyes crinkling at the corners. He held out both hands and said, "I'm sorry, I can't answer that question. It might endanger my secret identity."

Around him he heard some laughter from the news crew as well as his friends. He began to loosen up and relax. "Now, look—I just did what anyone would have done in a situation like this. You know, risk life and limb to help my fellow man. It's really just a matter of—"

From one of the news vans, a tech called out, "Hey! A fistfight just broke out across town between a pair of nuns! They're duking it out in front of St. Teresa's!"

Within seconds, the reporters were rushing toward their vehicles. The work crew barely managed to keep from getting trampled in the rush. Xander was left standing alone in a settling cloud of dust.

His mouth quirked to one side in disgust. "So much for fifteen minutes of fame."

Glancing up, he saw Mindy staring at him. The way she'd been acting before, he was expecting a look of adoration. Instead, her eyes reminded him of that moment when he'd stared into the camera. She seemed to be recording his every move. And staring into the depths of her eyes was like looking into . . . *nothing*. He shivered slightly. Then she realized he was looking her way. Suddenly her eyes lit up, a wonderfully bright smile exploded on her lips, and she rushed forward to give him another hug.

Looping her arm in his, she started walking him back toward the office trailer, keeping up a steady stream of praise and chatter.

Still disconcerted, the best reply he could manage was, "Um. Yeah, thanks."

As the day wore on, the strangest thing for him about the entire incident had been how unafraid he had felt throughout it all.

It was almost as if he was becoming a new man.

And he had no idea *why*.

Chapter Six

Willow shielded her eyes from the glare of the setting sun. A cool breeze kicked up and eagerly sifted through neatly arranged piles of leaves on either side of Sunnydale University's central walkway, stirring them into a gentle frenzy and sending them like columns of troops against the leather boots of the auburn-haired witch. She giggled as they snapped and crackled against her, some bolder than others, stealing up high against her long paisley skirt, others billowing and slapping against her silk forest-green peasant blouse. The wind rushed in, a near magical force, the earthen purity of nature itself shoving against her so boldly, and with such strength, that she had to turn away from it for several seconds to keep from losing her breath. Willow was still laughing—until she saw the building where she had met Tara for the first time.

Suddenly, she was no longer certain the dying breeze had been so playful. Had the wind been trying to turn her back, to send her away from this place? Its touch now felt like a warning, or a reminder, however unwelcome, of times past and love forever lost.

Sitting on the steps of that fateful building were two young women, one a honey blonde, the other with darker hair, possibly reddish. They were laughing— and holding hands.

Whirling in the direction of this evening's class, hurrying to catch up with several other students prowling the walks of the sprawling campus, Willow couldn't resist the temptation to look back and see if both figures were still there, or if her imagination—or some darker force—had been playing tricks on her.

Both women were there. They were real, not shadows or illusions. Yet the sight of the couple now embracing was more than Willow could stand. Her view of the world wavered, and she realized she'd caught a little speck of something from one of those pesky leaves, or from the earth itself, in her eyes. Why else would they be tearing up?

Sweetie, sweetie, this isn't what I'd want for you. You know that.

It was Tara's voice, seemingly carried on another soft breeze. Willow was certain she had only imagined it, but the sentiment expressed was true—she knew that in her heart. Bucking up, forcing her smile back in place, she strode on, the trees above reaching across with spidery arms to shelter her from the fierce golden light streaking down from the all-seeing heavens.

Even though she'd been back in Sunnydale for a while, Willow didn't quite feel as if she'd stepped back into place yet. She wasn't the old Willow, after all. The dark specter of magic had changed her, so it didn't make sense that she'd be able to snap right back into the swing of things. It was a bit like trying to wear her prom dress to her ten-year reunion. Or so she figured, since that reunion was still a ways away.

Life seemed particularly out of whack at school. It wasn't that she was behind the other students. Willow never had a problem catching up in class—usually it was more a matter of trying not to get too far ahead.

No, again, it was being out of step. It was post-magical meltdown, post-Giles packing her up and taking her to England, where he and the coven could watch her brain to see if it was going to sprout a broom and take off flying like the Wicked Witch of the West and finish killing Jonathan and Andrew and their little world too. Though that wasn't the real reason nothing felt right.

The real reason was the one she hated to remind herself about, and the hardest one to forget.

Willow had met Tara at school. She had met her *here*. In fact, it was right over there, in that building, the very first time. . . .

That's all it took, really. One little detail. *There's the building where we met, there's the tree we used to grab a few precious moments under between classes—* any aspect of their life together could start a chain reaction of memory. Random details, jumping out of nowhere and doing more damage than any run-of-the-mill vampire skulking around the alley behind the Bronze.

It depressed her even further that details were now the enemy, since once they had been her friend. Details were always what she and Tara enjoyed. The new discovery, the previously undiscovered clue. Tara used to have this spell where she would bend her fingers to form a circle and it would act as sort of a telescopic magnifying glass, and they'd spy on bugs living their lives in the grass. Bugs suddenly became very non-*ick* when they didn't know you were watching them. In fact, they were kind of cute, bopping around in their little bug world. And they didn't have any of those creepy hidden secrets you might find out about when spying on actual people. Tara always liked the ladybugs best, and Willow would say, "Of course you do. You have a gender bias." Didn't matter how many times she said it, that always made Tara smile.

Of course, by the end of it all, Willow could zoom in a thousand times faster and closer than her lover. She could do it right now, find a ladybug somewhere in the campus garden without even really giving it much thought. She *wouldn't,* naturally, but she *could.* If she were looking to do such things.

Which she wasn't.

Willow closed her eyes, shook her head a little. The details were tumbling out of control again. They stacked up like a game of Jenga, and it would be such a mess if she knocked them down. It was best to stay focused. She was here to try to resume some kind of normal life. School was always the one thing she was really, really good at. School never came crashing down on her—*except maybe when mayors were turning into giant snakes and destroying it, but that really doesn't apply here.*

Ooops. It was nearly six o'clock. If she didn't get a move on, she'd be late for Dr. Sands's computer class. It was time to step out of the clouds.

Only maybe she should have looked before merging into traffic.

Whammo! Willow had run straight into another student. Books spilled out of hands, papers went flying, and the other girl was stumbling back. Willow caught a flash of arms, a striped sweater, khaki pants, dark hair. This girl was very Gap. Nice, neat, well put-together. Without realizing it, she did that zoom thing and was locked onto the girl's eyes. It was like a Clint Eastwood western. *You think you're fast enough, kid? When I say draw, you draw.*

Except the other girl wasn't in fight mode. Her eyes were looking every which way, flicking about quickly. Her pupils were big and black. The girl was startled, a bit scared and, most of all, feeling dreadfully *weak*. In fact, now that she thought about it, Willow could smell it. Along with the vision, her abracadabra had heightened all of her senses.

"I hate that weakness smell," she whispered, something terrible rising in her. "It's like old clothes dipped in tomato sauce."

The other girl looked at her strangely. She didn't

have the first clue—and that made Willow even more . . . cross.

Willow felt her anger start to crackle. It ran through her like currents of electricity, zigzagging through her bloodstream. She started to feel it in her fingers. There were little sparks just under the nails, tingly like when you touch a battery to your tongue. *How dare such a trivial person bump into her!* The world started to go dark, shadows started to creep in. It was the black milk in her eyes that told the world, "I am the big, evil thing that you fear, and you are about to die."

It was a feeling Willow didn't like. She liked even less that it came over her so fast. There was no reason for this. Someone knocking her books out of her hand shouldn't elicit the same response as Warren killing the love of her life.

Willow swallowed the feelings, fighting hard to let the currents run dry. Just in time too. The girl had turned away, but now she was looking up at her. "Shoot, I'm sorry. I was trying to sort my folders, I was in a hurry . . . I wasn't looking."

The girl hadn't noticed. It had happened that fast, as if it existed in a moment shuffled between the other moments. A bad card trick of time. An ace of spades mixed in with a bunch of hearts, and this poor kid had nearly picked it.

"It's okay," Willow replied, feeling her racing thoughts begin to slow. Banter. She needed banter to stabilize her engines. "I'm just as guilty. My mind was somewhere else, otherwise I'd have seen you before we went all *kerploofy*."

They both knelt down and started to gather their things. "I'm such a klutz," the girl said. "I swear, they should make people like me get a license to walk."

Willow kind of liked the idea. "Ooooh, they could issue them at shoe stores. And they could have different kinds. Like, you have to have a different license to wear sneakers than you do high heels."

There was more small talk, and it made Willow feel better. A little.

Even so, as quick as she made with the jokes, it wasn't enough to block out that this disturbed her. It was like the girl had hit some kind of button, and before she knew it, Dark Willow was taking the wheel and careening toward the cliff at full speed. She had worked so hard to try to make it so this would never happen, but all that effort was undone just like that.

The whole walk to class, she tried to tell herself that the change had only come because she was thinking about Tara. She had let herself get worked up, and it put her on edge. All those feelings were there on the surface, and the collision had jostled them to life. She wasn't so out of control.

I'm not.

There was nothing she could really do beyond telling herself that—and praying that it was true.

The accident made her late. When she arrived at Dr. Sands's class, most of the seats were already full. There was one open in the front row, near the door, and she made a beeline for it. Sneak in and sit down, attract minimal attention, that was the plan.

It was one time that not really knowing anybody had paid off. No one had noticed she wasn't there, so they weren't waiting for her to come in. It was like she was never late at all—even if she was.

The sabbatical in England had put a swift end to most of the social life she had forged in the previous years. A lot of it had been stuff she and Tara had established together, as a couple, anyway, so it would be easier to let it all slide. Besides, college wasn't really about being social, it was all about the learning, right? Of all her new courses, Dr. Sands's class was her favorite. All the nights looking for information on smelly slimy demons with six nipples and twelve fingers had made her pretty familiar with the ways of the computer, so programming came naturally to her. She felt like this was the one class she probably could master. It was sort of fun to take code and all the secret nerd jargon and make it bend and do what she want—all without any threat of unleashing any ancient evil or causing the planet to collapse in on itself. The worst she might do is click on the wrong Internet site and see something with boobies in it.

Dr. Sands was still in his greeting phase, talking about what they had in store that hour, so she hadn't missed too much. She liked the computer lab. Her monitor was already humming, and there was a screen saver with cats surfing on pieces of toast, maneuvering around those strange flying toasters that someone had once thought was a good idea. She even liked the silly posters on the wall, the computer humor that no normal person would really get. The picture of the human head with the phrase "Intel inside" written on the cranium. Or the one of the car with a disc superimposed on the top of it that said, "Drivers usually warn you when they need to back up, but why stand in harm's way?" Okay, so they weren't very funny. They were more like that weird uncle who comes to the house on holidays and you like having him around because he reminds you that you're not the biggest dork in the gene pool.

"Before we start digging deeper into the possibilities of Flash animation," Dr. Sands said, addressing the class, "my teaching assistant, Mel, is going to hand back your assignments from last week."

Willow hadn't noticed that Mel was moving down her row, dropping papers on each student's desk as he passed. She wasn't sure what to make of that guy. He wore a lot of tight black T-shirts, seemingly to show off that he had a few muscles, that he worked out, and just wasn't some tech geek. He had a Caesar haircut, and even Willow knew that it was a style that was over several years ago. Once George Clooney moved on, so had the copycats. Maybe that was Mel's problem. His barber had sold him a haircut that had reached its sell-by date.

"Overall," Dr. Sands continued, "I have to say I'm pleased. Most of you did fairly well. Some of you did better than others, obviously, and one or two of you . . . well, I'm not sure why you bothered."

It was just then that Mel reached Willow's desk. He handed her the paper and also gave her a tight-lipped scowl. Could Dr. Sands be talking about her?

"Then again, at least one of you showed a knack for invention and creativity above and beyond the call of duty."

Nope. There was a big red "A" at the top of her paper—as well as a couple of plus signs and a poorly executed star.

Dr. Sands turned to her. "Ms. Rosenberg, I was most impressed with your ideas. I think it's about time that someone looked at making a virus protection program that is both effective *and* fun. But where did you get the ideas for the little icon characters?"

Willow felt that blush return, but she also couldn't help but smile a little. *Teacher likes me!* "Oh, gosh," she said, "it really wasn't much. Just some silly—"

"Nonsense!" Dr. Sands exclaimed, interrupting her. "Class, Ms. Rosenberg has crafted a variation of your standard virus detection system. It features a little animated red-haired witch who looks over your hard drive with her magic wand and, when she finds an infected file, her hair turns black and she becomes powerful and zaps the virus with bolts of energy. It's adorable."

Mel unleashed a rather loud *harrumph* from the third row.

"Do you take exception to my assessment, Mr. Turner?" Dr. Sands asked him.

"Sure, it's cute," Mel answered, stopping the return process, "but it's impractical. The RAM required to animate the completely superfluous characters would likely grind your machine to a halt. You couldn't operate other programs while your were running the scan."

"Sort of like how you can't continue to hand out papers and criticize at the same time?" Dr. Sands suggested.

The class laughed at the joke. Even Willow found it pretty amusing, especially since it was her idea Mel was dissing.

"Perhaps if you spent more time on your own programs," Sands added, "and less time finding fault with others', you'd fare better."

Mel turned on his heel and started handing out the graded assignments again. Willow could tell by the way he hunched his shoulders that he was pretty mad. She thought he may have even shot her a look—the sort of look she normally saw from vamps and beasties that didn't like the Scoobies messing with their fun.

She thought now would be a good time for one of those jokes to lighten the tension. Even a bad pun like what was on the posters. Certainly there was something someone could say about floppy discs.

As if to answer her wish, another student farther down the front row jumped up, knocking his chair back. It slammed loudly into the desk behind him. Willow had seen the boy before. He had straggly brown hair and thick, black-rimmed glasses. She had thought he looked like the singer of Weezer. He was wearing a T-shirt with the logo of an old-school breakfast cereal on it—*not* the sort of guy she'd normally expect to have an outburst.

The boy turned to the girl next to him, grabbed her

by her cardigan sweater, and pulled her out of her chair. Willow expected the girl to freak out, but before she could do anything, the boy planted a kiss full on her lips. It was like a kiss in an old movie, all smashed faces and mingling noses. The girl went with it without objection.

Dr. Sands saw what was happening and started to move out from behind his desk. He seemed taken aback, and stopped halfway there. "Mr. Sizemore!" he shouted. "John! What are you doing?"

John didn't answer. He swiveled around, taking the girl with him and plopping her down in his chair. He then turned back and moved to the next station over, where another female student, a blonde with a ponytail, waited with a wide grin. Willow remembered her from other class sessions, too, because she always wore a little too much makeup and her shirts were usually a little too short to reach the top of her pants. Not that Willow was complaining about that. The girl had a cute belly button, after all.

Willow's face flushed at the thought. *Geez, there's that blush again. . . .*

Today, the blonde had a shirt on that said, "I'll try anything *thrice.*"

Although the first coed had met John's advance with stunned indifference, the second girl leaped into it with a can-do attitude. She wrapped her arms around John's neck and was on him even before he could plant the kiss on her. Willow was reasonably sure that there was tongue involved.

When John extricated himself from the girl's

grasp, he pulled the same move he had pulled on his first victim. He spun her around like a dance partner, gracefully dropping her into the first girl's chair. "Don't tell me that's it, Tiger?" she said.

John giggled. "Sorry," he said, "I have to share the love."

"Mr. Sizemore! I must insist you sit back down!"

If John heard Dr. Sands, he gave no indication. He was busy moving to the next student in the line. It was a boy, though. A rather burly one, at that, and he was wearing a fraternity sweatshirt. John held up his hands and laughed. He was stepping very slowly, working his way around the frat guy's chair, almost like he was sidestepping a land mine.

"Take it easy, big fella," John said. "Don't get excited."

"That's right, buddy," frat guy replied, "keep moving."

Willow laughed at the predicament the two found themselves in, but then realized that *she* was in the next occupied seat in the front row. John was making his way straight toward her. Sure, he was cute in that sensitive rock-boy way that had made Oz so appealing, but Oz was a long time ago. She had left his species behind and had never looked back.

Trying to think fast, Willow got out of her seat and put her chair between herself and the kissing bandit.

"Come on, now," John said. "It's no fair to run. It's just a little kiss."

"Can't we talk this over?" Willow asked. "I'm sure we can come up with many alternatives for things to put to your lips besides me. A cup of coffee, maybe? A scone?"

Just when she thought she was going to have to shove the chair at John and bash his knees, he suddenly stopped short. He let out a small, throaty gurgle, and his arms flew out to the sides.

Dr. Sands had grabbed John by his shirt collar and was jerking him back. "Mr. Sizemore, that is quite enough," he said. His voice had dropped a couple of octaves. He had his authority cap on, big-time. "I don't know what's gotten into you, but you're going to cut it out. Ms. Rosenberg, if you'll kindly step aside, I'm going to escort Don Juan here down to security."

"Gladly."

Willow moved to the next row back, taking her chair with her. No sense removing the barrier between her and Sir Kiss-a-Lot. Probably a good move, too, since when Dr. Sands wrangled him from behind the computer table John had puckered his lips and made several kissing noises, aiming them all at her. She hadn't really had any doubts about her current feelings about men, but had there been any, this would have definitely erased them.

"You can't do this to me, man!" John protested. "Haven't you ever heard of freedom of expression?"

"You bet I have," Dr. Sands said. "Have you ever heard of self-control?"

"I have not yet begun to kiss!"

"Yes, you have. You just kissed your enrollment here good-bye." And with that, Dr. Sands pushed John out the door.

The class instantly erupted in laughter and gossip. The first girl stood up and started talking to no one in particular. "Can you believe it? I can't believe it!" She raised an eyebrow. "I sort of liked it, though."

The second girl started to giggle. "Please, honey, you were just a speed bump on his way to my mouth."

Chatter from the back of the class ranged from shock to outrage to one kid declaring John his new hero. "The Rock is so over," he said. "I wanna smell what John Sizemore has cooking!"

For her part, Willow didn't know what to think. As she sat back down, that uneasiness was creeping back in. Some of it had to do with the tranquillity of her favorite subject being shattered, but more of it was reminding her of her own outburst earlier. Sure, John didn't almost fry someone's organs inside their body, but he still seemed to have lost himself to the moment. Normally, he sat in class and doodled, listening to Dr. Sands and never saying a word to anyone. He kept to himself—not in a creepy serial-killer-below-the-surface kind of way, but more shy and daydreamy. She wouldn't be surprised if he'd never even made eye contact with a girl before today.

"Wake up!"

Willow was startled from her thoughts by the shout and the angry rapping of knuckles on her computer monitor. "Uh . . . hi," she said. As she realized who it was, she got a little embarrassed. "Listen, about what Dr. Sands said—"

"Save it, I don't care." Mel was glaring at her. "I don't know how you did it, but you clearly have the wool pulled over his eyes. He may not see through your empty subroutines and pointless light-show graphics, but I do. I've got you under surveillance, Red."

"What? Like you're on a stakeout?"

"Something like that. You know what I mean. You'll slip up sooner or later, and I'll be watching."

"Why do I suddenly feel like one of the kids on some bad high school sitcom?"

Mel didn't respond. He just pointed at her—it was a finger of warning!—and went over to his desk, a smaller one at the front of the class, next to Dr. Sands.

By the time Dr. Sands returned, the period was nearly over. Most of the students were surfing the Net or playing computer mah-jongg. Even Willow had used the time to hit some of her regular Web sites looking for news from the spooky world. Apparently there was a shortage in monkey fur among the Wicca community, and prices were skyrocketing. A Baggie weighing close to eight ounces went for sixty dollars on eBay. That was the sort of price normally reserved for albino monkeys, and she was glad she wasn't in the market for any.

"I'm sorry about that, class," Dr. Sands said. "It looks like Mr. Sizemore has eaten up all of our time together. I have no idea *what* has gotten into him. Perhaps it's the stress of the impending midterm, or maybe we're coming up on a full moon. I don't know. I imagine more than a few of you will be going cuckoo from too much studying as the semester progresses."

Oh, great, Willow thought. *If I'm cracking up now,*

imagine what I'll be like after an all-night cram session.

"Anyway, no sense trying to salvage the remaining time, so let's call it an early day."

There were a couple of cheers from around the room, followed by the rustle of everyone gathering their stuff. Since she was late, Willow hadn't taken any books out, so she was pretty much ready to go. She was about to make a break for the door, when Dr. Sands stopped her. "Not so fast, Ms. Rosenberg," he said. "Can I see you for a moment?"

Willow made her way to Dr. Sands's desk, maneuvering through several wavering lanes of oncoming student traffic. She wondered if she was in trouble, though she *knew* she hadn't done anything wrong.

Except . . . well, out in the quad, when she almost let Dark Willow out over *nothing.* That hadn't been so much filled with the chocolate goodness. But how could he know about that?

And why did she always fret so much? That was the one appealing thing about Dark Willow—she wasn't afraid of anyone or anything.

Not like the real Willow, who was scared all the time.

Dr. Sands sat in a large wooden chair with wheels at its base, leaned back, and clasped his hands behind his head. He was a man in his late forties, with a dark beard flecked with gray and a bit of a bald patch forming just above his forehead. "Willow," he said, "I just wanted to tell you again how much I liked your program ideas. Have you ever considered making this your major?"

Willow thought her blush was going to become permanent if the day continued this way, though, lest she become too full of herself, Mel was still at his desk looking over papers from another class—or so he was pretending. He was really giving Willow the stink eye.

"No, sir," Willow said. "I just like to dabble. Yup, just a dabbler."

"I talked to your computer science teacher from last semester, and she said you hadn't displayed nearly this much skill in her class. I thought maybe you took some comp courses in your summer semester in England, but she wasn't sure."

"Uh, yeah," Willow quickly lied. "Though, really, the focus was managing data and things. Moving this file here, dumping that application there, sorting out the good stuff and picking out the bad stuff."

Not really a lie, more a creative embellishment. Her time in the country with Giles and the coven was used to help her learn to store information properly, though on the soft drive of her brain rather than on a hard drive on a computer. And, truth be told, her idea for a little witch icon to help rid machines of dangerous, corrupting viruses came out of the other Wiccans' program for helping her clean out the residual effects of the darkness that had corrupted her in the wake of Warren murdering Tara. So, really, Dr. Sands connecting her summer in Britain to her current study focus wasn't too far off.

"Well, whatever they did, I think they only tapped into a natural aptitude that was already there," Sands said. "I don't know if you've given any thought to what you'll be doing on winter break, but there are a couple of internships I know of that you'd be perfect for. You should come by my office sometime and I can give you the lowdown."

Yup, the blush was permanent. Dr. Sands's interest made her realize for the first time what a hole Giles's departure had left in her life. She missed his encouragement and the affirmation he'd give when she'd done a good job. Most of what she'd learned about research had come from working with him back in the musty library of Sunnydale High. And even though she had gone to spend her summer with him under less than fantastic circumstances, it was good to feel his guiding hand again. Additionally, introducing her to the coven had given her a much needed sense of acceptance. Tara was the only one who understood her journeys into magic, and with her gone . . . well, the voids Tara left were numerous and varied. The coven had gone a good distance at filling at least one of them.

"To tell you the truth, I haven't been looking at much beyond getting through this semester," she said. "It's taking me a while to get my sea legs back. Which is kind of a bad idea, now that I think about it, given that I'm on land and all. Do people actually have land legs?"

Dr. Sands laughed. It sounded like it came from the bottom of his ample belly, but Willow decided that it came from slightly higher, somewhere around his heart. *Hey, is that why they call some laughs "hearty"?*

Mel got up from behind his desk. "Excuse me, Doctor," he said. "I'm sorry to interrupt, but you have a meeting with the dean of students in ten minutes. It's all the way across campus, so you probably should—"

"Okay, okay," Sands said. He waved Mel off without even looking at him, and then got up and slipped on his sport coat. "It seems, Ms. Rosenberg, that I am late, late, late for a very important date. If you'll forgive my hasty departure, as well as my paraphrasing Mr. Carroll's fine words, I would be most obliged."

"No problem. In fact, we'll just chalk up your paraphrasing *to* the haste, because who needs complicated sentence structures when they're in a hurry."

"Quite right. Do think about what I said and let me know. It would be no trouble to put together a list of contacts for you. I might even be able to summon up a letter of recommendation."

"I will."

Dr. Sands grabbed his briefcase and, without another word, left.

Mel threw his pen down on his desk. Willow could see he was tense, irritated. His shoulders gave it away every time. "You're welcome, you old fart," he mumbled to himself. It was becoming clear to Willow that Mel's problem really wasn't with her, but with what he assumed she was getting at his expense.

"I'm sure Dr. Sands just forgot to say anything," she said, hoping to smooth out the tension. "He sometimes seems like he can only focus on one thing at a time."

"Yeah, cute redheads," Mel snapped. He picked up a blue backpack and slung it over his shoulder. "Doesn't matter. He's not the only professor on this campus, and certainly not the highest on the totem pole. In fact, perhaps all I need is for him to engage in a little misconduct with a coed to take him down even lower."

"Hey, wait just a darn minute—"

"See you later, Red." Mel gave her a smug salute, and then he, too, exited.

Why, of all the—!

Great, this was all Willow needed. Clearly Mel was a bit off-center, and now he had it in for her. This wasn't the sort of fight she was used to. It was a human battle. Her enemies usually were demons and big ugly things, and they all had rules they had to follow. Sure, they liked to rip people's limbs off and eat kittens, but at least you knew which way they'd attack you from. Mel seemed capable of anything as long as it got him what he wanted, and he didn't seem to worry much about who was in his way or how dirty he had to play to get them out of it. Well, fine, if he wanted to make an enemy of Willow, he could go ahead, because she could take anything he'd throw at her and toss it back a hundred times worse.

Heh. Though not in a murderous-rage, black-magic kind of way. Of course not.

There she was, getting all super-duper mad again. It was like there was a temper leak, and one stray spark could set her off. *But maybe it's not just me?* Mel sure seemed all the rage today. Emphasis on rage. Could someone—or some*thing*—be messing around here, using the school as its own pressure cooker and making a big pot roast of anger? John's behavior was certainly weird, and she could mark that in the meddle-some magic column, as well, but it didn't make sense for someone to be playing with fury and amorous passion at the same time. The two things didn't match up the way naughty spellcasters usually liked them to. Your typical magical geniuses tended to prefer a chocolate and peanut butter kind of relationship, as opposed to ham and pineapple on pizza. You can call it Hawaiian, but it's still pizza. Willow was willing to bet that real Hawaiians didn't eat it that way.

Maybe Dr. Sands was right and everyone was just having their usual midterm freak-outs. Even so, she thought maybe she'd better be careful walking down the hall this time—

"Oh, my God! Willow?"

D'oh. Spoke too soon. But whose voice was that? Maybe whoever it was didn't mean me—

"Willow Rosenberg!"

Nope, definitely me.

Willow turned to look, only to see a perky blonde in a big pink sweater lunging at her. The sweater tossed her arms around her and gave her a huge squeeze. She suddenly realized what a Push Pop ice cream must feel like.

"Oh Willow, I am so excited to see you!"

"Yeah, I get that."

The sweater let go of her and gave her a playful shove. "Shush, you!" she laughed. "Don't you remember me? It's Amanda, from Dr. Fisher's philosophy class."

"Oh, yeah . . . Amanda!"

Willow had no idea.

"I am so glad I ran into you. I have the bestest news."

"Well, try not to run into me again. I think you broke a rib."

"Ha! You were always so funny. No, shut up and listen. Remember how I was dating that guy Geno and he so totally wanted to go to the next level and I was all, 'I dunno, that kind of makes me feel a bit oogy'?"

Amanda could barely stand still. She was hopping from foot to foot, and gesturing wildly. Willow's parents used to have a dog like this when she was a kid. It got really excited every day when Willow got home from school and would jump around making *yip-yip* noises and would pee on itself. She was hoping that today there would be no peeing.

"Um . . . okay," she said.

"There were just *sooooo* many scary things in the way, you know? I mean, we'd really only just met, and my dad so totally hated his guts, and we were only eighteen . . . but you know, we're nineteen now, and he's not marrying my dad, he's marrying me, and it is a year later, which is why we're nineteen. I was just way too wigged out by the whole idea of putting a ring on my finger."

"Are you trying to say you're engaged? Because I think I know a shortcut to getting there."

"You guessed! How did you guess?"

"I took a class in deductive reasoning."

"Well, you must have gotten an 'A,' because you're so super-deductive. It was, like, I saw him this morning and he was eating a banana muffin, and all of a sudden all those scary things didn't scare me anymore. It was like he was this big shadow on my bedroom wall in the middle of the night and I thought he was some monster, and then someone turned on the light and it's no monster at all, it's just a tree, and trees are stable and safe and give life, and I was, like, 'I trust you. You're like a tree I could climb. Let's get married.' You should have seen Geno's face. It was like he'd won a car."

"How romantic for you. Though it's usually not good to run a car into a tree."

"What?"

"Nothing." Willow knew it was mean, but she thought it was kind of funny, anyway.

"Aren't you happy for me?" Amanda asked. She clutched her hands to her breast and did a sort of swoon. "I'm happy for me. There is so much happiness out there, and I want some of it. I am glad I found you, because I want to tell *everybody*. Speaking of, there's Shari. Hey, *Shari*! Bye, Willow!"

Amanda took a run at Shari and hugged her with such force, they both slammed into the wall. Willow was glad Shari looked sturdy, because had Amanda hit her any harder, they might have broken through into the class inside.

What had gotten into these people?

Weirdness with a capital weird.

Willow didn't have any plans for the evening, so she decided to slack off a bit at the mall. The mall was a place where normal people went to sample wares and purchase items they had decided were necessary but really weren't. Normal people sounded good given the day she was having. She could also check out the latest cuteness the fashion world had cooked up. After all, she was looking to settle into a new stage of her life, and maybe what she needed was a new wardrobe. Fresh fall fashions always made a new school year start much easier, so maybe that's what she was missing.

On the bus ride over, she noticed a guy in the back who was trying to look inconspicuous. His trench coat and old-movie–style fedora weren't really helpful, especially given the sunny weather. His face was all wrinkled like a shar-pei puppy's, and he didn't have any of those regular features like a nose or an eye or a mouth. Willow had seen a similar-looking face in one of her demon books. If she remembered right, this guy was a lower-class devil and was often used as bait by other demons when they were hunting large prey. Poor thing looked like he was on the lam. This kind of bizarreness was the kind Willow was more accustomed to these days, and it brought her an odd sense of comfort. She smiled and waved at the creature, but he just pulled his hat down and sank lower in his seat.

At least some things seemed to be just as they should be.

Once inside the mall, Willow made a beeline for the store she always voted Most Likely To Have Something For Me. Off Our Rack carried contemporary fashions for young women at affordable prices. Or so their ads said.

Or so their ads normally said, to be more precise.

Today, Willow was greeted by a whole different campaign. There were posters all over the store publicizing a model search. Off Our Rack was looking for "a new face for a new century." Though her first thought was that they were a couple years late joining the rest of the world in the established time line, her second thought was to be offended by the model they were using as an example.

Incongruously waifish and buxom, she was dressed in a barely there shirt that on top emphasized everything she had and on the bottom everything she didn't. Was this really the look for the twenty-first century, because it didn't look all that different from the twentieth, as far as Willow was concerned. Maybe this store should be called Off Our Rack And Onto Yours. Did everyone have to be built like Cordelia Chase? Who had decided that? Wasn't this a democracy? Couldn't there be a vote to get rid of the people who had previously decided what beauty was and bring in some new leaders? Then again, why should anyone decide? Why be so small in the scope of our thinking that we can't say everyone is beautiful just as they are?

A sneaky thought snuck its way into Willow's brain.

Oh, it would be too easy. Just a little alteration spell. No one would be hurt, no one would have to know who'd done it. Maybe a little something to remove some of the weight from the model's chest and distribute it to the other areas where she needed it. What would be the harm?

No, no, no. What was she thinking? Using no magic meant using none, zero, zilch. Even if she was just goofing around, it was no better than earlier when she'd nearly annihilated that poor girl for having the audacity to experience a moment of uncertainty in front of her. When it came down to it, maybe the coven hadn't spent enough time zapping the corrupt files out of Willow's soft drive.

"I take it you don't like what you see."

Willow had been so caught up in her internal monologue of Hamlet-like indecision, she hadn't noticed anyone approaching. In fact, she was a bit surprised by how zoned out she must have been, because the woman standing next to her was stunning, almost regal looking—her face carved with sharp angles; her hair cut short and neat; a long, beautiful neck framed by the high collar of her black pantsuit. Just for an instant, Willow thought she understood the sort of compulsion that had seized John Sizemore and sent him on a lip-locking rampage.

"I don't like it, either," the woman said. "It doesn't really capture the spirit of the campaign, and I don't know about you, but I don't think that something so cosmetic can be beautiful."

"Uh, no . . . actually, I don't mind girls like her. I just don't think they should be the only women we see."

"Exactly. It's why I fought to take charge of the search. I wanted to make sure we didn't succumb to the usual clichés."

Willow couldn't believe her ears. Surely this was

some bizarre fantasy. She had fallen asleep on the bus and was dreaming. She quickly slapped the back of her hand against a metal clothing rack. "Ow!" she exclaimed. Okay, that *hurt*. Definitely not dreaming.

"Are you okay?" the woman asked.

"What? Oh, yeah . . . I'm fine." Willow smiled. "So . . . so you work here?"

"Not here, no. I work for Off Our Rack, though. I'm the regional advertising manager. Right now I'm in charge of this promotion nationally."

"Good deal."

"I think so. And I'm hoping you'll give me a hand at making it better by signing up for the competition yourself."

"*Me?* Oh, no. I couldn't. I'm not exactly model material. I mean, with the legs and the . . . well, the other things. Not me."

The woman squinted at Willow. Her face said she wasn't happy with that answer. "Why not you? Sounds like you're giving in to exactly the sort of beauty fascism you were just saying you hated."

"Well, yeah, I mean . . . there are other kinds of beauty, but certainly not—"

"I don't like where that's going—and I don't agree, either. I came over here specifically to ask you to sign up because I saw you walk in and instantly fell in love with that face. I mean, I don't know what face you're looking at in the mirror when you get up in the morning, but the one I'm looking at could make just about anyone weak in the knees."

"Okay, I get it now," Willow said. "The big evil

spell of the day is that everyone has to make my cheeks go red, is that it?"

"What?"

"Nothing. Look, I dunno. I'll think about it. If I wanted to do this, where would I sign up?"

The woman smiled. "That's my girl," she said, putting a hand on Willow's shoulder and nudging her slightly in the direction of the front counter. "When you're ready—and I know you will be—just fill out those forms next to that standup display for that new makeup line, Antwerp or whatever it's called."

Willow felt a surge of *something* go through her, though she had no idea where it was coming from. She blinked. Again. A few more times. And rocked a little on her feet, her brain on fire, then freezing, then pleasantly warm and breezy . . .

What in the Seven Hells was happening to her?

She let out a deep sigh, unaware of how much tension she'd been carrying around, how much fear she'd been holding close to her like a warm, happy puppy that of course wasn't really a puppy at all but had been close and all that.

Huh. She rubbed her forehead. Maybe she was coming down with something. A people virus, maybe. Not like the kind a computer might get, though it had come on all of a sudden, like a kakworm.dat infiltration.

She shuddered and realized the woman was still talking to her. "So just fill it out, and when it's time to bring you in for some photos, I'll give you a call."

"Okay."

"Just so I can be sure your card gets pulled, what's your name?"

"Willow. Willow Rosenberg."

"Well, that'll be easy to remember. My name is Gwen. I'll see you again, Willow."

Willow watched the woman walk away. There was a confidence to her stride that she might have envied on some other night. True, this was a woman completely in charge of her own life and, from the sound of it, in charge of several other things too.

And yet . . .

And *yet*.

There was so much energy running through Willow's body, she wasn't sure she could write her own name correctly, much less remember the specifics of her address. It was a good energy too. No magic, no spells or incantations. Just good old human get-up-and-go. The magic of self-confidence, the oldest magic there is.

Willow turned from the form. She wasn't going to fill it out. There wasn't a trace of fear in her over the prospect, over being judged and considering how others saw her—none of that mattered. She wasn't going to do it because she didn't feel the need.

Willow felt *great*. If she had to find two words to sum up how this strange encounter, the choice would have been simple:

No fear.

Maybe the world wasn't such a bad place to live in. It was certainly turning out to be all right today.

●●●

In the small back room of the clothing shop, Gwen shrugged off her current disguise: another wig to dispose of, along with, naturally, the body of the girl who had been working this shift until Willow had wandered in and Gwen had snapped the worker's neck so that she could take her place.

Withdrawing a small digital messaging device, Gwen typed in a few words: THE HUMAN TRIALS CONTINUE. ROSENBERG HAS BEEN ACTIVATED, ALONG WITH HARRIS. I WILL MONITOR THEIR PROGRESS TOWARD *BECOMING*.

THE THIRD AND FINAL TARGET FOR TONIGHT IS PRIMED. I HOPE THE SUMMERS RESIDENCE IS PREPARED.

SOON, IT WILL BE A WHOLE NEW DAWN.

Chapter Seven

Dawn had only wanted to look at the mirror, but her plan, and the mirror itself, had fallen all to pieces.

The mirror was Buffy's—handheld, with a faux-ivory decorative frame, and spattering of angelic cupids. The glass had fallen out and landed on the carpet when she picked it up, so it didn't break, but every time she tried to put it back in, it fell out again. It was getting really, *really* annoying. No matter how hard she tried to get control of this simple little task, she failed. Just like with everything else in her life. No control at all. And with this mirror . . . she *had* to make it stay in, or Buffy was going to kill her.

A muffled knock came at the door.

Oh, no. It's Buffy. She's going to see me. Dawn

froze, thinking maybe if she didn't move she'd fall off her sister's radar and it would be like she wasn't even there.

The knock came again. But it sounded funny. It wasn't at all like a door was supposed to sound; it was more like—

—the window.

Dawn swam up out of her dream, suddenly registering that she was awake, in her own room, in her own bed . . . but coming out of a heavy dream could be rough business, and the way her head felt, all throbbing and cobwebby, she sort of hoped she was still dreaming. At least that stupid mirror didn't really exist. But what was making that sound?

It came again. A tapping, not a knock. And it was definitely coming from her window.

Okay, she was *wide* awake now. Getting freaked out could do that to a girl. *Think.* She reached over to her nightstand and grabbed a wooden stake that she kept there in case of just such an emergency. She knew vamps couldn't enter the house unless invited, but she never wanted to rule out an accident. What if Xander or Willow—*or, let's face it, probably Anya*—flippantly gave some reptile-faced fangman a "Come on in." A neck Dawn's age was like *veal* in the vampire world, and chances are the Nasty would come after her first. So, stake in hand, Dawn kicked away the covers and inched her way off the bed. Whoever was gently rapping gave a third tapping, tapping on her chamber, um, window. Okay, they had just done Poe in English lit, and it wasn't her fault she couldn't rhyme on the fly.

She felt her breath become a bit forced. Her skin was tingling—and not just because it was cold and she was in a tank top. Certainly she wasn't as brave as she always liked to insist, but she had to be brave enough for this.

I mean, really, it could be nothing. All I have to do is peel back the curtain, and . . .

Dawn gasped as Tommy Jacobs peered in at her. He was propped precariously on a tree limb, leaning forward and balancing himself with one hand on the outside window ledge. He had been tapping with the other. Tommy used that free hand to give her a wave, and when he backed it up with that killer smile of his—well, if he'd said "Hello," Dawn would have been quite fine with going all Renée Zellweger on him and giving him the "You had me at hello" line.

A wave of relief flowed over Dawn. She had gotten so used to bad things coming out of the night sky, she had forgotten that cute boys didn't turn into pumpkins when the lights went out. Granted, there was a chance Tommy had been possessed by some dark and creeping thing out of a smelly old book, but frankly, when it came to cheekbones like his, it was worth taking the risk. And, at least, there was no chance he was a vampire, unlike her first boyfriend. She had seen Tommy in broad daylight just today!

But just as quickly as she'd experienced relief, she also had an *eek!* moment. She was in her sleep clothes, and her sleep clothes were not fit for public consumption. The tank top and boxer shorts bared her arms and legs, which she thought were too skinny. Plus, the boxers had Tweety Bird all over them. Girls in high school don't wear Tweety Bird stuff!

Dawn grabbed the curtain and put it in front of her. Hopefully, he'd gotten just a glimpse, hadn't really made out the details. She stepped away from the wall, too, and tried to block the bed some. If she had successfully hid the Tweeties, it wouldn't do to let him see the stuffed animals on her bed. If he saw them, he was going to think they should have kept her back in junior high! "What are you doing here?" Dawn asked.

Tommy laughed. He pointed to his ear and then shook his head. He put up his thumb and jabbed it repeatedly toward the sky, indicating she should open the window.

Dawn reached out from behind the curtain, leaning toward the window while trying to remain covered. It took a bit of effort, but she finally unlocked it and slid the window open.

"Hey, girl," Tommy said, "I didn't wake you did I?"

"Not really, no," Dawn replied.

Tommy laughed. "Then why were your lights out?"

Dawn hadn't expected that. It wasn't really fair to call someone on such an obvious lie, was it? "Oh, you know my sister," she dodged. "She's the guidance counselor who counsels the fun right out of everything. She lives to restrict."

Good save!

"Don't I know it, yo," Tommy said. "'S why I came to bust you out. I don't like seeing my girl on lockdown."

His girl? Really?

"Figured I owed you one, know what 'm sayin'?" He smiled again. "You came down to the Juvenile Hall to say hey. They didn't let you in, but I got the message. A girl comes to see me, I'm gonna go see her."

Dawn couldn't believe this was happening. Usually she had to throw herself in front of a guy's car for him to even notice she was alive, and even then she risked him running her over without ever seeing her. Perhaps there was something to that law-of-averages thing her math teacher had talked about.

Or maybe there was something to all that destiny stuff in *Romeo and Juliet.*

"You see what I'm sayin'?" Tommy continued. Dawn could have sworn there was a little flash of something in his eye. It probably wasn't dangerous, at least not in the sense that she would need the wooden stake in her hand to fend it off (*oops, better casually drop that*). It was a little mischievous and kind of sexy. "You don't want to hang here with your teddy bears all night, do ya? There's fun to be had."

The teddy bears! He'd seen them!

And he was still here. . . .

Dawn looked over her shoulder, biting her lip just a little. She wasn't sure what she was worried about, since she'd have heard Buffy come in; even so, she had a mental snapshot of her sister standing in the open doorway, arms folded over her chest, vexed, and very, very disappointed.

The door was closed. No one was there.

Still, better safe than sorry. "I don't know,

Tommy," she said. "It's late, and I could really get in trouble."

"You going to let that know-it-all sister of yours tell you what to do?" Tommy seemed to flash from sweet to irritated just as quick as someone would change a channel on a TV. "Give it a rest, kid. You rather take orders or live your life? Sunnydale is ours for the taking."

He had a point. No, seriously. This was a philosophy Dawn could wrap her head around. It's like these were the words she was waiting to hear. *Why be scared all the time?* "Okay," she said. "You're right. Just give me a second to get dressed."

"Awww, come on, do you have to? I thought you looked kind of hot in your jammies."

He tossed that smile at her. Did he know what a lethal weapon it was?

Dawn was suddenly feeling a little daring and she let the curtain drop when she went to close the window. She wasn't sure Tommy was looking, and she couldn't believe she was thinking it, but she kind of hoped that he was. Once the window was down, she gestured with her index finger that she would just be a moment, and closed the curtain.

Oh, my god! She fanned herself with her hand. A boy had climbed up to her bedroom in the middle of the night. How many girls did *that* happen to?

Well, besides Buffy, when Angel used to sneak into her room . . .

Different! Totally!

Tommy must like her, right? He wouldn't be here

if he didn't! But in what way did he like her? He'd seen her at juvenile hall, and that could have given him the wrong idea.

Well, she thought, *it's worth taking the chance. I've fought off worse if he turns out to be all grabbing hands and stuff. At least it won't be tentacles.*

There was no time to go for complicated coordinating, so "simple" and "functional" would be the buzzwords for the evening fashions. A denim jacket was an easy match for jeans, and a robin's-egg-blue T-shirt with a V neck pulled it all together. It said, "I'm a girl ready to go at a moment's notice."

Tommy waited for her on the front lawn. He was wearing a puffy, white ski jacket, and when he saw her coming he pulled a dark blue skullcap out of one of his pockets and pulled it down on his head. It had a white "D" emblazoned on the front. One side of Dawn's brain wanted to say, "Yeah, right, like you've ever been to Detroit," but the other side quickly told it to shut up in a voice menacing enough to make the first side listen. That was the sort of crack Buffy would make, and tonight was about *not* doing what Buffy would do.

Except, of course, for the sneaking out in the middle of the night with a strange, and possibly dangerous, gorgeous boy part. It was only fair that Dawn got her chance at that sort of fun.

Tommy rubbed his hands together and snapped his fingers. "A'ight," he said, "now we're talking."

"Yeah, here I am," Dawn said. Funny, she hadn't felt nervous upstairs, but she was starting to now. If only she could be fearless, like Tommy. "So, what's up? What're we going to do?"

"Well, we can do whatever you want, or you can just kick back and let me drive. I know some pretty sick places we can go. Whattaya say?"

What *could* she say? Were there options? *Doubtful!* "Sounds cool. Lead the way."

"Tight."

Tommy knew exactly where the crack in the fence was. Dawn wondered if maybe he was the one who had cut it, but thought better of asking him that. She knew his reputation well enough, and he'd probably find it insulting to be asked to prove it. Besides, he was holding one side of the fence back for her to pass through. You don't question chivalry like that.

The soil was soft under her tennis shoes, and a little wet. It made a *squish* noise when she stepped. The air smelled like damp towels.

"You ever been back here?" Tommy asked her.

"I don't know, where are we?"

"Yo, you can't tell?" Tommy laughed. "You don't hear 'dat?"

Dawn stopped. Now that he mentioned it, she could hear water. *Rushing* water. "Are we at the reservoir?"

"Straight up."

Tommy laughed again, and then leaned in close. He was right next to her, barely even an inch between their faces. She could feel his breath on her cheek, and it smelled like Juicy Fruit gum. She was scared to

move. He whispered in her ear, "Hey . . . you want to
see a dead body?"

Dawn's eyes went wide. She knew it was ridiculous to let them do that, but they went and did it, anyway. Dead bodies were common in the Summerses'
lifestyle, but that didn't mean they were ever expected.
"W-what?"

Tommy clapped his hands and laughed so hard, he
nearly doubled over. "What do you think this is, yo?
Freakin' *Stand by Me*? Do I look like that Corey Feldman dude to you?"

"Ha-ha, very funny."

Tommy grabbed her hand and shook her arm a little. "Awww, don't be mad. I'm just clownin'." He
moved his head in to find her eyes, and locked her in
his gaze. "You ain't mad, are ya?" he asked.

And there was that smile again. Hanging around
the Magic Box, she'd seen some pretty powerful
charms, but those pearly whites had them all beat.
"No," she said.

"Good, 'cause I really *do* have something pretty
cool to show you."

He kept hold of her hand and led her away from the
fence and into a patch of trees. They weren't very thick,
but it was completely dark inside the enclosure. The
lights of Sunnydale disappeared behind them. They
might as well have disappeared, it seemed so far away.
Dawn felt a twinge of worry, wondering if maybe she
had made the wrong decision, but then, almost as if he
could sense her doubt, Tommy gave her hand a little
squeeze. "It's not much farther," he told her.

They came to the other side of the trees, and the sound of the water had reached the level of a roar. The reservoir was in front of them, illuminated by the stars and a few stray lights on the fence on the opposite side of it.

"I haven't been out here before," Dawn said. "It is pretty cool."

"You think this is why I brought you out here? Girl, I ain't shown you nothin' yet. You feelin' me?"

Tommy led her along the edge of the reservoir. The water was flowing in the other direction. It would be there if someone back in town woke up and wanted to get a drink. They could always count on twisting their faucet handle and the water ready to fulfill their request. *Tsk, how predictable,* Dawn thought. How much better it was to be going someplace unknown.

About half a mile from the thicket of trees, there was a very small dam, holding back the lake that fed into the reservoir. Water was flowing through a hole in the center of the dam. That spot was almost like a little building—a big block of concrete and whatever machinery it was that opened and closed the portal for the water—and it was connected to the bank on the other side. The only way to get to that position from where they were was a very thin wall, about twenty yards long and only wide enough to maybe hold one person's foot at a time.

"This is the only place to get across," Tommy said.

"Are you sure?" Dawn asked. "It doesn't look very . . . safe."

"You scared?"

The truth? Yeah, she was. That was a long walk on a very thin path. It would just be an easy slip to send her tumbling into the water, where she would probably be crushed by the stream flowing through the dam.

But sometimes the truth is the enemy.

"No," she said, "let's go."

"Tight. It's easier than it looks. You just gotta go. Once you start, don't stop. It's best to do it fast." Tommy stepped to the edge of the dam. He looked over his shoulder at her, gave her a wink. "Watch."

He put one foot on the dam, then the other in front of it. He held his arms out like airplane wings and started heading across, one step following another—no pause, no looking back.

No fear.

When he got to the platform beyond the dam, he spun around and raised his arms in victory. "See?" he shouted.

Dawn realized she hadn't breathed the whole time he was on the dam. It made her head feel a little light. It looked a lot easier than she'd expected, though, and surely Tommy wouldn't bring her out here if he thought she'd end up plummeting to a watery grave.

"The first step's the hardest!" he yelled. "Once you've taken it, it's easy."

The concrete didn't crumble when Dawn touched it with her toe, and that was surprisingly reassuring. She put her whole foot on the dam, put it down flat, and she felt the strength of the structure move up her leg. She followed with the other foot. She had completely left solid ground behind. *Well, I'm committed now,* she thought. She gritted her teeth and headed across.

Tommy greeted her on the other side. He grabbed her off the dam and gave her a hug. "I told you," he laughed. "You didn't believe it, but here you are."

She giggled. "It wasn't so hard!"

He grabbed her hand again. "Come on. We're close now."

There was a small hill on that bank, and they quickly went over it and to the fence. Instead of open land on the other side, like it was farther down, there were a few buildings, along with some metal towers and wires. It looked like a power plant–type place, confirmed by all the DANGER: HIGH VOLTAGE and KEEP OUT signs. There were even a few placards with what apparently was some kind of international sign for "Careful, you'll get shocked." It looked like a guy had stepped on a lightning bolt and it had knocked him over. It made Dawn think of Glory and how she'd blast people out of their shoes. *And if a place makes me think of Glory, maybe it isn't a good idea for us to be here.* "Is this it?" she asked.

"Yeah," Tommy said. "Don't be disappointed yet, though. What I want you to see is inside."

"Inside? But didn't they put up those warnings for a reason?"

Tommy gave her a look that said, *What kind of world do you live in?* "The only reason for warnings is that someone wants to spoil our fun," he said. "If you wanted to go through this world listening to warnings, you should've stayed in bed."

A locked gate was only a few feet down the line. Tommy went over to it and pushed hard with his shoulder. It opened up just enough that he was able to squeeze his body through. He had to duck down to go under the chain, but he did it quick and got through before the gate popped back and the gap closed. Once on the other side, he pulled on it and reopened the crack. He looked at Dawn. "You in or out?" he asked.

Dawn took a deep breath. She hadn't come this far just to go back now. She exhaled, bent down, and followed Tommy inside the compound.

"You won't regret this," he said. "Trust me."

It was clear that Tommy had been here before. He confidently led her through the dark maze toward the center. All the little shacks seemed to be built with sharp angles, and with the towers pointing in every which direction and the cables separating them from the sky and the world outside, Dawn found it all rather ominous, like a mechanical spiderweb built by a robot spider, and she hoped she wasn't the predator's favorite flavor of fly.

Suddenly, everything opened up. At the center of the compound was an area where the ground was clear. There were no buildings, no steel or wire, nothing to obscure the universe above them. "Check it out," Tommy said. "Isn't it cool?"

"Wow," Dawn said, though it was more of a gasp than a real word. "How did you find this place?"

"I looked. It's amazing what you'll see once you bother to."

Tommy sat down on the ground. He patted the spot

next to him. "We're not really there yet, Dawn," he said. "There's only one way to experience this."

She sat down next to him, and he placed a finger to his lips. *Shhhh.* For the first time, Dawn became aware that there was a hum all around them. It was the hum of electricity, all the power passing through the wires and machines. It was a bit eerie, but it also made her feel powerful, like all that energy was actually passing through her.

"Now lie down on your back," Tommy said, "and look straight up."

She did what he said, and he followed her down, lying on his back right next to her. It was instantly obvious what he'd meant.

Above them was wide-open sky. No city lights to obscure the view, no power lines, no trees—nothing. Just miles and miles of stars, bright and shiny and completely beautiful.

"Sometimes I come out here when things are just too noisy, you know?" Tommy said. "If you look at the stars and you listen to all that electrical stuff buzzing around you, it's like . . . it's like you're actually hearing *their* power, like all the stars are buzzing inside your brain."

Neither of them spoke, and Dawn could see— could *feel*—exactly what Tommy was talking about. It was like they had tapped into the cosmos. She imagined this was what it would be like if she had all that power everyone said she had when she was the Key.

"Tommy . . ."

"Yeah?"

"This is awesome."

Tommy didn't say anything, but Dawn felt his hand on top of hers, felt his fingers slide between her fingers and rest there.

The walk back to town was sublime. Tommy held her hand the whole way. It was like in *Rebel Without a Cause,* when Natalie Wood had seen through to the real, tender side of James Dean. Tommy would probably think that movie was corny, but she thought it was romantic in that silly way that no one was allowed to be romantic anymore, so she kept that thought to herself lest she spoil the moment.

"You know, I heard about that trouble you got into last year," he said.

They had been quiet most of the way, but now they had entered a shopping district near the center of town, and pretty soon they'd be back to Dawn's house.

"What?"

"The shoplifting. My dad's a lawyer, remember? I know none of those stores pressed charges against you, but some of the owners didn't make that decision until they'd talked to their lawyer, and that was my pop."

"Oh . . ."

Great. Tommy probably thought she was really lame, being dragged in by her older sister and having to give everything back and apologize and stuff. He would never back down that way.

"My dad didn't tell me what you'd done or anything.

I just go through his notebooks and computer files when he's not around," he continued. "He had to charge for the consultations, so he kept records. Anyway, I thought it was pretty cool. Really, like, totally sick. I said to myself, 'That girl's got some deep stuff, and hardly anybody knows it.' I was pretty stoked when you showed up down at juvie."

Well, that's a relief. "Thanks," she said. "Most people wouldn't be as, um, understanding."

"Not me, Boo," he said. "I got much respect for someone who does what they please, who doesn't care about all that stuff society hangs on us."

Tommy stopped and looked around. There were stores up and down the street, stores with large windows and all sorts of different items behind them. He pointed to an electronics store across the way. "Let's check it out," he said. He let go of her hand and made a beeline for the window.

Dawn followed behind him. She was starting to get confused. It was like hot-and-cold running Tommy. She didn't know where she stood from one minute to the next, and suddenly she was starting to think again that he found her terribly dorky.

Tommy put a finger to the glass, leaving a smudge. "Check out that MP3 player, kid," he said. "I betcha that holds a couple thousand songs. I could download some bangers off the Internet and I'd never need nothin' else to play them."

Dawn took his hand and moved it down so it was pointing at a digital camera. "I want one of those," she said. "You don't have to buy film or get the pictures developed. I can take a photo of anything I want, and have it right then."

He pressed his hand on hers so it was flat on the glass. "Then why don't you reach in there and take it," he said. His voice had dropped low. His tone was almost hypnotic. "It's just glass. It's made to break."

"Are you serious?" she said, snatching her hand away. "I couldn't. I've been in enough trouble—"

"Awww, dude. Don't play. That doesn't sound like the Dawn I know."

"I'm sorry, but my sister would kill me. Plus, it's wrong."

Tommy shook his head. "You're still stuck on 'right' and 'wrong'?" he asked. "You think there is such a thing?" He held his hand up, palm out, right in front of her face. Without another word, he turned and headed off down the block. "I thought you were cool, but I guess you'd rather not be."

Dawn stood there and watched him go. *So that's it, then?* she asked herself. *Everything we've done tonight, and it ends like this? Maybe he's right, maybe I am just clinging to a concept that doesn't really apply to the real world. What's the big deal, anyway? It's just one camera, and they probably have twenty more inside. If I want it, I can take it, and then I'll have it . . . and I'll have him.* "Tommy!" she exclaimed. "Wait!"

He stopped and turned back to look at her. He shoved his hands into his jacket pocket.

It was trash day, and all the shops had taken their garbage out to the curb. Just a few feet away there were some empty paint cans. Dawn picked one up, lifted it over her head, and tossed it at the shop window. The glass shattered with a loud crash, and seconds later the alarm started to sound.

Before Dawn even had a chance to really register what she'd just done, a security guard came sprinting out of a department store across the street. He shone a flashlight on her as he ran, and she quickly pulled her hair in front of her face so he couldn't see what she looked like. Holding one arm out to further block his view, she plunged the other one through the hole in the glass. The camera fit right into her hand. She clenched it tight.

The guard had gotten across the street by that point. "Hey, you there!" he shouted. "What do you think you're doing?"

He lunged for her. The self-defense training Buffy had given her came flooding back, and she easily dodged his advance, grabbing his arm and twisting it behind his back. He cried out in pain, and she shoved him into the store's doorway, being careful not to slam him into the wall. This wasn't exactly what Buffy had trained her for, so the least she could do was not pervert it too much.

Then again, who *cared* what Buffy thought? She gave the guard a nice kick in the butt.

Before the guard could recover, Dawn broke away, running in Tommy's direction. As soon as she reached him, he grabbed her hand and they raced off together.

They didn't stop running until they got to the park. Luna and Big J were hanging out under the jungle gym. This was obviously the gang's regular spot, because Tommy had known a pretty complicated route for getting there, ducking through dark alleys and zigzagging across various streets—an escape route for eluding the long arm of the law. She and Tommy were the new Bonnie and Clyde. *Like the Beyoncé and Jay-Z version, though, and not the old ones.*

"Look who's here!" Luna said. "What have you two gotten into tonight?"

Dawn felt a quick jolt of fear. She stiffened up and put the digital camera behind her back. It made Tommy laugh. "What are you scared of?" he said. "This is your new family, Boo. They live on the same side of life I do. You live here now, too, so you don't have to be shy about nothin'."

He snatched the camera from her and held it up. "Check out what Dawnie scored," he said. "You shoulda seen it too. This doughnut-eatin' rent-a-cop tried to stop her, and she put him on his face. It was sick, yo."

Big J plopped down onto a swing. The chains vibrated all the way to the top. "Sweet," he said. "So, this your new lady, T?"

Tommy looked at Dawn. He dropped that smile on her and said, "Yeah, I guess you could say that."

"You gonna play that new CD for her?" Luna asked. "That Antwerp band?"

Dawn shuddered, a sudden rush of alien sensations making her every nerve tingle. She touched her forehead, wobbled for a moment, and had to fight off a sudden wave of dizziness. Sighing, she felt her body release all the stored up tension within her.

It felt amazing.

Tommy swam back into view. She thought she knew how it felt to be fearless before this moment. But . . .

"We got our own music," Tommy said. He leaned in and put his lips to hers. She felt her hand rise and grab the back of his head as she kissed him back. She tasted that Juicy Fruit now. She liked it.

Luna snickered. "Yup, Dawn," she said with a wild laugh, "I'd definitely say you're *definitely* one of us now."

Morning comes way too quick when you stay out all night and don't go back to bed until five in the morning. Dawn's mouth tasted like she'd been chewing on a sponge for several hours, and it almost seemed like there were bandages over her eyes, the way the world looked all hazy and dim.

She stumbled into the bathroom.

Reaching up to wipe the hair out of her face, she noticed in the mirror a black splotch on her right shoulder. On closer inspection, she discovered it wasn't a splotch at all. It was some kind of tattoo. It was a strange symbol, sort of Celtic looking. A star on top of a cross, and then something superimposed on top of them. At first she thought it looked like someone had run their hand across the ink, smearing it before it had dried, but as her eyes brought it into focus, it actually looked like it was some kind of bar code.

But perhaps before she worried about what it was,

she should worry about how it got there. She didn't remember getting a tattoo, and she wasn't sure when they'd even had time. She touched it, and it wasn't sore. Any kind of makeshift needle kit those guys would have used would most definitely hurt. So where did it come from?

Dawn threw a T-shirt over her tank top so that the sleeve would cover it up. She didn't want Buffy to see it. She could imagine what kind of conversation *that* would be over breakfast. She wasn't eager to explain herself—not because she was scared of her sister, but because Buffy wouldn't understand. Wherever this came from, whatever it was, it was part of her new, private life, and for now, it would stay private. She let Buffy butt in way too much, anyway, and it was about time that stopped. In the past, she'd only let her interfere because she'd been scared of what Buffy might do. She was done with being pushed around, done with being scared of her big sis.

In fact, she was done with being scared altogether. Nothing was so big that it could make her afraid anymore.

Nothing in the *world*.

In another bedroom of the Summers home, Willow stirred, feeling something tickle her right shoulder. Blinking a few times, she looked at the strange rash that was forming. She stared at it but couldn't figure out what it was, or why she should care, scratched it, settled back in bed, and didn't give it another thought.

• • •

Across town, Xander was showering and he, too, noticed a dark smudge or something on his right shoulder. What—had he leaned against something at the construction site? He couldn't remember, and it didn't really matter. Soap wouldn't remove it, but, then, he was in a hurry to get to work, so it's not like he worked hard at scrubbing it off.

He didn't notice in the slightest as the dark splotch moved a little, a few of the marks joining into lines, other shapes only beginning to come into focus.

They were all *becoming,* some much quicker than others.

Chapter Eight

Buffy stared at her peanut butter and jelly sandwich on white bread and wished it would turn into something more interesting, like sushi or even a hamburger. But no, every time she turned her head away and looked back, it remained the same old thing. It sure would be nice to have a little Willow wizardry to presto-chango the silly thing—Willow magic *without* all the dark mojo, that is.

The truth was, the Slayer really needed to do some food shopping or, before she knew it, she herself was going to turn into a peanut butter and jelly sandwich. Eat enough of them, that's what you'll turn into. Mom had said that plenty of times. And how would she fight demons if she were a sandwich?

Whoa. Major low blood sugar spiral. Eat now. Think later.

Buffy was stirred from her thoughts by the creak of the faculty lounge door opening. Glancing over, Buffy gave a little nod to Sally Harper, Principal Wood's new administrative assistant. Sally's slender, gorgeous body had practically been *poured* into her simple, tight, pink-and-white-floral print dress. Her short-cropped brown hair stuck out all over from the product she used, and her blazing red highlights shone even in this bland overhead lighting. Sashaying in on pristine high heels, Sally had one of those bodies that women hated on other women—and one of those weird mutant metabolisms that let her eat whatever she wanted without ever gaining an ounce.

But the worst thing for Buffy about Sally was her attitude. She was always smiling and bubbly. Even when tempers flared and the students appeared about ready to kill one another, she was optimistic and happy. There *had* to be something wrong with the woman.

Sally bounced over to the table where Buffy sat and chirped, "Is this seat taken?"

"I dunno," Buffy said with a fake smile meant to ward off high-heeled evil. "Define 'taken.' Is it taken with itself, losing hours at a time staring at its own reflection? Is it taken, as in tied up in a serious relationship with at least one of the other chairs at this table? Is it taken for granted by all those who don't even think to grant it a kind and nurturing word when it needs it the most? There're a lot of ways we can go here."

Sally's inhumanly friendly smile never faltered. "May I sit down?"

"Yeah sure, whatever," Buffy said, surrendering to the inevitable. Lunch with one of the beautiful people. Guh! Where was Simon and his demon attacks when you really needed them?

Buffy didn't mean to be cruel, but there was definitely something wrong with a person who could be this chipper at twelve o'clock in the afternoon.

Drawing up the chair she had been gingerly caressing, Sally sat down quickly, adjusting her dress, sliding in close to Buffy, and tenting her hands so that she could rest her chin on them mischievously.

Buffy waited for Sally to say something, to do anything other than stare. *Do I have a peanut butter mustache?* she wondered self-consciously. *A jelly soul patch?*

"I'll let you in on a secret," Sally promised.

"Oh gee, do ya have to?"

Sally's smile widened. She didn't make any move toward procuring lunch. No hunting, no gathering, no cracking open of the fridge or raiding of the junk food dispensers. This was an ominous sign. Maybe she was, in truth, a Sally bot. *That would explain a lot of things. . . .*

"I've been watching you for a while," Sally said, dropping her voice down to a kind of sexy conspiratorial level.

The Slayer glanced at her in surprise. "Me? Why? What'd I do?"

"Well, I'm new here, and you seem to have everything down pat, so I figured I could learn a lot from you."

Buffy groaned inwardly. So that was Sally's game. She wanted a mentor.

Great, just what Buffy wanted to do during her short lunch break: talk about work. Buffy took a huge bite of her sandwich and chewed with her mouth half-open, a grade-school gross out she hoped would dissuade Sally from seriously considering a long conversation.

"You're really good with these kids," Sally said nervously. "And you have *so much* style in the way you dress. You really seem to be comfortable here, and I really want to do well at this job."

Buffy was about to make a comment regarding the realities of just staying alive when you worked at Hellmouth High, but decided against it. She noticed that Sally was a fidgeter, genetically predisposed against sitting still. It was like the seat was hot, so the woman kept moving around on it, trying to find a cool spot.

Or she just liked waggling her butt around.

Practice makes perfect . . .

"Well, I've been here a long time," Buffy said. "I went here. Um—not here, exactly. The high school that was here before it blew up or burned down or whatever happened to it, *I sure wouldn't know!*" She laughed one of those short crazy-people laughs, then settled back to wash her sandwich down with some milk. "I mean, seven years in Sunnydale and a person's bound to know the ropes. You just have to give it time and get out there and meet people."

Y'know, when I say "meet people," I mean, like, other people. As in, not me. As in . . . please go away. Your niceness is getting to me and making me feel bad about thoughts like these.

"Oh, yes indeedy," Sally said, proving to be one of the last six people left alive on the face of the earth who could deliver that phrase and not have a roof collapse on their head for the affront. "I've met some people already. In fact, I ran into Willow Rosenberg at the bookstore last week and *she* said you and she are friends."

Buffy nodded. It was all she could do. The peanut butter had again stuck to the roof of her mouth, so she couldn't speak. Probably a good thing. *Willow, you're meat.* Buffy took a swig of milk to wash down the bite of her sandwich.

Sally's confidence suddenly ebbed. "But, I was just wondering . . . if you would be interested in, ah, um . . ."

Waitaminute. The girl was babbling. Why was she so nervous?

The whole thing came crashing in on her like a freight train carrying explosives. *Does she think I'm gay? Like Willow?*

That would mean she's . . . into me.

Swallowing hard, she decided she would have to set Sally straight . . . so to speak.

"Look Sally, you seem like a really nice person, but I'm—"

Sally cut her off, blurting out, "Would-you-be-interested-in-going-on-a-blind-date-with-a-friend-of-mine?" She gasped for air, then kept going before Buffy could get a syllable in, let alone a whole word. "He's-a-really-great-guy-and-I-could-really-see-the-two-of-you-together!"

Buffy recoiled as if she'd taken round after round from an automatic weapon of words.

A blind date? She had seen that TV show enough times to know how *badly* that could turn out. But, on the other hand, two of her past relationships had been with vampires . . . so who was she to trust her own judgment when it came to choosing men. And it had been a *long* time since she had gone out with anyone. Buffy made her decision. Gripping the edge of the table, she went for it. "Okay. Sure."

Sally squealed. *"Really?"*

"Yeah."

"Great! I'll give him a call and arrange everything. All you'll have to do is show up," Sally yelped happily. She jumped up and ran out the door of the faculty lounge before Buffy could say anything else.

At least now I can get back to my lunch, Buffy thought. But just as she was about to take another bite, the bell rang for next period. *Or not.* She gathered up the rest of her lunch to eat at her desk, wondering what kind of guy someone like Sally would call a friend.

Her mind beginning to boggle, Buffy chose to adopt a wait-and-see rather than a wait-and-worry attitude.

Too bad it didn't take.

• • •

Buffy slammed on the brakes of *again* as she drove to the downtown movie theater for her blind date. This was ridiculous! Traffic was way too crazy for this time of day, and the drivers who had chosen to make Sunnydale a new location for one of those wacky shows with the car chases and crazy stunts were *way* out of line. She was already late because she didn't have Dawn around to help her pick out the perfect outfit. Well, she did, but Dawn was busy being moody and alone in her room under the watchful eye of Willow. Buffy wouldn't have even considered going out when there was so much craziness on the home front, but she had been through phases like this with Dawnie before— maybe not this sudden and severe, but similar enough—to know her kid sister was only going to open up when she was good and ready . . . and that always took a while.

The outfit Buffy wanted was one that said, in just the right way, that she was available, but not easy. The clock taunting her, Buffy had finally settled on a brown peasant blouse, tan skirt, and brown boots.

Later in the work day, Sally had come to her office to inform Buffy that the date had to be set up for tonight because "Tad" had a business trip that he was leaving for tomorrow morning and he would be gone for a week. So much for doing the food shopping. Buffy was going to start having nightmares about peanut butter and jelly sandwiches coming to destroy the world.

On the upside, Sally had worked out a corny but easy way for Buffy and Tad to recognize each other. They would both bring a single red rose with them to the movie theater and hold it in their hand while waiting outside. For this, Buffy was relieved. She'd been worried that Sally would make her wear a certain color or something silly like that.

Butterflies, butterflies, butterflies. She had 'em. Her tummy was their home.

The traffic kept getting worse. Buffy didn't have Tad's telephone number so she could call him to let him know she was running late.

Cars flew by, running lights, passing illegally, blurring around her like she was sitting still. For the first time in her life she was convinced that she was the safest, sanest, and most skilled driver on the road.

What was going on here? It was like road rage had become the national sport of Sunnydale.

Then, because it had to, that's how this stuff worked, things went from bad to worse.

Buffy's cell phone rang. Opening her handbag, she slid it out and answered. "Hello," she said. "You've reached the voice mail of Buffy Summers. If you'd like to talk to a real, live operator, press pound or stay on the line for more options. Thank you and have a wonderful—"

"They're dying," Simon said. "I've seen them."

An ice pick the size of someone's arm drove itself down along Buffy's spine. Shuddering, she sat up straight, a surge of adrenaline helping her overcome the shock at hearing his voice. "Who's dying?" she asked, navigating around what could have been a ten-car pileup if two of the loonies on the road had zagged instead of zigged.

"All they wanted was a night out at the movies. Some popcorn, a light romantic comedy . . . it doesn't seem right that they should suffer, now does it?"

Simon's voice was flat, a marked contrast to the downright nastiness in his words.

"The movie theater?" Buffy asked, picturing hundreds of people trapped, being ripped to pieces by butt-uglies, even as she spoke. "The one downtown?"

"The one and only. A man in the theater stole a very powerful demon's woman away from him. The demon wants revenge and is sending a hit squad to take care of the problem and all the witnesses."

"Oh, you have got to be kidding," Buffy said. "We're talking a demon scorned?"

"This is no joke," Simon said. "The theater is filled with people."

"This is happening now?"

"I didn't say that. Only that I've seen it."

Buffy swerved to avoid another car, this one barreling toward her in the wrong lane.

"You know, I'm getting *really* tired of this," Buffy said, her heart racing from all her frustrations. Nothing was under control. She was losing Dawn again, Simon was running her around like it was all a big-time fun-fest for him, and her job was a nightmare.

"Try yoga," Simon urged. "It's relaxing and it invigorates at the same time."

"Who *are* you?" Buffy snapped, squeezing the cell phone so hard, its plastic case started to crack. "How do you know when these things are going to happen?"

"That doesn't matter. The only thing that's important is that you protect those you are sworn to protect. That is what you do, Slayer."

"Are you behind all of this?"

"What if I am? There are still innocents to be saved."

"I *will* find out who you are."

"A dangerous proposition, as your little red-haired friend can tell you. But, yes, you will. In time. That time is not now, Buffy. Hurry now, child. Tick-tock. Race the clock. Otherwise . . ."

A swell of screams rose up from his end of the phone—and the line went dead.

Buffy had to restrain herself to keep from hurling the phone against the dash.

Simon and more of his games. Great, just when she'd thought she was getting a little control over her life and doing something vaguely resembling normal—

BAM! Buffy had no choice. She couldn't risk innocents suffering . . . and she was heading for the theater already.

Coincidence? One wonders. . . .

Buffy quickly called every member of the Scooby gang on her cell phone, but couldn't reach anyone. She heard Willow pick up, then the line went dead. Ditto with Xander. Anya.

Willow had warned that Simon was powerful. He knew magic . . . and Buffy had an idea that he was using it now, forcing her to go this one alone.

Fine.

It took Buffy another twenty minutes before she

reached downtown Sunnydale and was able to find a parking space. By this time, she was steaming mad and ready to kill an entire army of demons.

She looked over at the red rose sitting on the passenger seat and frowned.

Maybe, if I'm lucky, Buffy thought, *I can down the demons and still go out on this date.* Well, she could hope. Buffy left the red rose in the car and instead grabbed a couple of daggers, which she placed in her purse.

Buffy reached the movie theater, half-expecting to find a flood of innocent people fleeing the main exits . . . but it all looked peaceful and blessedly normal. Which was actually good, in certain ways, bad in others. The overall calm *could* mean that the evil beasties hadn't attacked yet, *or* it could mean they were already inside, had blocked off the exits, and were slaughtering hundreds under cover of the film's loud sound track.

The Slayer turned to survey the area—then she saw him. The him. As in, her blind-date him.

He stood in front of the theater holding a red rose, just like Sally had said he would. Oh crap, and he was actually good looking. A hottie, even. Tall, tan, and blond, with wide shoulders and a physique that was hinted at by the cut of his expensive business suit. And he was human. *Normal.*

Not that she could worry about any of that right now. Innocents were in danger, and she had a duty to save them. Ignoring her date, Buffy looked for the fastest way in. That would be the glass doors in the front, of course, but if she went in without buying a ticket, people would try to stop her from going past the concession stand. She could overpower any theater workers, she knew that, but the police might be called, and when she got to the theater—well, Simon sounded like he was in a mood to make things difficult for her because of her attitude. What if the attack wasn't going to happen for half an hour? They wouldn't clear the theater on her word. Not unless she resorted to making up some story that would also cause a panic, and *that* could get people killed.

There was only one side alley with emergency doors leading out of the theater. Peering down it, she saw two employees taking a break. Okay, she could overpower both of them, too, and rip the door open even if it was locked—but more people were getting here now, a small crowd was forming, and that meant she was likely to be spotted, and that *again* meant there was the risk of the cops being called and her getting hauled off by them before the trouble started.

Frustrated, the Slayer darted in front of a mass of people deciding what movie they wanted to see and got on the still thankfully short line to buy a movie ticket. Buffy concentrated on the back of the person in front of her. She didn't want to risk making eye contact with the guy she was standing up.

Then the worst possible thing imaginable happened: The Slayer felt a tap on her shoulder. She turned around, and there, standing in front of her, was her blind date, complete with the requisite red rose held out in his hand.

"Excuse me," he said in a smooth voice, "aren't you Buffy Summers? I'm Tad."

He was cute. *Why did he have to be cute? Must be strong, Buffy. Must be strong.*

"Buffy? No, no Buffy here. Sorry, got the wrong one," said the Slayer in a tone that little kids used when they are caught doing something that they are not supposed to be doing.

Out of the corner of her eye, Buffy saw that she had finally reached the ticket booth. She jammed her money under the Plexiglas window and asked for a ticket to tonight's movie. The girl working the ticket booth squinted and shook her head. "Yes, you *are* Buffy Summers! I graduated a year ahead of you. What's the deal lying to this guy?"

Great. Just when I don't want to be recognized.

Buffy turned to Tad. "Look, I'm sorry I can't explain this right now. You look like a really nice guy. This just isn't going to work out."

"Buffy, what's going on?" Tad asked as he crossed his arms in front of his chest. "This isn't going to work out? This hasn't even started."

"I don't have time for this." She spun and slapped her hand near the ticket window. "Listen, Miss Nosey and in Everyone's Business, can I please have my ticket?"

"Yeah! What's going on?"

"I just need to get inside. Ticket. Now. It *can't* be this difficult."

"Here." The girl hurled a ticket at Buffy. She snatched it and ran into a hunky wall of Tadness.

"What? I'm not your type but you want to see the movie, anyway?" Blind date Tad said.

"You know . . . yes. That's it." Buffy thought, *Oh, kill me now.* This was getting far worse than Buffy needed. She hadn't wanted to create a scene, and that was exactly what was happening. *Nothing* was under her control. She slipped by Tad, ran inside, and handed her ticket to the attendant.

Bored, not even trying to make eye contact, he said, "Second theater on your right."

"Yuh-huh," Buffy said, snagging the torn shred of paper and sprinting toward the inevitable. *Slayers slay,* she thought. *It's what we do.*

Then she pictured Tad left standing outside the theater, probably wondering why he always got set up with the crazy ones.

That and make people's lives miserable.

After Buffy went inside, the manager of the movie theater came over to the ticket booth to see what was going on. "What's the problem?" the manager asked.

"I quit. I'm gone," said the girl as she grabbed her handbag from underneath the shelf. Her face was pale. She looked panicked.

"What? Why?"

"Buffy Summers was here, acting all urgent and stuff," she said as she tore off the movie theater employee ID on her white shirt.

He blanched right along with her. "Got a car? Can you give me a ride?"

They both ran out of the ticket booth and headed

for the alley, where the girl's car was parked.

Screeching tires quickly commenced.

Buffy carefully scanned the lobby's interior. The usual line stretched out from the concession stand, and a few kids massacred the video game machines in the corner. The strong smell of popcorn and butter wafted up through the air. No demons in sight, *but . . .* she felt that something was going to happen soon. She marched over to the auditorium, opened the door, and went inside. The only sounds she could hear came from the wall speakers, thundering out music and snippets of dialogue to accompany the previews playing on the movie screen. Some action flick about a superhero romance. Eeks. The room lights were dimmed but not completely out, and almost every seat was taken.

WHAM! Buffy spun as the air warped and glowed bright red as a mystical shield settled on every exit in the auditorium, blocking them. The Slayer could feel the barrier behind her like a blast of hot air striking when you leave an air-conditioned building on a humid August afternoon. The shield glowed bloodred around the outline of every exit in the place. They were *all* trapped.

That's when the creepy-crawlies came out to play.

A dozen in all, melting out of the shadows, three from each corner of the auditorium. Short and round, clothed in long, gray robes, they didn't look like what Buffy might have pictured for a demon hit squad, but experience had taught her that looks weren't everything. Light flickered from the screen as a daylight

scene washed over the crowd and illuminated the baddies. Actually, seeing what they had that passed for
heads, they actually *did* look very dangerous. They had
three eyes, large ears, and two horns that curled
upward six inches from their heads. Their mouths
made up almost the entire lower half of their faces, and
they were filled with enormous teeth that could tear a
person apart. Their hands ended in huge raking talons
that could slice open anything.

Just as Simon had said, one of the demons bee-
lined for a guy sitting in the front row. Tall, dark, handsome, and sitting with an inhumanly beautiful
woman—yep, that had to be the one they were after.
Before Buffy could run the distance down to the first
row, the demon grabbed the man, pulled him to his
feet, and sliced open the man's neck with its talons.

"No!" Buffy shouted, but it was too late.

In one quick motion, the hit was done. Buffy
stared in shock as the man's body fell to the ground,
blood pouring from his neck. All the people in the
auditorium followed the Slayer's example and just
stared, unaware that they were on the demon pack's
short list. The dead man's lover was on her knees,
screaming. Buffy had the feeling the demons would
either save her for last—or take her back to the
scumbag who had ordered her boyfriend killed.

The other demons had fanned out and appeared to
be waiting for a signal. When the head demon was sure
that the target was dead, he nodded his head in the
direction of the other demons.

"Move!" Buffy screamed at the people in the room.

The crowd turned and gazed at the Slayer with confusion. Where was there to go? A few jumped up and ran to the front exit, but they were violently thrown back by the mystical heat barrier. Buffy heard the demons chortle at the confusion they had engendered, and it really cheesed her off. It was bad enough that they planned to kill everyone in the room, but their arrogance and amusement were *really* annoying.

Snapping open her purse, Buffy pulled out her daggers and leaped at the head demon. Landing on one foot, she kicked it hard in the midsection with the other—and it was like hitting a brick wall.

Ouch.

The demon swung at her with his sweeping talons, and she fell back to avoid it, landing hard on the ground as she tripped on the leg of a panicked movie house patron.

Grabbing her by the hair, Mr. Mouth tossed her into the screen, which she tore through before slamming against the concrete only a few feet behind it. As she rose, Buffy heard screams of terror issuing from the audience, the sounds mixing with the sounds of the previews that accompanied the images still being played on the torn screen.

"Now I'm really mad," said the Slayer. Buffy ran forward and threw herself onto the head demon's back, driving both daggers deep into his chest. The demon let out a groan of pain and fell to the ground with a loud thump. The other demons turned at the sound from their own personal mayhem and came charging en masse.

Oh, good. The more, the merrier. . . .

Buffy took a few steps back to give herself plenty of room to fight the demon onslaught. The Slayer stunned one demon with a roundhouse kick to the head and stabbed another in the chest. She threw the other dagger at a demon and hit it squarely in the center of his head, splooshing right through its third eye.

Then it was just demon frenzy. One kicked her in the chest and punched her in the face several times in rapid succession. Buffy shook off the blows and countered with a volley of punches of her own, her dagger slicing through the demon's right arm.

In-coming!

A demon grasped her right arm, which held the dagger, and raked its talons across her face. She whipped her head back quick enough—good old Slayer reflexes—and only received a handful of light, stinging cuts.

Stamping down on its ankle, Buffy heard a yowl and a satisfying crackle of breaking bones. The demon released her arm, allowing Buffy to spin with the dagger, moving it across in a wide arc that tore through its throat and sent it spinning and gurgling away.

Buffy heard people crushing one another near the exits. She had to end this quick, but there were so many of them!

A demon backed away momentarily and then lunged at Buffy with its razor-sharp claws, slicing through the sleeve of Buffy's blouse.

"Do you know how hard it was to find a blouse that went with this skirt?" the Slayer asked the demon.

Then the Slayer grabbed the black curtains from behind the screen, threw them over the demon's head, and used the dagger to slice open his throat. The demons fell to the ground but not before gushing all over her—with a load of blood that ruined Buffy's skirt and boots.

"These stains are never going to come out, you know!" she screamed as she stooped down, snatched up the second dagger from the throat of a dead demon, and launched herself at two more of the creatures.

The daggers fell, shimmering in the ever-changing light of the images on the torn screen, and two more demons died. Slapping both daggers into one hand, Buffy grabbed the arm of another incoming demon and flipped it up and over her, sending it crashing into the now empty first row of theater seats. With amazing speed, the demon leaped up and over Buffy to come down behind her. It grabbed her from behind and held down her arms.

Buffy bent her knees and dropped forward, jamming the daggers into one of its arms to break its grip, then putting her back into it as she thrust the demon high and away, noting with some satisfaction when it crashed into the concrete wall she had met with a few minutes earlier. More demons came. Buffy hacked and slashed, finally landing on the last one, whom she held down with a knee to the chest while stabbing its chest until it stopped writhing.

Buffy whirled and took in the craziness around the theater. Dozens of people were hugging the walls and screaming or crying. Others lay dead in their seats where the demons had attacked them before Buffy had been able to stop them. A strange *whooshing* sound rose up, and Buffy breathed a sigh of relief as the mystical barriers disappeared from the exits. "Okay," Buffy said to the remaining movie viewers, "go! Get! Scoot!"

There was no way this crowd had enjoyed the show.

The group rushed for the doors, and no one even stopped to thank her. Well, at least something in her life was still the same. Then the familiar glow came, and Buffy watched three of the demonic forms congeal and coalesce until the only thing left behind was a foot-long chunk of magical sword. The Slayer scooped up her new prize and her purse, and made for a street exit.

Suddenly, one of the actors on screen turned to her and said, "Don't forget who that's for, Buffy!"

As if you'd let me, Simon.

Soon, she was on the street, heading for her car. Mourning the loss of her favorite peasant blouse, Buffy pulled a Handi Wipe from her purse and wiped the blood off her face. There was usually a fresh tarp in the trunk that she could use to protect the seats from stray blood and guts she may have bathed in during a typical evening out, but she just remembered she'd taken out the last one and had forgotten to replace it. Perfect.

Fortunately, vandalism seemed to be at an all-time high in Sunnydale, and a ripped-up awning for a closed-down business did the trick instead. In the car, she speed-dialed Willow.

This time, the call went through.

"Assemble the troops," Buffy said, "or whatever it is we do. Had a really great time on the blind date. Killed a bunch of three-eyed demons and got another chunk of sword. Not going to be much left to recover pretty soon, so we need some heavy-duty research—"

"On it," Willow said, sounding unusually confident.

"Okey-dokey," the Slayer said, hanging up.

She drove off slowly and carefully. There was no way in hell she was going to let Simon have the pieces of this sword before she knew a lot more about its possible powers.

A sword formed from dead demons probably doesn't bring about Heaven on Earth.

She didn't care how many innocents Simon helped her save—particularly if he was the one arranging the attacks. If this sword was dangerous, then she would not let *anyone* get their hands on it.

Buffy sighed. She was *never* going to get her food shopping done.

Chapter Nine

The Hideaway was one of Sunnydale's nicest restaurants. Or, more correctly, one of the nicest restaurants *near* Sunnydale. Although not common knowledge to the past or present populace, it was built in the 1920s by Malachi Stevens, a prominent Sunnydale citizen who began to realize that strange things were happening in his fair city. Fearing for his safety but unwilling to abandon his financial interests, he had an estate constructed several miles from town and named it the Hideaway. A sprawling combination of castle and hunting lodge, it sat on a hilltop at the end of a long and winding road. Behind the house was a deep ravine, and a stone wall surrounded the place. In the event that the evil from Sunnydale spilled out that far, he wanted his retreat to be as defensible as possible. He was almost disappointed to live to a ripe old age and pass the estate on to his children. None of them wanted to live in such an isolated place, so it was closed up. Sadly, most of them died in Sunnydale, victims of vamps, demons, and supernatural disaster. Almost to the last, their dying thought was that they should have listened to their father.

Not long ago, Malachi Stevens's last surviving grandchild, having devoured a case and a half of band candy, embarrassed herself immensely during a second adolescence. Afterward, she decided she'd had enough weirdness and moved to South Bend, Indiana. The property was snapped up by a celebrity chef from L.A. who decided it would make a perfect atmospheric eatery. These days it served as a retreat for the well-to-do of Sunnydale who wanted to get away from the stress brought on by the continual denial of what they experienced in their daily lives.

Outside, the restaurant remained a stately combination of stone and timber, but the interior was completely redone. Dark-paneled walls, shining brass fixtures, subdued lighting, and the occasional outdoorsy touch, every aspect of the décor was a seamless blend of good taste and style. There was only one thing that seemed out of place.

Xander Harris tugged on his collar, twitchy and uncomfortable in a coat and tie. Sure, he'd worn a suit plenty of times since becoming a contractor, and this was *supposed* to be nothing more than another professional meeting, but his partner's teasing words about

Rebekah's possible romantic interest in Xander had gotten to him. He hadn't worn a suit on a date in a long time. Of course, there was the tux at the wedding but . . . not a happy corner of his memory to visit.

Not that this *was* a date, or that he *wanted* it to be a date. . . .

The whole business was unsettling. Business and pleasure, and, well, pleasure and Xander . . . bad combinations all around.

After the incident at the downtown job site threw off his schedule, he'd called Rebekah Olschan to ask if they could bump their meeting back a couple hours. She'd been tied up and suggested getting together for dinner the next evening instead. He picked the Hideaway for the exact reason that Malachi Stevens had originally built it—it was outside the Sunnydale city limits and might prove exempt from the supernatural and sometimes fatal weirdness that tended to plague the city proper. More than anything, he wanted this meeting to go well.

He tugged at his collar again, convinced he shouldn't have gone so formal. He didn't want to come across as uptight and stuffy. After all, part of his charm, or whatever it was he had that passed as charm, was his offbeat sense of humor and casual attitude.

Oh, God. What if it isn't charming at all? What if Rebekah thinks I'm a complete doofus? Xander fretted. It was strange, too, because for some time now, he hadn't felt afraid of anything, yet . . . this was different. This was like the final frontier, only not in a geeky

Trekker way. He was being treated like a grown-up, a respected professional, being given credit for having a brain and everything. . . .

Ack.

Rebekah was a very together, very upscale kind of lady. Hence the sport-coat camouflage. Blend in. Draw no unwanted attention. He checked his fly for the fifth or sixth time. Can't be too careful. Thankfully, it was still closed.

Shrugging inside of his jacket to loosen the tension in his shoulders, he smoothed down his tie. Maybe he should have gone for something fun in neckwear instead of the plain tie he was wearing. Maybe a cartoon character or the fish tie his uncle Rory had given him in July as a belated Christmas gift. Merciful Zeus! He must be nervous to even consider wearing anything that had come from Uncle Rory.

Why? After all, it was just a business dinner. Not like it was his first. And Rebekah was a return client. He didn't have to wow her. The project he'd done for her company (okay, with a little help from the rest of the guys on the crew) had already done that.

He wiped his palms on his pant legs, hoping they wouldn't leave big, wet streaks. What if Rebekah showed up casual? She could stroll in any second wearing hip-hugger jeans and a belly shirt and there he'd be looking like a stiff. Xander shook his head to clear away the very pleasant but very unlikely image of Rebekah in jeans and a belly shirt. Not exactly easy to do. Of course, he'd never seen her like that. Every time they'd been together, it was obvious that Rebekah was the consummate L.A. businesswoman: sleek, sophisticated, and sexy. Not that she ever came across as aloof or stuffy. God, no. She was very sweet and down-to-earth, not full of herself or her success. Plus, she was smart. Very smart. Very savvy when it came to business, too. Like the girl next door made good. That is, if the girl next door was pure *Cosmo*. Not that he'd ever really read *Cosmo*. Just, y'know, the occasional survey like "Rate Your Partner's Prowess" and stuff like that. Can't hurt to know about women's expectations, right? He flashed on the image of her in jeans and a belly shirt again.

Get a grip, Harris. This is a professional meeting. Try to at least pretend *you're a professional. She's just a client looking to get more involved. . . .*

With the company. More involved with the company.

He glanced around the restaurant for the hundredth time, looking for some sign of impending doom. Vamps, werewolves, demon waiters from a nasty hell dimension, even some ancient god determined to crash his dinner meeting. He was certain something was going to go wrong. It almost had to. After all, she was a beautiful woman, and he had a track record. Xander Harris plus beautiful woman equaled some kind of catastrophe. Always. He tried to take comfort in the fact that the law of averages demanded that the streak had to break sometime.

Suddenly, a hush fell on the restaurant. Xander looked around warily.

Here we go. Fans, meet . . .

Rebekah stood in the doorway, obviously the cause of the sudden silence. Everyone who saw her had probably forgotten to take a breath. Xander had. She had her auburn hair up in a twist and she was wearing a dress. An amazing dress. A "They don't wear those in Sunnydale" dress. It was black and sort of layered, with a gauzy, see-through kind of fabric over the silky stuff underneath. The high collar wrapped around her neck like a scarf, crossing over her chest (her very, very nice chest) and angling down her sides, leaving her shoulders and stomach bare. The skirt it attached to was full and flowing, with the gauzy layer wreathed around it like a veil. He had seen every species of exotic female that Sunnydale had to offer, from mantis monsters to Incan mummies, psycho slayers to Cordelia Chase, and, in that dress, Rebekah had beaten them all cold. Maybe even not in that dress. That thought flashed another image across his mental movie screen, and he reddened.

As the maître d' pointed over toward the table, she caught Xander's eye and gave him a big smile. He grinned in return, but inside, all he could think was just how far out of his league she was—or would be, if this was anything but a professional meeting. Because that's what it was: professional. Strictly professional.

Realizing that the polite thing would be to pull out her chair for her, Xander bolted up from his own. The legs scraped loudly on the floor, and he ducked his head slightly in embarrassment.

Rebekah arrived, the maître d' at her side. The man

had a thin, sour face that puckered even more as he gave Xander a disapproving look and said, "Your server will be with you shortly."

Rebekah's eyes followed the man. She covered her mouth quickly, obviously trying to hide her amusement at his pompous airs. Then she focused on Xander and smiled again, brilliantly. "What a charming place, Xander." Then she made a quick turn so that the skirt swirled around her. "Well, what do you think? I thought I'd raise a few eyebrows here in Sunnydale."

Xander smiled back and wiggled his eyebrows. "I expect you'll raise more than that."

"I beg your pardon?"

Xander's eyes bugged. "More than a *few.* Eyebrows, I mean. Lots. Of eyebrows. Not that you'd raise anything else."

Rebekah regarded him coolly. "Oh?"

"Not that you wouldn't. I mean . . ."

Rebekah threw back her head and laughed. Not cruel, just honest amusement. "I'm sorry. I shouldn't tease you like that."

Xander grinned nervously in return. "Heh. No problem. I just express myself poorly sometimes. Like when I actually open my mouth and *speak.*"

She laughed again. Just then, the waiter arrived to help seat her and to take their drink orders. As he sat down again, Xander breathed a deep sigh of relief at the distraction.

"So," said Xander, "you found the place okay? It's a little off the beaten track."

Rebekah nodded. "No trouble at all. You gave

excellent directions." She winked at him. "Besides, I took a cab."

"Ah. If you need a ride home, I can do that."

"Sure. If it's not too much trouble. That'd be great."

"No trouble at all."

"So, honestly, what you think of the dress?" Rebekah asked. "I love it, but there's no point in wearing it up in L.A. I'd just be lost in the crowd of starlets and models."

Xander snorted. "More chance of a vampire not being noticed at a blood bank."

She gave him a curious look. "Um, thanks?"

Xander's eyes went wide. "I said that, didn't I? Out loud, I mean?"

"I'm afraid so, yes."

Xander covered his eyes with one hand. "Oh, ye gods."

"Hey, I can honestly say that's the most unique compliment anyone has ever paid me." Rebekah frowned just a touch. "That *was* a compliment, right?"

"Definitely. What I was trying to say is that there's no chance you'd ever be lost in a crowd."

Leaning forward, Rebekah rested her elbows on the table, one hand reaching up to touch her face. She smiled warmly. "Mmm. I like that better."

Was she flirting? It seemed like she was flirting. He sat for a second, mind blank, trying desperately to think of a response. "I mean, sure, you could get lost. Actually lost. That's not impossible. Crowds are kind of confusing, and everybody gets lost sometimes."

She laughed again, quietly, eyes sparkling. "You have the most bizarre sense of humor."

"Bad thing or good thing?"

"Oh, good thing. Definitely good thing."

Xander opened his mouth to reply, but was interrupted by the sound of giggling drifting over from a nearby booth. He and Rebekah both glanced over. The occupants of the booth were a man and woman in their mid sixties. They both sat on one side, snuggling close together and whispering into each other's ears.

Rebekah leaned forward and said in a hushed voice, "That's so sweet. Still frisky at their age."

Xander gave her a quizzical look. "'Frisky'? Did you actually say 'frisky'? Not the vocabulary I'd expect from a big-shot VP, Ms. Olschan. Besides, that's a little more than 'frisky.' More like 'gropey.'"

She rolled her eyes and waved away his comments. "Big-shot VPs are people, too, Mr. Harris. Anyway, I've seen worse than that in Europe. Much, much worse." She picked up her menu and opened it. "So tell me, what's good here?"

"Honestly?" asked Xander. "I have no clue. I've never been here before. It's just that it's in the area you were talking about for your new project and I've heard good things about the place. Thought you'd like it."

"Okay, then, test time. Exactly what is it that you thought I'd like?"

Nervously, Xander sat up a little straighter and smoothed down the lapels of his jacket. He cleared his throat. "Well, the Hideaway is very classy, yet unpretentious. Very much like yourself."

"Well, aren't you the fount of compliments this evening."

Xander shrugged. "I do my humble best."

"Your humble best is very good. Since you're doing so well, want to make a guess at what I might like this evening?"

"W-hat you'd like?"

She nodded. "Yes. You know, from the menu?"

"The menu? Right, of course, the menu. For eating."

She composed her face into a look of mock seriousness. "Exactly. Let's see how well you can guess my taste." She paused for a moment, considering her last words. "In food. My taste in food."

"Right." Xander flipped open his menu and scanned the contents. He immediately noticed there were no prices and winced. That usually put them in the "if you have to ask, you can't afford it" range. Still, no worries. It was a business dinner. Business expense. Deductible. Wallet-crunching for now, but paying off in the long run. After a couple seconds of that, he realized he wasn't actually looking at the offerings. "Hmmm. Let's see. Well, here you go—pan-roasted organic chicken with black truffles."

"I look like a black-truffles kind of girl?"

Xander nodded solemnly. "Oh, sure. Black truffles to go with the black ruffles. Besides, they're . . ."

A loud bump interrupted him, followed by the clatter and tinkle of plates, cutlery, and glass. Rebekah and Xander looked back toward the old couple in the booth. One of them had apparently bumped the table in their . . . enthusiasm. They were all over each other, kissing passionately and clutching each other tight. Blushing, Xander turned back toward Rebekah, trying to divert her attention. "Black truffles. We were talking about black truffles."

"Oh, don't worry. Like I said, I've seen worse. This one time, while I was living in Paris—"

"You *lived* in Paris?"

Rebekah nodded. "Just for six months or so. Business. Same with London and Hong Kong. I was in Amsterdam almost a year."

"Amsterdam? Wow. I've heard stories."

She gave him an evil grin. "They're all true."

Shaking his head, Xander said, "I barely manage to get out of Sunnydale."

Rebekah regarded him slyly. "From what I hear, you've found yourself a little excitement right here."

"What . . . um . . . what do you mean?" he asked warily.

Rebekah gave him another bright smile. "Don't be so modest. I heard the news this afternoon. You're a hero!"

"Huh?"

"Oh, c'mon. Rescuing a guy from a ten-story fall? That's pretty amazing."

He adopted an air of false humility. "Well, I don't know as I'd go so far as to say 'amazing,' but far be it from me to contradict."

She regarded him with an appraising look. "I admire a man who is willing to take some risks.

"Of course," she continued, "when you come right

down to it, risks are my business. Not life-and-death stuff like your caper this afternoon, but still, risks. Like this project I want to put together here in Sunnydale. Lots of investors seem to think the insurance costs are too high around here. Too much random vandalism, too many fires and natural disasters—that kind of thing. I think the area has a lot of untapped potential."

Xander nodded. "That's what you were saying on the phone. You said something about a two-phase development plan?"

"Exactly. The first step is an upscale, gated community or two. Right around here, like you said. It's a pretty area, and I bet this place would love the additional business. The second stage is to put up a number of strip malls to service the new communities. Everything they need would be close at hand—supermarkets, video stores, specialty shops, that sort of thing. They wouldn't even need to go into Sunnydale proper for the most part. We can take advantage of the low property values and get around the stigma of the town in one fell swoop." She fidgeted a bit. "No offense. I know Sunnydale is your hometown."

"None taken. It's definitely not . . ."

A loud crash cut him off. Leaping from his chair, Xander scanned the room for some sort of attack, some supernatural nasty ready to maim and devour. Instead, all he saw was the old man, standing at the end of his booth, tablecloth in hand. The plates, glasses, dishes, and silverware were all scattered on the floor. It looked like he'd tried pulling out the cloth without moving the dishes but had failed miserably.

Embarrassed by Rebekah's questioning gaze, Xander took his seat. "Ahem. Looks like his magic trick still needs some work."

The woman didn't seem to think so, though. She was clapping her hands together gleefully. As Xander watched, she scrambled out of the booth and into the man's embrace. Meanwhile, Rebekah glanced around, looking puzzled that no one else seemed to be paying the couple any attention.

"Just so you know, this isn't exactly everyday stuff," Xander explained. "It's just that people in Sunnydale have a . . . uh . . . highly developed capacity for screening out any unsettling events that happen around them. We're not all crazy, though."

Shaking her head, Rebekah replied, "Don't sweat it."

Another loud bump caught their attention. Much to her delight, the old man had thrown his companion down on the table. Xander's mind boggled as they began tearing at their clothes, the man climbing on top of the table.

Xander stammered, "Uh-oh."

"Oh. Whoa."

"Whoa, whoa, whoa!"

Jumping up from his seat, he stepped between Rebekah and the unfolding scene. "That is just not right. Why don't we find someplace a little more . . . a little less . . . why don't we find someplace else to eat? Okay?"

The woman from the other table, sounding very much like a cheerleader, started yelling, "Fred! Fred!

Fred!" Rebekah stood and slid her arm through Xander's. "Probably for the best. Hard to talk business with that kind of floor show."

As they headed for the door, Rebekah surveyed the room again. Every one else was studiously ignoring the thuds and grunts from the booth, with only the occasional curious glance. Reaching into her purse, she pulled out a pocket tape recorder. Clicking it on, she spoke into the mike. "Note to self: Seriously consider petition to allow Frederick's into mini-mall. Definite market here."

Soon, they were in Xander's car, and a minute or two of awkward silence settled between them as they drove back toward town.

Finally, Xander broke the stillness. "Look, I'm really sorry about that. There are some other really nice places in town."

Rebekah shrugged elegantly. Very French. "Don't give it another thought. Anyway, we don't need to go someplace fancy. I know it sounds shallow, but I already got my grand entrance." She gave Xander a quick and mischievous grin. "The look on your face was priceless."

As Xander started to protest his innocence, his stomach rumbled loudly.

Rebekah laughed. "Sounds like we'd better get you something to eat, sooner rather than later." She pointed ahead. "There's a Double Meat Palace."

"No!" Xander grinned feebly in response to her startled look. "Unpleasant experience. Not my favorite place."

She nodded. "That's okay. Suit yourself."

They ended up doing the drive-through at Happy Burger. Rebekah asked about the bars on the drive-through window. Xander shrugged. "Not sure."

As they pulled out of the parking lot, Rebekah asked, "Where to? I don't want to eat a Mr. Happy Double while we're cruising around."

Xander nodded. "Any preference?"

"Yup. Let's see the site of your heroic rescue this morning!"

He gave her a pleading look. "I hope you're not serious."

Rebekah just smiled innocently. "Deadly."

"Bad word choice," said Xander.

A few minutes later they were sitting in the car, staring up at the unfinished tower as they gulped burgers, fries, and sodas. Xander had finally given in to his unrefined impulses and had loosened his tie. Rebekah, much to his surprise, had tucked a paper napkin into the collar of her dress.

In response to Xander's questioning look, she said, "Hey, do you realize how much a dress like this costs to clean? I'm not about to get Happy Sauce all over it."

Xander glanced away, thankful that the darkness hid his blush.

Get your mind out of the gutter, Harris.

She raised a single sensuous eyebrow. "That didn't sound quite right, did it? Again."

Xander looked back to Rebekah. "Did I say that out loud?"

Rebekah gave him a confused look. "No. What? I was talking about what *I* said."

Relieved, Xander gave a nod. "I knew that."

They spent the next half hour finishing their food while Rebekah quizzed him on the morning's events. She was particularly interested in Davis's ramblings.

In the end, the only thing she could find to say was, "Fascinating."

Xander laughed. "Thank you, Mr. Spock."

Rebekah laughed as well. "I've never been mistaken for Leonard Nimoy before."

"Not a big surprise. He'd never be able to pull off that dress." After a second's panic, he continued. "I mean, *wearing* that dress. He'd never be able to pull off *wearing* that dress."

Rebekah just smiled. They sat there for a full minute, gazing at each other in the quiet car. Then Rebekah pulled the napkin out of her collar. Xander held his breath. She reached over, napkin in hand, and wiped the corner of his mouth. "Mustard," she said.

"Oh."

"Well, we should probably get going. Don't want the cops to roust us for suspicious parking. I mean, being parked suspiciously. I mean . . ."

Rebekah just chuckled and said, "Got it."

She gave Xander the name of her hotel, and he pulled out of the site lot. A mile or two later, Rebekah tugged on his sleeve. "Oh, look! I guess that's where the couple at the restaurant must have come from!"

Xander looked where she was pointing. In front of

the Sunnydale Villa Assisted Living Community was a crude, hand-lettered sign on posterboard:

TOGA PARTY!
COME ONE, COME ALL!

As they drove by, several of the residents, senior citizens and then some, came running out the front door dressed in sheets and began romping in the yard. As Xander watched, one of the old men made a grab for a blue-haired lady with a wreath of flowers in her hair. He only managed to snag her toga, which slipped from her shoulder.

"Sweet Christmas!" Xander blurted as he jerked his head away from the sight, jerking the steering in the process. The car swerved and skidded as he tried to bring it back under control. He glanced sheepishly at Rebekah. "Sorry."

Her eyes were wide and somewhat distant. It was possible she'd finally reached her limit on disinterested observation. "No, I understand."

Pointing upward through the windshield, he said nervously, "Look. Full moon. Heh. People do the craziest things, huh?"

She squinted upward. "It's not full—"

"But close," he interrupted. "Very, very close."

He tried to stay focused on the road, but his mind was churning. They couldn't have had just some nice, normal vamp attack. Maybe gargoyles or slime demons or something like that.

Still brooding, he pulled into the hotel parking lot.

As he drove toward the front door, Rebekah suggested that he come up to her room so they could continue their conversation. "So far, we haven't exactly had a comfortable evening," she said. "I've got a really great suite. We can kick back and relax a bit. It's not too late, is it?"

Xander shook his head. "What? No. Not at all. Sounds great."

A hundred conflicting thoughts were doing a solid imitation of a soccer riot in his brain. She was inviting him up to her hotel room. Her *hotel* room. What was she expecting? What was *he* expecting? Hell, he wasn't even sure what he wanted to expect. Fooling around with a client could seriously jeopardize the project. At least if things went wrong. Then again, how could they go anywhere but wrong? He was Xander Harris, and she was a very beautiful woman.

He decided to come up with some excuse and beat feet. Pulling into a parking spot, he turned to her. He looked up and saw her eyes looking back. Very nice eyes. Kind of blue gray. It seemed like that color should make them kind of cold, but it didn't. They were warm. Inviting, even.

He opened his mouth, but couldn't speak. After all, she was a *very* beautiful woman. One who seemed interested in what he had to say. One who seemed to respect his insights and his skills and . . . well . . . him. How often did *that* happen? Besides, it was just business. Didn't have to mean that she . . . that he . . . that they . . . didn't have to mean anything. Of course, it wouldn't exactly be *horrible* if it was more than business. Although the lines might blur. That could be bad. Or good. And it had been a long time. And she was so very, well, hot.

"Hello? Earth to Xander? You coming up?"

"What? Right. Of course. Sure."

After all, what could it hurt?

They strolled through the lobby, drawing secretive glances. Well, Rebekah did. Xander figured that if anyone noticed him at all, they would only wonder what a woman like her was doing with a guy like him. He could live with that.

Rebekah's suite was incredible, practically an apartment. The furniture in the main living area was all white canvas and blond wood, with an off-white carpet that was thick enough to muffle footsteps and give a cushy, comfortable bounce. At the far side of the room, beyond a wall of glass, was a huge balcony with redwood benches and lots of green and growing plants.

There was a kitchen nook off to the left. To the right, a dining room table was covered with plans and schematics.

"Wow."

"I thought you'd like it." Rebekah beamed at him warmly. "Why don't you make yourself at home? I'm going to slip into something more comfortable."

Xander gulped as she walked through the double doors to the bedroom. He caught a glimpse of a bigger-than-king-sized bed scattered with half a dozen pillows. Then the doors closed behind her.

Slumping into one of the chairs, Xander rubbed his face with both hands. "Oh, boy." Visions of slinky black negligees danced in the corners of his mind. Sure, she'd look phenomenal in a slinky black negligee, but this was supposed to be a business relationship. With a start, it occurred to him that maybe this was part of the deal. Maybe she expected him to be her boy toy to cinch it.

Lurching to his feet, he stared out the windows into the night. Quietly, he said, "Yeah, right. Like a woman like that needs to coerce someone to . . ."

The sound of the bedroom doors opening cut off that thought. Slowly, uncertainly, he turned.

Rebekah was strolling over to him wearing worn jeans and an oversized Irish sweater. Her hair was down, spilling to her shoulders in an auburn cascade. Her feet were bare. It was like someone had spritzed her with Vixen-Be-Gone and—poof!—she was Rebekah Olschan, everyday woman: someone, something he could deal with a whole lot easier.

"Not too casual, I hope?" she asked. "I just love the way this carpet feels without shoes. You should try it."

Xander gave a little shake of his head. "Maybe later. You definitely look more comfy. Not that you looked uncomfy before."

Dropping to the couch, Rebekah let out a big sigh. "I have a confession, Xander."

He took a seat in one of the chairs and tried to look casual. "Oh?"

She sat up on the edge of the couch, looking at him intently. "That dress? That was kind of, well, a stunt."

Xander looked puzzled. "Stunt? Not sure I follow."

"It's like this—there's been some definite local attention focused on my company's interest in the land outside of town. I sort of . . . um . . . leaked the location of our meeting to the paper. Y'know, put the word into someone's ear that you know will mention it to someone else who will mention it to someone else?"

Xander had no clue what she was talking about, but he wasn't about to let her know. "Sure. Uh-huh. Of course."

"See, I managed to set it up so that Sheila Ketrik was at the restaurant tonight. You know her, right? The 'Out and About' columnist? Anyway, she gets a little something for her column, and I laid the foundation for the image I want to have here in town. See, if I come across as a *très chic* sophisticate, able to bring some major *dinero* to the table, a lot of wheels will be greased in terms of permits and such. It's kind of a Hollywoodish flimflam, but it's all in a good cause, right?"

"Right," he replied, though he wasn't all that sure it was necessary.

"Truth to tell, I'd rather be on site, hip deep in plans with a hard hat perched on my head."

Xander stared at her, completely amazed. "You? In a hard hat? I can picture you in a lot of stuff, but not in a hard hat."

She gave a wry look. "Oh? What kind of stuff?"

Before he could answer, she let him off the hook. "Never mind. I'll let you in on my deep, dark secret. . . ."

He'd know it all along, really. She was too perfect and too interested. She had to be a . . .

"I'm a construction site brat."

"Huh?"

"Like some kids are army brats? I'm a construction site brat. My dad worked for a firm a lot like yours. He spent years tackling the day-to-day headaches that crop up on any major project. I loved visiting the site and watching him work. He was really great. When I was in high school, I told him I wanted to follow in his footsteps. He said I could be whatever I wanted to be, but if I was going to go into his business, I had to learn *about* business. Said I had to get at least an MBA. I told him that he didn't have one, so I didn't need one, either. You know what he did? He went out the next day and enrolled in college. While I was finishing high school, he was getting his degree. By the time I was in college, he was finishing his master's. That's the kind of guy he was. Wouldn't ask anything of anyone else that he wouldn't do himself. When I graduated, he got me started with another company. Didn't want me to be perceived as 'Daddy's little girl' getting all the breaks because I worked with him."

"He sounds like a great guy."

She smiled sadly. "He really was. He passed away last year. Heart attack. He worked himself a little too hard. Still, I was glad that he got to see me make good."

"I'm sure he was proud of you."

"He was. He made sure to tell me." Then her smile brightened, and her attention focused on Xander. "You remind me of him a little. Good head for business, but a lot of heart."

Xander smiled back. "Thanks. That's probably one of the nicest compliments I ever got." It was, too. Here was this woman, this amazing woman, and she compares him with the man she respected most in the world. Who'd have believed it? Him. Xander Harris.

Rebekah got up and went over to the table, sorting through the diagrams. "Let me show you what we've got planned for the first community."

Xander followed her and glanced at the plans over her shoulder. She turned her head, brushing her hair back behind her ear with a couple fingers, and smiled at him. He smiled back. It felt good. Finally, all the tension that he didn't realize he had been still feeling, eased away. Nothing had gone wrong. Well, not so seriously as to have an impact on his professional relationship with Rebekah, anyhoo, and that was the big worry. Here was a woman who seemed to be interested in him strictly for his brain. Who'd a thunk it? And, y'know? It was a mighty fine feeling indeed.

Maybe things weren't so crazy in Sunnydale tonight after all. . . .

Gripping the bodybuilder by the ankle, Gwen dangled the dumb-as-dirt slab of meat from the clock tower's roof. The fall was a good six stories, and he was mewling, crying, wetting himself. His club outfit was every bit as outrageous as hers: He had donned a mesh shirt, a "General Patton" jacket with an insignia that was custom made and cool (even if it was now carefully draped over the edge, Mr. Bo-Hunk here thinking something other than the Human Trials were going on here, like he was getting lucky—and, in a way, he was), chaps, and boots. His short, product-ridden blond hair kept its shape even though he was upside down, and all the change had already fallen from his pockets to the sidewalk below, though no one had noticed. Gwen wore a bright pink acrylic tank top, a new blond wig, this one an eighties punk retro that looked like it had been squeezed from a tube of toothpaste, and shredded black leather pants. Stiletto heels spiked downward from her shiny black shoes.

She looked at the blotch on his arm and frowned. It just wasn't coming together with this one. . . . "Hey, look up," she said. "Look at the moon. At least you'll have something pretty to look at on the way down."

"Please don't do this to me!" he cried shrilly.

"If you keep wriggling, you're going to get my hand all sweaty and I'm bound to just lose my grip."

He stopped flailing and went to vibrating, shuddering, and twitching. She thought she heard him praying and was about to let him go then and there, just for that, but the distinct *click-clacks* of the Progenitor's designer shoes sounded on the rooftop ledge.

"Problem, Gwendolyn?" he asked.

She hated it when he called her that, which is probably why he did it. "This one didn't turn out right, and it's making me grumpy."

"You think shaking him like this is going to make the process take any better? If it doesn't work, it doesn't work. And I can tell you right now—"

"It's not that," Gwen said petulantly. "I was wrong, okay? Fine."

"What is it, then?"

She frowned. "I liked it when we did the vampires. It didn't take with them, either, but at least it was fun watching them blow up."

The dangling man screeched, *"Why are you doing this?"*

"Hey, fun and games," Gwen said mildly. "Now hush or I *will* drop you!"

He quieted down again.

The man above looked down at the failed experiment and said, "This is nothing personal. Just consider it the luck of the draw. You had the same chance as anyone. Things just didn't quite work out where you're concerned. The world is moving on, and your kind will soon be extinct."

"Mah—my—k-k-kind?" Mr. Dangling stammered.

"Unevolved. Unable to progress further."

His wide, frightened eyes showed no hint of comprehension.

Gwen thrust her own shoulder forward, showing off her perfectly formed tattoo. "I'll make it simple for you. You have one of these?"

The little rash on his shoulder, which was already fading, said it all. "Please," he begged.

Gwen shook her head. "You don't have the Sign, you don't get to go on to the next round."

The Progenitor knelt close enough to reach the man's bare belly. He looked up at Gwen. "You really want to see something different, don't you? Like with the vampires?"

She bit her lip, looking kind of sexy, like the bad girl that she was. "Yeah."

"Well," the Progenitor said, "for you, then."

The dangling man let out a scream of incredible pain as the Progenitor's hand touched his flesh. Gwen's prize twisted, bucked, and flung himself in every direction as his flesh rippled and changed, something crackling within his body, which was quickly losing its shape. Even the bones in his face, those high, handsome cheekbones, were sagging like ice cream on a summer's day. Then a bolt of crimson and amber light exploded out from his chest, shredding him from within.

Gwen dropped him, smiling broadly as he crackled and popped like a firecracker before striking the sidewalk below with explosive and gory results.

"They'll be picking his teeth out of the walls for years," the Progenitor whispered.

"That was nice," Gwen said, stumbling back from the edge, her craving for excitement sated . . . for now. "So what's next?"

"We stick with the plan," the Progenitor said. "First Sunnydale . . . then the rest of this country . . . then the world . . . and beyond."

"I mean tomorrow. I want something pure. I want to take it and bend it into funny shapes. That's the funnest kind to turn around."

"We're talking Dawn Summers, I assume. She's already activated. You said as much . . . and I can feel it."

"Oh yeah, but she's not a hundred percent. She's

walked on the wild side a teeny weeny bit, but there are places to go with her before we start to bring in the new era. Things we can have her do. Fun things."

"Gwen, my dear," the Progenitor said with a thin smile, "*never* let it be said that I'd stand in the way of your fun." He laughed. "The child is yours. Do what you will."

In the near darkness, Gwen smiled, her eyes glowing bright amber.

Chapter Ten

Dawn practically ran to school. She passed Tommy in the hall and he waved, making her melt. When Tommy followed his wave with the universal teenage gesture of "What's up?"—a little jerk of the head, the chin pointed at your target, a slight wink—Dawn couldn't help but give the universal teenage response—the exact same thing. This is what her generation's communication was built on, a series of small signals and grunts. Some would call it primitive, but she preferred to think of it as a code devised by generations of adolescents, distilling human action down to the bare necessities.

Tommy's smile turned into a grin. *Message received.*

When they met up after third period, Tommy already had his plan all mapped out.

"Listen up," he said. "We can all hang around here for the rest of our lives and just kill time, and when we die, no one will even care we ever stepped foot on the planet. *Or . . .* we can take it off the chain and really do it up right."

"What do you mean?" Luna asked. She was chewing on the ring in her lip, which Dawn already knew meant the gears in Luna's head were turning, that she was hooked into what Tommy was saying.

They had all been hanging out on the lawn by the school's side parking lot. Big J was eating his second breakfast, and Dawn and Luna had been playing a game of cards with a pack of Luna's that were decorated with skulls and crossbones.

"Everything we've been doing is small-time," Tommy explained. "It's chump change . . . and they call it that 'cause any chump can do it. I don't want to go out like a chump. I want to go out like a playa."

Tommy held up his right hand and balled it into a fist. He had written the word "PLAYA" on his fingers in black marker. Only there were too many letters, so on his index finger, it had both the "Y" and the second "A." It made Dawn think of her tattoo, and she reflexively reached up and rubbed her right shoulder. She had been careful to pick a shirt that covered it, a pink top she really liked. Standing next to Luna, who was dressed head to toe in black, made her question whether or not it was good color choice.

"We've been doing little things here and there,"

Tommy continued. "Sometimes we'll boost some beer from the store, or we'll tag the gym, but even if we got caught, we'd barely get a slap on the wrist and everybody would forget about it tomorrow."

"You got somethin' in mind, T?" Big J said, putting down his egg sandwich long enough to ask the question, and then attacking it again as soon as he was done.

Tommy looked like he had just stumbled across all the winning lottery numbers for the rest of the year and was about to take a bath in a gigantic pile of money. "Yeah, I do. Total anarchy. I'm talking *rampage,* man."

A surge went through the group. They were all starting to see the bigger picture Tommy was trying to paint.

"Instead of doing one thing today, one thing tomorrow, another on Friday night, once we start today, we don't stop. We don't stop until this school is nothing but rubble or they take us out of here either in handcuffs or on a stretcher."

"Word," Big J said. He stepped up to Tommy, and they knocked their fists together. "You da bomb, T."

Luna pulled her textbooks out of her backpack and one by one tossed them onto the roof of the school. They jumped open in midair and their spines cracked, and the books landed in a crumpled mess high above them. She laughed like a hyena with Tourette's.

"I guess that means you're with me, eh?" Tommy said. Then he turned to Dawn and locked those sweet green eyes on hers. "What about you, Boo?"

A smirk passed over Dawn's lips. "What do you think?"

• • •

Step one, Tommy said, *is general destruction.*

The group dispersed and headed off in different directions around the school. Everyone was in first period already, so the corridors were mostly empty—meaning they had a completely open playing field for unleashing mischief.

Luna walked through the halls with a piece of jagged metal placed firmly between her fingers. Casually, she strolled past the lockers, holding out her hand and letting the tip of the metal slide across the locker doors, leaving a line of peeling paint in her wake. The metal on metal made a screeching sound that she could feel in her teeth. Luna liked that noise.

Elsewhere, Big J knocked over every garbage can on his way to the gym, dumping trash all over the floors and making a loud racket. He had to wait outside the locker room for a couple of minutes while the last of the P.E. students finished dressing and headed off to the field. Once the coast was clear, he went into the far back corner where the football team dumped their laundry every day after practice. The custodial staff wouldn't get to washing that stuff until midday. The bin was a cloth bag hung on a frame made of aluminum rods. It was full of sweaty T-shirts and other unmentionables. Big J could smell the rank residue of high school athletics from a couple feet away. It stank like a herd of sheep left out in the rain.

Big J unhooked the bag and took it from the locker room. As he walked, he reached into the sack and took out an item of clothing, tossing it randomly on whatever was convenient. He made a conscious effort to get the underwear and jock straps into the drinking fountains, but really, anyplace would do.

While Big J and Luna worked solo, Dawn and Tommy remained a duo. Their targets were the bathrooms. It was better to work as a pair on toilet detail because it would help reduce the risk of being caught. They'd switch off standing watch based on the sex of the bathroom. For instance, Dawn standing in the doorway of the girls' room would arouse a lot less suspicion than if Tommy did, so while she was on guard, he'd hit the stalls, stuffing the bowls full of paper. Once all three toilets were completely clogged, he'd hit flush and run out, leaving three overflowing porcelain thrones behind.

The pair was on its fifth bathroom when they hit their first glitch. A freshman named Shirley had gotten a rest room pass and had chosen the one they were working on. Dawn gave Tommy the coughing signal they'd worked out, and he jumped up on one of the toilets, holding the door closed and waiting for his Boo to take care of it.

"Where do you think you're going?" Dawn asked. She put her arm across the door frame, blocking the girl from passing.

"I have to pee," Shirley said.

"Not in here, you don't."

Shirley tried to look around. "What are you talking about? It looks fine in here. I had to walk all the way over here from the 300 rooms because the bathroom down there was a total mess."

"What makes you think this one isn't a mess?"

"Trust me, if you had seen the other one, you'd know. It looked like an aquarium had exploded or something. Come on, I've really got to go now."

"Listen, chickie." Dawn was trying to sound menacing. "If you try to get past me, it's *you* that will be the mess. I'll take you back down to the 300 bathroom and use your *hair* to mop it up. You got me?"

Dawn punctuated the last bit by shoving Shirley in the shoulder. This shocked the girl, who backed away. "Geez, fine," she said. "It's not worth it just to pee."

Watching Shirley leave, Dawn felt a small thrill, comparable to the best caffeine and sugar high she'd ever had yet without that nasty coffee aftertaste. *So this is what it's like to be the bully, huh?* she thought. Now she knew why there were so many bad guys out there always trying to wreck everyone's fun—because that was more fun than the stupid stuff everybody else was doing. Being bad was awesome. Why simply sing in the choir when you can be a Soprano?

Three flushes went off in rapid succession, and Tommy came trotting out. "Nice work, babe," he laughed, "now let's haul our butts!"

Step two: Mayhem.

The janitors drove small mechanical carts when it came time to empty the campus trash cans. To get around the school and collect all the garbage would be too large a task on foot. They'd only use them during the off-hours, either before or after classes, to avoid any insurance hassle about them driving through the halls while kids were there.

During the rest of the day they were parked in a small cage behind the cafeteria—essentially a chainlink fence with a locked gate to keep the bad elements of the student body from getting their hands on them.

The problem with the bad element, though, is that they're bad, and they weren't made to follow rules. The irony of this thought—which had initially come to her the night before when Tommy first came to her window—wasn't lost on Dawn. It just confirmed the age-old suspicion that vampires were inherently stupid.

Big J had swiped a set of large bolt cutters from one of the janitor's closets. The custodial stuff was rushing around trying to clean up the various messes the quartet had created, and they'd left one of the supply cabinet doors open. Tommy thought it was wonderful that all of the pieces of his plan were stacking up that way, creating new unforeseen benefits.

It only took one bite with the cutters, and the chain on the gate was no more.

"Grab some wheels," Tommy said, sliding into the driver's seat of the first cart, "and let's get gone in sixty seconds!"

Tommy and Dawn took one cart, and Big J and Luna took the other. The boys drove while the girls took the shotgun position. Big J led the way, smashing through the cafeteria doors, going straight through and into the classroom areas. Tommy followed, and as soon as they were in the corridor, he pulled up alongside a fire alarm. "Hit it, Boo!" he shouted. "It's yours!"

Dawn stood up in her seat and grabbed the handle on the alarm. It took her two tries to pull it hard enough to smash the Plexiglas protector, but as soon as she did, the entire campus was filled with the ringing of warning bells. Tommy stuck his fist into the air and cheered. He hit the gas hard, knocking Dawn back into her seat, and took the cart to full speed.

Students started to spill out of their classrooms. Teachers were trying to keep them calm and get them to follow the emergency plan and march out of the school single file, but no one was listening. Tommy and Big J were racing each other down the hall, dodging in and out of the crowds, tires screeching around corners. Kids were jumping out of the way, and with the joyriders threatening to run them down, it didn't seem like there was safety in any direction. Which way was the fire? Where was the nearest exit? Where might the janitorial carts of death strike next?

"Move it or lose it!" Tommy shouted. "You guys are the dinosaurs, and we're evolution. Get out of the way or get run down!"

Principal Wood could scarcely believe his eyes. There were teenagers all over the place, tearing through the halls like Spaniards at the running of the bulls. They didn't seem to know where the big horns were, they just didn't want them spearing their backsides.

How did this happen? There was no fire drill that day, and for all he knew, there was in fact a fire burning somewhere. "Everybody!" he shouted. "Please, stay calm! Stay calm!"

and it sagged under his weight. He bounced a little and then launched himself into the air. He tucked his body into a giant ball and hit the water hard. First there was suction, dragging a good bit of water down after him, and then there was a recoil, that same water shooting toward the ceiling and spraying everywhere. Some of it almost hit Luna. "You get me wet and I'll send you to the bottom of that pool, jerk!" she declared.

Dawn and Tommy were at the other end of the pool. They were swimming in circles, almost like they were chasing each other. Tommy was looking at Dawn, and Dawn was looking at Tommy. Her head felt airy, like a big helium balloon. She was pumped full of adrenaline from their vandalism and the fairy dust sprinkled on teenage girls in love.

"See, Boo?" Tommy said. "Did I tell you, or did I? No one is going to forget this anytime soon."

"You called it, Tommy," Dawn said. "We're going to be legends. Like the Wonder Twins, only we're not twins and we're the bad guys."

"Mos' def'," Tommy said. "We're outlaws, kid."

He paddled over to her and gave her a kiss. Even now, the soft touch of his lips took Dawn out of this mundane world and to somewhere she couldn't describe. It was like they were moving at a super-speed, and the rest of the planet's population was stuck in dull, snail-paced moments of drudgery. Were they too scared to feel like this? Because Dawn sure wasn't.

After a few minutes, they all got back out of the pool and started to get dressed. Dawn had left her clothes by the doors, near where they'd come in, while the boys had undressed on the other side, near the swim team's locker room. This had been one of the best days of her life. Destroying things wasn't nearly as exhausting as saving them. Buffy and the Scoobs were always so stressed out. Everything they did was just so futile, and it wore them down. They could stake five vamps, and ten would rise from the cemetery the very next day. Maybe it was time they realized that if you couldn't beat 'em, you're better off joining them.

She had her pants on and had just pulled on her shirt when Dawn heard voices out in the hall. "I think this is the last area that needs to be checked," one of them said. She didn't recognize who it was.

The second voice she definitely knew, though. It was Principal Wood's. "I keep telling you, it's just a prank," he said. "A bad one, but still a prank."

There were small windows in the doors, and Dawn peeked out the corner of one. Sure enough, Wood was coming her way with three firemen. This wasn't good.

"Guys! Guys!" Dawn was trying to shout and whisper at the same time. The others had to hear her, but she didn't want to alert the search party that they were there. "Seriously, guys! You have to get out of here!"

The doors started to open, and Dawn threw herself against them. The people outside hadn't been pushing very hard, since they hadn't expected resistance, but she was pretty sure that if they gave it a good shove, those fire guys could knock her across the room like Sammy Sosa hitting a baseball. She had to think fast. "Get out of here!" she screamed. She was gambling that the ambiguity of the lines would tip off her cohorts and still give her room to cover her butt when Wood and the others got inside. "You guys can't come in here! I'm not decent!"

"Dawn? Is that you?"

Oh, no! Buffy! She hadn't seen Buffy.

Thankfully, her ploy worked, and Dawn had gotten the gang's attention. They could see the bodies moving outside through the windows, and could see them giving the doors another light test push to see if there really was something blocking them. Dawn was waving at them wildly. "Get out of here!" she shouted again. "Leave me alone!"

Tommy and Big J snatched up whatever clothes they didn't have on yet, and they and Luna high-tailed it out the back way. It was just in the nick of time, too, because this time Buffy herself gave the doors a real shove. Dawn slid across the wet concrete, tumbling to the side as the search team came barreling in. Her big sister was at the head of the pack, hands on her hips, looking at Dawn spread out there on the floor. "Dawnie?" she said. Her voice was full of disbelief. "What are you doing here?"

"Um . . . nothing?"

"You're soaking wet," Buffy said. "You've been swimming? Don't tell me you didn't hear the fire alarm."

Principal Wood and the firemen had spread out across the room, checking for smoke and flames.

"I did," Dawn said, moving quick through her vocabulary to find the right words. "I heard the bells and I came in here. I mean, what place could be safer in a fire than a swimming pool, right? If I was in the middle of water, how could the fire get to me."

"You were in the pool this whole time?"

"Uh-huh."

Dawn reached out her hand to Buffy, and the older girl helped her up. "It's been, like, half an hour," Buffy said. "I can't believe you've just been floating around in here. You look like a drowned rat."

"Yeah, I kind of figured I was being pretty dumb and maybe it was safe to go. You guys nearly walked in on me getting dressed."

Dawn tried to read Buffy's face. She couldn't tell if her sibling was buying her story or not. She was giving herself fifty-fifty odds. Had it been last year, she wouldn't have gotten away with it for a second, particularly after the whole shoplifting thing had come out. But she had gotten a lot of Buffy's trust back, and now she'd put it to the test.

Principal Wood came up to them. His hands were behind his back. "Were you in here by yourself, Dawn?" he asked.

"Yup," she said, "just me. All by my lonesome. Swimming like a dolphin without a school."

"The not having a school part is relatively prescient," Wood said, "given that you're suspended."

Buffy and Dawn turned to him simultaneously and exclaimed, "What?"

"You heard me," he said, and revealed what he was hiding behind his back.

It was a gigantic tennis shoe. It had once been

blue, but now it was so filthy, it was brown. A big "J" was drawn with a black pen on the tongue.

"You weren't in here by yourself," Wood said. "This shoe belongs to Big J. One of the teachers said he was driving one of the janitor-mobiles. He had Tina Jameson riding with him."

"Tina who?" Dawn asked, honestly baffled.

"Luna," Buffy said. "That's what she likes to call herself. And if those two were involved, that means the peroxide punk, Tommy Jacobs, couldn't have been far behind."

"He wasn't." Wood paused for a moment. It was clear he didn't like what he had to say next. "I saw him driving the other cart myself. And I didn't believe it at the time, but Dawn was riding around with him."

"What?" Buffy turned on Dawn. "When did *you* join the Apple Dumpling Gang?"

"I don't know what you're talking about."

"Don't lie to me, young lady."

"Oh right, of course! I'm lying! I must be!" Dawn's chest rose and fell violently. "You always assume the worst of me!"

Buffy shrugged. "That's because the worst is usually true. At least, it was. I thought you were over this kind of thing."

"Look who's talking! I've seen the way you still look at Spike!"

The Slayer flushed. "*Dawn . . . ,*" she said in her harshest warning tone.

Principal Wood stepped forward and extended his hand between them. "Come on, now," he said. "Let's take it easy for a second before this gets out of hand."

Dawn slapped his hand away. "No, forget it!" she screamed. "You're right, Buffy! I'm just as bad as you always wanted me to be, and I don't care! You never just let me be who I am. You always have to try to make me someone else, like I was your Mini-Me or something. I'm sick of it."

"So your answer is to hang out with Kid Rocks-in-his-Head and his poseur posse? You're smarter than that, Dawnie. Tommy Jacobs is a capital-L loser."

"Don't say that about him! You don't even know Tommy! He doesn't care what I do, as long as it's what I want."

"It's not what *you* want that I'm worried about."

Dawn could feel her blood reach critical temperature. This was insane. Why was she standing here listening to this? "Forget it, Buffy," she said. "You don't get it. You have no idea what it's like to be a normal girl." Dawn bent over and grabbed her shoes. She'd had enough lecturing. She was out of there.

The rest of the gang were waiting for her at the jungle gym when she finally arrived. Tommy swung down off the bars and ran over to her. He gave her a big hug. "Boo!" he exclaimed. "How did you squeeze out of that jam?"

"I didn't, really," she said. "That chrome-dome principal and my know-it-all sister suspended me. My own sister!"

Luna came over and put her arm around Dawn. "Don't give it another thought, girl," she said. "Just because Buffy is related to you by blood doesn't make her your sister. If you want to be someone's sis, you have to act the part, not just coast by because you were born into it."

"It's like how you took the rap and let us bail," Tommy added. "That's what you do for your crew."

Luna led her over to the swings and sat her down. She kneeled in the sand in front of Dawn and held her hands. "Listen to me," she said. "We've all learned this the hard way. There was no one else like us to tell us. We all had families before we met each other, but they weren't *really* families. They were just some people we were stuck with. We figured out that we could choose our real family if we wanted to, and that's why we all hang together. I'm here for Tommy, and he's here for me. And we're both here for Big J."

"Word," Big J chimed in.

Tommy took the swing next to Dawn. He kicked off and started working his way up in height. "What do you say, kid?" he asked her. "You ready to free yourself from the ties that bind and pick a new unit to run with?"

"We can be your family, Dawn," Luna said. "We're yours to choose."

Dawn had never really thought about it that way before. There was a point, back when she was the Key and she'd thought Buffy would jettison her as soon as Glory was defeated, when she would have done anything to make sure she stayed in the Summerses' house and kept Buffy as her sibling. But even then, Buffy had made it so hard on her, and ever since, she had expected Dawn to act a certain way, to be a certain way, to do all sorts of things that were just unreasonable to ask a regular kid to do. It was almost like she expected Dawn to *earn* her position as little sister. That wasn't the way it was supposed to work.

She had been so scared for so long, letting her fears rule her. Her terror that Buffy would go away again, like Mom, or that her older sister would just run off as she had to California that summer, and that somehow, Dawn would be made to feel that it was all her fault . . . or that she would feel that way all on her own. She'd let her fears rule her.

Had let *Buffy* rule her. . . .

No more.

"You're right," Dawn said finally. "Buffy doesn't care about me, so why should I worry about her? I *do* have a new crew. I'm with you guys now."

Luna stood up. She was smiling. "Good," she said. "We're glad to have you. Only thing is, we need to do something about your wardrobe . . . *pink* is so very *square*."

Chapter Eleven

Willow could feel her heart start to mellow out as soon as she walked through the door. It was the first time her anxieties had subsided all morning. Most of the students had already arrived at the computer lab and were busy, before class officially started, gabbing about whatever latest film was topping the box office or who was seen flirting with whom. Dr. Sands was sitting at his desk, sorting through some papers, and that was a nice, comforting sight. Old, reliable, routine.

Unlike the whole nasty business with Simon, that is. Simon—whoever, whatever he was—had been so unpredictable, and so cagey about letting the Scoobies figure out his plan that, well, it was just nice to be back in a place that lived and breathed according to schedule.

The seat on the front corner was open again, so Willow scurried over to grab it before anyone else did. That way, if anything went down and Buffy had to page her, she could make a quick exit.

"Hey, Willow, did you hear?"

Uh-oh. What now?

Willow turned to see the two girls who had gotten attacked with kisses at the previous class session standing behind her. They both looked extremely giddy. In fact, the dark-haired girl didn't really look like herself any longer. Gone were her glasses and cardigan sweater, gone was the ponytail. She now had her hair down and was wearing a tight T-shirt and had rouged cheeks and lips. The bookish girl was now replaced by someone almost identical to her new, blond bud.

"Hear?" Willow asked brightly. "No, what? I've been socially deaf."

"About John Sizemore!" the brunette giggled. "Apparently the good professor shouldn't have taken him to see a female administrator. No one knows what he did once the door to Dr. Sireci's office was closed, but as soon as it was open again, he was a free man."

"Apparently he was at just about every frat party there was last night," the blonde continued, "and believe me, there were *a lot* of them. I saw him at Tri-Delt, and he was totally off his face. His technique had certainly improved, though, if you know what I mean."

The brunette looked a little confused, as if maybe she hadn't gone as wild as her new appearance would suggest. "No, we don't, what do you mean?"

such graphic detail! Laughter billowed down from the higher tiers of computer stations behind her, then enfolded her from every corner. People were shuffling in their seats and whispering to one another. Willow glanced at her neighbor's screen and saw that he also had a new message flashing there. Was she right and she had heard the *bling* come from all the other students' computers? Did they all get the same message?

"Oh. My. God. *Willow!*"

The blonde kicked her chair. Willow was afraid to turn around and look. The worst feeling of dread was creeping over her. She looked at the message again. At the very end, it was signed, *xoxo XXXWillow.*

What? No! This can't be happening! I didn't send this!

The shock of the revelation was still registering when there was another *bling.* A second message popped up. It was even more detailed than the first, going on at length about the various places where Willow wanted to enact the alleged fantasies from the first message. The library, under the bleachers in the gym, right here in the computer lab taking full advantage of the professor's *hard drive* and promising she had an *empty socket* ready and waiting anytime he wanted to *interface.*

Yow! And that was just in the dirty geeky tech-talk foreplay parts.

"I can't believe you'd cheat on John, Willow!" the brunette hissed, kicking her chair hard.

There was a third *bling.*

Willow glanced at Dr. Sands. He looked like he

could tell something was going on but wasn't sure what, so he was soldiering on.

The third message was more hysterical. *Why aren't you answering me?* it asked. *You can't tell me you can do better than me. Who else would do the things I will do to you?* It then outlined the various acts that apparently Willow was unique in being able to perform, many of which she was certain were physically impossible for anyone human. She would at least have to be double-jointed.

Willow was scared to look around. Her face felt like it was on fire. She glanced at the boy in the station next to her, who smiled and gave her a thumbs-up.

That is so ick!

The laughs and the whispers grew so loud now that Dr. Sands could no longer ignore them. "Let's get quiet and focus, people!" he instructed.

And then he looked at her. For the first time since the session had started, Dr. Sands looked right at her. He held her gaze for barely a second, but that was long enough. It was all so clear now. The students weren't the only ones to receive these letters. Whoever had created them had sent them to Sands, as well, certainly before class. That was why he was giving her the arctic treatment. Now the prankster—or saboteur—wanted to make sure the rest of the class saw them. That would mean this was being done by someone who really knew the professor's habits, who could count on the man to ignore the blings and bling-blings of the good-goddess-almighty naughty missives that were supposedly from her!

Willow instantly decided that this was the worst thing that had happened to her at school *ever.* Worse even than the time in third grade when Xander had told everyone she had worn green underwear because it was St. Patrick's Day. She hadn't actually worn any green, and he was trying to be sweet and keep people from pinching her, but Willow was mortified nonetheless.

This didn't compare, though. There was no sweetness in these salacious tales. These were only sweet if you considered late-night cable sweat-a-thons to be touching and tender. Who would do such a thing . . . and why?

The answer was so obvious, it was literally right in front of her. Willow felt stupid for not noticing before: Mel sat at his desk behind the professor, a huge grin on his face. She was certain he was hiding a canary behind it. He blew her a kiss and mouthed the words, "Gotcha, you little witch."

Willow felt her anger bubbling inside her. It was struggling against her nerves and humiliation, struggling to find the switch to get her juices flowing.

It wanted to turn her into Dark Willow.

But no, she couldn't allow that to happen, not under any circumstances. She had to keep it together, especially now, because, with her being this mad, there was no telling what she'd do if even a little of her power was unleashed. Mel would have to wait. . . .

Still . . .

He had called her a little witch. He hadn't known how right he was.

At least not yet.

• • •

"Earth to Buffy."

Principal Wood's mellow voice startled Buffy back from her musings. As she glanced up at his questioning look, she suddenly felt like she was back in her student days at Sunnydale High, caught daydreaming when she should have been paying attention. In a burst of guilty energy, she sat up a bit straighter and busied her hands straightening the papers and pens on her desktop. A quick glance at the clock showed that she'd been sitting there, spaced out, for fifteen minutes. Hopefully he hadn't been standing there the whole time.

Clearing her throat nervously, Buffy said, "Sorry, just drifted there for a sec. Pondering how to help deal with all this student badness that's been going on." She pursed her lips, and her brow crinkled as she ran back over her words in her head. "Guess 'student badness' isn't exactly proper counselor-speak, is it?"

Sitting on the corner of her desk, Principal Wood gave her a friendly grin. "I'm pretty sure that 'counselor-speak' isn't exactly proper counselor-speak, either, but I think we can overlook it just this once. You seem kind of distracted."

Buffy shook her head. "No. Not really."

He raised a skeptical eyebrow.

After a second, she gave an embarrassed shrug. "Okay, maybe a little. This morning was kind of crazy, and this thing with Dawn getting herself suspended kind of threw me. I mean, it's like I don't even know who she is these days."

The principal gave her a comforting look. "Buffy,

you have to remember that Dawn, that all the kids here, are going through one of the toughest times of their lives. This is where they push the boundaries and try to forge *their* own identity, apart from family and societal expectations." He gave her a wry smile. "I sound like a beginning psych text, don't I?"

Buffy smiled warmly. "Not at all. Well, okay, yes. Doesn't make you wrong, though. It's just that Dawn . . . well, she's had a hard time these last couple of years." She couldn't help thinking what a good listener he was. It always seemed like you had his undivided attention, and that made her want to say more, to share more.

Before she could follow up on the impulse, the phone rang. She gave Principal Wood an apologetic glance and picked it up. "Buffy Summers."

"Well hello, Buffy. It's Simon. So pleasant to talk to you again."

Turning away from the principal, Buffy spoke to the mystery caller in a hushed whisper. "I really can't talk now."

"You needn't talk at all. Simply listen. Another unfortunate incident is about to occur. It will take place at the Sunnydale Historical Museum in just a few minutes' time. Sadly, it will interrupt the visit of Ms. Bennett's fifth-grade class from Stevens Elementary."

Exasperated, she asked, "How do you *know* this stuff?"

"That's not particularly important right now, is it? All those children in danger—I'd think you would be more concerned for them. If you want to save them, you'd better run. Tick-tock, tick-tock." Then the line went dead.

Turning back to Principal Wood, Buffy gave him a dazzling smile, hoping her nervousness didn't show. "Well, time for lunch!" she said brightly.

He looked puzzled. "At eleven o'clock?"

She stood up and fumbled for her bag. "I know it's a little early," she said, "but I didn't have a chance to grab breakfast this morning." She rubbed her stomach briefly. "Feelin' kind of rumbly."

Buffy headed briskly for the door, trying not to think how flaky this made her look.

A few minutes later, she was bounding up the marble steps of the museum four at a time. Her leather backpack bounced against her spine, the weight of the weapons inside strangely reassuring. Dashing between stately pillars, Buffy pushed through the heavy, brass-bound glass doors.

In the lobby, she paused to let her eyes adjust to the change in lighting. Her gaze swept the immense foyer, but she didn't see any kids.

They must already be on their tour.

As she raced for the archway that led to the exhibit halls, a shrill voice called out, "Excuse me! Excuse me, miss!"

Confused, Buffy turned and looked around again. Finally, she noticed a woman waving at her frantically from behind a cashier's window set into the wall on the other side of the lobby. Buffy rushed over. "What is it? What's wrong?"

The woman, thin-faced and primly dressed, gave

her a disapproving look. She pointed toward the sign in the window in front of her. It read: VOLUNTARY DONATION REQUIRED.

Buffy resisted the impulse to complain about the contradiction. The woman didn't look like she'd care, anyway. "How much?"

The question brought a tight-lipped, disapproving glare. "There is no set amount. The donation is voluntary."

Rolling her eyes, Buffy fumbled in her pockets. She came up with a crumpled five-dollar bill. Holding it out, she asked, "Can you break this?"

"I'm afraid we are unable to provide change." The woman looked pretty happy about it.

Tossing the five into the slot at the bottom of the window, she sprinted through the archway and down the echoing hallways. She poked her head into four different rooms, hoping to spot the students. No luck.

The clatter of hard-soled shoes on the floor drew her attention. She spun in time to see a security guard in a light gray shirt, dark slacks, and a flat-topped police hat clattering her way, a walkie-talkie in his right hand. He skidded to a stop and gave her a stern look. "What's the big hurry, miss?"

Buffy grimaced. "I'm looking for the fifth-grade class. Where can I find them?"

He gave her a puzzled look. "Why do you—"

A chorus of high-pitched screams echoed down the hall.

Buffy smiled sweetly and said, "That would be

why." With that, she bolted toward the children's voices.

She passed a sign that read, MYSTERIES OF EGYPT EXHIBIT and darted through the entrance beside it. The room—the museum's main hall—was huge, two stories tall, with observation windows set high in the walls so that people could look down into it from the second-floor hallways. It was filled with tall stone tablets, sarcophaguses—*or maybe sarcophagi,* thought Buffy—and an assortment of smaller artifacts all displayed in a pseudo-Egyptian setting complete with sand piles and artificial palm trees. There were even a couple of battle-chariots crewed by mannequins and hitched to what Buffy *hoped* weren't actual stuffed horses. She noticed two other entrances to the room, one to her right and one to her left, about halfway across the room.

The children's cries came from the far end of the hall. She saw the mass of young students huddled in one corner, behind a display case. Three teachers were with them, two women and a man, all looking almost as scared as the kids. No big surprise considering the couple *dozen* creatures were swarming the place. The demons were nothing Buffy recognized. They stood about seven feet tall, with long-snouted, doglike faces, pointy Doberman-style ears, and thin, strangely jointed legs. Most of them wore nothing more than short, kilty looking skirts, minus the plaid, and gold-plated straps crisscrossing their chests. One of them had a gold headdressy thing on his head, kind of like what King Tut wore. Buffy breathed a sign of relief.

Right at the moment, anyway, they seemed more interested in trashing the displays than in menacing the innocents. Still, they weren't letting anybody near the exits.

A demon dog looked her way, and his eerie, undulating howl echoed through the hall. Great. The dogfaces had spotted her. She rushed toward the monster with the big yap and launched herself at him in a flying tackle. As they crashed to the floor, a rib snapped in its chest and it yelped. Buffy put one hand at the back of its head and used the other to twist its snout back over its shoulder, snapping its neck.

"Someone wasn't eating his Alpo," she quipped, considering how easy that one had gone down. But, behind her, more howling erupted. One of the dogfaces, the one in the headdress, raised its arms, and his howl rose above the rest.

"This must be the Slayer, of whom we were warned," he growled. "She must not be allowed to interfere!" With that, he barked out a phrase in some strange language.

Literally, *barked out.*

A crackling sound split the air like thunder. The overhead lights blinked, then faded. Suddenly the only light coming into the room was streaming through the observation windows and the entranceways. These, including the one Buffy had just come through, were all blocked with shimmering red energy that painted the room with a dusky crimson glow.

Warily, Buffy squinted into the gloom. *Bet the Beagle Boys can see just fine,* she thought. She heard several coming straight for her, panting and snapping, while others darted into the fake terrain.

Buffy spotted a nearby display case with a couple of weird, crescent-bladed swords inside. The case's plaque said they were Khopesh weapons, but Buffy wasn't really in the mood for a history lesson. Smashing the glass, she snatched up one of the heavy blades, testing its balance as three of the monsters closed on her.

As the first of the creatures growled and leaped at her, she swung the sword in a broad arc, slashing the monster across the belly. It hurtled past, streaming intestines, and hit the floor with a wet slap. *Ewww . . .* Buffy made a face. The second dogface slashed at her with clawed hands. Buffy whirled the heavy-bladed weapon to her left to intercept them, thinking how the balance felt a lot more like an ax than a sword. The sword connected, and with a shriek of pain, the creature jerked back, its hands falling at Buffy's feet. The third monster came from her right, trying to tear into her before she could bring the sword back around. Darting back, she brought the sword up and slashed down. The blade bit deep into the dogface's chest and stuck. Buffy tried to drag it free, but even with Slayer strength, it wouldn't budge, so she let it go.

Three others rushed her, their taloned hands slashing as she ducked, darted, and dodged. She launched a low kick at one of her attacker's legs, which gave way with a brittle snap as the creature yowled. In the corner of her eye, Buffy caught a glimpse of reflected light. She spun away from the slashing blow—too slow! The razor-sharp claws missed her, but sliced through her pack, sending her weapons clattering into the shadows.

As she sized up the five beasties who moved between her and her gear, a quiet clicking sound was behind her, a curly little demon dog's toenails tapping the floor as one of the beasts tried to sneak up on her. *Much in need of the manicure, Fido.* She leaped high, backflipping behind the stalker who had been sneaking up behind her, snapping a kick at its head before she dropped lightly to the floor. It stumbled into the others.

"Bad doggie woof-woof," Buffy said. "No milk bone for *you* tonight."

A shadowy form launched itself from behind a fake palm tree. Another demon dog!

The dogface hit hard, slamming her into the ground. These things were stronger than she'd thought. *Too strong to play with one-on-one,* thought Buffy. *Better lose this puppy quick and figure out a better strategy.*

Buffy remembered reading that a dog's nose was really sensitive. *Really* sensitive. Probably because of all the nerves and stuff that helped their sense of smell. If the same thing was true for these guys . . .

She smashed her forehead into the creature's snout. It reared back, and a pain-filled howl split the air, confirming her hunch. "Pretty sucky having an Achilles' heel in the middle of your face, huh Rover?"

The creature lashed out blindly. She dodged, rolling to her feet. As it tried to rise, she threw a spin kick, hitting it squarely on the nose again. It staggered back, stunned.

Her eyes swept the room and locked on the chariot

not far from where the kids and teachers crouched in terror. Smiling, Buffy darted that direction.

One of the creatures tried to block her path, but she somersaulted over him, catapulting herself into the chariot. Her landing knocked over the charioteer dummy, but as it fell, she managed to wrench the bow it was holding out of its hand. Buffy grinned. It wasn't often she got to practice her archery. Grabbing an arrow from the quiver attached to the front of the chariot, she nocked and took aim at the dogface she had hurdled. It howled defiance and kept coming.

The arrow whistled through the air and into the monster's jaws. It struck the back of its throat with a meaty *thunk,* sending the critter to demon dog heaven. Or hell. Or whatever.

Buffy snatched up another arrow and looked around for Mr. Headdress. Unfortunately, he was shielded by another pair of pooches coming her way. She let fly at one of them and reached for another arrow as it fell dead, feathers seeming to sprout from its eye. She nailed the other point blank as it was trying to scramble into the chariot.

Mr. Headdress howled with rage. "We must find the bowl and complete our sacred mission!" He jabbed a clawed finger toward the school group. "Use the whelps to shield yourselves!"

In the bloody glow from the sealed doorways, the slavering monsters stalked toward the children.

Buffy fumbled for another arrow. Finding no more, she looked down and saw that the quiver was empty. "Wonderful. Now what?"

Glancing at the back of the chariot, Buffy realized there were two javelins sticking out of a slender sheath there. She hauled one out, took a moment to judge the distance, and hurled. The javelin struck home, its head buried deep in a dogface's back. The monster fell at the feet of the male teacher. Disbelieving, the pudgy, balding man stared at the body at his feet, then at Buffy. She figured it could go either way—he'd either cope or collapse. After a second, Mr. Science Guy yanked the javelin free and gripped it tight. Buffy smiled grimly. "Good for you, teach."

The other javelin in hand, Buffy jumped out of the chariot and charged toward the horde of creatures converging on the screaming eleven- and twelve-year-olds. Two of the kids squirmed out from behind the display case, scrambling on hands and knees, trying to make a break for the door. One of the teachers, a thick-bodied, red-haired woman, followed after, trying to bring them back. Jaws slavering, a pair of dogfaces raced after all three.

Buffy knew it was too risky to throw the spear— the demon dogs, the teacher, the kids : . . they were all too close together. If one suddenly stopped or fell, or anything, she could impale an innocent.

She put on a burst of speed and used the javelin to pole-vault over the children and into the closest monster. Her feet slammed into its chest, and she felt several ribs give before it staggered back.

The other creature's claws tore at her left thigh. She thrust the javelin, instinctively driving it through the monster's heart. It lurched away, taking her weapon with it. Another dogface slammed into her, knocking her to the ground. She did a backward roll, coming to her feet, but another was on her in an instant. Buffy did her best to block as it clawed at her, but she felt a sharp pain as a talon tore a shallow furrow in her forearm. She launched a forward kick, catching her attacker under what passed for its chin. Fanged jaws clacked shut, blood spurted, and its severed tongue dropped to the floor.

Blah! Major yuck!

Suddenly, there was a moment's respite. Wary, she peered through the red twilight. The creatures had backed off, just a little. Most of them were forming a loose semicircle, surrounding her. It figured. They were canines, sort of, and their instinct was to hunt in a pack. If they came at her together, they'd overwhelm her for sure.

"Neat. Everything I've been through and I'm gonna get munched to death by a pack of dogs."

A tentative voice behind her said, "Jackals."

Despite herself, Buffy couldn't resist a quick glance behind her. The speaker was the last of the teachers. Her blond hair was peppered with gray, and she wore glasses with thick black rims. Behind the lenses, her eyes met Buffy's with a serious and determined gaze. As the Slayer looked back toward the foe, the teacher continued in a soft, sure voice. "I recognize them from my reading. They're jackal warriors. Servants of the Dark Ones, the evil gods that preceded the Egyptian pantheon."

Buffy's brow furrowed. Exactly how many Dark

Ones were there in ancient times, anyway? Did they have unions? Play bridge? This was about the six hundreth variation she'd heard on this particular theme.

A triumphant cry sounded from beyond the circle of monsters. Mr. Headdress was holding something over his head with both hands. "I have found the bowl!" he hollered.

The pack's attention wavered back and forth between their leader and their prey.

"Oh no," whispered the woman behind her.

Buffy's stomach clenched. There was something about that bowl that scared the woman more than being devoured by jackal warriors.

"What?"

"It's just . . ." She hesitated.

Buffy's voice took on a harsh, commanding tone. "WHAT?"

"Legends tell of a silver bowl. A sacred bowl. Filled with pure water and blessed by the priest of the jackal warriors, it will open the way for the return of the Dark Ones. It will grant them ultimate power. Dominion over mankind." She paused. "But . . . that's just a *myth*. Except that they *aren't* a myth. They're real. If they're real, then . . ."

It was hard to make out in the red light, but Buffy was pretty sure the bowl in Mr. Headdress's hands was silver. His muzzle opened in an evil leer as she watched.

"Slaughter them all," Headdress Head commanded with a slaver.

Time seemed to slow down.

The pack surged forward, and Buffy braced to meet their charge. Mr. Headdress threw back his head and howled, then, from overhead, a tremendous crash of shattering glass rang out.

Every eye turned upward.

A black-clad figure streaked downward in a shower of diamond-bright shards, black leather flapping around him like a pair of midnight wings. He landed gracefully, unfazed by the two-story drop, his platinum hair tinged with scarlet in this light.

Spike brushed bits of glass from his shoulders. His mouth twisted into a satisfied sneer. "Always wanted to pull that one."

Buffy breathed a sigh of relief. Not only was he here, but Spike was sounding like his old self. She assumed that being a kind of demon himself had helped him get through the mystical barriers that usually kept everyone in or out of a Simon Sez battle zone.

Spike turned back and looked past the jackals, meeting the Slayer's gaze. "So, what's the deal, Slayer? What bone are the bow wows after?"

Before she could answer, Mr. Headdress barked fiercely to his pack. Spike tilted his head like he was listening—like *maybe* he could understand. "Wot's that? Rip us to shreds? Not a good choice. Not a good choice at all."

As part of the pack surged forward, Spike leaped to meet them. At the same time, the rest swept toward Buffy and the helpless civilians behind her. She lost sight of Spike as the wave of jackals crashed over her. She was buried in a maelstrom of violence: kicks and strikes, blocks and feints, breaking bones and tearing flesh.

The flow and crash of bodies soon brought her back to back with Spike, his game face in place, demon ridges glistening with sweat on his forehead, fangs out, a fevered light in his eyes.

"Wooo! I tell ya, Slayer, you do know how to throw a party!" Without missing a beat or looking away, his hands lashed out and grasped a dogface by the head. One quick twist later, the body fell lifeless to the ground.

Buffy's fist moved in a blur, crushing the windpipe of another creature. Gagging and gasping, it dropped to its knees and she kicked it away.

"Spike, we have to get the bowl. If they fill it with blessed water, they'll spread darkness over the earth." She paused, realizing that wasn't quite right. Her left foot shot out, shattering a jackal's thigh with a wicked side kick. "Or something like that."

Spike's jaw dropped in surprise. "What?" He ducked as a dogface slashed wickedly at his throat. Catching the hand, he yanked hard, driving it back into his attacker's own belly. Then he burst out in wild laughter. Not a pretty site. Buffy shuddered as she swept the legs out from under her latest opponent.

"You're so right!" Spike said with a laugh. "Bloody brilliant, it is! Demon dogs after a sacred water bowl."

Despite herself, Buffy gave a grim smile. It *was* kind of funny. Unconsciously, she pulled Mr. Pointy from under her belt at the small of her back and plunged it into the nearest demon dog's heart. He wasn't a vamp, so no dust, but it killed him just the same. She spun, the stake in hand, wishing she'd thought to use it before. Bad habit to think of it as *just* a vamp killer.

She looked around for another jackal to tackle and was surprised to find that none were left standing. Her eyes swept the rest of the room. The light was no longer tinged red. The mystic seal was broken. She looked back toward the civilians, who were blank-faced, overwhelmed by what they'd just seen, the children and the teachers staggering out from behind the display case. The blond teacher met her eyes and mouthed, "Thank you." Then she pulled a couple of children close and moved toward the exit. As the man passed her, javelin still in hand, he gave her a nod. She returned it.

One of the little girls stopped, staring wide-eyed at Spike. Buffy looked too. He seemed oblivious to the fact that he was still wearing his game face. As he looked down at the girl, at the fear in her eyes, Buffy saw realization wash over him. He covered his face with his hands, turning away from the girl.

"No! Don't look. Don't look. This isn't me." He huddled against a wall.

Saddened, Buffy turned back to the girl. Smiling, she told her, "Go on now. Go catch up to your friends."

Behind her, Spike waited as the last of the children cleared out.

"We should go," she said softly.

Spike nodded. "Right. Time to head back." Then, a

curious expression came over him as he craned his neck to look beyond her. "*That* ain't right, I'll tell you that much for free."

Buffy looked around to see what had caught his eye. It was Mr. Headdress. His crumpled body still lay sprawled across a couple minions, the silver bowl upside down on the floor not far from his head, but the body was *changing*. His flesh melted away, oozing through his harness and kilt in a hundred tiny quick-silver streams. The two bodies he touched began to do the same. The eerie, reflective fluid flowed together on the tile floor, condensing and then expanding slightly as it hardened. Buffy had a sinking feeling, knowing exactly what was going on.

Before long, another sword fragment lay on the floor, the partial crossguard and blade an obvious match to the piece from the cemetery. *Major wiggins.*

Spike eased past her, obviously fascinated. "Not much use, pet. Missin' some important parts." He looked back at her with sad eyes. "I know the feeling." He reached down to grab the sword, but Buffy was on him like lightning, grabbing his wrist. He looked a question at her.

"Bad idea. That's a whole lot of trouble and you're"—she struggled for a kind way to put it—"not at your best."

Spike shrugged. "No bother. Like I said, not much use now, is it?"

Buffy nodded. "Look, why don't you help me gather up my weapons? We should probably . . ."

She stopped. A skittering sound whispered

through the hall. The glass shards, the shattered remains of the observation windows that Spike had smashed while making his entrance, were sliding along the floor, coming together. They eddied, twisting and coalescing from chaos into order as if manipulated by invisible hands. Words and letters took shape, spelling out a kind of message that was becoming all too familiar.

SIMON SAYS, the glittering characters read, *YOU WILL ADD THIS PIECE TO THE LAST.*

Buffy's fists clenched. Anger and frustration washed over her. "That is IT!" she shouted at the bits of glass. "I am not a puppet. I am *sick* of you jerking my strings and expecting me to run your twisted errands. No more!"

A quiet snort drew her attention. She glared at Spike's bemused grin. "What's your damage?"

The grin vanished, and he shrugged. "Hey, we both know *I'm* crazy, but you're the one yellin' at some busted windowpanes."

Before she could reply, the glass spun, swirled, and skittered to form new patterns on the floor: *WE BOTH KNOW YOU'LL DO AS I SAY, SLAYER. OTHERWISE, MY WARNINGS WILL CEASE AND INNOCENT BLOOD WILL FLOW IN RIVERS. YOU DON'T WANT THAT, DO YOU? OF COURSE NOT.*

Rage washed over her, and she lashed out, her left foot shattering the nearest stone tablet. Dust swirled in the air around her as she tried to regain control of herself. Lord knows she didn't seem to be in control of her life. Then she strode forward, stomping Simon's message, kicking the bits of glass in all directions.

She rounded on Spike, her face tight with anger, and poked a finger at him. "Not. One. Word." Then she looked upward, defiant, and called out, "We'll do it your way for now, you arrogant bastard, but you better believe this isn't over. Eventually, we're going to track you down. When that happens, believe me, you and I are going to have some serious face-time, mister. The kind that involves me kicking your smug butt from here to Maine."

Taking a deep breath, she decided to focus on something else. Anything else. "Look, Spike, I just want to say thanks for . . ."

She was talking to his back. In seconds, he disappeared down the corridor, leaving her alone in the vast silence of the exhibit hall.

Slowly, Buffy made her way back to where her pack had been shredded. As she began to retrieve her weapons, voices sounded in the hallway and she heard the sounds of a whole lot of running feet.

In the distance, someone shouted, "Down this way. I think she went into the new exhibit!" Probably the guard she'd bumped into before. There might even be cops with him. Gathering the last of her gear, along with the new sword fragment, Buffy slipped out the same way that Spike had. She was just hoping she could make it out of the building without having to explain the mess she was leaving behind.

Chapter Twelve

W illow frowned. Computers were funny things.

On days when they ran smoothly, when much needed Web pages loaded fast or software efficiently spotted the ghastly typo in a midterm that would have embarrassed one to no end, it could be a user's best friend. On days when it froze every time a simple print was attempted or an e-mail with a big attachment crashed the machine and cost a user hours of work, it could be one's most hated enemy.

Usually, Willow was on good terms with the computer world. She understood how things worked, the ways to lobby its congress and get what she wanted, even where to find the good spots with the best information that it didn't advertise publicly. She was a citizen of the nation of source tags and codes.

But today, she wondered if somehow her citizen-ship had been revoked. Nothing was going her way. Her research was a collection of dead ends, and she couldn't Google to save her life. Literally. If a vamp busted through the window and tried to fang her, she wouldn't even be able to find a Web page that told her how to kill it. Not that she needed one, with the number of vamps she'd staked, but that wasn't the point.

Mel's efforts to sink her with Dr. Sands had really ticked her off. Much is made of the bullies in school who pick on the nerds and make geek jokes and do the clichéd bully things, but Willow was all too aware that there was another substrata of the bully species. Brainiacs were not free of the tormentor gene. Some very smart people were also very mean, and Willow had dealt with them her whole life. It had started in kindergarten when Jason Shields had advanced faster than the rest of the class in building blocks and had used them to spell "Booger." He'd point at the blocks and then at Willow and laugh and tell everyone that *she* was the booger. She had wanted to stick those blocks in various places of his anatomy, spelling the body part they were entering as they went in.

College so far had been relatively free of the brainiac bully. But Willow had known they were out there, and it had only been a matter of time before someone like Mel had come along.

And now Willow wanted to beat him at his own game.

The advice she'd always heard for dealing with

playground tyrants was to stand up to them. It was said they were really cowards and they'd back off. So, it stood to reason that if you fought violent bullies with violence, the brainiacs would have to be brought down with intellect.

This was how Willow wanted to handle Mel. Dark Willow could reduce him to dust in a blink, but she didn't want to set that side of herself free. Besides, there would be no real satisfaction in that. She'd only get a second of revenge, and possibly a lifetime of regret if things got out of hand. No, what *she* was after was the same kind of humiliation he had dished out to her.

She had thought it would be easy to dig up dirt on Mel—he was an arrogant jerk, and arrogant jerks are usually sloppy show-offs—but so far very little was coming up. A few infractions here and there, but certainly nothing to cry over.

Still, there had to be *something* out there. He was far too territorial to have earned his position cleanly. Perhaps check one or two places more. . . .

Bingo!

Willow couldn't help smiling to herself. "Oh, you are so mine, little man."

Mel sat at his desk cleaning his nails. Dr. Sands was late, and that gave him power over the room. He had given the class a JavaScript problem to solve, a small patch of a program with a bug in it for them to debug. He liked the idea that it would stump a lot of them. He found it pretty simple, himself. Then again, just about everything they did at this level was pretty basic. Sands wasn't really the most challenging professor in the computer science department. Mel could run this course a hundred times better.

Willow wasn't in class, either—which was just fine by Mel. He figured one of two things. Either the little witch couldn't take the heat and had made a run for it, or Sands was sending her packing right now, and that was why he was late. Whichever scenario was true didn't matter, because either of them would be happening as a result of Mel taking the matter in hand. It was almost beneath him to have to manipulate such small minds.

As if in answer to his mental query, Dr. Sands entered the classroom with a man and a woman following behind. The man was dressed in a blue suit, was a little overweight, and balding. The woman was attractive, but seemed a bit cold. The ruffled blouse suggested she was somewhat out of date as far as fashion was concerned. Mel smirked. They seemed just about Sands's speed.

And if they'd been occupying the professor's time, it meant he'd scared Willow Rosenberg away all by his lonesome. No faculty advisement needed.

"Sorry I'm late, class," Dr. Sands announced. "I had some unexpected visitors." He motioned at the pair who had come with him. "I'd like you all to meet Mr. Johnston and Mrs. Reader from Eyetel Digital Systems."

Johnston and Reader gave a little wave to the students. Some of the kids looked up, most of them didn't care. Sands didn't seem to notice one way or the other.

"You keeping them busy, Mr. Turner?" he asked.

"Yes, sir," Mel replied. "I have them working on today's practical."

"Excellent," Sands said. He put his hands on his hips and surveyed the class. "Good."

Sands motioned for his guests to follow him, and they all walked over to Mel's desk. Mel stood. He wasn't sure what was going on, but he did know that this was one of the companies that was looking for an intern, and maybe it was even more fortuitous that he'd gotten rid of the teacher's pet when he did.

"Anthony, Christie . . . this is the young man I was telling you about."

Sands presented Mel as if he were a major appliance, gesturing the way a spokesmodel does. *This is our latest design. It comes with all the special features, including an ice maker.*

Mel extended his hand and said, "It's a pleasure to meet you."

"Likewise," Johnston said. "Dr. Sands has told us a lot about you."

"Oh, nothing good, I'm sure," Mel laughed.

Sands patted his shoulder. "Quite the contrary, and you know it!" he said. "In fact, I've been talking their ears off in regard to your filling that intern position they have coming up."

Just then, there was a *bling.*

Mel knew the sound well. He also knew that the volume meant that it went off on all the computers at once. *But that's impossible,* he thought. *I didn't set anything up for today.*

By the look on Sands's face, Mel was pretty sure he knew what the sound was too. The professor had stopped dead in his tracks.

"Dr. Sands, you were saying . . . ?" Mel was hoping to reignite the conversation, let the moment pass. He glanced quickly at his monitor out of the corner of his eye. Something was loading.

The pop-up screen suddenly came to life. There was movement, there was sound.

"You're welcome, you old fart."

It was Mel's voice, and it echoed around the room. The whole class began to laugh.

"I'm sure Dr. Sands just forgot to say anything." It was Willow speaking now. She and Mel on the screen, talking. It was an mpeg of the conversation they'd had in class the day John Sizemore had gone wiggy.

Mel was horrified. He felt as if the earth were slowly swallowing him, like a pelican had caught him in its beak, was tilting its head back and was slowly wobbling him down its gullet. The process quickened when Sands made his way around Mel's desk to see what the commotion was. His two followers followed. "Hey, that's you there," Johnston said, pointing at Mel's digitized image.

The moment seemed to be taking a lot longer than it had a right to.

"He sometimes seems like he can only focus on one thing at a time," Digital Willow said.

John knew what was coming next.

"Yeah, cute redheads," his digital self said.

The students let out a collective "oooooh," sounding a little too much like a bloodthirsty *Jerry Springer* audience.

"Doesn't matter. He's not the only professor on this campus, and certainly not the highest on the totem pole. In fact, perhaps all I need is for him to engage in a little misconduct with a coed to take him down even lower."

"Hey, wait just a darn minute—" Digital Willow tried to protest, but the file ended there.

The video stopped. It stayed frozen on Digital Mel, making his exit from the classroom. Real-life Mel knew it was likely an all-too apropos image.

"Mr. Turner," Dr. Sands said, his voice gruff and low, "I think you and I will be having a talk after class."

"Yes, sir," Mel replied.

Sands motioned for Johnston and Reader to follow him. "I'll be in my office, Mr. Turner," he said. "Feel free to release the class early."

Mel sat back down in his chair. He felt completely defeated. How did that stinkin' witch get video of their conversation? It was impossible for her to know that their confrontation was going to occur. She couldn't have come prepared.

Then it dawned on him.

Every computer in the lab had a Webcam mounted on top of it. Small white orbs with their accusing eye, all pointing at him. Someone must have broadcast that day's lecture to record so some absent student could take notes. They must have left it running.

That's how Willow got her hands on it.

Mel felt his face go white. He looked at himself in the monitor screen, more a shadow than a reflection. If a cloud rolled by and blocked the sun from coming through the window, he'd probably disappear completely. And there would be nothing he could do about it.

Willow stopped in at the campus coffee shop for a quick drink of something warm before class. She ordered her usual Peppermint Patty, took the steaming cocoa, and grabbed a seat by the window. She wanted to try to familiarize herself with Sartre's "The Wall" before her lit class. She'd read it once, but the night before had been a bit hectic, preventing her from absorbing it fully. From that initial breeze-through, she had decided that Sartre was trying to say that life is ultimately beyond our control, that circumstance has a way of coming around and biting you, but she wanted to make sure prior to committing to that interpretation.

Before she could crack open the book, there was a loud slapping noise on the window. Mel had come from out of nowhere. He had both hands pressed flat against the glass. His eyes were wide, and his jaw was set like stone. Soaked with sweat, his hair matted in clumps on his head, Mel looked like he was about to keel over from a clogged artery. "You!" he bellowed.

Mel tore himself away from the window and headed for the door.

Uh-oh.

He stumbled into the coffee shop, flinging the door

open with a *bang*. He pointed an angry finger at Willow. "You think you're pretty clever, don't you?" The last two words seemed to be spit through his teeth. "Well, you're not. You're definitely not."

"I'm not sure you're any kind of Oscar Wilde yourself," she replied, taking a sip of her cocoa. She was enjoying his meltdown. "You look really tense. I think you should loosen up. Have you ever considered acupuncture?"

Mel raised his hands in the air, closing them into fists while simultaneously inhaling a big gust of air. He exhaled an exasperated grunt. "You stupid little slut!" he yelled. "Who do you think you're dealing with? You're nothing. You're a . . . a . . . a paramecium. A zygote!"

Willow put her cup down and got up from the table. She took a step toward Mel, noting that there didn't seem to be any other customers in the shop, and the barista must have gone to the back for supplies or something. She was alone with Melvin Jeckyl, watching him turn into T. A. Hyde.

Mel leaned forward. "They say it's men who have the defective chromosome, but it's really you if you think you've gotten the best of me, you amoeba."

He was seething with anger—literally. His shoulders were hunched, his lower jaw extended, spittle was splashing out of his mouth. "You think you've ruined everything," he said, "and maybe you have . . . maybe almost. But I won't go down that easy, nuh-uh. I'll take you down with me!"

"You need to relax before your eyes pop out of

your head," Willow told him. "You also need to take a second look at reality." She felt the power rising within her. "You touched first, Mel. I merely touched back."

"Maybe it's time I touched you harder!"

Mel pulled his arm back, screwed up his face, and launched his fist toward Willow's face. Without so much as an extraneous twitch, her left arm swiftly shot up, knocking his arm away with a curving arc. She instantly followed with her right arm, giving him enough of a shove with the palm of her hand to send Mel back a couple of steps. He hadn't seen it coming. For all he could tell, that blur of motion might not have even been her.

Wow, Willow thought. *Fancy stuff.*

How'd I do that?

"Seriously, Mel," Willow said, "don't make me bring you back down to earth the hard way. Opt for that reality check I suggested earlier."

Her taunts only enraged Mel more. He lurched forward again, screaming, throwing his whole body at her. Willow centered herself and executed one quick chop, striking with the edge of her flat hand against his throat. Mel instantly dropped to his knees like groceries falling out of the bottom of the bag. He clutched at his throat, gasping for air demonstratively and loudly.

"Oh, take it easy, you big baby," Willow scolded. "You'll be fine. I hit you with only enough force to shut you up. If I'd wanted to hurt you so bad that you'd have choked on your own windpipe, I could have. But I didn't. So don't start blubbering, you dumb blubberer."

Willow sat back down and took a sip from her cocoa. This was getting more and more satisfying, seeing Mel kneel before her. A girl could get used to that.

"Consider this the game-winning point, Mel," she said. "My little video show was just the tip of the *Titanic*-sinking iceberg, okay? I know all about your little schemes—your cheating and grade fixing, your test and term paper retail outlet. You've been using your position as a teaching assistant to milk the most out of your college experience. But for a computer guy, you sure aren't very bright . . . or maybe you're just careless because you're arrogant. We both know that just because there's no paper, it doesn't mean there isn't a trail, right? I've got all the dirt on you, yessiree bob."

She finished the last of her cocoa and gathered her books. "I could wiggle my little nose and you'd be buried good and proper," she said. "Don't give me a reason. Clean up your act, cut out the shenanigans, and I'll never mention any of it to anyone. Don't think you can get away with ignoring what I'm saying and going back to what you were doing, either, because I'll be watching. And you'd be surprised how much I can see."

Willow stepped past Mel. He let go of his throat and let himself fall forward, so that he was on his hands and knees. He was still struggling for breath as she neared the door, but he managed to gurgle out a couple of words: "Stinking . . . *witch*!"

Willow stopped. *Hmph. He likes that word,*

doesn't he? she thought. *Wonder how he'd react if he knew how right he was?*

She put her books down on the nearest table and turned back to face him. *What the hell, why don't we show him?*

Since anyone could walk in without warning, the first thing Willow did was cast an invisibility spell around her and Mel.

Once this was done, she lowered her hands to her sides and turned them so that they were palms out and facing Mel. "Pay attention," she said. "You're going to be shocked by what this stinking witch can do."

Blue bolts of electricity began to sparkle around her fingers, surrounding her hands, crackling and popping loudly. Willow brought her hands up, pointing them at Mel. The energy shot from her hands, circling his head, making his very passé Caesar hair stand on end. Mel was screaming and wailing like he was actually on fire, even though he wasn't being hurt at all. Maybe a slight irritation as the electricity charged his fillings, but that was about it. As usual, he was overreacting.

Willow was feeling pretty good about the little magic trick she was playing. It was nice to be using her powers again, and she didn't feel a hint of the darkness that had consumed her several months before. She decided to take it a little further, letting the energy snake out around the room, joining with light sockets and electrical gadgets, creating a web of sparks all around her panicking victim.

Still no side effects. Take it a bit further.

The electricity picked Mel up, levitating him about two feet off the ground. His screams were silent now, but they were still visible on his face. His mouth was open wide, lines and wrinkles stretching his visage to grotesque proportions.

This is incredible! Willow thought. *I'm flexing all sorts of magic muscles I haven't let myself touch since I squashed my dark side. I was so scared it would come out again, I had no idea I could still fire up the ol' batteries. I don't feel any Dark Willow at all. I have my power firmly in my grasp.*

"You enjoying this, Mel?" she asked, giving him a wink. "Because we're only just getting started."

When it came time for bed, Willow felt more relaxed than she had been the entire time since she'd returned to Sunnydale. Sleep had been a patchy relief, as it was hard to get through the night without worry and doubt creeping into her dreams. She was confident the problem had been cleared up.

After giving Mel's fear threshold a run for its money that morning, Willow had to hurry to get to her next class. She was nearly there when she heard her name being called from behind her. It was Dr. Sands. He was sprinting after her, trying to flag her down.

"Thank goodness I found you," he told her between heavy breaths. "Listen, I feel like such a fool. I should have known that you'd never send those notes. I backtracked everything and they led me to Mel's terminal. I checked his account history, and it was all there."

Dr. Sands put a hand on Willow's shoulder. "I'm so sorry I didn't have more faith in you," he said.

Willow smiled. Her plan had worked perfectly. "Oh, don't worry about it," she said. "Really. I knew the truth would come out."

"Listen, Mel obviously isn't going to be my assistant any longer," Sands said. "It's a lot of work and some heavy responsibility, but I think you're the girl for the job."

She hadn't really expected an offer like that. Sure, they'd talked about her getting an internship, but that was in the future—the near future, admittedly, but still some time and distance away, and that had been comforting. Why was that? Was she that married to life with the Scoobies, to magic and thwarting evil, that it was all she should consider being? There was more to life than vampires and demons and ancient prophesies about Chosen Ones. And there was certainly a world outside of Sunnydale.

Was it so wrong for her to consider all that? Couldn't she be more than Buffy's research person?

"Okay," Willow said. "I'll do it. Thank you, Dr. Sands."

It had been a day full of unpredictable happenings, but she didn't regret a one. And tonight her slumber would be free of anxiety. She'd sleep straight on to morning, and then start her new job and quite possibly her new life.

Willow's left shoulder began to tingle. An itch was growing there. She tried to scratch it, but it didn't do any good. In fact, it almost made it worse, like when you try to wash a stain out of the carpet and only end up spreading it around.

Going over to the mirror, she dropped her night-gown off her shoulder and looked at the back of it. That was no itch. Well, it was an itch, but it was itching because she had a tattoo.

A new tattoo that she hadn't gone to any tattoo parlor to get.

It was black, and it looked to Willow like it was some kind of old symbol—a star and a cross, and quite possibly a bar code superimposed over it.

She didn't know why or how it had gotten there, but she knew it must have appeared for a reason. Maybe this was an outward manifestation of her new power level, of her discovery of increased abilities of control. The bar code was a bit odd for a magic symbol—but then, if the tattoo was a symbol, that meant it was symbolism. Maybe this represented her newfound balance between technology and the occult.

The sudden appearance of the tattoo should have bothered her. On some level, she knew that she should have been bothered, that she should be flipping out and looking for answers, an explanation. That's what she would have done only a week or so ago. That's what the old Willow would have done. But she didn't feel like her old self anymore; she felt better, more accepting, like the responsibility for things like these really wasn't hers anymore, and she could just let others worry about stuff, she was here to feel good. Looking at the tattoo, she thought, *Wow. Cool. Instant hipness.*

Willow turned out the light and crawled into bed,

not thinking anything else about the tattoo. It was as if someone had run a computer subroutine in her mind, letting her know the tattoo was nothing to worry about, and so that was how she felt—peaceful, calm, and relaxed. As soon as her head hit the pillow, she drifted away into a deep, dreamless sleep.

Chapter Thirteen

That sleep didn't last long. Shortly after midnight, Buffy was at Willow's door, unable to sleep, looking for help on the good old research front. Xander was already at it downstairs.

Sometimes Willow suffered from a strange research nostalgia, and she felt well rested, stronger than she had in a long time, so she bounced out of bed, threw on some clothes, and came downstairs with her pal.

The missing of the old-style research business didn't make a lot of sense, she knew, because Buffy's house was way nicer than the old high school library. Yet, there was something about that dank and musky backroom that she missed from time to time. Maybe it was the essence of Giles. She was there most often with him, and when they'd be working into the wee hours, a certain droll sense of humor would come to the fore. A tired Giles was a silly Giles, and he didn't let that part of himself out in front of the others. It made Willow feel special.

Or maybe it was times like now that she missed him in other ways. She sure could use his knowledge. Just having some of his books wasn't always enough. The man had a knack for getting through to the good bits, a skill he really couldn't lend their missions while he was in England.

She and Xander had been at the old research game on and off for days, and they weren't finding anything about Simon, the shattered sword, or the demons Buffy had been sent to fight among the moldy and cracked pages of the Watcher's tomes. Her Internet scavenger hunt wasn't turning up much either. Results on even their general search for demons that turned into stuff were equally *nada*. Plenty of stories about stuff turning into demons, but the reverse was apparently a modern wrinkle in the fabric of demon mythology.

Buffy had gone downstairs to pound out her sorrows on a punching bag. They could hear the impact of her fists on the canvas, faint *fwap* sounds in the background.

"There she goes again," Willow said wistfully. "She says hitting things helps her concentrate."

"A lot to concentrate on, clearly," Xander replied. "Maybe we should take a cue from the Buffster, only we can pound our heads against the wall. It will do as much good."

Anya was there, too, but she was curled up on the couch, sound asleep. The *fwapping* was like a lullaby to her. Xander had told Willow of his fond memories of watching her nod off with a happy smile to the sounds of explosions and screaming from such favorites as *Platoon* and *Saving Private Ryan*. In her best of days, carnage was like candy, and the sounds still comforted.

The former vengeance demon had helped earlier, but there was only so much reading time they could get out of her. It was far more practical to rely on her for firsthand knowledge about various demons—even if she *did* go too far sometimes, like earlier tonight when she gave more details about a Ridwid demon's digestive system than anyone really wanted. She had fallen asleep about an hour ago, and was snoring loudly in an easy chair—creating a sort of natural music with Buffy's punching. "It's like *Stomp*," Xander quipped, "but for the violent and lazy."

"If only that were a more common combination," Willow said. "Too many of the violent nasties we know are so hyperactive. How much better would it be if Glory had decided to take a nap rather than destroy the world?"

Xander rubbed his eyes. "I'm running out of gas, Will. This is useless, there's nothing here. Plus, I used up the last of the chocolate syrup forty-five minutes ago, and I refuse to drink regular milk. I can't work under these conditions."

Willow was afraid he was right, but she didn't want to admit it. There was always something to be found, some key to the mystery's locked door that was right in front of them all along only they weren't seeing it.

What were they missing?

"Okay, let's break it down," she said, determined not to throw in the towel—her towel, Buffy's towel, anyone's towel, and no matter its condition—without one more shot at this. "We have *three* things we're looking for. We're looking for stuff on demonic swords, on demons that turn into pieces of swords, and on some dude named Simon who seems to know what's going to happen before it does, quite possibly because he manipulates events to make them happen."

"The triple," Xander said with a frown.

Willow looked up from her notes. "What's that?" she asked.

Clasping his hands behind his head, Xander leaned back in his chair. "It's the classic formula for comedy," he explained. "It's all about the triple—the setup, the build, the payoff. Something about stuff coming in threes appeals to audiences or something."

Both of them sat in silence, listening to Anya snore and Buffy *fwap*. Xander's words hung between them. They looked at each other, eyes widening, so much of it suddenly coming clear. "Hey, Will . . . you thinking what *I'm* thinking?" Xander asked.

"I'm going to make a phone call," Willow replied, getting out of her chair and making for the kitchen.

"You do that," Xander said, "and I'm going to work up a schematic. I think we're onto something."

• • •

Buffy was still sweaty from her workout. Willow and Xander's excitement had been so pronounced, she couldn't take the time to clean up. She was scared if she didn't let them talk now, they might explode. And research guts were hard to get out of the carpet.

They'd woken up Anya, who said it had better be good. She had dreamed of diving into a big swimming pool full of coins, like that duck who wore a top hat. "Why don't more ducks take an interest in haberdashery?" she asked.

"I don't know," Xander said. "Maybe their hats fall off when they fly?"

Anya frowned. "Maybe there's an answer in one of your books. Why don't you look for that?"

They'd also tried to get Dawn to come down, but she was conked out, huddled under the covers, and they didn't want to wake her. Buffy didn't know what she was going to do with her. It was normal for teenagers to act like they were being wronged when they were being punished, but the stunts Dawn had pulled at the school were so extreme, it didn't make sense for her to try to pretend her suspension was unfair. Then again, when did sixteen-year-olds ever make sense? Buffy sure hadn't when she was that age.

The Slayer wasn't so much worried about what Dawnie had done than *why* she had done it. Unfortunately, Buffy's surrogate-parental woes were going to have to take a backseat to the dog-and-pony show Wil and Xander had whipped up. Of course, Buffy had never really gotten that phrase. Did the dogs chase the ponies? Did the ponies do tricks with the dogs? What was the deal with that, anyway? "Okay, whattaya got?" Buffy asked.

Willow and Xander exchanged quick smiles. "You ready?" Willow asked.

"Yeah," Xander said, "but why don't you start."

"Oh no, I couldn't. You're the one who stumbled onto the idea."

"Sure, but you let your fingers do the walking and got the info."

"Yes, but you made visual aids."

Buffy waved a hand between them. "Hello?" she said. "Remember us? Remember the whole Simon and his pet Slayer and his whole, hey, I'm gonna need that sword for something big and dark and world threatening, more likely than not?"

"Heh. Sorry." Willow gave her a sheepish smile.

Buffy shook her head. "Don't worry about it. Just make with the 'splaining."

"Okay," Willow said. "Basically, it came down to looking at what all the demons we've encountered have had in common. Two things became immediately evident."

"First, there were Simon's warnings," Xander said. "Before each demon attack, our mysterious psychic phone friend gave us a jingle."

"Second," Willow continued, "are the pieces of the sword they left behind immediately upon their demise."

"And, if I may," Xander added, "great job on the demising, Buffy. Top-notch Slayer work."

Buffy nodded to him. "Thanks. Continue, please."

"Right," Xander said. "The less evident third commonality is where the visual aids come in."

Behind them, the duo had displayed a poster board with crudely drawn versions of the bad guys they'd run into. Willow explained, "If you notice, each demon, while seemingly different from the others, actually has something on their bodies in the quantity of *three*. This one has three eyes, the other one three arms, and another three legs. It was easy to miss these details because they were all so fundamentally dissimilar, we didn't even consider looking closer. Ghouls, reptiles, dog soldiers—it just seemed too random."

"Plus, among the types of demons you fought, there are several different kinds in the same family," Xander continued. "But once we started working under the triple theory, it was easy to narrow them down."

There was a stack of printouts on top of all the books. Willow handed them to Buffy. "I called down to Wesley in Los Angeles, and he e-mailed these over," she said. "My resources were dry, but he really came through in a pinch with more accurate images of what we've been up against. I got Cordy when I called, and she said he's looking pretty hunky these days—which I suppose is good to know if you're into his type. You know, men. Those things I gave up."

"Anyhoo," Xander interjected, "the three-eye thing made us think all these races might have something in common, and they do. They all came from the same place, they all had a common foundation, but over the last thousand years they've forgotten that and so have most of the people—and thingees—who've written about them. Again, props to the Wesmeister for supplying that bit. I mean, really, looking at the way they've evolved, reverse-engineering it, the whole scheme is a lot like putting up a building. It has a basic foundation upon which everything else is built."

"It's actually really fascinating, when you think about it," Willow added. "The roots of magic start in the physical world, so by transforming these fragments into demonic creatures, and coding them by their body parts, Simon has built his magic spell on the very structure of life itself."

Buffy was starting to think this was way too complicated. Had she been honest, her dance session with the punching bag had ended up being more to clear her anger over Dawn's acting up than it was to sort out the business of Simon. "This is all very neat in a 'yay school' kind of way, but how is it going to help me kick this creep's butt?"

"We're getting to that," Xander said.

"How typical," Anya snorted. "When you need to go fast, you slow down. Usually it's the reverse problem."

Xander felt the blood drain from his face. He pointed at Anya. "See this finger?" he asked. "This is my scolding finger. You were so quiet up until now, and that was a good thing, so the finger hasn't been seen until now. The finger suggests you go back to shutting up."

"Whatever." Anya folded her arms and looked away. "Stupid finger."

"So, as the story goes," Xander said, trying to recover, "in ancient times, in another hell dimension, all these demons were manifestations of a single evil being called Netrazzi. Once we had it figured out, the pieces of the sword puzzle started to come together. It also started to explain why Simon has needed *you* to get the fragments."

"Okay, then," Buffy said, settling back. "I'm all ears." Her hands automatically shot up to the sides of her head. "No, I mean . . . not really. All ears, not. Not covered completely in ears." She sighed. There were times when wish magic was so prevalent in the air of Sunnydale, it could make anyone paranoid about how they put things. "I'm listening, is what I'm trying to say. Go ahead."

Willow was shuffling through the Wesley pages. "The weapon you're slowly 'reassembling,' Buffy, is called the Soulsword. When it's put back together, it will regain its powers, not the least of which is the ability to slice the soul straight out of the victim and grant its raw energy to the evildoer that did the slicing. Some texts suggest that it can also be used for resurrection and body-switching spells."

She finally found the sheet she was looking for. "Here we go," she said. "This is an entry Wes gave me, out of the journal of an honest-to-goodness sorcerer's apprentice. . . ."

Master warned me never to tell, and I have not. Words of what I have seen and done have never passed my lips. I am a sanctuary for the greatest of secrets, a keeper of dreams, ambitions, and tragedies, the silent hope of a scattered handful who have experienced majesty and wonder on a scale few mortals could comprehend.

I have not told. I have not spoken. Yet the knowledge I possess must not become dust, as I will be soon, old and frail as I have become, particularly if the quest I set out upon this evening ends in anything less than triumph. Thus I write in these yellowed pages, honoring the wishes of the sorcerer who took me in and gave me life when all others sought to release my head from my shoulders because of the strangeness that occurred wherever I would go.

My name is unimportant. I am, what is called, an Adept. The potential, I now realize, to become a mage every bit as powerful as my lord and master was within me all along, but I was only a boy when he found me, the ax of an ignorant zealot about to kiss my scrawny throat. He deflected that ax with a bolt of lightning that leaped from his eyes, and I watched him tear my attackers to pieces with little more than a few whispered words and arcane gestures. I gave my life, and my power, to him that day, and even now, I have no regrets. Power I may have wielded, yes, but not wisdom. The world would have suffered and bled had I lived and not given the strength of my soul to my master as tithe for my life.

The trouble began a century after the fall of Rome, in an age of fear and shadows. My master, hallowed be his name, though I will not write it here, ruled a small kingdom by force of will—and arms. Chief among the *weapons he wielded was a blade he called the Soulsword, a shimmering, beautiful thing I touched only when he was weakened from war and took the strength from my body, the power of magic from my very essence, to restore himself. Master forged it with spells culled from the many tribes of the demon Netrazzi, the force of great darkness from whom he first gained powers. He won many battles with this blade and conquered many enemies.*

The sword was highly coveted. Ultimately, it was an alliance forged of his rival mystics and their enemies, the human zealots, that laid siege to his kingdom and forced us all to retreat to his high castle. Despite my master's power, his resources were not without limit, and after many bitter months of combat, magical and otherwise, the outcome was clear: The castle would fall, and master would die. He accepted this, confiding in me and only a few others that death would not mean his end. Shocking us all, he shattered the Soulsword, then performed a ritual transmuting the shards into monsters. These newly made creatures had the many and varied shapes of the Netrazzi, and they knew nothing of what they had been, how they had come into existence, the role they were meant to play in times to come. What they did not know, they could not tell.

My task was simple. While my master bravely opened his gates and attacked his enemies with all the magic left to him—while wielding a weapon created to look like the true Soulsword—I was among a small group of protectors who led his wife and son away

*through an exit his enemies abandoned once their
prize was in sight. We also freed the very demons who
had been the sword, three for each of the shards, and
marked by the covenant of three upon their bodies.
With a spell I had spent difficult months perfecting, I
sent them to wandering the four corners of the earth,
charged with the task of remaining hidden and alive
until they were again summoned.*

*Myatsa, beloved of my master, mother of his single
child, carried with her a book of spells that would
allow us to recall them at an appointed time ten years
later . . . but both lost their lives in a simple carriage
accident and Master's spellbook was taken when
thieves descended upon the wreck.*

*I have spent a lifetime looking for Master's book,
despairing that it had been tossed into a ravine or
burned to ward off a chill by the ignorant fools who
absconded with it. This day, however, I have been
given hope that it exists still, and I leave tonight for a
rendezvous with one who says he can take me to the
tome—for a price. I have stolen much from others in
anticipation of this day, and pray the book will soon be
in my hands. If so, I will open it to a page Master
pointed out to me many times in the final days, where-
upon is writ a spell of resurrection.*

My heart is light.

*Master will soon be alive before me once more, the
Soulsword in his hand, and our day of vengeance will
come at last.*

*Or so I hope. If I fail, and these words are read by
another, find the book, recall the sword from hiding,*

and resurrect my master. In his glory, in his brilliance, all others pale.

Buffy shook her head. She stretched her arms, pushed her sore muscles a little bit. It felt good.

She needed a smidgen of feeling good. She was glad she still had the power to do *something* positive, even if it was just a quick stretch. Sometimes the business of being a Slayer was nothing more than stopping the bad from happening, which seemed a lot less affirmative as time wore on. It was rarely about helping something good to occur. So, allowing herself a nice stretch in the face of Simon's badness was something she'd take. Hooray for small victories.

"Sounds like our boy Simon has found himself a little nighttime reading material," Buffy said. "He sorted out this Soulsword's history and has been bringing these demons to Sunnydale for me to destroy."

"To destroy and change back to the sword bits," Willow clarified.

"Right," Buffy said. "But shouldn't these demons be ancient? Wouldn't they have died from old age a long time ago, rather than being healthy and spry and hitting me and things?"

"The spell he cast must have had regenerative properties," Xander said, "making our demon friends those hip and groovy senior citizens they have in movies. You know, like *Cocoon.*"

Buffy laughed. "I get it. And they've been keeping their heads down, hiding out, even if they didn't know why, all this time. When they were summoned, they joined up with others like themselves, and were drawn here, probably still not knowing *exactly* why, just thinking the Hellmouth is the place to be. The thing is . . . why me? Simon's 'mister all-powerful magical mojo guy'—why didn't he just pop these critters?" Buffy waited . . . but no explanation came, just uncomfortable looks between Wil and the Xan-Man. "You said you knew how I fit in with all this," she prompted.

Willow took a deep breath. Buffy recognized the expression on her face. You don't know someone as long as she and Willow had known each other and not know how to read her mood by little things like the shape of her mouth. Willow was unhappy about this part.

"It's because you've been dead," Willow said, "and have come back to life."

Ah, that was it. Willow still felt guilty about resurrecting Buffy last year. Not like she needed to have been brought back that time to make her eligible for the wizard guy's employment plan. Not the first time she cheated the reaper.

"Only someone who has had their life restored after it's been destroyed can put the Soulsword back together," Willow continued. "It's like a fail-safe, so that not just anyone could rebuild the sword—and particularly not his enemies."

"Which means the sorcerer probably set it up so his wife and kid could bring him back from the dead at the right time, I'd imagine," Buffy said. "I don't think we can count him out of the picture just yet."

"Great," Xander said. "Like there aren't enough

unidentified supervillains in this scenario already, we've got to have Saruman show up, as well."

"*The Lord of the Rings*?" Anya chimed in. "I know which one of us around here has the hairy feet to be a Hobbit."

Xander held out his finger. "Anya, remember what this is?"

"Yes," she said, rolling her eyes. "Wouldn't want to upset the finger. Shutting up."

Buffy picked a stake up off the table and absent-mindedly started chewing it. So many things were still unanswered. Finding out about the sword only meant Simon, as powerful as he was, wanted even *more* power, though for what purpose, none of them had a clue. Body-swapping wasn't the easiest magical trick in the world, but it could be done without this do-hickey. That *lovely* time she spent with everyone thinking she was Faith and the other way around proved that.

Unless, like, one was incredibly ugly, and needed a major power source to pull off a switch—and that might fit with Simon not showing his kisser. . . .

Nah . . .

Resurrection spells? Buffy wouldn't be here right now without one.

The soul-suckage business . . . that was kinda like what Glory did, and the idea that Simon was after power on her level made things a little scarier than before.

Hmmm . . .

Buffy suddenly became uncomfortably aware that

everyone was looking to her to lead the way out of this mess . . . or, were they just looking at her? Why were they all staring?

The taste of stake nibbling came to her.

Ewwwwwww! She realized what she was doing. Stake gnawing. *Icky habit! Why can't you just bite your nails?* Maybe it was better to think out loud. . . .

"Okay, so we have the whole sword thing sorted," she said, putting the stake down. "But that still doesn't tell us who Simon is and what he wants the weapon for. And, more importantly, once we have all the pieces of the Soulsword, what do we do with it? I can't just hand it over to him, can I?"

"Nah, I don't think so," Xander said. "Giving the evil dudes their weapons doesn't strike me as a smart plan. It's not like banks hand guns to the robbers when they come to set up an account."

"Except bank robbers usually announce themselves," Willow argued. "Simon is playing his game all secretive. If we offer to give him the Soulsword, he'll have to come out of hiding to get it. I mean, it's not like anything else we've tried for smoking him out has worked, and he's hurt enough people already. Tell him forget it, no sword, and no one knows what he'll do. Turn it up to eleven or something!"

Buffy's ponytail had started to become dislodged. She reached back and began to straighten it out. "I don't know," she said. "I'm not sure if that's a good idea. I'm also not sure what the alternative might be, but until I've worked it out, I think the best thing to do is to leave the fragments where I've hidden them.

That'll keep them safe. Here, there are too many variables, and particularly with Dawn in full-on teenage rage, it's probably best not to keep bringing them back to the house."

"So what'd you do with them?" Xander asked.

"It's better if you guys don't know. If you get in a bind, you can't reveal information you don't have."

Xander swept the books off the table with one sweep of his arm. He stood up with such force, his chair went tumbling over backward. "That's just typical!" he yelled.

Buffy was startled. "Whoa," she said, "settle down. I don't get it. What's wrong? This is just standard operating procedure."

Willow slammed her laptop shut. "That's just it, Buffy," she said. "It's *too* standard. You always do this. You always do whatever you feel like. It's Buffy's way or no way, because Buffy is so much better than the rest of us!"

"Exactly! Thank you, Willow. God forbid any of us should ever question 'the Chosen One.'"

Everyone was on their feet now, including Anya. The sudden eruption of tempers from both Xander and Willow had jolted the room. There was a crazy energy in the air. "Xander, you're being weird," Anya offered. "Even for you."

Xander snapped at her with a savage ferocity. "Don't make me whip out the *second* scolding finger, Anya! I've had just about enough of you!" He turned his attack back to Buffy. "But *you* . . . I would think that after all this time, all the things we've done *with* you and *for* you, you'd give us just a little bit of your trust. You think we'd crack so easy that we'd give up your precious secrets? I might work with my hands, Buffy, but that doesn't make me a mental midget."

Buffy was at a loss. "I didn't—"

"Save your excuses," Willow interrupted. "We don't need another run-through of your cursed-and-alone routine. I know how much you hate us to trample over your brooding with our friendship and our help, how it's so much easier to keep us in the mush pot while you play Hellmouth duck-duck-goose. We're not inferior to you, Buffy. In fact, I think it's safe to say you're not even the most powerful one in this room."

Buffy threw up her hands. "Hey! Now hold it! No one said anything about anyone being inferior or superior. All I'm trying to say is that if you don't know, that lessens your desirability for Simon. His attention is on me right now, and it's better that way. Not because you can't handle yourselves, but because I *need* you. Without you guys, I'd never know what I was up against."

Xander flapped his hand like a puppet. "Blah, blah, blah," he said. "I'm out of here. Hopefully I can find my way home all by my lonesome. My mom forgot to pin my name and address to my jacket."

Willow tucked her laptop under her arm. "Hey, Xander, on your way out can you help me find the stairs? I need to go to my room and do some homework. Maybe if we work together, we can locate them faster."

"Come on, guys," Buffy protested.

But they weren't listening. They left the room without even looking back.

"What's eating them?" Anya asked. "Did someone put jerk sugar on their cornflakes?"

"I don't know," Buffy replied. "I'm hoping it's just stress, and that they haven't been affected by whatever has this whole town acting grumpy. It's bad enough the rest of Sunnydale has gotten up on the wrong side of the bed, I don't need my friends against me too!"

As far as Dawn could remember, she had never gotten any kind of reaction when she walked into the Double Meat Palace—now open in the wee hours—before. She always saw herself as the sort of person not even automatic doors would pay attention to, forever trapped outside the grocery store of modern life.

Not so now. Just about everyone looked at her. Some faces were shocked. Those mostly belonged to adults, parents who were old enough to have been there when her new look had first started, and yet also old enough to forget that they themselves may have adopted this fashion once. There were some teenage boys who clearly weren't drooling because of their BBQ meatlet sandwich (back for a limited time!). Fast food rarely got coyote howls. Typically, the girls sneered at the competition.

She had gone back to Luna's house with her, where they'd have access to her closet and makeup kit. "What we're going to do is tear it all down and start from scratch," Luna told her. "Anything you're going to find at the mall is out. We're dropping *Sweet Valley High* for *Tales from the Darkside.*"

Dawn had used one of the oldest tricks in the book—some pillows and stuffed animals gathered into the shape of a sleeping girl and covered by many blankets left on her bed—to allow her to run wild and free without worrying about Big Sis coming looking for her.

Luna showed her pictures of Sally from *Nightmare Before Christmas* and Siouxsie Sioux and said they were going to be their foundation. Ultimately they'd work their way toward Marilyn Manson, something with a little edge.

The transformation took over an hour, and what emerged was a new Dawn, the head-turning Dawn. They'd adopt Tommy's term-of-endearment for her into a full-fledged nickname. She was Boo, both sexy and scary.

The gang took a seat by the window. There was no light outside, just the black night, and as a result, Dawn could see herself in the glass. It was the first time she could take a real gander at the new look since they'd left Luna's. Her hair was teased and sprayed so it stood up like Robert Smith's from The Cure (Luna had even played their album *Disintegration* while they'd worked). It reminded Dawn of a smaller version of the helmets that the guards wore outside Buckingham Palace.

Her makeup was slightly "death clown" in nature. They'd covered her face in a white base, and then played the rest of the makeup off it—Cleopatra-style outlines around her eyes, bright red lips, a star drawn on her cheek with eyebrow pencil. It was sort of like what *The Crow* would have looked like if they'd cast a cute girl for the part.

And the clothes. The clothes were put on in layers to create effect. She had a tank top on, and then a mesh shirt over that—both of which allowed her to show off her tattoo. She had a wristband with metal studs on her right arm, and about ten little rubber bracelets on her left. She also had on a studded belt, holding up a short miniskirt. The final touches were striped tights, and heavy shoes with soles four inches thick. Everything was *black*. Black as the night she was seeing herself superimposed against.

Tommy gave a "what's up?" nod to the jocks at the next table over, all of whom were still checking Dawn out. He dramatically leaned over and cupped her face in his hand, turning her head toward him. He gave her a big kiss, almost overdoing it, taking a little bit of her lipstick with him. "How you doin', Boo?" he asked.

Dawn smiled. "Not bad. How about yourself?"

Tommy looked back at the jocks, who really couldn't believe their eyes. "It's *all* good."

Luna signaled Dawn that Tommy had messed up her makeup by making a quick hand gesture around her lips. Dawn quickly grabbed the Johnny the Homicidal Maniac lunchbox Luna had given her and dug out her compact and lipstick. Luna had warned her when they left, "Maintaining your fashion will require constant vigilance and dedication. Always be prepared."

"Hey, you guys want to hear something lame?"

Dawn said. "My stupid sister actually used to work here. Can you believe that this is the best job on her résumé, and they think she's qualified to tell kids how to run their lives?"

"I think the only thing your sister runs is her mouth," Tommy laughed.

Big J held up his hand and gave Tommy a high five. "You got that right, T."

"Maybe that's why she's so determined to hold you back," Luna said. "She can't do anything productive with her own life, and none of the kids at school are going to listen to her, so she takes it out on you."

"When her and Principal Dud were hassling me," Dawn said, "they were all, like, 'You shouldn't hang with Tommy, he's no good.' That's when I straight-up walked out on them. I wasn't hearing any of that."

This seemed to irritate Tommy. He kicked away from the table, tilting his chair back and straightening out his baggy jeans. "Luna's right, yo," he said. "Your sister has a whacked sense of reality because she doesn't want to admit her place in it is over. She's scared of you because she knows that when peeps get old, they fall behind. She didn't make anything of herself when she had the chance, and you're going to leave her in the dust."

"Tell her, T," Big J said. "It's time."

Dawn was confused. "Tell me?" she asked. "Tell me what? What's it time for?"

"He's right, Tommy," Luna said.

Tommy let his chair drop back down to all four legs. He leaned in toward the center of the table and motioned for everyone else to do the same. Once they were close together, he said, "Okay, you're right." He was speaking in hushed tones. These were secret, sensitive matters, and it wasn't for outside ears.

"Your sister is scared," Tommy explained. "That's no joke. She can sense something is up. She knew it when she rounded us up and tried to interrogate us in her office. She knows you might become something greater than she is, something greater than *you are*. She knows we're all . . . becoming."

Big J and Luna nodded. They agreed. They got what Tommy was laying down. Unfortunately, Dawn didn't. "Becoming?" she asked. "What are we becoming?"

Tommy leaned back in his chair again. He adjusted his skullcap, pulled it down so it was just over his eyes, and squinted out from underneath it. "Something more," he said. "That's all you need to know right now. Just trust me that everything we're doing isn't for nothing. Everything means something, even that thing on your arm."

Dawn looked out of the corner of her eye at her tattoo reflected in the window. She still had no memory of where it had come from, and she didn't want to look like a dork by asking about it. Now Tommy was saying it meant something—but what could that be? "When will I be ready?" she asked.

"Soon," Luna assured her, clasping Dawn's hand in hers.

"You've just got one more thing you have to do," Tommy said. "It's almost like a clean-up job. If you think about it, too, I bet you already know what I mean. Somebody has it in for us—not just you, but all of us now. Somebody wants to tell us what to do, wants to control our lives, but we're not going to stand for it."

"Ain't nobody gonna hold us down," Big J agreed.

Dawn looked at all three of them. It was starting to sink in.

"You know what we mean, don't you?" Luna said. "Get rid of Buffy, your troubles disappear, almost as if by magic."

Dawn looked at herself in the window again. She looked through her reflection, out into the darkness. When she thought about it, yeah, just about everything that wasn't right in her life was somehow connected to Buffy and her various rules and regulations. The guys were right: There really was only one source of all her problems.

And if she looked to the darkness for answers, then somehow it answered her. She knew exactly how to get rid of this blemish. "I get what you're saying," she said, "and don't worry. I know just how to wish it all away."

Chapter Fourteen

At first, Xander thought it was the low roll of thunder in the distance that woke him. The room was still dark, no morning light glimmered in the windows. Gritty eyed, he glanced at the clock beside his bed: 4:30 A.M. He stifled a yawn. *Plenty of time to get back to—*

The phone rang again, bringing him wide awake. A thousand scenarios ran through his mind as he fumbled for the phone, all of them bad. With all the screwy stuff going on, he should have stayed at Buffy's that night instead of coming home. If anything happened, he would never be able to deal. Images of Buffy, Dawn, and Willow being torn apart by some Big Bad flashed through his mind's eye. Then he thought of Anya.

Oh, God. What if something happened to Anya?

In his rising panic, he knocked the cordless phone from its cradle, sending it clattering to the floor. Diving after it, he landed with a dull thud. His neighbors would be on him for that in the morning, not that it mattered. Not if anything had happened to the people he loved, the *fear* he lived with constantly. . . .

Shuddering, he finally brought the receiver to his ear. "Hello? Hello?"

"Xander? Is—is that you?" The man's voice caught him off guard. He didn't recognize it, though there was something familiar that tugged at the back of his brain, something underneath the obvious tension and uncertainty.

Aching from his fall, Xander sat up and leaned back against the bed. "Who the hell is this?"

"It's . . . it's *Dan.* Oh, God. Xander . . . she . . . she won't get up. I keep trying to make her get up, but she . . . she isn't moving, Xander. Oh, God. There's so much blood."

Stunned, Xander tried to put the barrage of conflicting impressions into something he could comprehend. He'd never heard Dan angry or worried or anything less than calm, cool, and collected. It was hard to reconcile that longtime sense of the man with the near-hysteria he was hearing over the phone line. Dan wasn't the kind of guy who made panicked calls at 4:30 in the morning. He was the guy *you* called when everything was going to hell—dependable, rock steady, and completely under control.

Recovering from his surprise, Xander managed to

sputter, "She?" It hit him that something must have happened to Dan's wife, something *awful*. That would explain everything. "What's wrong, Dan? What happened to Annie?"

A muffled sob came over the line. "Annie? My God, you're right, what am I going to tell Annie? How am I gonna explain this?"

That hit Xander like a two-by-four between the eyes. His mind reeling, he asked, "Where *are* you?"

Dan choked out, "I didn't mean to do it . . . she just made me so mad. . . . She kept telling me how she could make me do anything she wanted, that she was the one in control. You've got to help me, Xander. You have to. I didn't know who else to ask."

"Dan!" Xander shouted, trying to break through his friend's confusion. "Of course I'll help. You just have to tell me where you are. I can't help if I don't know where you are."

"I'm at the apartment. I know I shouldn't have come over here this late, but she made me do it. She *made* me. Oh, God. What am I going to do?"

Xander's mind was racing, trying to figure out the right questions, the right approach, so he could calm Dan enough to get the information that he needed. Meanwhile, his friend just kept up a steady stream of incoherent rambling in the background.

Suddenly, it struck him. Scrambling to his feet, Xander ran to the kitchen. He hadn't had the chance to replace all the phones yet, but the one in the kitchen was brand-new. Switching on the light, he squinted at the number on the Caller ID display. For once, he was grateful that his mother was such a gigantic pain. The woman at the phone company had told him it would take a week to get the service, but he'd used his momentary fame from the other day to rush the process along, telling her that he was getting flooded with calls from reporters. Would she have been as accommodating if he'd been honest? Probably not.

The number on the display looked familiar. The name listed was *M. Wells.*

His stomach felt like he'd just swallowed a chunk of dry ice. A sense of dread overwhelmed him, and he mumbled into the phone, "Stay put, Dan. I'll be right there."

He was dressed and on the road in a couple of minutes. The sky was completely dark, with not even a single star visible. Brief flashes of light flickered above, revealing the clouds that stretched from the horizon. Thunder followed, vibrating the windows on Xander's car. Storms were rare in sunny SoCal, even over the Hellmouth, but it looked like Sunnydale was for a major blow. The rain hadn't started yet, but it was coming.

Every shudder of thunder hit Xander like a fist. His friend's call had turned his universe upside down, placing everything he thought he knew about the supposedly normal side of his life in doubt. Before long, he was pulling up in front of a six-story apartment building just outside of downtown. He'd been there before a couple of times, just giving a friend a ride home. He'd never been inside.

Digging in his coat pocket, he found the scrap of

paper he'd shoved there. The next flash of lightning lit it well enough for him to see the apartment number he'd scrawled on it. Getting out of the car, he started for the door.

The rain began to fall in sheets.

Upstairs, Xander pushed the wet hair back from his face as he knocked on the apartment door. A shadow fell across the peephole, then the door opened. Dan was standing just inside, barefoot and bare-chested, wearing only a pair of jeans. His eyes were red and wide with fear. Quickly, Xander stepped inside.

Dan latched on to him—not with a friendly bear hug like he'd given after Xander had rescued Davis—but with the desperate, urgency of a frightened child. "You came," Dan whispered. "Thank God, you came."

Awkwardly, Xander patted his friend's back. As he did, his eyes scanned the room. It was a lot like he'd expected. The walls were a cool blue, with lots of chrome-and-glass furnishings: end tables, coffee table, and entertainment center. The floor was hardwood, the couch and chairs dark leather. A couple of movie posters hung on the wall in chrome frames. The whole place was very sleek and very modern. . . .

Except for the body, of course.

Mindy Wells lay near the couch in the shattered remains of the glass coffee table, her face bruised, her lips and one cheek split and crusted with blood. She'd obviously been beaten, but whether that was what had killed her was hard to say. Her back must have been slashed open by the shards of the tabletop, because there was a lot of pooled blood congealing on the floor. Her long, bare legs stretched out from under a faded denim work shirt . . . the one Dan had been wearing earlier that day.

Xander pulled away from his friend's clench. He kept his hands on the man's shoulders, shaking him to get his attention. "What's going on, Dan? What happened? Hell, what are you *doing* here?"

The big man's eyes dimmed, and it was like something broke inside him. He slumped bonelessly into the nearest chair, then covered his face with his hands. His reply was soft, "Isn't it obvious? I was cheating on Annie."

Xander nodded. "I guess I figured that out. I'm just having a hard time processing the information. I mean, you and Annie are so happy, and you and Mindy never seemed that close. Besides, she was always . . . um . . ."

His friend barked a short, bitter laugh. "Always hitting on *you,* right? I'm sorry, man. I'm so sorry." Dan looked up at Xander, his red-rimmed eyes wet with tears. "Honest, Xander, it could have gone either way. She . . . we started fooling around right after she hired in. She was looking for a guy with some money, somebody who could help her live in style. Me being married was just a bonus. With me, there was no chance of putting demands on her, of crimping her style. I know it was stupid. It's just that she was so sexy and so full of life, I couldn't help myself. I've been married for eight years. We've got three kids. We've got a nice, quiet, boring life. Everything is exactly how it's supposed to be. . . . I needed something crazy.

Something out of control." His eyes flickered toward the body. "I guess I got it, huh?" He laughed again, this time with an edge of hysteria.

"I was scared you'd figure things out," Dan went on. "You know me too well, and you've got that damn knack, that way of seeing things. I *told* her to flirt with you. I've seen the way you are around women since things fell apart with Anya. It's like you think any woman who likes you must have some deep, dark, terrible secret. I figured if Mindy put the moves on you, it'd just make you suspicious and keep you away. Plus, if she seemed interested in you, she couldn't be fooling around with me, right?"

Xander worked hard at keeping his face from showing what he was feeling inside. It all made a kind of sick, twisted sense now. Of course Mindy wasn't really interested in him. How could she be? Then he thought of the look that she gave him after the rescue, that cold, calculating look. Was she sizing him up? Maybe reconsidering her choice of meal tickets? He let the question go. Neither answer was going to make him feel better. His eyes fell on her body again, bringing home the simple fact this wasn't really about him. "Tell me what happened," Xander asked softly.

Dan leaned forward in the chair, elbows on his knees, cradling his face in his hands. In the momentary silence, Xander could hear the rain slapping against the windows.

"She called the house, Xander," Dan said angrily. "She even talked with Annie for a minute before she asked for me. Told her that there was a problem at the work site and that I needed to come check it out. When I got on the phone, she told me to come here. She didn't ask. She *told* me. Like I was a puppy that was supposed to run over whenever she called. I was mad, but I said okay. I was going to come over and set her straight, y'know? Tell her she couldn't do stuff like that. I . . . I was putting on my coat, telling Annie how sorry I was that I had to go, and y'know what she did? She kissed me on the cheek and she smiled and told me that she understood. She's such a good woman, Xander. She trusts me. She *loves* me. Look at how I pay her back."

Xander hunched down, trying to look his friend in the eye. His face was stern. "Try to focus, Dan. Annie isn't the issue now. Mindy is lying over there, dead. How did that happen?"

Dan looked up, shaking his head slowly. "When I got here, she jumped me as soon as I got in the door. I mean, she was all over me. It was incredible!" He paused, remembering. "After, I tried to tell her that it wasn't right, that she couldn't just call me anytime at home and expect me to come running. She . . . she just laughed."

Dan leaped up out of the chair, not even noticing as he nearly knocked Xander down. He threw up his hands and started ranting as he paced over toward the couch. "She laughed! She said she'd call me whenever she wanted, that I'd better do what she said." He paused for a moment, looking down at the woman. "She threatened to tell Annie, to say that I had made her do it to keep her job. Said she could ruin my life."

As Dan turned back, thunder boomed loud, shaking the windows. The lights flickered. "She said *she* was in *control*!"

Xander went over and grabbed his friend's shoulders. "Look, Dan, we'd better call the cops. We'll get you a lawyer—"

"NO!" Dan twisted his fingers into the front of Xander's shirt. "You don't understand! It's not my fault!"

Xander tried to pull away. "Let go of me, Dan. I don't want to have to—"

Dan just clenched his hands tighter, pulling Xander toward him, his eyes wild and glaring. "It was like it wasn't me. Like I was *possessed* or something. I couldn't stop. I knew I shouldn't, but I started hitting her. I grabbed her and hit her and hit her. I couldn't stop. Then everything went dark."

His eyes, empty and lost, bored into Xander's. "When I came to, I was just standing here, looking down at her. The table . . . oh God, the table . . . the blood." Then his hands fell away from Xander's shirt as he sank to his knees, sobbing.

Xander stood there, looking down, torn. He knew he needed to call the police. Still, he hesitated. He'd known Dan for a while now. Even allowing for the secrets he'd just learned, this level of violence—this brutality—seemed beyond anything his friend could ever do. Dan's words echoed in his mind: *It was like it wasn't me. Like I was possessed or something.*

This was Sunnydale, after all. Possession was about as common as coffee shops.

He looked over at Mindy, as if somehow she might hold the answers he was seeking. He couldn't help thinking that bruises and blood had become an all too familiar part of his life. When exactly did he gain the capacity to stare down at the corpse of a friend and not fall completely apart? As his eyes took in the sight, he noticed something that had eluded him before—a glint of metal on her left wrist. Easing around Dan, he crouched beside Mindy's body and lifted her arm. She was wearing a bracelet that he'd never seen before. It looked like brass or bronze. Something coppery, with hints of that blue-green verdi-whatsis, like on the Statue of Liberty. There were markings, too, swirled designs and some kind of what might be weird writing. That was enough.

Xander walked back over to hunker down next to Dan. "Look, buddy, we need to get some help here."

Dan looked up, panicked. He reached out and grabbed Xander's sleeve. "Not the police! You can't turn me in. I didn't mean to do it, Xander. I couldn't stop. I couldn't stop."

Putting a hand on Dan's shoulder, Xander tried to reassure him. "Not the police. Some friends of mine. They're good with stuff like this. You just trust me, okay? It'll be all right."

Standing, he pulled his cell phone from an inside coat pocket. His first call was to Willow. She might know something about the bracelet or the markings. On the fourth ring, he heard Will's bright, perky voice coming over the speaker, saying, "Hey there!"

"Will, it's Xander. I . . ."

"This is Willow. Well, okay, it's actually Willow's voice mail. Can't make with the talky right now, so leave the usual stuff and I'll call ya right back! Thanks!"

"Dammit." Xander waited for the tone and said, "Look, Will, I need to talk to you pronto. Call my cell." He hit "End" and dialed again. The markings on the bracelet looked kind of rune-ish. Thankfully, he happened to know someone who had started out reading runes, back, back, back in the day. The ringing stopped.

"Greetings. This is a recording of Anya's voice. As I have not answered your call myself, it is safe to assume that I am unable or unwilling to speak with you at this time. Please wait for the beep, then say your name, recite the phone number at which I can call you, and speak any other message you may wish to convey, and if it suits me, I may return your call."

Xander rubbed his forehead. "Anya, it's Xander. Pick up. This is important." He waited a little longer. "Pick up!" After a few more seconds, he ended the call.

With a wry smile, he punched the first speed-dial number on his phone. "When all else fails, call the Slayer."

Buffy answered after two rings. "Hang on a sec!"

Over the phone, Xander could hear grunts, cracks, and thumping.

"Hey, Xander. Sorry. Little busy." That was followed by a kind of *chik* sound and then a loud *poof.* "Can you give me another minute?"

"Sure, I—"

"Whoa!"

In the background, Xander heard the ring of steel against stone. From experience, he was guessing sword and headstone. He winced, hoping that he hadn't just gotten one of his best friends killed. Things hadn't been so great when he left Buffy's house earlier, that business with the sword had really cheesed him off, and it was like, hey, look, it's the new no-impulse-control Xander, wind him up, make him rant!

Still . . . she wouldn't hold that against him, not now, under these circumstances.

Would she?

A loud boom of thunder sounded outside, and the lights flickered again. In the quiet that followed, he strained to hear any sound at all coming over the phone. There was a loud crack, and a muffled thud.

"Back," Buffy said warmly. "Vamps brought along a demony knight guy. Had to borrow his sword so I could give it back to him. What's up? You're up early."

"Buff, it's bad. Really bad. Really, really bad. You remember Dan Martin?"

"Your hunky work buddy?" her voice was full of concern. "Sure I do. What's wrong?"

He took a few minutes to run through the events, from answering the phone to finding the bracelet. When he finished, there was dead air on the line. "Buffy? Are you still there?"

"Uh-huh."

"Well, what do I do?"

"Are you *kidding* me? For God's sake, Xander, call the police!"

"But what if he was under some kind of mojo?"

"Look, Xander, from what you've told me, it sounds like your 'good guy' pal isn't quite so white-hatty after all. In fact, it sounds like he's gone completely whack job. Did it ever occur to you he might turn on you next? If you don't call the cops, I'm going to, for your own good."

"I know it looks bad, but what about the bracelet?"

"Xander, the bracelet is on the dead girl. Emphasis on the *dead*. Emphasis on the *girl*. Most of the time, evil doodads put the whammy on whoever is wearing them."

"Okay, true, but . . ."

"Tell you what—if you want us to look into this, we will. If you're right, we'll figure out a way to fix things."

"But—"

"Until then, you're not going to help anyone by ending up an accessory to murder! Now, do you dial 911 or do I?"

Frustrated, Xander snapped, "Fine. I'll call. Thanks for your help."

Dan looked up at him, his eyes full of hope. Xander's heart sank at the complete faith he saw in that look. More than anything, he hated to let his friend down.

"So, are they coming?" asked Dan.

Xander shook his head slowly. "Not right now, buddy."

Dan looked at him, puzzled. "What do you mean? You said that your friends would help. You said that *you'd* help." He started to rise, so Xander helped him to his feet. Once he was standing, he shoved Xander's hand away. "You said you'd help!"

There was a flash of lightning and another peal of thunder, so close, it rattled the windows. The lights flickered, then faded to a feeble glow.

"Great," said Xander. "Brown-out. Look, Dan, we—"

He was interrupted by a blare of sound coming through the wall. The neighbor's stereo system was cranked full blast, bass line thumping like a giant's heartbeat, guitars screaming like banshees wailing. Xander's first impulse was to pound on the wall and yell for them to keep it down. Then he looked at the flickering lights and wondered how it was that they had enough power to make that much sound.

Lightning strobed in the window again. Thunder roared, drowning out the stereo. The lights went out completely, then surged to full intensity and cut out again.

In that full burst of light, Xander thought he saw something moving, over by the coffee table . . . over by the body. He peered through the shadows, moving closer, trying to make out any sign of motion.

Again, the lightning strobed. The thunder, almost simultaneous, was deafening. In that brief illumination, Xander saw that Mindy's body was gone.

He felt strong hands grab him from behind. Spinning, Xander just barely managed to restrain his battle instincts and avoid punching Dan across the jaw as another streak of lightning, farther away, lit the room.

His friend was growing even more frantic. "We've got to get *out* of here!"

Xander tried to calm him. "It's okay. It's going to be okay."

Dan clenched his hands into Xander's coat, shaking him roughly. "It's not okay! It's never going to be okay again!"

Another flash of lightning gave Xander a glimpse of Dan's face. In the split second of light, he saw fury turn to terror. "What? What is it?" Xander spun to look in the direction Dan was staring. He saw nothing in the darkness, then more lightning lit up the room once more in a flickering glow. Mindy's body, bruised and bloodied, was back. The dead woman's face was turned toward his. As the light faded again, she smiled at him and winked.

Stumbling backward, Xander bumped into Dan. He turned, heart pounding. Another brief second of illumination showed the man standing rigid, trying to keep completely still, like a rabbit trying to avoid the predator's gaze. Mindy's body was behind him, her arms sensuously draped over his shoulders, her hands caressing his bare chest. She smiled wickedly at Xander as she licked Dan's ear.

Howling in fear, Dan lurched forward, grabbing Xander's shirt again, pulling their faces close. Xander could feel flecks of spittle hit him as Dan yelled, "You said your friends would come! You promised me! Liar! *You damned liar!*"

Suddenly, the lights wavered and came back on. Xander could see Dan's face, red with anger, just inches from his own. He tried to push his friend away, to get a little room. Unexpectedly, all resistance stopped and Xander's shove sent Dan staggering backward. His friend's face was white, and his eyes were wide. Turning sideways to keep Dan in his peripheral vision, he glanced in the other direction.

Mindy Wells's body lay in the shattered ruins of the coffee table, as if it had never moved.

Xander stumbled backward, putting some distance between himself and the corpse. Turning back to Dan, he saw tears streaking down the man's cheeks. His eyes were full of despair. In a barely audible voice, Dan whispered, "You said that they would help. But no one can help."

Stepping closer, Xander reached out to his friend. Without warning, Dan lashed out with both hands, shoving him away, yelling at the top of his lungs, "Nobody can help!"

The force of his shove sent Xander tumbling backward. His head struck the twisted frame of the coffee table.

Everything went black.

Groaning, Xander opened his eyes slowly. Light was streaming in the window, the glare making his eyes ache and his head throb. Reaching back, he felt a substantial lump. He winced. Probing tender lumpiness, the touching was definitely a bad idea.

With a grunt, he staggered to his feet. Through the window he could see blue sky and fluffy white clouds. Unfortunately, inside was still pretty much the same:

Mindy's body, shattered glass, and lots of blood. Dan, however, was gone.

He staggered toward the door, not quite sure why. Maybe he could catch up to Dan. Maybe he should get out of there. In the hallway, a wave of dizziness hit. Sagging against the wall, he closed his eyes. Maybe if he shut them, he wouldn't see the place spinning.

Footsteps sounded loudly. With a sense of relief, he waited for help. Suddenly, rough hands grabbed him and shoved him across the hall to the far wall. His eyes flew open as he slammed into it. His arms were wrenched up behind his back, and he felt the cool metal of handcuffs close on his wrists. Definitely *not* the usual context for handcuffs.

He was grabbed again and spun around. His vision titled slightly, and a wave of nausea swept over him. When things came back into focus, he saw two policemen, one holding him against the wall, the other using a two-handed shooter's stance to aim a pistol at him. Okay, it was the usual context for handcuffs, just not the one he was used to.

Xander tried to speak and found his mouth dry. Swallowing a couple times, he tried again. "What the—"

"Shut up!" shouted the policeman holding him. For good measure, he thumped him against the wall again. The hallway spun.

The second cop looked over his shoulder into the open door of Mindy's apartment. "We got another one in here," he said.

"Another one?" asked Xander.

The first cop grinned. It wasn't a friendly grin. "Well, looks like it's about that time. You have the right to remain silent—"

He ran through the Miranda litany. Xander couldn't help thinking it sounded different than it did on TV. Then again, maybe that was just because he was on the receiving end this time. While the cop was finishing, more officers ran up the hall. After exchanging a few terse and cryptic phrases, the first two dragged Xander down the hall to the elevator.

As they neared the doors, Xander could hear sirens blaring. Outside, the parking lot was chaos. There were more police, ambulances, and even reporters. Xander recognized the lady in the silk trench and the old guy in the rumpled suit. He blinked in the morning sun. Apparently it was the *same* rumpled suit from two days before. For the second time that week, he found himself staring into the cold eye of cameras. This time, the human eyes regarding him looked the same.

The reporter in the rumpled suit called out to the cops, hauling him toward a black and white. "So, did the jumper have some help?"

Jumper? Xander wondered about that for a second. Then his gaze turned toward a gathering of paramedics lifting a body from the parking lot pavement. A man's body, barefoot and bare-chested, wearing only a pair of jeans. There was a tape outline showing how it had landed.

Dan.

Xander stumbled. If it weren't for the policemen holding him, he would have fallen.

• • •

He'd been in the interrogation room for over an hour and things weren't getting any more pleasant. The room was about fifteen by twenty feet and painted an institutional gray-green. There was a hint of yellow, too, but from the smell, that might have been residual cigarette smoke from back before California pretty much banned smoking inside. A big table took up most of the space. There were chairs. Xander was in one, on the far side of the table from the door. Across from him was a big mirror. A one-way mirror. He'd seen enough cop shows to know there were probably people on the other side, watching the interrogation and listening over an intercom.

Xander raised his hands, now cuffed in front of him, and gave a little wave. "Hey, guys," he said, "why do they bother with the one-way mirror when everyone knows it's a one-way mirror?"

The detectives handling the investigation were a mismatched pair, but both of them glared in response. The younger guy was black, with a shaved head and a tailored suit. His name was Jessup. The other, Baker, was an older white guy with salt-and-pepper hair who apparently shopped at the same place as the reporter in the rumpled suit. Xander was no expert on police procedure, but these guys seemed to know what they were doing. Unfortunately, what they were doing just then was trying to pin two murders on him.

Baker said, "Sounds like you haven't quite figured out just how much trouble you're in, wise guy."

Xander swallowed. Hard. "No, I have. Sorry. I

just babble a little when I get nervous."

Jessup spun a chair around and sat down near Xander. He leaned forward, leaning on the chair back, and said, "What d'you have to be nervous about, bro?"

Xander shook his head. "Here's the thing—a lot of people, myself included, get nervous when a police car pulls in behind them on the street, even if they're doing the speed limit and obeying all the laws. Why? I don't know, but we do. Likewise, here I am, being grilled by two of Sunnydale's finest, and I'm nervous. I shouldn't be. I didn't do anything wrong. Still, hard not to be nervous." He looked quizzically at Jessup. "Does that make any sense?"

Baker leaned forward, slamming his hands down on the table. Xander jumped.

"It doesn't make any more sense than the rest of your story, Harris. For example, you say you got to the apartment and found your buddy, the jumper—"

Jessup chimed in with, "Dan Martin."

"Dan Martin with a dead girl. So what do you do? According to the call history on your cell phone, you place three calls. One to Willow Rosenberg, one to your, apparently, ex-fiancée and one to Ms. Buffy Summers, with whom you spoke for a couple minutes and with whom, by the way, the department has more than a passing acquaintance. Yet, while you were doing all that dialing, you never considered calling us? Why is that?"

Xander shrugged. "I already told you. Dan was pretty freaked out when I got there. I was afraid that if I tried calling the police, he'd run or he'd jump me. I

310 BUFFY THE VAMPIRE SLAYER

was trying to get in touch with one of my friends so I could try to figure out a way to suggest they call the police—you—without setting Dan off."

That wasn't exactly the truth, but it was close enough. No way these guys would be interested in theories of possession and dark magic.

Baker interrupted, "Your ex-fiancée is a friend of yours?"

Xander nodded.

"My ex-wife wouldn't help me out of a jam for a million bucks. What makes you so lucky?"

Xander shrugged again. "We've got lots of mutual friends, so we've sort of had to figure out a way to deal."

It went on for a long time, the same questions, phrased slightly differently, endless attempts to poke holes in his story. Then the detectives' boss entered, an older African-American woman, short and a little stocky. She was wearing slacks and a sweater. She didn't look like a hard-nosed cop. She looked more like somebody's mom. She asked, "Detectives, can I have a minute?"

"Please. Take several," Xander said, his arms sweeping expansively.

He didn't hear what they talked about in the hall, but he knew they would have to cut him loose once forensics was over the place. They had nothing on him. *Nothing.*

Strange, he should have been afraid. . . .

But he wasn't.

They returned, not making a lot of eye contact, and

told him he was free to go. Xander decided to take a
risk and ask about the bracelet Mindy had been wearing. He wasn't about to let on his theory that there was
something supernatural about it. If pressed, he would
simply say that it looked like a very expensive gift that
his friend must have purchased for his mistress (a story
he had just made up) and that selling it might get some
truly needed money into the hands of the dead man's
family. But the detectives didn't have a clue.

The lieutenant shrugged. "No sign of any bracelet.
You had your bell rung pretty hard. Maybe you're confused."

Xander rubbed at his temples. It was getting so
hard to think. Even now, he could no longer remember
exactly what the bracelet had looked like. . . .

Within seconds, he had forgotten it completely, as
if someone, from some far off distance, had thrown a
switch inside his head.

Anya came charging through the front doors of the
police station as Baker and Jessup were escorting Xander out. Spotting Xander, she made a beeline right for
them.

"Xander! I came as soon as I heard." Rounding on
the detectives, eyes blazing with righteous indignation,
Anya pronounced firmly, "It is my understanding that
you have no right to detain this man without counsel."
She waved a finger under Baker's nose. "If you do not
release him at once, I will be forced to resort to drastic
measures."

Baker exchanged glances with Jessup.

Xander tried to calm her down. "Anya, it's okay. They're letting me go."

That stopped her. She looked from Xander to Jessup to Baker, puzzled. "They're letting you go?"

Xander nodded.

She smiled. "I had no idea I could be so persuasive outside of a retail environment."

Baker's eyes widened. He looked at Xander. "This the ex-fiancée?"

Sheepishly, Xander nodded.

Baker slapped him on one shoulder. "Good luck, kid."

As Xander and Anya walked down the steps, she couldn't stop asking questions. She wanted to know what "prison" was like and was he accosted by any of the other prisoners and did the police resort to brutality? She particularly wanted footnotes on the brutality.

At the foot of the steps, he turned to face her and set a finger on her lips to stop the torrent of questions. "Anya, I have had a really bad day, and it isn't even noon. One of my best friends killed himself after murdering my secretary, and now I'm going to have to try to explain this whole thing to his wife, Annie, and I don't even understand it myself."

Anya nodded sadly. "Poor Annie. I know we didn't spend a great deal of time together, but she seemed like a very good sort."

Xander snorted bitterly. "Yeah well, Dan seemed like a very good sort, too, and look at what happened to him."

Anya gave him a brief hug. "Xander, what happened to Dan was not your fault. You shouldn't blame yourself."

Xander pulled away, face red. Anya backed off, frightened. She'd never seen him this angry before.

"Blame myself? Blame *myself*? Of course I don't blame myself. I blame *Buffy*!"

Anya looked confused. "Buffy? I don't understand."

Grabbing Anya by the shoulders, he shook her. Hard. "How many times, Anya? How many times have I been there for her? No matter what. Vampires, demons, apocalypse—hey, I'm there and ready to do whatever needs doing. Right?"

Anya tried to break free. "Stop it, Xander. You're scaring me."

It was like he didn't hear. He just kept on, venting, raging, his emotions spiraling up and out of control. "Hell, I even saved the world, all by myself, when the Slayer couldn't manage. So what do I get in return? The one time that I call her to help with *my* problems, she tells me she's busy and we'll worry about it later."

Suddenly, he released Anya, turning away, ashamed but still angry. "Well, there isn't going to be a later, is there? Not for Dan."

She tried to move closer, to comfort him, but he held up both hands to keep her away. "Well, that's it. No more. You go back to Buffy and you tell her that if she wants her windows repaired, she can look in the phone book. Seems like that's all she wants me for these days, and there are a lot of other guys who would be glad for the work."

Afraid to get close, Anya called out to him as he stalked away, "Xander! Come back! She needs you for more than window repairs!"

As he moved out of earshot, she looked down, tears welling in her eyes. Looking back up, she said softly, "I need you."

He was too far gone to hear.

Xander wasn't sure how long he'd wandered along the streets of Sunnydale. He just wanted to be alone—and that made him laugh bitterly. He already was, very definitely, alone.

His stomach rumbled loudly, reminding him that he hadn't eaten in twelve hours or more. Glancing at the street signs, he remembered a diner just a few blocks away. He began walking with more purpose.

Before long, Xander was hunkered down over a buffalo chicken sandwich and a pile of seasoned fries. From time to time he cooled the spicy goodness with a chocolate milk shake. Weird combo, yes, but still tasty. There was a TV behind the counter. It was tuned to one of the countless, cookie-cutter daytime talk shows with semi-celebrity hosts discussing topics that no one much cared about but everyone seemed willing to watch. A news bulletin interrupted the broadcast. The word "morgue" caught Xander's attention.

"The latest in the string of strange events sweeping the streets of Sunnydale took place this afternoon at the city morgue. The victim of a brutal killing has disappeared. Administrative Assistant Mindy Wells, age twenty, died last night after a brutal assault at the hands of a coworker. Sadly, someone has decided to deny Ms. Wells her opportunity to rest in peace. Police believe that her body was removed from the morgue between one and two P.M. this afternoon, by a person or persons unknown. Keep tuned to Action News for updates as this story heats up!"

A loud laugh sounded from the booth behind Xander. He glanced over his shoulder and saw a couple of men scarfing down steak burgers and chili fries. One of them, a burly guy in a too-tight checkered shirt, was the one yucking it up. His buddy was wearing a Dodgers baseball cap and a faded maroon golf shirt with enough greasy spots to display his inability to get a fry into his mouth without dripping chili or cheese on himself.

"Geez, only in Sunnydale. How the hell is a story about a corpse gonna 'heat up' is what I want to know."

Xander dropped a few dollars on the table to pay for his meal. Picking up his shake, he stepped over to the next booth. Checkered-shirt looked up at him, sneering. "What's your problem, boy?"

"My problem? My problem is loud, insensitive jerks who don't know enough to have a little respect for the dead. That's my problem." With that, he upended the shake over the man's head.

With an angry roar, checkered-shirt started to work his bulk out of the booth. His pal in the Dodgers cap grabbed his arm. "Don't."

The other man looked at him in surprise. "What?"

The man in the cap nodded nervously at Xander. "I saw that guy on the news this morning. They was takin' him out of the building where they found that girl."

His friend looked disdainfully at Xander. "Him?"

"Yup," he said. Then he added pointedly, "In handcuffs."

Checkered-shirt's eyes went wide. "Oh," he said. He reached for napkins.

Disgusted, Xander walked out. He wanted to talk to somebody, to anybody. Anybody but the so-called friends who had let him down. Problem was that his other options were pretty limited. In fact, now that Dan was dead, they were pretty much nil. He stood on the corner, trying to figure out where to go and what to do. He was determined to leave his old life behind, but had no clue how to build a new one.

It occurred to him that he had one more option, someone who understood the importance of building something new. He took out his phone and dialed.

An hour later, he stood in front of another unfamiliar door. He hesitated, and suddenly, the door opened. Rebekah stood in the doorway, wearing a T-shirt and jeans. Her hair was pulled back in a loose ponytail. She smiled. "Were you planning to knock?"

Xander smiled sheepishly. "Eventually. This isn't a bad time, isn't it?"

Rebekah shook her head. "No. The bad time was when my phone rang in the middle of a meeting with the mayor."

Xander's mouth dropped open. "Oh my God. I am so sorry. I didn't—"

She waved it off. "Hey, I'd been in meetings since eight this morning with investors and town council members and concerned citizens. Under those circumstances, cutting a meeting short and getting out of two more isn't such a bad thing." She looked Xander directly in the eyes, her concern obvious. "Besides, you sounded like you needed to talk."

"Well yeah, but I didn't mean to interrupt. I—"

"Hey," she said, smiling, "what are friends for?"

Xander returned her smile and walked inside.

She asked, "So, how about some coffee?"

Xander nodded. "Yeah. Coffee sounds nice."

The door closed behind them.

Chapter Fifteen

It was *way* past breakfast time as Dawn came through the door. Buffy and Willow would probably be up and gone by now. Those two were slaves to their alarm clocks. Schedules weren't going to put a drag on Dawn's life anymore. The world didn't come alive until nighttime, anyway, so why did everyone rush home at the first sighting of the moon?

She ran her fingers through her hair. There were few tangles where the industrial-strength hairspray had held its own against the onslaught of time, but she could tell other spots were starting to go flat. She hoped she could replicate the style on her own after some shut-eye and a shower.

Dawn's foot had barely touched the first stair when

Buffy decided to reveal herself. "I hope that you were in some serious, life-threatening danger that you barely escaped," she said, "because I'm not sure that anything less than a raisin-faced vamp is going to cut it as an excuse."

At first, the familiar sinking feeling, the way her stomach started to plunge through empty space, took over Dawn. It was that parental tone her sister adopted when she decided to stop playing sibling and start playing mom.

Ew, Dawn thought. Buffy checks on me in the middle of the night? *What am I, two months old?*

For a flickering instant she felt guilty and worried over disappointing her sister, then the emotions passed. Dawn realized that letting Buffy make her feel that way was stupid, it was all based on being afraid of one thing or another, and she was getting rid of all that nonsense. She slapped her hand against the stairway banister and hopped down to the floor. Buffy was sitting in the living room, on the couch. The morning light was coming in through the window behind her, and she was just a silhouette against it. Dawn figured she had planned it that way. She liked being dramatic. "What makes you think I have to give you *any* excuse?" Dawn asked.

Buffy rose up off the couch and stalked toward her. "Why wouldn't you?" she snapped. "You're suddenly making all your own decisions now? I spent the whole night looking for you. Well, part of it. The part when I wasn't slaying and stuff, but I only walked into that because I had my eye out for you. Dawn, I had no idea what kind of bad beastie might have gotten its hands on you, and I was—"

Buffy stopped in her tracks. She had finally gotten a good enough look at her younger sister to see that a radical change had occurred. "Are you kidding me?" Buffy laughed.

Dawn didn't like the way Buffy had said that. She wanted to throw her lunchbox at her sister's head. Instead, she just said, "Excuse me?"

"If a beastie did snatch you, it clearly has terrible fashion sense. You look like the *Addams Family* decided to play Barbie dolls—with you as Barbie."

"Oh, I'm sorry. The blond bimbo is going to lecture me on looking like a plastic toy?"

If Buffy had an anger switch, Dawn definitely flipped it. "What did you just say?" She was shifting into *über*-Mom mode now. From concerned sister to angry matriarch in two seconds flat. "I'm not sure how joining the spook patrol makes you think you can talk to me like that, but you can't. Not to mention that you're in serious hot water as it is. Most kids aren't dumb enough to follow getting suspended from school with staying out all night."

"Why not stay out? Not like I have to be up for class."

"You know, of all the stupid things you've done—"

Before Buffy could complete that statement, she was interrupted by a loud banging on the front door. "Don't you go anywhere," Buffy warned Dawn. She stomped over to the door and angrily threw it open. "What?!"

Two uniformed police officers were waiting on her porch. There were two more by the cruisers parked at their curb. Both cars had their lights going.

A female officer stepped forward. She had bright red hair and freckles. She looked like Pippi Longstocking, but super ticked off. "Buffy Summers?" she said.

Buffy's anger gave way to concern. *If it isn't one thing, it's another. What's going on now?* "Yes," she said. "Is there something I can help you with?"

Buffy wasn't sure how she should mean that statement, and hoped the officers would infer from it what they needed. Over the course of her time living in Sunnydale, Buffy and her ragtag group of misfits had crossed paths with local law enforcement several times. While the boys in blue had no real clue what kind of things went bump in the night around the Hellmouth—or even what the Hellmouth was—they knew that many of the unexplained events involved the Scoobies. Buffy had been particularly wary of bringing attention to herself following Dark Willow's assault on the jail last spring. It's usually a bad thing when someone staying in your house sets a couple of suspects free. Then there was that whole thing with Xander . . . it had been all over the news this morning. A couple of detectives talked to her on the phone, and Buffy had sent Anya to do what she could to get Xander out. She had to stay and deal with Dawn first.

"Ma'am, we need you to come with us," Pippi squeaked.

"Me? What for?"

Pippi's lantern-jawed partner stepped inside. He

got behind Buffy, so that there was an officer on either side of her. He surveyed the room, including giving a nod to Dawn. She returned it with a wink. It made his brow furrow, but he didn't say anything to her. He turned his attention back to Buffy. "Ms. Summers, where were you last night?"

"Specifically, where were you around four o'clock this morning," Pippi clarified.

Let's see, four in the morning. It was about that time she was in the backroom of one of the local demon dives, asking one of the regional crime bosses if he'd seen a young lady with long brown hair and a perpetual pout. The boss's name was Angus, and he had three horns on top of his head, two tusks growing out of his nostrils, and he smelled like creamed corn.

For some reason Buffy didn't think *that* was an appropriate alibi.

So, she opted for the easiest lie. "That early in the morning I was in bed. You know, the way *normal* people are."

"Can anyone confirm that's where you were?"

Oh, okay, that was a tough one. "Ummm, no," Buffy said. "I sleep alone and, well, everyone else was asleep, too."

Everyone but Dawn, that is. But she thought volunteering that her teenage sister had been out all night in her new getup wasn't a good idea either.

"Seriously, is anyone going to tell me what's going on?" Buffy asked, vexed.

Lantern-jaw grabbed Buffy by her left wrist. Her first instinct was to use her free hand and give him a nice, clean chop to the neck, but she caught herself. This was the Sunnydale PD she was dealing with, not a gaggle of rowdy vamps. "Ma'am," he said, "I'm going to have to place you under arrest."

He attached a cuff to Buffy's wrist, and then grabbed her right arm. He brought it around and cuffed it to the other one.

"Arrest?" Buffy was actually starting to freak out. "Arrest for what?"

Pippi held up a dark green stocking cap. "Do you recognize this, Ms. Summers?"

"It's a ski cap."

The officer turned the hat inside out. "Okay, but do you recognize this label?" She held the cap up so Buffy could see it.

Sure enough, there was a label inside, and it said, PROPERTY OF BUFFY SUMMERS. Shortly after her late mother had found out her daughter was a Slayer, Joyce had gone through all of Buffy's things and sewed tags into each one. Buffy tried to explain to her that being chosen to save the world from destruction wasn't like going away to summer camp, unless that summer camp involved a lot of demon guts and the sucking of blood, but it was too late. That maternal instinct she'd passed on to her eldest daughter had caused Joyce to spring into action, and now all of her clothes declared whom their owner was.

"This has to be some kind of mistake," Buffy protested. "I haven't worn that hat for two winters now. I retired it. Where did *you* get it?"

"Someone left it by the cash register at the Double

Meat," Pippi explained. "If you're going to rob your former employer, you might want to be more careful what evidence you leave behind."

"And there were a *lot* of people who've ID'd you as being on the street last night," Lantern-jaw said.

Buffy thought about it. Her search for Dawn had taken her in the general vicinity of the Double Meat at one point, and there were more people out late, acting crazy—more regular people—than she could ever recall seeing at that hour.

So they already had her in one lie. This wasn't good. . . .

Lantern-jaw kept his hand on her wrist and started to direct her toward the door. "Buffy Summers, you have the right to remain silent," he began.

Buffy whipped her body around so she was facing her sister. "Dawn!" she exclaimed. "Find Willow!"

A hard shove from Lantern-jaw put her facing the doorway again. He leaned his weight on her and starting physically thrusting her out onto the porch. "If you *choose* to give up this right, anything you say may and will be used against you in a court of law."

Buffy yelled, "Dawn, get someone, anyone, and get me out of this!"

"You have the right to an attorney—"

Then Buffy was out the door, being led down the walkway and out of view.

Pippi took off her hat. Her face changed from stern to concerned. "I'm sorry you had to see that, young lady," she said. "Is there anyone else home who can look after you while this is settled?"

"Yeah," Dawn said, motioning over her shoulder, "our friend Willow is just a phone call away."

"Okay," Pippi said. "That'll do until we can have social services drop by."

She put her hat back on and left, closing the door behind her.

Dawn chuckled to herself. That had worked better than even she had expected. Buffy didn't have the faintest suspicion that she had set her up, and with no one else to pin it on, she'd be going down the river faster than a Jamaican bobsledder on ice. She had been mad that Dawn had stayed out all night, but now she was going to be staying out for a long, long time.

Dawn went to the phone. Buffy had wanted her to call someone, and she had said it could be anybody, so why not Tommy?

"Hey, babe," she said. "My sister just caught a black-and-white taxi downtown. Gather up Luna and Big J and come on over whenever you want. We're going to throw a party that's guaranteed to bring the house *down*."

"That's wicked tight, Boo," Tommy replied. "I knew you could do anything you wanted. Buffy never should have underestimated you."

"That's all over now, Tommy. I got rid of the source of my problems, and I'm ready to take that next step."

"Don't worry, kid. It's all good. Before this day is over, your every little question will be answered, and nothing will ever stand in our way again."

• • •

The air five hundred feet up was cooler than it was on the ground. It blew through Willow's hair, massaging her scalp, relaxing her into a state of pure delight.

With her magic completely under control, Willow was fulfilling the most basic of human dreams. It was a simple spell, really. She'd have expected something so wonderful to be more complicated, but *flying* was one of the easiest things she had ever done.

She had often dreamed about flying. Really, who hadn't? It was a great dream to have. Actually doing it was another matter entirely, though. In a dream, one was still subject to outside forces, and you were as much a slave to your anxieties as your desires. Flying for real, doing it on her own free will, there was nothing to hold Willow back. She was feeling her own power, revving it up as high as it would go. She understood how birds felt, how amazing it was to be released from the restraints of gravity.

And Dark Willow felt like a distant memory.

Sunnydale passed beneath her. She could practically see the entire town at once. There was the Magic Box. It looked like it was closed for the afternoon. The Bronze was over there. They were getting a delivery.

Willow veered to the north and headed toward campus. She imagined flying right into Dr. Sands's class, touching down in the middle of his lecture. It was a safe bet that none of his previous teaching assistants were capable of doing *that*.

There was a commotion over near the student store. People from all over campus were running there to see what the fuss was about. Willow dipped to the right and started to descend toward the activity. A voice in the back of her head said she probably should land behind one of the buildings where no one could see her, but she didn't see much point in that. She touched earth in an open spot on the periphery of the crowd. No one seemed to notice, not that she'd care any if they did. She was fearless, for once in her life.

And happy.

Willow stood on her tippy-toes and tried to peer over the mass of students to see what was going on, but the pack was too dense. She considered shrinking everyone to four feet tall, leaving her plenty of airspace to watch whatever action was taking place, but before she could start to put together her shrinking equation, a girl sprang from the crowd and began running up the side of the cafeteria. Really running up it, defying gravity, feet flat on the wall. When she got to the top, she spun around, pushed herself off, and dropped back into the crowd, her foot extended in a judo kick.

Wait a minute. Willow knew that girl. It was the blonde from the computer lab.

Willow began to ram her way through the crowd, setting any stubborn coeds aside with a nice magical push. When she got to the front, she saw that everyone was watching two girls locked in a kung-fu catfight— the blonde and the mousy girl, the two women who had been kissed by John Sizemore. And there was John, off to the side, watching the whole thing—along with a quarter of the student body and a handful of professors.

The blonde threw a punch, and mousy girl jumped out of the way, spinning in the air like a tornado.

Mousy was nearly six feet off the ground. She came down, smacking the blonde across her face with the back of her hand. "I told you, wench, John is mine!" she declared.

So, that was it! These girls were still fighting over John. No wonder he was hanging around, smiling like the king of Christmas. He was living out his sicko male fantasy of having two women fight over him.

Of course, if she was being honest, Willow thought it would be pretty cool for two cute chicks to fight over her, particularly if it was going to be this hyper-drive, chop-socky wire-fu—though free of the wires. Why was this happening? And how?

And why didn't *not knowing* the answers to those questions bother her all that much?

Willow watched as the blond girl did a sweeping lower kick, unbalancing Mousy. But Mousy was more agile than she looked. She quickly righted herself, using the momentum to flip over backward, doing a handspring off the ground. Blondie was quicker, though, spearing her between the breasts with all four fingers of one hand. "Take that, you little whore!" she screamed.

Blondie jumped at Mousy, kicking her in the same spot on her chest—but before she could bound away, Mousy got both hands on her foot. Mousy tossed the blonde over her head, taking the first couple rows of onlookers. Blondie got up and began to charge, and Mousy charged too. Both of them sprang off the ground, soared through the air, punching and kicking at each other as they passed.

Well, even if this is cool, it's just silly, Willow thought. *What're they fighting about? The way John, the kissing bandit, had been acting, he certainly had love enough for more than one person.*

Willow was about to step in and relay her theory to the gladiator girls, when someone tapped her on the shoulder. When she turned to see who it was, her face collided with the person's fist.

Whack!

As she struggled to regain her senses, Willow thought, *Wow, they ain't kidding. You really* do *see stars.* It was like paparazzi flashbulbs were going off around her head.

"Where're your fancy tricks now?"

That voice! Her eyes started to clear up. It was Mel!

A second fist slammed into her stomach. She felt her flesh give way to the impact, felt her feet leave the ground. Everything was rushing past, and she found herself smashing into the battling girls like a bowling ball knocking over the pins. *Strike!*

All three of them ended up in a heap on the ground. Willow was getting onto her hands and knees, trying to gather herself and stand, but Mel was on her again, kicking her in the gut. She was off the ground once more, flying through the air, but this time not by choice. She smashed through a second-story window in the building across from the cafeteria, landing in a deserted science lab.

Using one of the tables to pull herself up, Willow got to her feet. The room was moving in a seesaw

action, and she thought she was going to be sick
Who'd set the college adrift on the ocean?

The room came into focus just in time for her to
see Mel right in front of her, perched in the same win
dow she'd come through. How did he jump all the way
up here?

Then again, she didn't much care. Forget being
disoriented. She was mad now.

"You never should have messed with me," Mel
said, stepping down. Bits of glass were crushed into
even smaller pieces under his feet. "To use your phras
ing, my touchbacks are so much worse than yours
You've been tagged, and I do believe you are it."

Willow was seething now. She took a deep breath
seized her anger, and began to convert it to power. He
fists were glowing with it. "I underestimated you
Mel," she said. "You're not as dumb as you look. No
you're even dumber."

Willow threw a curveball of energy. It smashed
into Mel's side, sending him across the room. His body
plowed through several desks and skidded to a halt on
the floor.

"You think I showed all my cards last time around
huh?" she said. "My tricks are fancy, sure, but
wouldn't use my entire repertoire at the matinee show
ing."

She threw another burst of energy, this time at the
floor. It traveled the length of the room until it hit Mel
bouncing him and the floor tiles around him into the
air, pounding him into the ceiling. Willow raised
hand, extending a force field to hold him there. Let him

hang over the classroom, let him see how far he was going to fall. "I haven't even pulled my rabbit out of my hat," she laughed, and then let go.

Mel plunged to the floor, landing with a loud smack.

Willow held both hands out in front of her, balled into fists. She opened them swiftly and blew across her palms. Flames erupted all around Mel. The boy screamed in terror, feeling the heat of the very real flames.

Willow audibly inhaled. The fire extinguished itself.

Why kill him? she asked herself. *He's beneath me. He's a waste of power. Besides, if I keep him around, he may still prove to be a viable asset.*

Willow paused.

Asset? Why would I consider him an asset?

She felt a pulsing on the back of her shoulder. Her skin was growing warm. That was where her tattoo was.

Mel moaned. He was crying now, looking completely pathetic. She had no time for this. A quick gesture, and an invisible hand grabbed the back of his head and pushed him down, crashing his face into the floor, knocking him out cold.

Okay, something weird was going on. Were thoughts being inserted into her brain? And what was up with her tattoo? Was it heating up because she had expended so much power?

"Well done, Ms. Rosenberg."

Dr. Sands was standing in the doorway.

"Oh, Doctor . . ." Willow was fumbling around for

an excuse to try to explain all this, but she stopped herself. Why should she worry what this fuddy-duddy thought? It was none of his business what was going on. She wasn't going to give him the standard "This isn't what it looks like" routine, because it was *exactly* what it looked like, and Sands could just deal.

"I saw almost all of it, if that's what you're wondering," Dr. Sands said. "I was watching the melee from my window downstairs, and I saw Mel kick you through the window. I must say, I'm impressed."

Normally, Sands seemed to her like a man who was never really completely in the moment. Part of his mind always seemed to be occupied somewhere else. Not now, though. Now he seemed focused, clear.

Which is also how Willow felt. *Interesting.*

Sands motioned toward the hallway. "Do you have a minute?" he asked. "I think we should talk. If you come down to the computer lab with me, I think I've got some information you might find . . . illuminating."

Willow was suspicious, simply because Dr. Sands wasn't. He was too slick. He should at least have been a little bit surprised when his prize pupil was revealed to be a powerful witch.

Still, she went with him. What was he going to do to her? A flick of the wrist, and she could squash him like a bug. Or maybe even turn him into one.

In the classroom, Sands took a seat at the edge of his desk. "Don't worry, Ms. Rosenberg, this isn't an ambush," he said. "I'm here to help, not hurt. Besides, I think we know you could smack my butt into oblivion if you wanted to."

Willow clenched a fist, loading it up with magic in case she needed to strike. "Yeah, about that . . . ," she said. "Well, how did you know?"

"It's my job to know things, Ms. Rosenberg. I'm a teacher. Knowledge is my business, and you're my star student. Your progress is important to me, and you've been progressing at a phenomenal rate lately. Do you know why?"

Willow shook her head. "No."

"A lot of people think that science and magic are two different things," Sands explained. "That's not true. Sure, there is a division between them, but it's not a natural one. It's been manufactured. All things in life are connected, forming the tableau against which reality is played out. Science and magic are built on the same principles. I think you've realized this, even if you haven't put a fine point on it. Unless I miss my guess, you've built your computer programs the same way you've put together incantations."

Wow, he really did have the inside scoop.

"Your power has been increasing, Willow, because the two disciplines are coming back together, returning to the way they should be. With your power and intelligence, you understand how both things work, you see the blueprint of life and how they fit in side by side. In you is the perfect fusion of science and the arcane arts. You are exactly what they need."

"They?" Willow said, puzzled. "They who?"

"All of them." Sands made a sweeping gesture with both arms, as if to indicate the whole room, the whole world. "Everyone—including myself. Including you. There's something happening, Willow. The world isn't so much changing as it is falling back into place, getting back to where it belongs."

A fly buzzed through the air around Willow. She absentmindedly flicked a finger in its direction and incinerated it. It felt like her magic was churning up inside her, growing, and it brought her some relief to release a little bit of it. "But I still don't understand how I got involved in all this," she said. "I thought I was simply taking control of my magic."

"You are," Sands said. "And that's an important part of this plan. For this new world to be forged properly, we need power. They sensed that power in you and activated it. It was like they just had to open a valve, let what was already in you come out, making you everything you ever wanted to be. The beautiful thing is, you've only just begun to imagine what you're capable of. The power is still growing, evolving. There's nothing wrong with it, either, it's just nature at work.

"Everyone is becoming what they were meant to be, Willow. Some are growing faster than others, but that's just natural too. You and one other have been helped along with special care, because the two of you have the inner strength required to take humanity to the next level."

Sands stood. He approached his student. Placing his hands on her shoulders, he looked into her eyes. At first, her shoulders tensed, but as his fingers eased around them, Willow let them relax. "Whatever you want, Willow, it's yours," he said. There was an even tone to his voice. It dropped an octave or two, and she could feel it in her chest. It was as if it was filling her up. "As all of this change comes to pass, there will be a place for those who will stand up and take it. There is a place being held for you. All you have to do is decide to be a part of the development."

An amber flame had been kindled in Willow's eyes. It burned around her pupils, casting its light on everything she saw—and what she saw was no longer what was there, but what Sands was telling her was.

"I'm ready," she said, though the words were perfunctory. The decision had been made for her. "I want to take my place."

Chapter Sixteen

Anya couldn't believe her eyes.

A kid had opened the door. He had no shirt on, and his boxer shorts were sticking out of his baggy jeans. He had a baseball cap on his head, turned around backward. "Yo, whatchu want?" he asked her. "Aren't you a little old to be here?"

"Excuse me?" she replied. "Who are you, and where is Buffy?"

"Who's Buffy?"

"Only the person who owns this house."

"No, *mamácita*, this *maison* be Boo's."

What language was this guy speaking? Anya wondered if even he knew.

"Boo? Who is Boo? Is it that Buffy is too big a word for you to say?"

"Snap! No, it's Boo! You know, *Dawn.*"

Finally, this shirtless boy said something Anya recognized.

"Yes, Dawn," she said. "Where is Dawn?"

"Inside, yo. Where the party's at." He looked Anya up and down. "You can party wit' me if you want."

"Yeah, right," Anya said. "I'd sooner have a Gorsack demon freshen my coffee with his spitting-neck gland."

Anya shoved her way past the kid. He stumbled back, nearly falling down. "Awww, why you gotta play me like that?" he whined.

As soon as she got to the living room, Anya saw it.

It looked like the high school had thrown up in the Summerses' house. There were teenagers everywhere. They were on the couch, on the floor, back in the kitchen—there was even one standing on the mantel of the fireplace, using the ceiling to balance himself. He had on a T-shirt that said, "It must suck to be you."

Hip-hop music was playing on the stereo. Heavy bass lines and incomprehensible lyrics blaring at window-shaking volume. The only thing in the room that was louder was the kids themselves. There was at least twenty of them in that room alone. That didn't count whoever was in the kitchen and, judging by the pounding coming from above, upstairs.

Anya couldn't believe her eyes. She also couldn't

believe no one was charging a cover at the door. Teens are full of disposable income.

A blond girl in a red-and-black-striped halter top was dancing by herself. Her eyes were closed, and she was smiling. She seemed lost in some distant fantasy. Anya grabbed her by the arm. "You!" she said. "You are close to me, so you will do. Where is Dawn?"

The girl looked like she was waking up from a particularly happy coma. She blinked her eyes, leaning in close to Anya, so that their noses were nearly touching. "Who?" she wheezed. Her breath reeked of stale alcohol.

"Dawn. The hostess of this party. Dawn!"

The girl shook her head. The name wasn't registering. *Shoot. What had that boy called Dawn?*

"Not Dawn, but . . . Poo. Do you know Poo?"

"Boo?" the girl asked.

"Yes!" Anya exclaimed. "That's it! Now, answer me. Where's *Boo?*"

The girl put her arm around Anya's shoulder. "Boo is so cool. She's upstairs."

Anya pushed the girl's arm away. "Thanks," she said. "Now go vomit somewhere."

She turned back around and went to the stairs. None of what was going on was making sense to her. Buffy would never allow this kind of chaos to come into her house. She wasn't that much fun.

Halfway up the stairs, Anya heard Dawn's laugh, but she still didn't see her. There were just a couple of girls in dark clothes and freaky makeup sitting on the top step. They were smoking strange cigarettes that smelled kind of like pepper and glazed ham. One of the

came into her head. It was embarrassing. "Good," she said, "she left."

"Who left?"

Tommy had slid in behind her, wrapping his arms around her, putting his feet on the step beneath them. He pulled Dawn close.

"Nobody," she said.

"Sweet. I'm glad Nobody ain't here."

"Nobody was obnoxious," Luna said, blowing out a big puff of smoke. "And her choice of outfits made the old Dawn wardrobe look like Gwen Stefani's."

"Oooooh," Tommy laughed. "You gonna let her diss you, Boo?"

Dawn clicked her tongue. "It doesn't matter," she said. "She can say what she wants, just as long as you keep your promise and tell me what's going to happen."

Tommy gave her a playful slap on top of her head. "You don't quit, do you? My word is bond, yo. I'll tell you. Just not here, not now. I gotta do it in the right place. A'ight?"

The floor began to shake. Big J came thumping out of Buffy's bedroom. "Peep this, T," he said. He was dragging an old chest along the carpet. "There's some weird stuff in here."

Big J flipped the lid, reached inside, and pulled out a spiked mace. He started twirling it around.

"That's tight," Tommy said, "but check this." Tommy dug a hand into his jacket pocket. He pulled out a violet crystal. It was round with jagged eruptions. He held it in the palm of his hand, and it was pulsing with purple light. "That's *magic,* yo. I got it out of one of the upstairs bedrooms. Looked like a chick lived there."

"That's Willow's," Dawn said.

"Well, Willow has one sick stash, you know what I'm sayin'?" He closed his hand over the rock. The light leaked through his fingers. "This party's about to get started *right.*"

Luna leaned forward. "Is that a bliss crystal?" she asked, excited.

"Yeah, girl," Tommy said, "and it works. I'm getting a total happiness buzz off it."

Big J had put the mace back and was playing with some of the crossbow arrows. He stuck one under his armpit and started to stagger around like he'd been shot. "Ohhh, the pain!" he moaned.

"What else has she got in there?" Luna asked.

"All sorts of stuff," Tommy told her. "Lots of witchcraft seasonings, some charms. She's got a miniature vision orb, but it looks like it's been burned out."

Dawn was shocked. She wasn't sure what to think of all this. Tommy sounded like he knew what he was talking about. "How do you know about all that magic junk?" she asked.

Tommy rolled his eyes. "Come on, Boo, I grew *up* in Sunnydale. You can't hang around here that long and not pick up a few things."

Tommy stood up. He put the bliss crystal back into his pocket. He looked in the weapons chest and pulled out shiny silver sai. He held it above his head, let the light bounce off it, admired its polish. Then, without warning, his arm snapped forward and the sai flew from his hand. It stuck into the wall just above Luna's head. It was vibrating from the impact. "Didn't anyone hear me?" he asked. "I *said,* let's get this party started *right.*"

Tommy had put on some real dark hip-hop. "This is the Gravediggaz," he said. "They call it horrocore."

The band rapped about zombies and ghosts and killers. The afternoon sun was at its peak. The kids had been partying all morning. Dancing and drinking and everything else had been taken as far as they'd go. The couch cushions were ripped, and the stuffing was everywhere. There wasn't a picture frame that hadn't had its glass cracked. All of Buffy's weapons and Willow's left-over Wicca material had been uncovered and passed out, and swords were stuck into chairs.

The coffee table was flipped over, its legs broken off. A pentagram was drawn in the center of it. Tommy had carefully laid out a pile of magical ingredients in it, and he was now sprinkling a fine white powder over it. He had a sword in his free hand. It was stained with demon blood.

Big J's sword looked worse. It had a big chunk of mottled green-and-gold flesh stuck to the blade.

Luna was reloading her crossbow.

"Here us, Offishall," Tommy cried, "and arise!"

There was a brief explosion of smoke, and then it imploded, sucking back into nothingness, like it was disappearing into a hole in the air. A skinny-legged, winged demon with scaly skin the color of brick was there in its place. The air smelled like hardboiled eggs and burned wood.

"Who daresss sssummon Offishall?" it hissed.

The demon attempted a snarl, but before it could fully curl its lips, Luna fired her arrow. It lodged into Offishall's neck. There was a small splatter of yellow goo. Offishall screamed as Tommy and Big J leaped on him, plunging their swords into his body. Tommy's thrust, augmented by his super-strength, was so deep, his hand disappeared into the yellow guts. He pulled his hand out, and Offishall stumbled sideways. Tommy lifted the sword above his head, then brought it down fast, slicing the demon's head right off.

Offishall's body silently fell to the floor. His head landed near the kitchen. A boy gave it a kick and sent it flying over everyone's heads and through the front window. The glass would have shattered, had it not already been knocked out.

This was the fourth demon they had summoned to the house just to kill. Dawn knew it was wrong, that they risked pissing off some mighty demony force, but she didn't much care. It was fun hearing them scream, fun seeing Tommy jump into action. She liked that he wasn't scared. None of them were.

Not even Dawn.

"Too cool, T," Big J guffawed. "Let's get a bigger one next time."

"Bigger than you, Tubby?" said a familiar voice tinged with a sharp English accent.

Big J spun around. "Who said that?" he shouted.

He held his sword up. "I'll cut you in two."

Spike was crouched in the broken window, the heavy blanket over him sizzling from the sunlight as great gusts of smoke were billowed off the vamp. He held Offishall's head by one of its horns, the demon's yellow blood dripping from its neck. "What's this, then?" Spike asked. "Someone throwing a soiree and not tell me?"

Dawn was stunned. She had figured if Willow or Xander came by, they'd be easy to get rid of. There would only be one of them, and the kids at the party were legion. She hadn't factored on someone like Spike. Spike wouldn't be so easy.

Tommy stepped over the coffee table and stood next to his friend. "I'm with Big J," he said. "I say we slice you in half."

"Yeah?" Spike laughed. He stepped down onto the wrecked couch, letting the smoldering blanket fall to the floor. "Come and have a go if you think you're hard enough."

Spike tossed Offishall's head at Tommy's feet. Tommy started to step forward. Dawn realized that he likely had no idea who William the Bloody was, had no idea that he couldn't take Spike on. She rushed to him and grabbed his shirt. "Wait!" she said. "I know him!"

Spike hadn't noticed her before. Not in her new getup. He barely recognized her now. If it wasn't for the voice . . .

"You know this dork?" Tommy said. "From where? You go to a lot of Billy Idol look-a-like contests?"

"Billy Idol?" Spike spit. "Piss off! It's been a while since I've killed a child, but any more talk like that and I'll be willing to give it a go."

"Stop!" Dawn screamed. "Spike, stay where you are!"

Spike glared at her. "Dawn, what are you doing?" he asked. "And where's Buffy?"

"Where I put her," Dawn said with a wild grimace. "You can figure out the rest yourself."

"What's that you got on? All that paint and what-not on your face, there. We used to have a word for girls who look like that."

Dawn brushed past Tommy, crossing the room to Spike. "Yeah?" she said. "You better just keep it to yourself. Buffy doesn't want you here, and neither do I!"

That stung the vampire. He pushed the palm of his hand into his eye and moaned. "Nnnngh! We told you coming here was going to be bad."

Dawn didn't know who he was talking to. For a second, she almost didn't recognize him, either, like he had become something else. He then shook his head, shook off the mood that was threatening to take him. "Never mind. What are you messing about with, pet? I'm not sure what to think when I find demon heads on the lawn and the house trashed worse than an Irishman on St. Patty's."

"It's none of your business, Spike. Take your own advice and piss off."

"Now see here, Nibblet, who are you to talk to me that way?"

He reached for her, and Dawn reacted on reflex. Her hand balled into a fist and shot through the air, landing square on Spike's nose. She felt the cartilage give way beneath her knuckles just before her fist collided with bone, then Spike was off his feet, flying backward through the window. A panic seemed to take hold of him as he sailed toward the sunlight, and he only had a split second to put it to use, grabbing the curtains, tearing them from their rods. He landed half a dozen feet away out on the lawn. He rolled over the grass, charring the green blades and releasing puffs of smoke into the sky.

Dawn opened her hand and stared at it. It seemed the same size as always. The fingers were just as thin. *Wow!*

She watched as the humiliated vamp rolled over and got into a crouching position, peeking out from under the smoking drapes. His face had gone ugly—all wrinkles and fangs—and he was growling. His nose was bleeding. If she was reading him right, then if she were going to spill some of his blood, he'd spill some of her little friends.

Chip or no chip.

The glass being shattered wasn't the only damage to the window. The frame itself was completely torn apart, and Dawn grabbed a piece of jagged wood, gripping it tightly in her hand. She looked at Spike, who was all gnarly and nasty on the lawn, inches away from bursting into barbecue. Maybe it was time someone took this beastie down.

"Hey, everybody!" Dawn shouted. "There's a big

jerk of a vampire on my grass! First one to drive a wooden stake through his heart is gonna get a big sloppy kiss from yours truly!"

There was a mad scramble around the room. At least six guys and one girl grabbed whatever stray piece of wood was around and rushed for the window. Even Big J got into the act, lumbering through the window, catching his foot on the sill and doing a faceplant into the shrubs.

Spike looked up sharply at the teens, armed with stakes, spilling out onto the lawn. He was angry and a bit disoriented, but he wasn't stupid. He quickly got to his feet and took off running. A couple of the guys chased him down the block, but he knew the right yard to duck in, vaulting over the backyard fence and leaving his teenage pursuers in the dust—a necessary procedure to avoid *becoming* dust himself. He didn't know what was going on, but he knew he was outmatched—so live to find out another day. Let them eat his smoke.

Back inside, Dawn turned back to her friends. She balled her hand up into a fist and held it in front of her. "Did you see that?" she asked. "Pow! He shot through the sky like he was made out of paper!"

Tommy reached out and grabbed her wrist. "See?" he said, pulling her close. "You think I'd lie to you, Boo? That was proof. You're *becoming*. Pretty soon your sister is going to be a distant memory. Next to you, she's going to be nothing. Less than nothing."

Dawn leaned down and nibbled on the fingers wrapped around her wrist. She looked at Tommy coyly. "Did it bother you that I might have had to kiss someone else?"

"Nah," he said. "I thought the way you were getting all those people's blood boiling was dope. It was kinda hot. 'Sides, anyone who tried to claim their prize would've just been chopped up into little pieces by me."

Dawn laughed. She yanked her arm, using his grasp on her wrist to pull him close. She threw her arms around his shoulders and planted a giant kiss on him. He opened his mouth to accept it.

His sweet-tasting mouth that told her the sweetest things.

For Dawn, the day had been a blur. Looking back at it, she wasn't even sure if she could say she was in it. It seemed to begin with Buffy being hauled off to jail and end with her punching Spike in the nose—but in between, she felt like she had been more inactive than active, like she had been an observer in her own life. It felt like she had gotten her own reality show and could now sit back and be entertained just watching the trouble she was getting into.

And yet, she also had a new vigor for living. There was more strength coursing through her body now than there had been in all the years of her life combined. She was evolving—or, as Tommy called it, becoming.

Big J was flat on his back, lying in the grass and staring at the late afternoon clouds. They had stopped at the Double Meat on the way—giggling to themselves that they were buying the food with the DM's own money—and Big J was absentmindedly chewing on the straw from his soda. Luna had just gotten fries, but she was still picking at them. She liked to eat slowly.

Big J looked over at Luna. "Hey, babe. Wanna make out?"

"Ew!" she cried, closing her hands over her ears whenever she heard anything so oogie. "Sterile bunnies! Sterile bunnies!"

Dawn grinned. That was one of Luna's coolest catch phrases. Dawn dangled her feet over the edge of the reservoir. She watched the water rushing back toward Sunnydale, remembering how only a couple of nights ago she had mused on its predictability, on its always running to get to the same place. That's what her life had been. It had just been rushing toward now, to the woman she was—the word again—becoming.

She was happy that Tommy was sitting beside her. It made her feel incredible that he wanted to be close to her. They were heading for their own fairy tale–romance ending.

Tommy reached over, putting his hand on her shoulder. He started to pull down the edge of her shirt. Dawn thought maybe she should be startled. They had been kissing a lot, but this was going a step further. Plus, Luna and Big J were right there. Really, though, she couldn't find a reason worth getting upset about. She liked his touch, and Boo, the girl she was now, went with what she liked.

He touched the back of her shoulder, touched her skin. She realized he was touching her tattoo.

The one she still didn't know the origin of.

"You know I got one of these, too, right?"

"No, you don't," she said, denying it while simultaneously wondering if this meant he knew how she'd gotten hers. Maybe she could trick him into explaining it.

"I do. We all do."

"Nuh-uh. If you did, I would have seen it in the pool yesterday."

"Nuh-uh right back. Mine's not in the same place as yours. There's divisions, see? That's how they set it up. They. Him. Whoever, whatever . . ."

He stood up and turned around so that his back was to her. He hiked up his shirt, then bent back the waistband of his pants. There it was, the exact same cross-star-barcode design, on the small of his back on the left side, just below his pants line. "See?" he said. "I told you, I don't make this stuff up. Luna, show her yours."

Luna got up. She pulled her shirt over her head so that she was standing there in just her sports bra. She twisted around so that Dawn could see that she had the tattoo on her back, dead center above her waistline. Big J followed suit and showed her his, on the right side of his lower back—opposite of Tommy's. Dawn realized that if all three of them stood side by side, the symbols would all line up.

"They just showed up one day," Luna said. "The way I'm sure yours did."

"Yeah," Dawn said. "I had no idea how it got there."

"Wanna see something cool?" Tommy asked. "Watch this."

He had unbuttoned his pants so he could keep them rolled down just enough in the right place to keep the tat' visible. Tommy went over next to Luna. When they were side by side, the tattoos began to glow with a yellow light. Big J's came on, too, and when Dawn looked back over her shoulder, it had gone bright, as well. And it was warm. "Neat," she said. "But what do they mean?"

Tommy didn't answer. Instead, he walked back to the edge of the reservoir and lay down on his stomach. "There's a reason we come here," he said, stretching his hand down toward the liquid. "It's the water. There's something in it."

As soon as his fingertips touched the surface of the water, it began to ripple and rise. Four spouts shot up into the air, shimmered, and settled into four separate figures—doppelgangers of each of them. They stood there, a quartet of liquid statues in midair, the light from the sun glistening off their bodies.

"It's been going on for a week now," Tommy continued. "Whatever it is, it's everywhere. Every person has drank it or showered in it. The sprinklers soak it into the ground. It's unavoidable."

Dawn flopped down onto her stomach next to him. She dipped her fingers into the water. As she did, she thought of birds, and each of the water apparitions formed a pair of feathery wings, so that they looked like angels. Then Tommy stuck his hand back in after hers, and they changed from her

Dawn got up too. She was all wet, and her legs felt shaky. She didn't like the rage that had consumed Tommy. "But who gives someone something like this for free?" she asked. "What if whoever it was is going to want something in return?"

"She's got a point, Tommy," Luna said.

"No, she doesn't!" Tommy was shouting now. "If whatever did this to us wanted something for it, then we should be grateful and do it. Whatever the request, it would be worth it. Would you tell them to shove it and give them their powers back? Huh, Luna? Big J? I wouldn't!"

He turned to Dawn and looked her straight in the eyes. "What about you, Boo? You want the Wonder Twins to deactivate?"

Tommy brushed past her. He was angry and walking fast, following the reservoir back toward Sunnydale.

Dawn didn't know what to do. Luna and Big J were staring at her, like her answer was what everything hinged on. Their tattoos were flickering. It reminded Dawn of the time her mom had left her car lights on when they'd gone to the movies, and when they'd gotten out, the juice was running dry, the lights were slowly losing their shine.

She looked, and Tommy was getting small, just a shape on the horizon.

Seeing him, she knew.

It was just a short sprint to catch up to him. He heard her coming, and turned to face her. His arms were crossed, his face stern.

"No," she said. "I wouldn't care. Whoever it is, whatever they want . . . you're right. What we have is too good. As long as it's you and me, and if we're like this, it won't matter, because nothing can stop us. I'm not afraid anymore."

"Fear is for mortals," Tommy said, unfolding his arms, his whole body seeming to relax. And he was smiling again.

That smile. Dawn would do anything to make sure it stayed on his face.

He moved in close to her, ran his fingers through her hair, brought her mouth to his.

The kiss was perfect. The sort of kiss that could go on forever.

For the first time in her life, Dawn felt like everything was exactly as it should be, and she thought to herself, *This is what heaven must be like. Like resting your head on a pillow the size of the universe, and never wanting to wake up again, never wanting to let the moment fade.*

Whatever it was she had to do to keep this feeling, she would do.

Just then, she heard a thought in her head, a whispering voice that was not her own.

It would tell her soon enough.

For now, she was at peace.

Chapter Seventeen

Xander was sitting on the couch in Rebekah's living room and he was *worried*. He'd woken up right there, just a few moments before. Then he sat up, squinting in the late afternoon sun as it shone through the balcony windows. He yawned, stretched, and scratched his bare chest. That jolted him wide awake. Bare. As in naked. As in he was wearing nothing more than his jeans. That's when panic started setting in.

Through the half-closed doors to the bedroom he could hear the shower running. Rebekah was in there, also naked. Okay, more naked.

Xander was desperately trying to remember exactly what had happened earlier that day, but his recollections were kind of fuzzy. He remembered

Rebekah listening intently as he'd given her a slightly edited version of the events at Mindy's apartment and Buffy's unwillingness to help him out. He remembered talking to her for a long time, sitting close together exactly where he was sitting now. He was pretty sure there'd been some hugging. Innocent stuff. Comforting-friend kind of stuff. He shifted uncomfortably on the couch. The shower had stopped, and the sound of running water replaced by the hum of a blow dryer. Rebekah would be done soon. Then she'd be coming into the living room.

Oh, God. What if he'd done something stupid? Had he made a pass? Had she? Had . . . *things* happened? Talk about complicating a solid working relationship. He cocked his head to one side, thinking back. Worse than that, as he'd come in yesterday, Rebekah had said they were friends. Friendship was something Xander took seriously. Very seriously. Mostly because he'd had so little of it before the Scoobs had come together in high school. If he'd screwed up this new friendship, if he'd done something to drive her away . . .

Smiling, Rebekah breezed out of the bedroom. She was wearing a dark blue business suit, very much as he was used to seeing her, except that her auburn hair was still swirling loose around her shoulders. She was carrying his shirt. A memory of Mindy wearing nothing more than Dan's shirt flashed across his brain.

"Hello!" she said warmly. "How's my hunky hero doing this afternoon?"

Xander's heart sank and soared at the same time. *Hunky hero?*

"Um, good. Great. Never better. Swell. Super. Nifty. Aces."

Rebekah laughed and tossed him his shirt. He caught it reflexively, barely noticing he'd done so. It was warm.

"I've got some meetings tonight, but I thought maybe we could grab something to eat first."

Xander nodded. "Sure. Sounds great."

Rebekah bobbed her head toward the shirt he was holding. "Can't help with the rest of your stuff, but at least your shirt is clean."

Xander looked down, realizing that what he was feeling was just-out-of-the-dryer warmth. "Look, about earlier—"

Rebekah cut him off with a smile and a dismissive wave. "It's okay. You were tired."

Eyes wide, Xander gulped loudly.

"Next time I'll know better than to let you hold an open beverage when you're about to nod off."

"Huh?"

She chuckled. "You spilled it all over yourself, remember? Faded out right in the middle of telling me a story about your uncle Rory. Lucky for you, I've got a washer and dryer in this suite. Otherwise you'd be parading around with a big, crusty stain on your shirt." She paused and gave him an amused look. "That is, unless you're planning to stroll around with your shirt off the rest of the day."

Flushing red, Xander stood quickly and started

shrugging into his shirt. As he did so, he noticed that the rash on his shoulder had changed. It was more defined, forming a weird kind of pattern. Almost like a tattoo. Strange. Well, not really strange. He regarded it for another moment, then finished putting on his shirt. Not really that strange at all. Almost like it belonged there. He could feel the tension draining out of his body, both from his concerns about Rebekah and about the marking. He gave Rebekah a broad, confident smile and said, "So, you mentioned food."

"There's this fantastic café downstairs."

"Sounds good. I'm *starving*!"

They took the elevator down and began strolling through the lobby, as Rebekah told him about her schedule for the evening. A tremendous, barely muffled crash interrupted their conversation.

Through the wide glass windows of the lobby, they could see a huge pileup of cars just in front of the hotel. Drivers were hauling themselves out of the wreckage, swarming around the tangle of steel. As Xander watched, one man kicked the door of his car, trying to free himself. With a shriek of metal, it flew twenty feet and crashed into a hydrant. The hydrant snapped off at ground level, and a geyser shot into the air.

Then, a tiny older woman, probably in her late sixties or early seventies, grabbed the rear bumper of the truck beside her and tore it loose. She used it to swat at the burly man she was arguing with about the accident. He staggered back a step, then snatched the bumper away and twisted it into a knot of metal.

Another man, whose tweed jacket and glasses kind of reminded Xander of Giles, thrust his hands under the front end of the vehicle nearest him. Then he flipped it out of his way. It rolled over half a dozen times, until a teenage girl, probably just a little younger than Dawnie, slapped it away from her with both hands, sending it crashing through the hotel window. The cacophony of shattering glass was followed by a roar of chaos from outside.

The car came to a screeching, scraping halt just a few yards from where Xander and Rebekah were standing. Not far from them, a terrified bellhop abandoned the cart full of luggage he was pushing toward the elevators and ran. Xander watched him run, thinking he had the right idea, then glanced toward the window again. The people from outside, unfazed by the jagged shards of glass still clinging to the window frame, were surging into the lobby in a wave of crazed humanity.

Xander couldn't believe what he was seeing. Almost everyone in Sunnydale had been turned into a super-Buffy type!

Not him, naturally, but there you are. And, of course, all the super-charged crazoids wanted a piece of him and Rebekah. They were being pulled toward the couple like some giant magnet from the Fortress of Solitude's trophy room was right above their heads!

A woman in a waitress's uniform came hurtling over the car in an impossible leap, a wild light in her eyes. Xander pushed Rebekah back and grabbed the bellhop's cart, interposing it between himself and the crazed woman. She slammed into the shining brass bar that arced over the cart, smashing it to pieces and sending the garment bags hanging from it flying in all directions.

As the woman staggered to her feet, Xander shoved her toward another wild-eyed crazy. The two of them squared off, raining punishing blows on each other as they howled with incoherent delight.

Taking a second to wrench one of the brass poles off the cart, Xander urged Rebekah back toward the elevators. As they threaded their way through the mob, he realized that several of the deranged had already pushed beyond them.

"Xander!"

The sound of his name stopped him cold. He looked around to see who had called out to him. It might be one of his friends. It might . . .

His eyes stopped dead on the impossible sight of Mindy Wells, glaring at him with nasty bloodshot eyes. She was wearing a bright dress in a sunflower print. It was a couple sizes too small, stretching tight across her chest and riding high on her thighs in a parody of the sexy clothing she loved to wear back when she was . . . well, alive. There were bloody handprints smearing the shoulders, and the seam underneath one arm was split. It looked like Mindy had probably torn it right off the body of someone else. Someone who had lost a lot of blood in the process. Eerie green veins stood out on her bare arms.

"Where ya goin', lover?" Mindy leered at him. Her eyes flickered to Rebekah and narrowed to a glare.

"Oh, I get it. Little Mindy wasn't *good* enough for you, but you know this tramp for a couple weeks and you're all over *her*!"

For a second, Xander was stunned. "Huh? No, it's not like that. I . . ." Shaking his head, he continued. "I can't believe I was about to make excuses to a walking corpse."

Mindy ran her hands over her body and winked at him. "What, you don't like looking at me anymore?" She moved toward him. "C'mon, give me a little sugar."

Recoiling, Xander swung the brass pole with all the force he could muster. It rebounded off her skull with a dull *bong*. Mindy staggered. Then she tossed her hair and gave him a petulant sneer. "Now you're really pissing me off."

Xander caught a glimpse of movement from the corner of his eye. A heavy suitcase slammed into Mindy's head. It burst open, showering the girl with shirts, slacks, and underwear. As Mindy swatted the clothes away with distaste, Rebekah dropped the broken suitcase and grabbed Xander's arm. "Come on! We need to get out of here!"

Xander shouted back, "If we can make it to your room, I can set up a safe perimeter!" Then he smashed the knee of a fat man who jumped at them, eyes blazing with gleeful insanity. Sheesh. His army boy training was kicking into gear again!

Rebekah and Xander ducked and dodged and fought their way to the elevators. Behind them, Xander could hear Mindy screaming with rage as the crush of patrons and lunatics shoved her farther from her escaping prey.

At the elevator door, Rebekah pushed the Up button and turned to face the crowd with Xander. The old lady from the street suddenly popped out of the mob, her fists clenched and a wild grin on her wrinkled face. Xander swung the brass pipe, but she was too fast. Grasping the pipe, she ripped it from his hands.

"Let's see how one of you *boys* likes it when someone takes away *your* toys!" With that, she twisted the pipe into a pretzel shape and tossed it aside. Xander heard a quiet *ding* behind him, but it didn't register. He was trying to figure out how to deal with Supergranny without a weapon when a hand grabbed his collar and hauled him backward into the elevator.

Rebekah smiled grimly and said, "Going up!"

Xander was sure the doors would never close in time. Then Mindy shoved her way out of the press of people, bumping Granny in her rush to get at him. The older woman bristled. "Watch where you're going, girlie!" She shoved Mindy. Hard. The girl flew up and over the crowd. Xander watched with relief as the elevator doors slid shut.

He sagged against the elevator wall and grinned at Rebekah. "Thanks for the save."

She returned his smile. "Least I could do."

Pushing himself off the wall, Xander watched the numbers over the door flicker as they ascended. "What I want to know is just what the hell is going on down there. Those people were all mega-strong."

Rebekah shrugged. "You know what they say about crazy people."

Xander shook his head. "Suddenly the entire town goes nuts? I don't buy it. Something is happening. Something . . ."

The elevator jerked to a stop, throwing them both off balance. They clung to each other to stay upright. The overhead light flickered, and the emergency light came on, bathing the elevator in a faded, yellow glow. Once they'd regained their equilibrium, they exchanged embarrassed glances.

"Sorry," said Xander. "Don't mean to be clingy."

Rebekah laughed nervously. "Um, I don't mean to be focusing on the negative, but what are we going to do now?"

Xander jerked a thumb toward the ceiling. "We go up."

Within a few minutes, he'd managed to open the roof hatch and get them both up on the roof of the elevator. They were stuck between floors, the next door about chest high as they stood in darkness. Rebekah glanced over the edge, into the pitch-black elevator shaft. Xander put a steadying hand on her shoulder. "Trust me," he said, "when you're in an elevator shaft, you do *not* want to look down."

She gave him an appraising look. "You've done this before?"

He gave a nonchalant grin. "I'm full of surprises."

It only took him seconds to work open the doors for the floor above. First he boosted Rebekah up, then scrambled up behind her. They stood in a dimly lit hallway. Apparently the power for the entire building had been cut.

Rebekah brushed her palms against her slacks, slapping away the dust she'd accumulated in their climb. "Now what?"

Xander glanced down the hall in both directions. "Stairs." He pointed to the left. "I think the nearest ones are down here."

They moved quickly in the direction he'd indicated. As they neared a bend in the hallway, a strange thumping echoed from around the corner. Xander put an arm out, stopping Rebekah. He held a finger to his lips and quietly moved forward. Slowly, he glanced around the corner.

"Great Googley Moogley!"

Xander sprinted back toward her. Behind him, a gang of crazies rounded the corner. They were grunting and cackling and hollering like a herd of soccer hooligans.

As Xander rocketed past, he grabbed Rebekah's arm and pulled her along. "Then again, let's try the far stairs!"

She stumbled a couple steps and then found her stride. "A little exercise never hurt," she replied.

Both breathed a sign of relief when the way to the second stairwell was clear. Then, as they started upward, footsteps rang out from the darkness below. The faster they climbed, the faster the tempo of steps drifting up out of the shadows.

Sides aching and breathing heavily, they burst out of the stairway door on Rebekah's floor. Briefly, Xander's eyes swept the hallway, looking for something—anything—to block the door. There wasn't anything useful in sight, so they plunged down the hallway toward Rebekah's suite, hoping to stay ahead of the mob. Unfortunately, there was another mob emerging from the gloom ahead of them.

Mindy was in the lead, her too-small dress even more tattered and bloody. Granny had apparently put aside their differences, because she was there, too, her dentures glinting in a nasty, predatory smile.

Behind them, Xander and Rebekah could hear the rattle of the other stairwell door.

He met her eyes and admired the determination he saw there. "We gotta make a dash for your door. You concentrate on getting it open. I'll keep 'em off your back."

"But—"

He shook his head. "No buts. Go."

Together, they turned and sprinted full out toward the suite door, just a few yards closer to them than to Mindy's mob. The dead woman's eyes went wide with surprise at their charge. It bought them a couple more second's grace. Then Mindy screamed and rushed forward, the others on her heels.

Rebekah reached the door and slid in the key card. The green light flicked on and off, and she twisted the handle and shoved open the door. Mindy was almost there. Xander dove through the doorway and hit the floor hard. Aching, he rolled onto his back as Rebekah shoved the door closed.

She was just a second too late. The door flung

inward, knocking her to the floor beside Xander. From the doorway, Mindy glared down at them with hate-filled eyes. Rebekah and Xander looked into each other's eyes. "I'm sorry," he said quietly.

She shook her head slightly. "No, I'm sorry. I've been holding out on you. I had wanted the timing for this to be just right, but the timetable seems to have been moved up and no one sent me a memo. Typical. From the Human Trials to the First Wave. I should have been told—and that I was kept out of the loop makes me really, really *pissed*!"

He blinked in surprise. "Huh, what?"

Rebekah sprang up, effortlessly. Mindy made a grab for her, but Rebekah sidestepped, backhanding the other woman as she staggered past. To Xander's amazement, Mindy was thrown across the room, shattering the balcony windows. She continued through, her legs slamming into the railing outside and pitching her head over heels. She plummeted from sight.

Stunned, Xander watched speechless as Rebekah casually turned to face the crazed mob.

She spoke two words, very distinctly. "End run."

They all stopped like a switch had been thrown. Not one of them moved, not even a tiny bit. They were completely still. Then, one by one, nearest to farthest, they toppled unconscious to the floor.

Struggling to his feet, Xander stared. "How? I mean . . ."

Rebekah turned to him and smiled. She reached out a hand and caressed his cheek. "Shhh. It's okay. I'll explain everything." She turned his face toward hers and looked into his eyes. "Are you okay? Did any of this scare you?"

Xander looked at her, momentarily confused. He shook his head. "No. No, of course not." To his own surprise, he found he wasn't lying. "I mean, sure, definitely something to get the old heart a-pumpin', but scared? Definitely not." He looked back at the crumpled forms on the floor, then back into Rebekah's eyes. "What the hell is going on, Rebekah?"

She took him by the hand and led him toward a door he hadn't noticed before. It was on the opposite side of the room from the bedroom doors. As they walked, Rebekah spoke in a calm, reassuring voice. "Something bigger than both of us, Xander. Something very special and very important."

She opened the door to an office area. A conference table took up the near end of the room. It was covered from end to end with some sort of stark-white building blocks. Xander picked one up to examine it. They were like Klik-tites, plastic blocks he'd played with as a kid. The little bumps on the top fit into the indentations on the bottoms. You could build just about anything with Klik-tites. He remembered some massive structures he'd constructed: castles and bridges and even skyscrapers. He smiled.

"Good," said Rebekah. "That's exactly what I want. Touch them. Touch the table. I want you to close your eyes and picture something. A building. A *city*."

He looked at her, confused. "What do you mean? How?"

She beamed at him. "Don't worry about the how.

Just let your imagination go. Think of this as the ultimate commission." She took both his hands in hers and gazed deep into his eyes. "Just try."

She let go of his hands, and he turned back to the table. What she was saying didn't seem to make any sense, but . . . it *felt* right. Laying both hands on the table, he closed his eyes and *imagined*. Within seconds, he heard the *snick* and *snack* of the blocks snapping together. Only he wasn't putting them together with his hands. *Maybe Rebekah,* he thought. He began to open his eyes.

Rebekah's hands, soft and warm, slid over his eyes before he could see anything. "Don't. Just concentrate on the image in your head. *See* it. *Believe* in it." He did as she instructed, constructing a gleaming skyline in his head, mixing things remembered with things he'd never considered before.

Slowly, the *snickersnak* of blocks ceased. Rebekah removed her hands. Xander opened his eyes.

He gasped in amazement and joy. The table, from end to end, was a beautiful model of a futuristic skyline. "It . . . it's like Metropolis and . . . well, Metropolis." He turned to Rebekah. "Y'know, like Superman Metropolis and the movie. The one with the robots?" He blushed. "I'm such a geek."

She only smiled, completely accepting. "Visionaries must feed their imaginations. Never be embarrassed that you're open to all kinds of input."

"How . . . how did this . . . is this some kind of magic trick? I close my eyes and you have some guys bring in this awesome model?" He glanced from her to the table. "Did you do this?"

She shook her head, still smiling. "No. *You* did. Can't you see? Isn't it *exactly* what you envisioned? How could I know what you would design? How could anyone? It was you."

Seeing his confusion, she explained, "You have a gift, Xander Harris. An ability to take the visions of others—or your own—and transform them into *reality*. Do you realize what a wonderful and rare skill that is?"

Rebekah led him back toward the living room as she continued. "Plus, you've been exposed to things that others have never even imagined." At his panicked look, she squeezed his hand reassuringly. "It's okay. You don't have to hide anything from me. I know you've had to learn to deal with concepts and . . . things . . . that would make most men collapse into a whimpering heap, and you've stood tall among all of it. You should be *proud* of that."

They sat down on the couch. Her eyes blazed with enthusiasm. "There are others, like me, who have been given gifts. The strength that let me save us from that girl was the least of them. There are things inside us now, Xander. Tiny, living machines called nanites. They're self-replicating, microscopic, and imbued with magic. These things are capable of making us gods. That's what we're . . . becoming."

"But who . . . who's doing this?"

Rebekah ignored the question. "We were given our gifts for a reason. We intend to bring about a new world." She grabbed Xander's hands and pulled them close to her. "It will be Paradise, Xander. We'll rid the world of chaos and conflict. Everything will be completely under control: peaceful. Tranquil. Calm."

Her expression changed, from rapture to deadly serious. "It won't be easy, Xander, and we'll need your help."

"*My* help? What can I do?"

"What you did in there, Xander. You can build. You can help remake the world into a shining example of harmony and order. Your vision makes it possible. All you need is the power."

He looked away. It always came down to this. His lack of power.

Rebekah grabbed his chin, forcing his eyes back to hers. "It's okay. None of us can do it on our own. We must all work together, use our own special gifts."

"Okay, so where does this power come from?"

"Don't worry about that. We have someone working on that right now. What I need to know is whether you're with us. Are you, Xander?" Her eyes filled with an almost desperate anticipation.

"Yes." His eyes flashed with an amber light. His dark pupils flickered as glowing lines of arcana and circuitry scrolled across them. "I'm so there."

"Excellent," she said, a cool, satisfied smile playing on her lips. "If all goes according to plan—"

She gasped, winced, and her eyes lit up as she smiled, nodded, and mumbled something to someone who wasn't there.

The strangest thing was that Xander almost thought he heard a voice, too, somewhere in his head.

"Yes, yes, it's confirmed," Rebekah said excitedly.

"You will be working with a very good friend of yours. Someone who has all the power we need."

"Who?"

Rebekah's smile widened. "Willow. Willow Rosenberg."

Chapter Eighteen

Buffy paced back and forth across the ten-by-ten-foot-square women's holding cell. The few pathetic rows of fluorescent lighting outside the bars cast a yellowish tint to her skin. The damp and musky cell reeked of sweat, alcohol, and tobacco smoke. The Slayer glanced at her companion, who was also pacing the chamber. She was a couple of decades older than Buffy, attractive, with deeply tanned skin. Her platinum-blond hair, pulled back into a loose ponytail, sprang up and dropped behind her as she stalked the short length of the tiny room. She was rough looking. It was obvious she had seen a fair amount of living.

The guard had called her Karen. Karen Pliskin, believe it or not. Buffy caught a little tattoo of a snake near her wrist and thought Xander would love that.

Was he here? Had he been released? She was worried about him, worried for him . . . just plain worried. For them all.

Karen didn't look worried. She looked ticked off. She was of average height, a little thin, but finely cut with an athletic build. She wore a burgundy silk blouse tied off to show her abs; low-riding, tight black jeans; and high-heeled black boots.

"So, what are you in for?" Buffy asked nervously.

Karen stopped and stared at Buffy like the Slayer was a bug she wouldn't mind squishing under her biker footwear.

Buffy shrugged self-consciously. "Sorry. It's what everyone seems to say in the movies when this sort of thing happens. My friend Willow tells me they say other stuff in, like, that *Prisoner Cell Block H* TV show, and Cinemax movies with Linda Blair where she's in a women's prison, but, uh . . . didn't much seem like the right sort of somethings to say."

"Are you coming on to me?" Karen asked.

"What? What? No! I was honestly asking what your story was."

Karen cracked her knuckles, one at a time, using her thumb to move from finger to finger. "You're looking for story time, is that it, little girl?"

She sort of laughed when she asked it. Buffy realized that, to this woman, she probably looked like a blond socialite who'd ended up in the hoosegow for something mundane like running a red light. Karen probably saw her as . . . well, as a girl named Buffy.

And this was even before they'd been introduced.

"It's okay," Karen said. "You're scared, and a story will make you feel better. Fine. You'll get your story."

Karen leaned back against the bars. She crossed her arms and looked Buffy straight in the face. "We were having a barbecue," she said. "Me and my old man and some of our friends. I was in charge of the grill, and I was making my special burgers. It's what I season the meat with that makes 'em special. 'S why they give me the spatula. Anyone can toss some seasoning salt or soy sauce on their ground beef, but my secret ingredients put those patties to shame.

"Anyway, I've been with Larry, my old man, since we met at a bikers' rally back in seventy-nine. We've had a lot of barbecues over the years. He's gotten fat on my hamburgers. I know how to make it so he likes them. Doesn't stop him, though, from flapping his gums and telling me every single time how to cook his meat. It's always, 'Karen, make sure it's black!' 'Karen, leave mine on longer than everybody else's!' 'Karen, make sure it's dead. I don't like my food to moo at me!'

"For the first decade, it's kind of cute. It's all so fresh, you can forgive just about anything. The second decade, it's annoying, but you've learned to swallow it, to just ignore the foible and get on with it.

"It's not like I didn't *know* that he was going to say it today. I was waiting for it as soon as I loaded up the charcoal. Sure enough, he came around, and all serious-like, Larry says, 'Karen, put it in the center so the fire can make it look just like one of them pieces of charcoal. I don't want nothin' raw touchin' me.' It was a variation on an old favorite, but today . . . it was just different today. Something snapped inside of me. 'You scared of it being raw, Larry?' I asked him. 'You think I'll give it to you still pink inside? Well, you're right!'

"I didn't really know what I was doing. I started picking up the uncooked patties and throwing them at him, as fast as I could. Wham! Wham! Wham! One after the other. When I ran out of beef, I started throwing briquettes at him. Then the utensils. Our friends tried to stop me, but they couldn't. I didn't want to be stopped. I wasn't going to take his stupid instructions anymore. It was my turn to be in control!"

As Karen told the story, she practically relived it. The anger returned, as did the righteousness and self-belief. Buffy could see that this woman honestly thought her partner had deserved to be pelted with cow bits. There wasn't a doubt in her mind.

"Finally, the cops came," Karen continued. "Larry didn't want to press charges, but since he's my husband, I got dragged in on some cockamamie domestic disturbance law. I guess regardless of whether your spouse wants you arrested or not, they have to book you and hold you for twenty-four hours so you can cool off. Joke's on them, because when I get out of here, I plan to go home and brain Larry with a pot roast."

Buffy's eyes went wide. She reflexively took a step back. She'd been up against a lot of bad dudes in her time, but Karen Pliskin actually scared her.

Karen burst out laughing. "I freaked you out good,

didn't I?" she said. "Sorry. The story is true, but that last bit about the pot roast, that's just a joke."

A sigh of relief shuddered through Buffy's body. "Oh, thank goodness . . ."

"Nah, if I'm going to do it, the ham I've got in the freezer is a lot heavier."

Karen started laughing again. Buffy chose to think it was still a gag.

"Okay, I spilled my beans," Karen said, "it's your turn. What got *you* tossed in the pokey, little girl? You lift the wallet of the wrong rich admirer?"

"No," Buffy said. "They think I knocked over the Double Meat. I didn't do it, though."

"Honey, none of us did it. You know that from those movies you watched, I'm sure."

"Yeah. I guess that means this is the point where I insist that I really am innocent, and you smile and say, 'Of course you are.'"

Buffy went to the bars and pressed her face between them. The air outside the cell wasn't much better, but she'd take whatever tiny improvement was available. "I never realized how long it took to get thrown in jail," she said. "Booking was hellacious. I've had to give less information to get credit cards. Why do they need to know all that stuff? It's not like I'm going anywhere."

"Cops're just nosy," Karen answered. "They think everything is their business."

"I would have at least expected them to be more polite," Buffy said. "Talk about attitude problems. They could have just said, 'Please step this way,' but *nooooo,* it was always a shove over there, a yank over here."

"Sister, you're making the mistake of thinking Johnny Law plays fair," Karen said. "Not when they can get away with it. But you're right—something is making them think they have free reign to do whatever they want tonight. It's like they're looking for a fight."

"I've been here all day!" Buffy said. She kicked at the floor as if there were something there. She really wanted to pound something, to release her frustration. Where were her friends? Hadn't Dawn told them what had happened? At least one of them should have come to spring her. She had been saving up her one phone call, assuming Dawn would have sent someone to help her. Now she would have to use it . . . provided a guard ever came around to check on them. It was all so frustrating.

Worse than the frustration was the *boredom.* She couldn't read the graffiti on the wall anymore. She knew it by heart and, quite frankly, could have lived without having some of those images in her brain. If she could pop open her skull, she'd pour acid in there just to make sure those thoughts were good and dead.

Hoping to see something interesting, she peeked into the next cell over. Three women sat together on the single bed that was the only article of furniture in the cramped room. Looking at them, Buffy was reminded of stuff Willow had told her about pagan rituals—these three were the perfect images of maiden, mother, crone.

The maiden was a girl about Dawn's age, with

thick, long, wavy black hair, dark eyes, and olive skin. She looked every inch a gypsy with her loose, red peasant blouse, her multicolored skirt, and her brown leather sandals.

The mother was a woman of about forty, with short salt-and-pepper hair, sallow skin, a few wrinkles around the eyes and mouth, and gray eyes. Everything about the woman appeared to be gray. She was even wearing a gray jogging suit and sneakers.

The third and last woman, the crone, was at least seventy, and her pure white hair was slicked back into a tight bun at the base of her skull. She was dressed in her floral-print flannel nightgown over which was a blue terry cloth robe and matching slippers.

Buffy didn't know where they went shopping, but clearly it was the same place. The Fashion Outlet That Style Forgot, located just south of civilization, where indoor plumbing and mass communication cease to be.

"Hey, Karen," Buffy said. She kept her voice kind of low, to avoid her neighbors from hearing.

"What's up?" Karen asked.

"You have any more stories?"

"Sure. What do you want to hear?"

Buffy cocked her head, indicating the next cell. "You have the scoop on who these ladies are?"

Karen went over and took a look at their fellow prisoners. "Oh, sure," she said. "They came in after I did and were gabbing up a storm."

Karen pointed at the maiden. "You see Maria Vardouleas?" she asked. "They've got her on grand theft auto. She stole a Porsche off some fat cat when he stopped for his morning latte. She says when she was crossing the street in front of his car, he revved the engine at her and said something stupid, 'Hey, mama, you wouldn't have to walk so much if you had one of these!'

"Maria was on her way to her cleaning job at the Motor Inn. She realized that she was probably working three times as hard as this bozo in his midlife crisis car, and that she didn't have a hope of ever saving up enough money to have a ride anything like his. So when she saw him pull into that Java Hut, she started to think that maybe she should Robin Hood the vehicle for herself. The more she thought about it, the more she thought it was her right to do it. She said she wasn't scared at all, just walked over and hopped in, cracked the steering column, started it up, and hit the highway. The cops chased her until she ran out of gas."

Buffy couldn't believe that such a sweet-looking girl would toss caution to the wind and hijack a sports car. Then again, she'd seen plenty of bad guys come in not-so-scary and feminine-looking packages. Most of them ended up dating Xander.

"Contestant number two," Karen continued, "is Valerie Parker. Valerie is a divorcée whose ex-husband traded her in for a younger model. For some ridiculous reason, the rat and his new cheese moved into a house directly across the street from the one he left Valerie in. This meant every morning she could see him leave for work, and every night he'd come home. Some mornings he wouldn't go to work at all, but would take his cheese out for a joy ride. Valerie had become numb to it, she'd thought, but when the two of them left this morning dressed for a day on the tennis courts, she decided that enough was enough. She'd spent fifteen years being the dutiful Mrs. Parker, doing what she could to make her husband's life easier while he inched his way up the corporate ladder. Everything the rat was giving his cheese to enjoy was rightfully hers. She'd earned it as much as he had.

"So, she decided to take it back. Valerie grabbed the poker from their fireplace and marched across that street. She smashed a window in and climbed through. When the cops arrived, having been tipped off by the rat's silent alarm, Valerie was on her way out, her pockets stuffed with jewelry. She had taken the cheese's stash in its entirety. The cops refused to listen when she said that every necklace, bracelet, and bauble belonged to her. They also found that she had smashed the rat's prized collection of Limogen figurines. She said she had dusted them the entire time they'd been together, and she had never knocked one over. Today, she had seen no reason not to."

Buffy shook her head. "I guess she was done waiting to exhale."

"Sure enough," Karen laughed.

There was a thread to all the stories so far. Buffy could see it plain as the dirty drawings on the cellblock wall. It was even in Karen's. Something had happened to them all during what had been a very routine kind of day. They had somehow been wronged by a man, and his actions had made them decide to forget every boundary they had and just react. They each believed

100 percent in their right to do what they did.

No fear.

"What about contestant number three?" Buffy asked. She was eager to hear how the theme played itself out.

"That one is the strange one," Karen said. "That old lady is Samantha Endicott. You know, from *those* Endicotts. They found her at a grocery store at the crack of dawn. She'd rammed a shopping cart through the glass doors and walked right in. The cops nabbed her in the ice-cream aisle, standing in a pile of melting cartons of the stuff. She said she was looking for a particular brand of strawberry that was her favorite, and she was taking the cartons out one at a time and tossing the wrong ones aside. She said she was hungry for it, but her brother had set rules in the house regarding when everyone else could have access to the kitchen. He was in charge and always telling the family what to do. She didn't see any reason why she should have to wait. She'd been trained to wait and be polite her entire life, and for once, she wanted something when she wanted it."

The crone looked up at them. Was it possible she had heard them discussing her? She sneered at Buffy. "You have a staring problem?" Samantha snarled.

"No, no problem," Buffy said. "I stare just fine."

Oops. Old playground reflex.

"Is that a joke?" the crone asked. "You a funny lady?"

The maiden kicked at the crone's feet, extending her leg across the mother, who was in the middle.

"Why don't you lay off her?" Maria said. "She's probably just horrified by your hideous choice in nightwear."

"Hey, if you're going to kick her, then kick *her*," Valerie insisted. "You kicked me, too."

"Yeah well, you were married for how long?" the maiden asked. "Shouldn't you be used to getting kicked by now?"

"I'm not too old to slap you, you filthy tart!" The crone waved a crooked finger at her.

Maria stood up. "You want to take a shot, you old bat?" she taunted.

Valerie jumped to her feet. "Since you went through me the first time, why not try it again?"

"Hey, you guys need to settle down!" Buffy shouted.

"Shush!" Karen said. "This I *have* to see!"

Just before Karen's wish for bloodshed could be fulfilled, all the lights in the prison began to flicker. The three women halted their fight.

"What's happening?" the crone asked.

Her answer came in the form of a scream. It was another woman, and the sound of it was so shrill, it made Buffy's blood run cold. It echoed through the cavernous hallways. A lightbulb a few cells down popped, raining sparks everywhere. *The scream wasn't that loud,* Buffy thought. *Was it?*

As the sparks cooled, the lights settled at a dim level. The women were starting to get excited. The trio had moved to the bars and were pushing their arms out through them, trying to fit their heads in between. They were shouting for the guards. Conversely, Karen had backed into a corner. "Get against the wall!" she said, balling her hands into fists and spreading her legs. "You can't have anything sneaking up behind you! I ain't scared of these bastards, but I'm also not going to let them get the drop on me!"

A gunshot rang out from the same direction as the scream. Another lightbulb at the opposite end of the passageway exploded immediately after. What was going on? This was getting too weird! There was definitely something happening on down near the entrance to the holding cells. There were loud voices now, shouting. It sounded like everything was going to hell . . . literally.

Buffy went to the door of her cell. She placed her hands on the bars. She was feeling them for weaknesses. She might have to get all macho and bend the bars. Or maybe go one step further and just rip the doors off the hinges. If things were as a bad as they sounded, she couldn't stay locked up any longer.

"You really want to waste all that strength pulling a George Reeves, love?"

Did her ears deceive her?

"Spike?"

"None other." The blond vamp was standing in the corridor, wearing a wry smirk. "It wouldn't be chivalrous for me to let you bust *yourself* out."

Buffy couldn't tell whether she should be happy or angry to see him, since obviously he was the source of all the commotion at the front of the station. She buried her face in her hands. *What a day!*

"Spike, you can't just come barreling in here and tear the place apart. I—"

Just as Buffy was really getting ready to go into chastise-mode, Spike dove to the floor to avoid being hit by a rather large object hurtling through the air. It crashed into the ground and rolled into the wall at the end of the corridor. It was a police officer. A now-unconscious police officer. Someone—or *something*—had tossed it about twenty yards, nearly taking Spike's head off in the process. Maybe she shouldn't have been so quick to assume Spike was the one wreaking all this havoc.

Spike got to his feet. He had switched to his vampire game face—all ugliness and wrinkles and ready for action. Karen and the maiden, mother, and crone all stared at him warily—but without fear.

"Step back, Buffy," he said, clasping his hand on the bars at the center of the cell door and yanking it right off its hinges, breaking the lock with a loud *bang*. "You had enough of finding out why the caged bird sings, then?" he asked.

Buffy stepped out into the open hall. "You bet," she said. She turned back and gave Karen a wave. "You take care of yourself! No more food fights!"

"Always watch your back!" Karen replied, not moving an inch away from her wall.

The trio thrust their arms at Buffy, tried to grab her, demanded she take them with her. She ignored them, but could swear she saw Samantha bending two bars apart out of the corner of her eye.

The design of a jail only afforded them one way

out—the same way they had come in. The room outside the holding cells was where the detectives did most of their office work—sitting at desks and typing up reports, questioning their collars, drinking coffee, and shooting the breeze with their buddies.

Well, on a normal day, that is.

What Buffy and Spike ran into resembled more of a barroom brawl. And one with no clear sides. Cops were fighting cops, criminals fighting criminals, and one or two from the normally opposing camps were trading punches as well. Desks were dumped over, paper was everywhere. And Buffy saw the pot that normally served the coffee get smashed over a uniformed officer's head.

Two criminals in matching black outfits were kicking and scratching at each other. One of them, a blonde, broke free and grabbed a toppled filing cabinet by its bottom. He swung it like an oversized bat, shattering the teeth of his former partner in crime.

Buffy grabbed Spike and pointed. "Did you see that?" she said.

A policeman took a flying judo kick at Spike. The vamp sidestepped him and punched the officer in midair, knocking him into a water cooler. "You only just noticed?" Spike said. "It's bloody mad all over town."

A skinny teenage kid with his hands still handcuffed around a chair was on his feet, swinging the chair around and knocking people over. Once he had cleared a circle for himself, he flexed his arms and busted the cuffs. The chair dropped to the floor. An overweight cop in a shirt and tie charged at him. The kid lowered his body and got underneath the cop's gut. He lifted the officer over his head and threw him at the front wall. The cop went right through, leaving a gaping hole in the reception area.

"Come on, pet," Spike said. "There's nothing we can do here, and I see our way out."

The path to the hole was not an easy one. Buffy didn't like having to hit cops, but when one of them tried to introduce her face to a computer monitor, the appropriate measure of self-defense had to be taken. Things were just as crazy at the front of the station, but Spike had a plan. "Over here, to the janitor's room," he said.

There was an old woman who had an officer on the ground, and she was beating him with her umbrella. Her tiny dog stood by and was barking nonstop. Buffy snatched the umbrella from her hand as they passed. "It's not even raining today," she said. "You shouldn't even have this. There oughta be a law!"

Spike had thrown open the door to the janitor's area. "Hurry up!" he shouted.

Buffy sprinted through before the woman could react, tossing the umbrella behind her. Once she was through, Spike slammed the door and bolted the locks. "They won't last long if they decide to come after us," he said, "but we should be far away by then."

They were on a stairway that leads to the basement. "I came in through here," Spike said. "It leads to the underground tunnels."

He took Buffy through to the back, where a small,

round door opened up into the sewer system. They both went through.

"Okay, now that we're out of there," Buffy said, wrinkling her nose up, yet doing her damnedest to ignore the stink from the gunk at her feet, which would follow her around all day, "can you please tell me what's going on?"

"I haven't the foggiest idea," Spike replied. "The whole city seems to have gone a bit mental. Here I thought I was the only nutter in Sunnydale, but it looks like the insanity plea is catching. Even your little sis has caught the bug."

Buffy stopped. "Dawn? What's Dawn done?"

"What hasn't she, from the look of her?"

"Specifics. As in, make with the. Now."

"She set you up, for one. Who do you think arranged your stay in the county facilities?"

With a quick and savage swipe, Buffy grabbed Spike by the collar of his leather jacket, spun him around, and slammed him against the tunnel wall. "Listen, Count Screwloose," she said, "you'd better not be feeding me any of your sick fantasies."

The vamp started to snicker. "You want to rough up mad ol' Spike? Go ahead. If that's what it takes to get you to touch me, I'm not choosy."

Buffy pulled her hands away roughly and held them in the air, palms up. "Forget it," she said. "You're wrong. You're making things up again."

"Maybe so," Spike said, "but maybe not. The city is cuckoo for dodo birds, and if you don't believe me, ask *them*."

The echo of footsteps was working its way down the tunnel, getting close. Three men came around the bend. They were dressed in work outfits—overalls, hard hats, tool belts. They were grunting, but it didn't sound like it was from the running. It sounded more like the hum of rage. The grunts came through gritted teeth.

The first one to reach them was the smallest. He had a long face and a hooked nose. Buffy didn't notice until it was swinging at her, but he had a hammer in his hand. She was able to block it, but it made her wrist throb with pain. The man pulled a swift move, where he flipped the hammer around in his hand so that the claws were out. "I'm going to tear you down, blondie."

The second man was there now. He was big—both tall and wide—and he had sweaty curly hair peeking out from under his hard hat. "I want a piece of her, too, Ash," he said. "Don't hog!"

The big man raised his arms and lunged forward, ready to scoop Buffy up. "Back off, mate!" Spike shouted, diving between them. He smashed a fist into the big guy's head, but then instantly clutched his own, screaming as a charge from his chip shot through his nervous system.

Buffy took the second that he was distracted and knocked the hammer from Ash's hand. She grabbed him by the overalls and kneed him in the stomach. But the third man was there now. He was more portly, unshaven and perspiring, blond. He threw his whole body on Buffy, and they dropped to the ground. She was able to get under him, pivot her weight. "If you guys were interested in a tumble class . . . ," she said, tossing the man backward over her head, "you should have tried the YMCA." She then pushed herself up with her hands, landing on her feet and pivoting into a fight position. "Or maybe the young ladies' gymnastics class at the country club."

Spike was just shaking off the effects of the chip when the big man rose up to grab him. A sharp, reflexive elbow sent the big man back down, this time for good, but it also activated the chip again. Spike staggered and hit the wall, feeling the sharp shock in his teeth.

Ash pulled a screwdriver off his belt. He ran at her with it held over his head, ready to stab. Buffy executed a perfect roundhouse kick, clipping him across the jaw. He spun around and folded over, crumpling into a heap on the ground. "Sorry, guy, just had to stop you before you made a 'you're screwed' crack," Buffy quipped.

Weakened, Spike stumbled over to Buffy. "You hanging in there?" she asked.

"Just barely," he said.

Both Ash and Big Blonde were getting up again. These guys seemed normal enough, but something had put them on a rampage. They didn't seem too bright, though, and maybe she could use that to her favor. "Hey, Ash," she said.

Ash looked at her blankly. She pointed at Big Blonde.

"Word on the street is that he goes and sees your wife on lunch breaks, and they aren't just having sandwiches, if you catch my drift."

Ash turned to his friend. "Carl? How could you?"

Big Blonde didn't care to explain anything. He just let out a roar and grabbed Ash around the throat. The two men started to thrash around, cursing at each other.

Buffy grabbed the sleeve of Spike's jacket. "Let's go," she said.

A quick sprint down a couple of the tunnels took them to a ladder leading up to an open manhole. Sunlight flowed through the gap, settling in a pool on the concrete below. "Looks like this is your last stop, Spike," Buffy said. "I'm going topside."

Spike stopped her as she stepped onto the ladder. "Don't," he said. "It's not your Sunnydale. It's more like someone split open my skull and dusted the streets with my brain. They've all lost it."

The vampire looked genuinely concerned. Buffy appreciated the sentiment, but she wasn't going to hide down there with him. "I'll see you later, okay? Head back to your old crypt and rest up. I need to check on my sister, make sure you haven't damaged her reputation too badly."

"Ha, bloody, ha. Never listen to Spike, do you, Slayer?"

Buffy scampered up the ladder, disappearing into daylight.

"Never say bloody thanks, either."

With a sudden outburst of anger, Spike banged his fist into the wall, cracking the stone, ripping open the skin of his knuckles. "See for yourself, then, Buffy girl," he whispered, "see for yourself."

Chapter Nineteen

When Buffy was really young, there was a rash of films about nuclear war. Her mother let her stay up one night and watch one on TV. It was about two girls who were trapped in a mall after the bomb went off, which was a concept Buffy could get behind with hardly any effort. Who wouldn't want to have unlimited access to a shopping mall?

Unfortunately, this blissful scenario was shoved to the side by scenes that had horrified her—shots of empty streets with abandoned cars, random fires, crazed survivors looting. It had marred her sleep for several days to follow.

That movie was the first thing Buffy thought of

when she saw the mayhem that had taken over Sunny dale. The mangled remains of fender benders dotted the streets. There was movement everywhere, with people running in and out of doorways, accompanied by the constant sounds of shouting, and breaking glass.

Down by the drugstore, a group of boys had pushed the trash Dumpster to the front of the building. Buffy watched as one of the boys leaped off the roof of the store, his friends cheering him on. He missed his mark a little, crashing into the side of the Dumpster before falling back into the trash. He only laughed, and another boy got in place to do the same thing.

A middle-aged woman was dancing in her undies on the sidewalk, twirling roses in her hands. "Be free!" she declared. "What are you afraid of? This is how God made me!"

An overweight man stood on the hood of a pickup truck, singing Whitney Houston songs off-key and at the top of his lungs. "Thank you!" he shouted, having just finished "The Greatest Love of All." He blew kisses at Buffy. "Thank you for letting me finally fulfill my grandest dream!"

These people were shameless. They were all doing whatever they wanted, with absolutely zero fear or thought of consequences. Their inhibitions were gone. It was all starting to make sense. All the events of the week, they were escalating, moving toward this point. Buffy hadn't realized that they were all connected, but something had clearly taken over the people of Sunny dale. Something was causing everyone to act weird. But what was it, and who had set it in motion?

And why was Buffy unaffected?

It reminded her of one of Xander's comics, where men all over the world dropped dead without warning, except for one. No one knew what made him special, his heart just kept beating.

Buffy was the last man.

The chaos at the center of town had been pretty bad, but Buffy was still unprepared for the state in which she found her home. Buffy figured she could have been living at Animal House and it still would have seemed totally wrong to get home and see your couch sitting on the front lawn. That just seemed to be a lot of work to relax in the sunshine.

All the windows were broken, the front door was off its hinges, and when she looked inside, the place looked like a hurricane had blown through. "Dawn?" she called. "Are you here?"

Buffy didn't know whether to panic or feel relieved that no one answered. When whatever had wrecked the place had done its business, it probably was better if Dawn had been elsewhere. The problem was, she didn't know if Dawn had been there and had been carried off by the monsoon. And even if she had avoided this destruction, that meant she was out on the streets, in the midst of the madness.

And what about Willow? Xander? Anya? Was Principal Wood trapped at the high school?

Trash and debris were all over the living room floor. It looked like someone had detonated a bag of cheese puffs and had either ripped open some pillows or killed a few geese.

Buffy's heart sank.

Her weapons were everywhere. Some were stuck in the walls, some were strewn about the floor.

Even worse, some of the weapons had demon guts on them. There were also a few stray body parts among the beer cans and ceiling plaster. It looked like a slaughterhouse in Hell.

Something had gone down here. There was a fight, a struggle. There were demons. Given what Buffy had already seen today, she knew that anything could have happened . . . and likely had.

She searched the whole house, and it was trashed from top to bottom. The only sign of life was a shirt-less teenage boy passed out in the bathroom. He had thrown up on himself, and an empty bottle was still in his hand. He wasn't waking up anytime soon.

Buffy's mental inventory showed the weapons list was not complete. From what she could tell, a good portion of her arsenal was no longer there. Whoever had attacked had left with them.

The Slayer racked her brain for a clever line, some sort of cynical witticism to show she could still titter in the face of danger, but nothing came.

Her sister, her friends . . . they could be in big trouble.

It was time to hit the streets and find them.

Buffy tried to keep a cloak of stealth around her, but this wasn't like patrolling for fangly beasties in the dead of night. This was bright daylight, and people were everywhere. She was trying to check Dawn's favorite places, but getting to each one took tremendous effort. On the way to the Hello Kitty store, Buffy got in between two guys who were having a contest to see how hard their heads were by smashing things over each other. When Buffy showed up, the bearded gentleman of the duo had a cinder block in his hands. He raised it above his own head, but before he could drop it on his friend's, Buffy grabbed it from behind and yanked it out of his hands.

"Seriously, guys," she said, "let's not examine the irony of how you started using your heads at the same time you stopped."

Of course, what was intended as a good deed backfired on her. The men didn't like having their contest interrupted, and they decided to try to bash Buffy's brains in instead. They came at her at the same time, and she jumped in the air and did a double-split kick that impressed even her.

Except it didn't really faze them. And why should she have expected it to? These guys had worked their way up to smashing cinder blocks on their heads, and from the looks of the junk scattered around them, that meant going through garbage cans, a milk crate, and quite possibly a newspaper machine. "You guys wouldn't beat up on a poor, defenseless girl, would you?"

The clean-shaven man answered her question with a punch in the jaw. Buffy stumbled several steps backward and nearly fell down. These guys were exhibiting way too much strength. In fact, most of the things she had seen showed not only an incredible lack of fear, but everyone seemed to be ten times as strong as they should have been. Could whatever was making people go nutzoid be enhancing their physical prowess, as well?

A bumper had been dislodged from a station wagon and rested in the remains of the car wreck behind her. Buffy grabbed it. It was a bit unwieldy, but it would work. "Time for you to kiss the bumper, fellas," she said, before smacking them in another agile double-shot.

Both men went down. They weren't out, but they were dazed. Buffy took the window of opportunity and motored out of there. Her ego would have preferred to leave the goons breathing, yet incapacitated, but finding everyone else—and particularly Dawn—was more important. The Scoobies had gotten good at taking care of themselves, but her baby sister was still her baby sister.

Buffy checked the ice-cream parlor and the greasy hovel that sold nothing but french fries—sidestepping the daredevil juggling hacksaws, the brawling debutantes, and a man with a handlebar mustache who was wandering around shocking people with his taser, laughing as they twitched and writhed on the ground—and still no sign of Dawn. The obstacle course of insanity was tiring her out, and she hadn't found a single clue of her sister's whereabouts.

The sun was starting to set when she had finished sweeping the arcade. The kids playing nearly naked Dance Revolution were pretty disturbing, as was the whole seminaked dancing trend in general. Was it really that many people's deepest fantasy to let everything go free as if body parts were lab rats that had to be released from their cages into the wild, lest horrible things happen to them?

When she got outside, there were three people near the doorway. One was an older gentleman with silver hair, including a goatee, dressed in hospital scrubs. Another was a girl who was probably no more than eight years old. She had on a cute belly shirt with a cartoon character that had two big hair buns on either side of her head and was sticking out her tongue. The third was another man, in his thirties, wearing the green smock uniform of the Java Hut.

They were all standing very still. They were quiet and calm.

They didn't seem right.

"You guys lost?" Buffy asked. "Did you forget the way to crazy?"

The little girl stepped forward. Her eyes were glazed, her face blank. "It's you who have lost your way," she said—only she said it in a man's voice, a voice Buffy recognized.

Simon's.

"You've become unfocused and forgotten the task at hand."

"I don't think so, Simon," Buffy said. "More like you got confused, thinking I was hear to serve you, when really I'm here to kick your butt."

"I wouldn't suggest threatening me, Slayer," the old man said, also speaking in Simon's voice. "You were chosen to protect the innocent, were you not?

You should be more concerned about the citizens of Sunnydale than you are with besting me."

"Wait a minute, *you're* doing this? You made everyone lose their marbles?"

"Guilty as charged," the coffee *barista* said.

"But only you can keep them from ever getting their marbles back," the little girl chimed in. "I want the last piece of the Soulsword, and you're going to find it for me."

"I want it by this time tomorrow," the *barista* continued, "or I'll turn the insanity up to eleven. The games will be over, and the evisceration will begin."

"I'll make sure the innocents you are here to protect are ripping one another to pieces," the old man said, "and there won't be a damn thing you can do about it."

As soon as he finished the sentence, the old man's eyes began to flutter, and he fainted, drifting to the ground and landing in a heap. The little girl and the *barista* fell like dominos. Simon had left them.

Great! Buffy thought. *Just get the last piece of the sword. Easy peasy. Except I don't know where it is, and I can't find my research partners. What's the deal, Simon—can't help a Slayer out with a clue?*

Then it dawned on her: He didn't know. Simon liked to lord his knowledge over others and act like he was some kind of god; so if he'd known where the final fragment was, he'd have been crowing about it.

On top of that, he always talked to Buffy through some other means. Telephones, graffiti, and now he was possessing people. He didn't like to show his face.

Why? It probably wasn't something as simple as a big zit on his nose. He must have weaknesses. All the big bads did. And keeping his distance meant she couldn't find them out.

She and Simon were doing the usual dance of Slayer and evil being, only he was staying a foot away from her, like a shy nerd afraid to touch a girl.

Buffy was broken from her contemplative state by another familiar voice. "Should've known I couldn't trust you to stay where I put you . . ."

Dawn?

" . . . seeing as how you always have to have everything your own way."

Buffy was elated. She wanted to rush over to her sister and grab her in her arms and hug her. "Thank goodness you're okay, Dawnie. I've been looking everywhere for you."

Dawn stepped toward her. Her hair was teased as high as it could go. She was wearing a black half-shirt with the sleeves ripped off. It left little to the imagination, both top and bottom. Her miniskirt didn't exactly scream "shy," either. In fact, her studded belt was possibly the thickest article of clothing on her body.

Tommy and the gang stood behind her. Buffy was pretty sure that the ax that Big J was carrying was actually hers. "We got your back, Boo," Tommy said.

"It's all right, Tommy," Dawn replied, "I have this."

Dawn stepped close to her older sister, and then jutted to the left. She walked out into the street. A VW Bug was up on the curb, its interior on fire. There was an upside-down SUV, with a small Japanese car underneath it. A trash can on the other side of the street was also burning. Buffy thought again that this place looked like a bomb had hit it.

And there was Dawn, dressed head to toe in black, from the stiletto-heeled leather boots to the dark raccoon makeup around her eyes.

"You've been telling me what to do for a long time, Buffy," Dawn said. "All my life, in fact. I used to be scared of you too. You were the tough and scary Slayer, so I did what you said."

"Dawn, this isn't the place for this," Buffy protested. "We need to find Xander and Willow. Someone trashed our house—"

"*I* trashed our house!" Dawn exclaimed. "I did! You want to know why? Because I could. There was nothing anyone could do to me. There was nothing *you* could do to me. I'm not scared of you any longer. I'm not worried about what you think of me. I don't *care!*" Dawn picked up the burning trash can, lifted it over her head, and hurled it across the street. Buffy barely had time to jump out of the way before the can exploded on the sidewalk, spewing burning garbage shrapnel everywhere.

She should have noticed it right away. Dawn had that look in her eyes. It was a glint, a small spark. She was infected, just like everybody else.

Dawn *belonged* to Simon.

"Dawn," Buffy said, "don't do this. Calm down. You don't know what you're doing."

"That's just like you, isn't it?" Dawn's voice seemed to grow in anger. "You don't agree with what

I'm doing, so it must be wrong. I must not know the right way, because I don't know the Buffy way."

Buffy thought maybe she was starting to go crazy now, too, when Dawn lifted up a downed motorcycle by its front wheel. Wielding it like a club, Dawn came running at her. Buffy tried to move, but Dawn swung the bike, hitting her in the center of her back, sending Buffy skidding across the concrete. Dawn laughed and tossed the motorcycle over her shoulder. It bounced end over end down the center of the road.

"Big, bad Slayer," Dawn mocked. "Thousands of years of tradition. Oh so frightening. Too bad they forgot to give you some real muscles."

Dawn was feeling cocky now. She turned her back on Buffy to tell her friends, "I've totally got this under control, guys. If you just want to chill out, it's cool."

That was her fatal mistake. Buffy sprang into action. She hit Dawn in the back of the knees with her forearm, knocking her feet out from under her. But as she went down, Dawn reached back and got a handful of Buffy's hair. Buffy couldn't believe the force of the girl's grip, the strength of the tug. The next thing she knew, she had been tossed through the air and had landed on the hood of the Bug. She could feel the heat of the flames licking at her neck as she gasped for breath.

Tommy and the others were clapping. "No, no," Dawn said, righting herself. "I didn't do it right. I was trying to throw her *through* the window. I wanted to see how Barbie dolls melt."

Buffy had nearly regained herself. Landing on the car had sent shock waves of pain through her whole body. Thankfully, she was built to take a beating. She could already feel the bruises starting to heal.

Dawn slapped her hard in the mouth. "Have you ever wanted to wipe a look off my face as bad as I've wanted to knock a few off yours?" Dawn asked. "It feels good. You should try it—"

She punched Buffy in the stomach.

"—that is if you can ever get up long enough to fight back."

A backhanded smack in the face.

"Dawn . . ." Buffy was struggling with the words. "This . . . this is Simon. Simon's making you do this."

Dawn grabbed Buffy by her shirt, ignoring the Slayer's words about Simon. "What's the matter, Buffy? Are you scared? You should be proud of me."

Dawn cracked her forehead against Buffy's. The older girl felt her whole brain rattle. Her vision went blurry. *Oh gawd, that really hurrrrrt.*

"Think about it. You always wanted me to take out the trash, and I did just that. You always wanted me to ride a bike rather than bum rides off people, and I did that, too. And you were always harping on me about how I needed to bone up on my self-defense. I'm doing that right now."

With a quick fling of her arms, Dawn tossed Buffy back across the street and through a bakery window. Buffy crashed into the display items. She was covered in frosting and cake.

"Way to go, Boo."

It was Tommy. Lying among the smashed pastries, Buffy could hear the kids talk.

"Don't hold back. Let it all go. If you do, it'll be all good. You won't have a care left in this stupid world."

Not a care? Is that what this was about? Simple teenage depression? No. More like trying to rid herself of all emotion. Dawn hadn't really recovered from their mother dying, then Buffy dying, all of these bad things piling up on her at once. Buffy had tried to be sensitive to this, but maybe she hadn't paid enough attention. It had to be hard for this kid to be caught up in her world. It should have been more obvious to her, given how hard it was for Buffy to adjust to it herself. Dawn wanted to shut down the hurt, and Simon's spell—or virus—or whatever, was helping her do that.

It all went dark around Buffy. Dawn was standing over her, holding the burning Bug in the air. Buffy was in the shadow of it. "Look, sis, I got you a car!"

Buffy had just a split second to move, and she had to keep moving, keep rolling. The car came through the wall, crashing down on the floor. Buffy stayed just inches ahead of it, inches away from being crushed by it.

As the dust settled, she stayed still, hoping Dawn might assume the plan had worked. Sure enough, Dawn stepped away to gloat once more. "Hey guys, check it out!" she bragged. "You ever think you'd see a girl get squashed by a Bug? You know, rather than the bug getting squashed by the girl . . . like an insect thing."

There would just be one chance. Dawn's strength had reached superhuman levels, and Buffy had to take her down quick. Her whole body ached, but she had to suck it up. She saw an electrical cord still plugged into the wall, grabbed it, tugged on it. Its other end was connected to the cash register, and she broke it off.

Dawn was still flapping her gums. "I've heard of a buff-and-wax before, but this time Buffy got waxed."

Buffy leaped on her from behind, wrapping the cord around her upper torso, binding her arms. She twisted it tight and started yanking her sister away from the scene. Tommy and the others were starting to get up as Dawn struggled to free herself. "Stay where you are, you wastoids!" Buffy shouted. "I'm sorry, Dawn, but this is for your own good."

Dawn flexed her arms. The cord snapped, and Buffy was thrown to the ground. "My own good?" Dawn said. "What do you know about my own good?"

Buffy clutched her ribs. One or two might have broken. That didn't go how she had planned it.

Dawn walked over to the corner and ripped the street sign from the ground. She went back over to her sister, who was still lying flat on her back, and strad-dled her. She held the pole to Buffy's chest. "You think you know what's good for me," she said, "but you don't even know what's good for yourself. If you did, you wouldn't be here hassling me, you'd be out doing what Simon says. I know how hard it is for you to *follow* orders since you're usually so busy giving them, but you're gonna have to get used to it. You're in the army now, big shot."

"You're going to be feeling pretty silly, spooky girl, when the boot is on the other foot."

Dawn whipped around. *Who said that?!*

Two dozen vampires had surrounded Tommy, Luna, and Big J. The kids were lying facedown on their stomachs, vampire feet on their backs, the points of vampire swords tickling the bases of their necks.

Dawn tossed the street sign aside and stood. "Who do you guys think you are?" It was all crumbling in front of her, and she didn't like it.

Buffy sat up. She looked across the pruned faces of her rescuers. This was indeed a strange sight. One of them nodded to her. "Look's like you're in a bit of a spot, Slayer," he said. "What's say we cut ourselves a deal . . . ?"

Chapter Twenty

Seeing their *compadre,* Hugo, get taken over by a flesh-eating techno virus and burst into flame had chilled the vampire gang—at least as much as creatures whose bodies are normally as cold as corpses *could* be chilled.

Centuries of tradition had given the vampire nation a pretty static list of options for how their lives could be snuffed out. Stakes, sunlight, beheading—those sorts of things were the deaths they were aware of, tactics they could *deal* with. Slayers had been using them since the very beginning, and everyone was fine with that.

But now, it looked like this current Slayer had gone out and gotten innovative. She'd invented a new way to kill her prey, and it wasn't pretty.

"Our mission is clear," Billy Bob had said. "We need to hunt this Slayer down and kill her. Until we do, it won't even be safe to feed. Not if she's spiking our punch."

It didn't take long for them to realize they'd gotten the wrong idea, however. Their initial hunts for Buffy had put them in contact with Sunnydale's newly unrestrained residents. No one was scared of them any longer. In fact, people were taunting them. One night, they were attacked by a gang of teenagers who worked at the movie theater. They tried to beat the vampires with the faux-brass polls that held up the velvet ropes for the ticket line. One kid even had one of the ropes and was swinging it over his head. Mordo had gotten beamed in his left temple. There was still a scab.

But they knew things had seriously gone south by way of the Hellmouth when a priest had ripped his collar off and dared them to bite his neck. "I'm not scared of the Devil's minions," he said. "In fact, I look forward to seeing where they live."

That was then. This was now. . . .

"We knew it wasn't you, Slayer, when we saw all that weirdness," Billy Bob told her. "That just didn't seem like something one of your kind would do. You folks generally protect people, you don't use them as weapons. Even if you wanted to, I doubt you'd have the *cajones* for it. Even if you had the skills to mess with their blood, you'd never be able to get around using human life like that."

Buffy was holding a wooden stake against Billy

Bob's left breast. She had a chunk of his shirt in her other hand and was holding him against the arcade wall. When the vamps had arrived, taking Dawn's friends hostage, Dawn had had no choice but to let Buffy up. The Slayer's entire body was throbbing with pain, but she knew she had to move fast and get the situation in hand. Billy Bob had addressed her, so he was the one she targeted. He had been sputtering out his story ever since.

"Once we eliminated you as a suspect," he continued, "I have to admit, we didn't have much left to go on. Someone is poisoning the herd, and we have to find out who or we might die of starvation. Seeing as how this someone is making your life miserable, too, we figured we might be able to help one another out, wash one another's backs, as it were."

Big J had begun sobbing. "Let him go," Dawn hissed, "or so help me, I'll put a stake the size of a redwood through you."

Tressa pushed Big J harder with her foot. She gave a flick to the sword she was holding, creating a small opening of skin on the back of his neck. The blood that trickled out was a shocking red. "Go ahead," Tressa said. "We'll see who's faster, Scrawny—you or me. Think you can get here before I can take his head off?"

Buffy let go of Billy Bob's shirt, and instead put her forearm up under his chin, pressing on his relatively useless windpipe. "No one loses their head just yet," she said, "or the Soggy Bottom Boy here gets turned into a Sooty Nowhere Boy."

Billy Bob smiled. "I do believe this is what they call a Mexican standoff," he said.

Buffy twisted the stake in her hand. "I ought to stick you just for the Tarantino reference," she said. "Like we didn't get enough of that from you wanna-be tough guys years ago."

Billy Bob held up his hands. "True enough," he said. "Besides, we're not here to kill you. We're here because I think we need one another. This time, Slayer, we have a common enemy, and it may take all of us to get rid of him."

"Why should I trust you?" Buffy asked. "You're a vampire. You guys lie all the time."

"Fair enough," Billy Bob said. He transformed his face from his scary, oogy-boogy vamp look to his smooth-skinned human face. He signaled his troops, and they all did the same. "We want to show you we mean business. We're here to negotiate."

Buffy stepped away from the vamp. She stayed on alert, though. This could be an elaborate trick. It wouldn't be the first time the undead had tried to pull the wool over her eyes.

Billy Bob rubbed his throat. "Shoot," he laughed, "I bet my neck really *is* red now."

"Tell them to let the kids up," Buffy said, motioning toward Tommy and the others. "You should probably still keep an eye on them, but they don't need to be facedown on the street."

"Do what she says," Billy Bob ordered.

Tressa stepped away from Big J. Phillipe was holding Tommy down, and Fitz had taken Luna. The vamps released the juvies, but they kept their swords on them. More vamps closed in on them from the front and sides, making sure the teens couldn't make a run for it and attempt a counterattack.

Enraged, Dawn stormed at her sister. "Buffy, you're letting these bloodbags keep my friends as prisoners!" she screeched. "Who do you think you are?"

"Who you calling 'bloodbag,' bloodbag?" Tressa laughed. It was clear she didn't much care for Dawn.

"Both of you shut up," Buffy said. "I'm sorry, Dawn, but for right now, only the vamps seem to know how to behave themselves."

"This is whack, yo," Tommy complained.

"Shut it," Phillipe said, "before *you're* whacked."

Buffy didn't like the position she was in. She hated being forced to deal with this kind of scum, but brute force wasn't going to work at that moment. There was no way she could kill Billy Bob and then get to the others before they seriously hurt the kids. As much as she disliked Tommy and his posse, they were innocents under Simon's control, lives still worth saving, and if Dawn had to watch them become a vampire smorgasbord, Buffy wasn't sure she'd ever get her baby sister back.

Billy Bob must have amassed all the vampires in the city. Seeing them all standing together like that— she couldn't even begin to count how many there were—made Buffy start to wonder if maybe her efforts weren't a little bit futile. She was constantly turning the bad guys to dust, and there were still enough of them for a small army. Could she ever really turn the tide?

"So what's it going to be, Slayer?" Billy Bob asked. "You going to join with us, or is this going to be a three-sided war?"

This was one of those ridiculous situations where no answer ever seemed right. These kinds of things made her wish she was a young Slayer again, one who had her Watcher around to make the tough choices. Simon was a pretty bad cat, and one she may not have been a big enough dog to take down—but, at the same time, teaming with the fangs felt like the worst possible thing she could do.

Had she been on death row, the clock would be at 11:59 and she'd be hoping for a call from the governor, something to give her a little more time.

And sure enough, the "phone" rang.

Spike appeared out of nowhere. He plowed into the crowd of vamps, mowing them down like a tractor attacking crops. The element of surprise only lasted for a second, and while Spike struggled with the vampires he had knocked down, half a dozen of them piled on him. He was thrashing among the bodies, throwing fists, yelling. "Buffy!" he shouted. "Are you—"

His words were drowned out as he disappeared beneath his attackers.

Anya had also come out of the shadows. She was on the periphery, and she hit one of the vampires in the back of the head with a steel pipe. He instinctively put his game face on, the wrinkles and fangs and demony eyes returning. He turned on her, and growled.

"Hey, now, don't get all defensive," Anya said. She gave a weak smile, a strained laugh. "Sometimes it's hard to get a guy's attention, you know?"

The vampire growled at her.

"Hold it!" Buffy yelled. "Stop! Everyone stop!"
She turned to Billy Bob. "Call them off."

Billy Bob looked perplexed, but did what she said.
"Cut it out!" he ordered. "Leave the traitor and his
hoochie mama alone."

The vamps froze. They started to pick themselves
up, to step away from Spike. He stood up among them.
He looked as confused as Billy Bob.

Anya, on the other hand, was offended. "'Hoochie
mama'?" she said. "Just because I slept with him
once . . ."

Buffy stepped through the crowd. She grabbed
Spike's sleeve and pulled him out. As he passed, Tressa
bared his fangs at him. "They should have given you
what you deserved."

"These two are with me," Buffy said. "Nobody
touches them. Just like nobody hurts my sister or her
friends."

Buffy looked at Dawn. She had hoped that the girl
was starting to get a grip on the situation, but Dawn
only shot scorn back at her, murderous looks that
would make even the baddies who were all around
them shudder.

"It's bad enough that you want us to work with the
Slayer," Phillipe complained, "but now you want us to
work with Spike, this bleach-blond Benedict Arnold?"

Billy Bob was exasperated. "We knew he was a part
of the group," he said. "We knew this might happen."

Buffy only then realized how much his own kind

hated him. When the military had put that antiviolence chip in his head, he'd joined up with the Scoobies to fight the demon underworld, since he was only permitted to attack nonhumans or else suffer an electroshock to the brain. He had turned his back on his species, and they hadn't seemed to care that it hadn't really been his choice. They *despised* him.

Spike bit his fingernails, his eyes darting everywhere. "Buffy, what are they talking about?" he said. "Work with you? They must be barking."

Buffy motioned Spike and Anya in close. "They're trying to form a truce," she explained. "Whatever is driving the town bonkers is killing them when they try to drink the crazy-people blood. They want to team up to find Simon."

"Might not be such a bad idea," Spike said, surveying the gathering. "This Simon guy is pretty heavy duty."

"I hate to agree with loony tunes here," Anya said, "but he may have a point. With Willow and Xander gone AWOL, and your sister dressing like *Pretty Woman* going to a funeral, the last thing you need is to be fighting an army of vampires, as well. Having them on your side at least means you know where they are."

"You're as crazy as he is," Buffy said, flipping her pointy finger from Anya to Spike. "Both of you must be infected, as well, if you think I'm ever going to fight alongside those killers."

"Buffy, come on, you—"

Another ruckus interrupted Spike before he could finish his thought.

And it was out of control before Buffy had even realized it was happening.

Seven of Sunnydale's senior citizens had happened upon the vampire brigade and started to pick a fight. They were attacking with canes, smacking the vamps around like they were toy dolls. One of them was holding his walker by its legs and was knocking vampires down three at a time. Once Tommy and his cohorts got free, getting Dawn to jump in, it had erupted into a full-on brawl.

In all of their talk of Simon and unholy alliances, Buffy had forgotten about the people of Sunnydale. They posed a large and entirely random threat, and they seemed to be getting crazier and more savage with each assault.

Now the undead were having their clocks cleaned by grandparents.

Buffy went at the old man with the walker first. He had the biggest weapon, and he needed to be taken care of the fastest. She was about to grab him from around the back, when he pushed himself up, using the walker as his pivot, and swung both his legs behind him. He kicked Buffy in the chest, knocking her backward. Clearly he didn't need that walker for actual walking in his current condition.

That was actually good news. Buffy had worried that their bodies might be frail, that the strength was all in their heads, and that by fighting back, she could injure them permanently. It was going to be hard enough to beat them without having to hold back.

The man lifted his walker. He was going to strike

Buffy with it, so she went in low, knocking his legs out from under him. As he crashed down, she snatched the walker from him, tossing it far from his reach. Before he could gather himself, she gave him a sharp chop to the back of the head. His lights went out.

Buffy quickly surveyed the chaos. Two of the old men were being taken down by groups of vampires. The men weren't going easy. They were beating the vamps' heads with their canes, opening up big gashes that would heal soon enough, but likely hurt nonetheless. Dawn was tossing around one of the vampires, hitting him with punch after punch until he dropped. If nothing else, it was keeping her from beating on Buffy.

Tommy, Luna, and Big J had surrounded another vampire—a bald guy in black leather with tattoos on his skull.

Suddenly, a mole-like man with only a couple of wisps of hair lurched at Buffy. He was wearing a hospital robe. These guys must have busted out of somewhere, a nursing home or something. Buffy was quick enough to leap out of his way and avoid a confrontation.

She looked around again. Dawn was no longer in view, but the vampire with the tattoos on his skull was in plain sight. He was on the ground, and Dawn's punk friends were kicking him with fury.

Buffy sprang into action. She went for the biggest first, sucker-punching J in his kidneys, followed by a kick to the back of his knees. She used the large boy's momentum to knock him into his cohorts, taking all three of them out at once. They went unconscious pretty easily, not nearly made of the stuff that Dawnie was; it was like they were just worker ants and Dawn was a hive queen. "You guys need to learn to respect your elders," she said.

Of the last two guys, Billy Bob and Tressa took down one. They had him pinned down and hit his head against the concrete a couple of times until he lost consciousness. The wound wouldn't be very nice, but he would still be alive when he came to.

The final old man was in a fistfight with Spike. They were trading punches pretty evenly, but Spike was being dealt the double whammy of every time he tagged his opponent, it also sent a wave of feedback into his head. Buffy could tell it was becoming too much for him, and with a final cry of pain, Spike grabbed the man's shoulders, spun him around, and ran him straight into a wall. The old guy passed out.

There was too much going on. She had to get things back under control. She scanned the perimeter. No one else was on the attack. Anya had gotten out of the way and avoided harm. Perhaps the best thing to do was try to turn back the clock and return everything to the status quo they'd established before the senior citizens had struck.

"Billy Bob!" she shouted. "Get your people back on those kids!"

Billy Bob signaled, and several of his men once again surrounded Tommy, Luna, and Big J. They were all still out cold, but it was better to be safe than sorry. Dawn reappeared, and having her so-called friends as hostages looked to be the only way o keep her from flying off the handle again.

Billy Bob stepped over to Buffy. "We just showed you that we can be trusted," he said. "We stopped these old farts without killing them or drinking from them. We're ready to fight on what we presume will be your terms."

He was right. All the crazy old people had been taken down without any of them being killed. Some blood was shed, but they didn't have a choice, and no one had taken a free sample—that part, of course, was kind of a *duh,* considering what had happened to their pal when he'd drunk from someone who was infected. Still . . . they had no idea when any more of the Sunnydale-ites would attack, and if she was going to try to take Simon down, she couldn't contain his legions of crackerjacks at the same time, nor could she keep Dawn and the wild bunch in check, not without help. Superpowered baby sis had already swept the street with her once, and she could probably do it again.

"Yes, you did," Buffy said, finally acquiescing. Spike was sitting up now. He was rocking back and forth, but he was starting to compose himself. Buffy stood. "You've got a deal, Billy Bob. We're now allies."

"No, we're not," Billy Bob said.

All the breath left Buffy's body. "What now?" she asked, exhausted.

"We proved ourselves to you, but now you have to prove yourself to us."

"Prove myself? I'm the Slayer. The position speaks for itself."

"It's not you we're worried about, it's *him*."

Billy Bob pointed at Spike. Like a guilty child who knows he's been caught, Spike looked up.

"We need to know why we should trust that one," Billy Bob said. "Not only has he completely abandoned his true nature, but I've heard he's also gone totally crackers. He's already got the strength and skill of one of us. We don't need him getting all Supervamp on us and going berserk. That's one piece of unpredictable I can do without."

Buffy looked Billy Bob in the eyes. "You can trust him because I say you can," she said. "You can trust him because that's part of the deal. He's with me, and I'll take him with me. You'll just have to live with it."

Dawn stared daggers into her from across the street. She looked as if she might launch herself at any moment at the vamps keeping their weapons trained on her pals, but she also gave off the impression that the calculator—or voices—or whatever it was in her head that was allowing Simon to size up the sitch and send messages to her was letting her know even she couldn't reach them in time. One attempt and who knows what the vamps might do? Buffy had said not to kill. But she hadn't restrained them from serious maiming. . . . "I won't ever forgive you for this," Dawn spat.

"Probably not," Buffy said calmly. It was like seeing Angel when he'd turned to Angelus. "But my real little sis just might, if I can get past you to talk to her again."

Buffy extended her hand to the vampire, not taking

her gaze from Billy Bob's. He took a deep breath, and took her hand in his. They shook.

"You got yourself a deal, then, Slayer. We're now fighting on the same side."

Xander couldn't quite believe where Rebekah had taken him. "The mall?" he asked, stunned. "This is Mecca? I mean, maybe for chicks—um, I mean ladies—I . . . ah, you know what I mean."

Rebekah smiled. "This is the greatest community center in Sunnydale. It's central to all, and will draw those who have been activated quickly when we need them."

"Right," Xander said, still feeling as if he were watching a movie unfold around him, his sense of bliss and calm interrupted by minor flurries of emotion when he thought of Buffy and the way she had treated him. . . .

And just then, something in the wide, abandoned food court *changed.*

All the glass around the mall's latest addition, its very own Java Hut, crackled, then melted, and every burner in the place fired up at once, sending streaks of flame high into the air . . . before zipping around like possessed fire elementals and spiraling around the entire kiosk, changing it into a clanging, popping mess of molten metal.

"Geez, Harris, I knew you didn't like that place, but—extreme much?"

Xander turned and was confronted by Willow and a pudgy older guy, a professor type. She looked stronger than he'd ever seen her—save for that time when she'd almost destroyed the world. Yet this wasn't Dark Willow, it was his Willow, his pal, an aura of magical light seeping from her pores, amber circuitry glowing in her eyes.

She held out her hand. "Professor Sands says all we need to do to get this party started is hold hands. Whatdya think, X-man? Wanna dance?"

He thought of all the times in his life when he'd been younger and dancing had been only a smidgen of the things he'd wanted to do with Willow. Yet this request was innocent, at least in terms of anything that might lead to smoochies or gropings and so on . . . yet it was, at the same time, a more intimate and physical request, a chance for a bonding deeper than sweaty skin-on-skin (not that he'd ever run down the merits of that either). How he knew all this was a mystery to him. The information was just there, like it was being uploaded to his brain on an as-needed basis.

And maybe it was.

He took her hand and gasped, feeling like he had jacked into a source of ultimate power. It was like a caffeine rush a thousand times squared, and it made him feel light-headed, euphoric. His vision turned all Terminator-like, with view screens and digital readouts spilling information about every sector of this place, giving him its exact schematics, structural weaknesses and strengths, everything he'd need to tear it down and build it back up again in any way he so desired.

Willow gestured, and a sparkling emerald and amber podium sprang into existence before her. She winked, and a high-tech laptop whipped into existence before it. A little twitch of her nose—she'd always been saying she wanted to master that *Bewitched* move—and the screen flared to life.

"Enter password: GothWiccan4," she said. Tendrils of energy snaked out from the computer, forming a spiderweb of arcane forces throughout the floor of the mall. "Primed and ready to go."

"Now it's up to you," Rebekah said, her beautiful hair cascading to one side. "Just imagine what you'd like this place to look like, what it could be if you had all the money, all the time, all the resources in the world . . . because right now, you do."

The professor guy put his hand on Rebekah's shoulder. "Use it wisely. Use it to carry out the will of the one who is many, the many who are one."

Xander shook his head, wishing these guys would just speak English. Then, suddenly, clear understanding came to him again. They were all connected by the force that was—Simon. And he, or it, in turn, lived through all of them.

How had this happened?

"I'll tell you the story," the professor said. "Once you've begun your divine work, take the power now, both of you. And do what you will . . ."

The power they were talking about was surging up through Willow, all the magickal force in the world reaching up and slamming against her like killer waves bouncing off Superman's chest, leaving as much energy as her body could handle, no more.

It was more than enough.

Xander closed his eyes, feeling his every nerve joining with that of Willow's, and listened as pictures of a new world, a techno-organic Heaven on Earth, formed in his head . . . and elsewhere.

A shadowy ripple swept the walls in spastic fits and starts. Behind the wave of darkness, lights began to flicker. Tracings of circuitry and arcane glyphs began to pulse with a ghastly green light. The surfaces shuddered and took on a dull metallic sheen. Irregular shapes bulged and twisted into some kind of hyper-advanced machinery. As the effect surged along the walls, a dull hum sounded through the mall, a jaw-aching vibration that sent an unsettling sympathetic shudder in all those present.

Xander had control of this—up to a point. The flares in design, the look of the place, all that, was his domain . . . so long as it served the Progenitor's/Simon's purpose.

So long as it gave Simon what he wanted.

"It is only human to be curious," the professor said. "My name is Dr. Julian Sands. By all rights, I should not be alive, not standing before you now. But strange things have happened to me. Portals of discovery have opened in my mind, and I have journeyed to places few have seen without losing their sanity—and returned. It began when I was told I was dying and there was no cure for my illness. There are few motivators stronger than that to spur one into any and every desperate course of action, I can assure you. Since I was a boy, I had been in love with the idea of nano-technology, microscopic robotic entities with practically limitless power and potential uses. In my spare time, before I fell ill, I had been examining every breakthrough in this largely theoretical science, so I knew it all by rote."

Xander took it all in—while he engineered further changes to the world about him, Willow was silently encouraging him and providing the magickal resources necessary. He could feel the nanites within him, communicating his desires, merging them with their own. Through the now-polarized window of what had been a Gap, the display lighting snaked out of the ceilings on long conduits, their spotlight gaze illuminating inexplicable corners of the vast machine that the mall was becoming. The mannequins, awash with glowing traceries, bent and twisted, shifting into strange engines, pistons pumping, throbbing with powerful energies.

"I also knew it was impossible," Sands went on, "at least without our understanding of the natural world. But there was more here in Sunnydale, so much more . . . magick, mysticism, beings capable of more than the impossible. Thus I delved into a study of this town's hidden face, and I ultimately came into possession of the sorcerer's book, which revealed the secrets of the magickal world to him. Using a magickal energy source to power my microscopic machines, he tried again, and this time, found success."

Xander knew the success that Sands was talking about. The phenomenon, the transformation he had begun, swept on, over lingerie shops, jewelry stores, knickknack kiosks, candle emporiums and shoe stores.

Across the mall, the changes left metal and plastic monstrosities in its wake. Hoses and wiring snaked across the surfaces, connecting disparate mechanisms like a vast circulatory and nervous system. It was as if the building were becoming a single, immense techno-organism.

"Interestingly, I put something inside myself that has literally taken on a life of its own," Sands said calmly. "In order to deal with all the unpredictable challenges the disease within my body would throw at me, the nano-machines had to be able to think for themselves. What I didn't take into account is that once they had defeated the disease, replicating from just a few tiny machines to millions to ultimately win their private war, they would *still* be able to think, still desire to exist and serve a purpose. Their initial mission was to turn chaos into order within my body by destroying the ravaging disease, so they united under a single machine consciousness to do so with every part of me. They simply kept making one improvement after another, making me stronger, faster, and so on . . . and when they had done all they could within me, they looked out through my eyes and saw the disorder of the world in which I lived, and set their sights on creating order there."

Yes, Xander thought. *Order.* Change swept on, engulfing the food court. The metal supports attaching plastic seats to the center pole of each table squirmed and shifted. The seats, flowing into peculiar shapes, flipped over and plunged deep into the floor. The table-tops spread, becoming translucent. An oil-slick rainbow of light rippled beneath their surfaces, like some deranged LCD display.

The professor wasn't done. "What they found in Sunnydale was a chaotic collision of the natural and supernatural world that they found unacceptable. The best way to reconcile these rogue forces was to impose a single controlling will upon them. So they joined up into a single consciousness—calling themselves 'Simon'—and have begun a campaign to take control of the natural and supernatural worlds. This is where the two of you come in . . . where we all, finally, fit."

Behind the vendors' counters, fry machines drained, grill tops rose into spiky patterns, and timers unleashed a cacophony of eerie high-pitched wailing. Metal squealed as it contorted into fantastic devices of uncertain purpose.

One last, rippling wave of green light swept along every surface. Lights dimmed and came back to full intensity, casting stark light on a pulsing engine that was once the Sunnydale Mall.

And there, at its heart, was a place where the Soulsword would reside, a black marble slab with an indentation mapped specifically to the sword's dimensions. That was the altar where a new world would begin to take shape, where, somehow, Simon would spread his message not only throughout Sunnydale, but to everyone and everything in this world.

It was the forge of creation. Paradise's starting point.

Opening his eyes, Xander, only partially himself,

gloried in the sight. Beside him, Willow, also not herself, laughed joyfully.

"All that's left is the sword itself," Sands said. "Then Simon may be revealed, and our great work will begin. And that is in the hands of the one you call the Slayer . . . and the one she calls her sister, though it is not true in many ways, and the child, the Key to all Simon desires, is truly so much more."

Chapter Twenty-One

Buffy took another deep breath. She'd always heard that taking a deep breath and counting to ten was a good way to bring your temper under control. Only she had already counted to 234 and it didn't seem to be working. Maybe it was time to start over. Again.

She glanced at Dawn, at her new goth wanna-be look, and realized she would just have to deal with being pissed. Counting away her troubles wasn't going to cut it.

She and Dawn, along with Anya and Spike, had been prowling the streets of Sunnydale for nearly an hour and a half, trying to figure out a way to get a line on the final chunk of the Soulsword. Or, to be more precise, the demons that needed to be taken down so she could get it. So far, nothing had worked.

Spike seemed to be holding it together, though he appeared just as angry about the change in Dawn as Buffy. "Once we find this thing, I wanna be the one to lop this Simon sod's noggin from his neck." He glared at Buffy, daring her to challenge him. "Got a problem with that?"

Buffy shrugged. "You, me, whoever. No problem."

Anya nodded emphatically in agreement.

Dawn stopped dead in her tracks. "NO! We're finding it *for* Simon." She laughed wildly. "Besides, I won't let you kill him . . . and I *can* stop you."

Buffy rounded on her sister, jabbing a finger at Dawn's face to make her point. "Look, Dawn, right now it doesn't matter what *anybody* wants to do with the sword once we find it because we've got no idea *how* to find it. Your precious Simon didn't tell us squat this time around, and we're not getting anywhere wandering through Sunnydale in the middle of the night."

Anya looked thoughtful. "Perhaps we've missed some vital clue. That's generally the case on the television dramas when the investigators have reached a dead end. For example—"

"Fine," Buffy interrupted, "so what do we know? We know the demons who ooze together to form the sword pieces always have three of something. Three arms, three eyes, three fingers, whatever. Problem is, some stuff isn't going to be obvious. What if it has three hearts or three kidneys?"

Anya bobbed her head excitedly. "Right! I mean,

MORTAL FEAR   431

what if it had three—oh, um, smallfry in the house, never you mind . . ."

Dawn sneered at her.

Buffy's went on. "Anyway, the point is that it isn't necessarily going to be easy to figure out. It's not like we can spend the night chopping every three-somethinged demon to bits."

Spike snorted. "As appealing as that sounds."

"What else do we know?" asked Buffy. She stared toward the ground, scowling with concentration. "There's got to be something." Suddenly, her face lit up. "Wait a second. When the demons die, the ooze all pools together."

Spike shrugged. "Yeah? So?"

She turned and looked him intently in the eye. "It's like they're being pulled together by some invisible force. . . ."

Anya gave a happy squeal and clapped her hands together. All eyes focused on her. "Buffy is right! It's just like with those sword fragments on the kitchen table last night!"

Buffy gave her a confused look. "What are you talking about?"

"When you were out of the room. They got all frisky, sliding around like they were trying to come together. I was forced to move quite swiftly to prevent them. They were positively rambunctious." Her voice dropped, and she looked at each of them as if conveying an important secret. "They were hopping around like . . . well, you know. The bad things. With the floppy ears and the fluffy tails and the big feet?"

"Wot?" laughed Spike. "You *still* going on about bunnies? Off your rocker about bleedin' carrot-snarfin' animals?"

Anya sniffed indignantly. "You're certainly not one to be talking about sanity."

Dawn, grinning maliciously, leaned toward Anya and put her hands up like bunny paws. She bared her front teeth and made nibbling motions with her mouth. Anya shrieked and shied away.

"Stop!" yelled Buffy. "Will all of you just knock it off? In case you haven't noticed, we've got a city in chaos here." She turned to Anya. "Now what was that about the pieces?"

Anya gave Dawn a distrustful glance, but said, "When you left the room, they were trying to come together. Then somebody came in, I forget who, and they stopped."

Buffy nodded. "Okay. So they didn't move when there was a human in the room."

Anya stood up straight and said defensively, "I'm a human. At least, I am *now*. Everybody knows that."

Buffy gave her a puzzled look. "Sure. Then what . . ."

"Perhaps it's because I *used* to be a vengeance demon. Of course, I'm not *now*, but since I *was* at one time, maybe the fragments felt more . . . um . . . comfy. Around me. Because I was a demon. Before."

"Maybe," said Buffy. "But why with the sliding?"

Anya gave a self-satisfied smile. "Well, you know, these artifacts often have a will of their own, even if they lack an intelligence. Like calling to like, and that sort of thing. You know, like"—her voice dropped lower, and she scrunched her face to simulate wrinkles,—"*The ring* wants *to be found.*'" She smiled. "It's very traditional, you know."

Buffy shook her head. "And you're only mentioning this *now* because . . . ?"

Anya shrugged. "Nobody asked me."

Buffy took a deep breath and started counting.

Fifteen minutes later, they arrived at Spike's old crypt. Spike appeared a little uncomfortable there, and it was clear from various items they found strewn about—backpacks, pizza boxes, books, and more—that, in his absence, squatters had taken over the place, then abandoned it. Buffy dragged the pieces out from where she had stashed them, each one individually wrapped. She dumped them all on the table.

Dawn sneered. "Fine. So now what?"

Anya pursed her lips. "Perhaps you should leave me alone with them?"

Buffy gestured for Dawn and Spike to follow her outside.

Spike looked surprised. "Why me? I'm all big baddy. Well, sort of."

Buffy hauled on his arm. "'Sort of' might not be good enough. Or bad enough. Whatever. Come on."

As the three of them stood outside the crypt, noises echoed through the doorway, *clicks* and *clanks* and *shonks*. Then a momentary silence. Anya called out, very excited, "Come in, come in! It worked!"

The sword lay on the table, nearly whole. Buffy picked it up. She couldn't see any evidence that it was ever shattered. Only the point and the last couple inches of the blade were missing. "Nice work, Anya," she said, patting the other woman lightly on the back. Anya beamed at the praise.

"Whoa!" Buffy turned as the sword gave a slight but insistent pull against her grip. " 'Like calls to like,' huh?" She gave them all a quick smile. "Let's move it. The sword apparently has places to be."

Ultimately, it led them across town. Buffy and the others stared at the Farmer Ted supermarket, convinced that something must have gone wrong. The place seemed to be open, all the lights on inside, but it was pretty trashed. A couple windows had been smashed, but no one had bothered to board them up. Shopping carts were overturned and heaped in piles in the parking lot.

"Well," said Buffy. "This is different."

"This can't be right," Dawn said petulantly. "You must have screwed up. As usual."

Buffy gave her sister a look. "Nope. This is where the sword led us. This must be where we're supposed to be." She slid the blade underneath her long leather coat. "C'mon, let's go."

As they walked inside, the market seemed to be deserted. Buffy scanned the aisles warily.

A flicker of movement caught Dawn's eye, and she yelled, "Over there!"

All eyes shifted to a figure emerging from the back room, using a motorized hand-truck to wheel out a wooden skid piled high with cereal boxes.

Buffy looked twice, not sure that what she was

seeing was real. The baggy, saggy skin, the floppy ears. It could only be . . .

"Clem!" Spike called out, grinning. "Whatcha doin' in here, mate?"

Clem's eyes lit up. He hurried over. "Spike? You're up and around. That's *great*!"

Spike shrugged. "Some days better, some worse."

Clem nodded, his ears and chins and jowls flapping as he did so. "I hear ya, buddy." He smiled to the rest of the group. "Hey, Buffy. Dawn. Um, interesting new look. Hey, Anya. Really sorry about the wedding thing. How you holdin' up?"

Anya looked pained for a moment, but she forced a smile. "I'm quite well. Why shouldn't I be?"

Clem looked uncomfortable. "Um, no reason."

Buffy couldn't contain her curiosity. "What *are* you doing here, Clem?"

He grinned. "I'm a packer here. Night-shift people don't seem to mind if you look a bit different."

"Okaaaaay. Then where's everyone else?"

"Oh, I'm the only one who showed up for my shift."

Dawn crowded forward. "You really work here? Why? You're a demon."

"Hey, even a demon needs cash. I'm not big on mayhem and looting, so I work here. Plus, you meet interesting people." He smiled brightly. "Like you guys!"

"So you're here alone?" asked Buffy. That wasn't good. She looked him over for three somethings. Except for chins, she wasn't sure. She'd known Clem for a long time. She hoped that there was someone else around.

Clem shook his head. "Not exactly. The norms have been holding up in the back room for most of the day. Trying to stay away from the scaries, y'know? The human ones, I mean."

Buffy raised an eyebrow. "The 'norms'?"

Clem nodded. "Sure. Humans who haven't been possessed or infected or whatever it is. They're lying low and hoping the crazies don't find 'em. Of course, this time of night they're also trying to keep from getting spotted by the clientele."

"Clientele?"

"Demons have to eat, too, y'know!" said Clem. "Fiend cannot live on kitten alone. Personally, you couldn't pay me to munch a person. Anyway, some demons get by on the furry little fellas, and people of course, but in this day and age, with all the endless food choices being paraded on TV, it's almost impossible to keep from developing a taste for other stuff. I mean, there's cookies and crumb cakes and pretty much everything in the candy aisle. Plus, lots of 'em like some variety in their meat." He gave a low whistle. "Woo boy, they do love the meat, I'll tell you." He slapped his stomach where it bulged over his belt. "Me, I just have to watch the baked goods. Hard not to put on a few pounds."

A deep voice called out from behind them: "Hey, little help over here!"

They all spun around, ready for trouble. Except for Clem. He just strolled casually toward the cash register, where a slim, handsome man was waiting with a cartload of groceries. The rest of them followed cautiously.

The customer looked fairly normal, until you noticed the spattering of greenish spots on his forehead. His long, black hair hung down, concealing them pretty well.

Clem moved behind the register. "Wow. I was just telling my friends how careful I have to be about my weight. How do you manage to stay so thin? You were just in yesterday with a cart this full. What, do you have three stomachs?"

Inside her coat, Buffy felt a tug on the sword. The slight motion was enough to give Mr. Freckles a glimpse of what she was carrying. Eyes wide, he bolted for the back of the store.

Bingo!

She raced after him, but doubts swirled through her mind. Unlike the others, this guy didn't seem to be doing any damage or looking to do any harm. There were no innocent churchgoers or kids or *anyone* in danger. Could she really just run him through? Besides, there were always two others around to help form the sword shard. This guy was alone.

He burst through the stockroom doors, moving fast, but Buffy was right behind. Ahead of her, she could see a small crowd of people huddled near the back door. They looked up, terrified. Buffy couldn't blame them. They had been hiding out from the madness that was washing over Sunnydale, and now it had come to them.

Realizing that his exit was blocked, her quarry turned. His eyes were panicked and seemed to glow with an eerie light. His body began to expand, and there was a loud tearing sound as his shirt split and fell away. His eyes bugged out, turning iridescent and multifaceted. Coarse hairs sprouted from his skin and wings, shimmering like an oil slick in the sunshine, burst from his back.

Buffy tried not to gag. In seconds, the man had become a thing. Something very much like a giant fly. As if that wasn't bad enough, its spiky legs began to hack and tear at its own body. A wet, trembling mess squirmed on the floor for what seemed forever, then resolved itself into three distinct shapes: the fly, smaller now; a disgustingly green and yellow butterfly, but with sharp and jagged pincers in the center of its face; and . . . something else. Something gooey and revolting. Like a giant slug, but with quivering tentacles writhing from what might be its head. The stench was awesome.

The creatures all moved toward the people, buzzing, fluttering, and oozing. Not quite an attack, but definitely threatening. Buffy pulled out the sword, sizing up the situation, trying to be sure no one would get hurt.

With a savage cry, Dawn hurled herself at the butterfly creature. She grabbed it around the neck, keeping the pincers away as they clattered feebly, trying to slice at her face. Her weight was enough to bring it crashing to the ground.

The monster fly zipped over toward them, even as

a sickening crunch made it clear that Dawn had savagely—and without thinking—crushed her foe. "It has to be me," Buffy hollered. "Simon said!"

Buffy leaped forward, swinging the sword with all her might. It sheared off the monster's wings. Crippled, the thing plummeted to the floor just a few feet from Dawn. The sword whirled overhead once more, and Buffy brought it slashing down. The fly twitched and lay still.

Behind her, Buffy could hear the squelching sound of the slug. She imagined its slime-coated tentacles reaching for her.

Spinning, she saw Spike standing over the squirming body of the slug, dumping box after box of salt on the shuddering creature. She got to it and ran it though instantly before it would have shriveled and died. "Impulse control, people! Watch it!"

Hurling the empty salt containers at the body, Spike grinned. Then his face clouded briefly and he said, "Bad luck, that, spilling salt. Very bad luck indeed." He bent down and grabbed a handful off the floor. Standing, he threw it over his shoulder. He glanced at Buffy, uncertain. "That'll be better, yeah?"

Buffy turned away. She stared down at the body of the monster fly at her feet. A second passed. Two. She waited, expectantly.

"It's not melting."

She looked over to Dawn, who was wiping butterfly gunk off her hands. Dawn glanced at the twitching mess at her feet and back at Buffy. "Well?"

Buffy finished it off—and they waited.

"Nothing," Buffy muttered.

Dawn snorted. "Duh. Now what, genius?"

Buffy pointed the sword at the slug, then at the butterfly, then at the fly. Nothing. No pull. The weapon drifted up and over, yanking itself in another direction entirely. She stared down the glittering blade at the huddled people by the door. "I don't get it," she said. "Why would it be pointing at a crowd of normal people?"

Anya cleared her throat loudly. Buffy looked over. "Not all demons are obvious, Buffy. Most of the time I was a vengeance demon, I looked no different from how I do now." She paused. "Now, when I'm completely human, I mean."

Buffy scanned the frightened faces, trying to determine if any of them might be hiding a monster underneath. They all looked so terrified, so vulnerable. How could it be any of them?

Her gaze faltered on a cluster of three women: one old, one young, one middle-aged. She recognized them. They had been at the jail, in the holding cell next to hers. Mother, maid, and crone. It was a phrase she'd heard from Willow at some time or another and it had just seemed to fit.

Their eyes locked on the sword that pointed toward them. They stood, moving forward in a kind of trance.

Buffy was kicking herself. Back at the jail, she'd figured them for possessed. It made sense, considering the amount of damage they'd done to land there in the first place. Then again, maybe it was just their demon nature asserting itself in a time of danger.

The youngest of them looked at Buffy, her eyes

full of sadness and confusion. "I don't understand. What's happening?"

The one Buffy thought as the mother put her hands on the younger woman's shoulders in a comforting gesture. She looked to Buffy. "Can you tell us? We've been wondering for so long."

Uncertainty flickered on Buffy's face.

The old woman watched her expectantly. "We have no names. We have no past. Can you tell us these things?"

But . . . they had lives, just this morning.

Buffy looked at her friends, then back at the women. "I . . . I don't know. I think maybe . . ."

Anya stepped forward, grabbing Buffy's arm. "I know them, Buffy. I've seen them before!"

"What?"

Anya frowned, not looking at Buffy at all, just focusing on the three women. "It was so long ago. Maybe four hundred years. In the Rhineland. They looked . . . different." She nodded. "But I'm sure it was them. The Three Faces. Maiden, Mother, Crone. They symbolize the stages of a woman's life, though I'm not sure of their practical function."

"Okay, yeah," said Spike. "Heard of them. Strange birds. Never quite figured 'em. Reborn every decade or something like that."

The Crone squinted at Anya, then at Spike. She was terrified and confused.

"Um," Buffy began, "I don't suppose it was, I dunno, ten years to the day that each of you came to Sunnydale?"

The trio regarded one another with confusion.

"I'll take that as a yes. Sheesh. That must suck, get mind-wiped every ten years . . ."

"Part of the sorcerer's plan," Anya said. "Hide the last piece of the sword in plain sight, with the pieces having no clue!"

Dawn gave Buffy an impatient shove. "Go on," she whispered. "Kill 'em."

Buffy gave her sister a withering look. "Dawn," she said under her breath, "they don't even know what they are. Forget about the sword—they don't even realize they're demons! I can't just kill them."

"Why not?" Dawn retorted. "They're not real. They're not even human. They're just a thing in human form. We don't need them like this. We need them to be the sword."

Buffy looked deep into her sister's eyes. She flinched at the bloodthirsty enthusiasm that burned in them. "Just a thing in human form? Forget about what they look like and use them for what we need? That sounds familiar, Dawnie. It sounds *exactly* like something Glory would have said about *you*."

Doubt dimmed the fanatical light in Dawn's eyes. "That's different."

"How?"

"It just is. This is about what Simon wants." Her brow furrowed, and she looked away as she tried to reconcile what she was saying and what she felt. "How could he want something bad? He's just trying to make the world better."

Buffy put a hand on Dawn's shoulder. "Is he? If

he's so good and righteous, how can he be asking us to kill three defenseless women?"

Dawn wrapped her arms around her slender body as if warding off a chill. "You don't know anything about him."

"Why don't you explain it, then?"

Dawn spun toward Buffy, shrugging off her comforting touch. "Fine!" she said bitterly. "You want to know about Simon? You want to understand him? I'll take you to him! He'll make you see!" Then she jabbed a finger at the three women. "But *they* have to come too!"

Within an hour, all seven stood before the sprawling, glittering mass of high-tech madness that had been the Sunnydale Mall. It now looked like a futuristic small city—one out of a cartoon, or a comic book. It was sleek, with walkways strung across its highest reaches, regimented, steel towers shaped like cylinders, rectangles, and pyramids, tons of pipes and Gothic-inspired steeples and so much glass, much of it awash with strange inner luminescence, pulsing green, amber, gold, and back again, Matrix-like data lines flowing across every surface like nerves. . . .

Buffy didn't even bother counting this time.

"Xander," Anya said in a small voice as she took in the scene. "This . . . this is Xander's work. I know it."

Buffy nodded. Xander had been acting wiggy, ditto with Willow. Their vanishing acts, and the appearance of this . . . new addition . . . it all added up.

"Simon will take everyone who's worthy," Dawn said, her voice distant, her eyes fixed on nothing in particular. "And he'll make sure they're used to their fullest advantage."

"Stow the company rhetoric," Buffy groused to her possessed little sis. "See the flashing light? I'd say that's a way in . . ."

And it was. The light was a blinding white spotlight angling one way, then the other, set just over a huge steel door with shining silver columns posted at either side like sentinels.

Inside, a glimmering series of long, greenish glowing lines led them through the complex maze that had been the mall.

Buffy felt like a rat in a stainless-steel trap. "So what do you think Simon will be like in the flesh?" she asked.

Anya shrugged. "Unimpressive. Balding. Fat. They usually are, when they go to this much trouble to make themselves seem cool."

Their journey led them to a central command center that looked like it had come from a big-screen science-fiction epic. Roman-style archways, columns, and sweeping floating stages made of dark matter that might have been filled with stars reached up and around them, digital screens bigger than Buffy's living room curving around the rounded courtyard. Four figures stood on a high platform, each engulfed in a light sheen of emerald on black mystical energies, surging with marking that might have been runes, complex mathematical equations, computer language, or tiny bits of magickal energy waiting to be plucked and used. A place that had been set specifically for the sword, a kind of altar, was only half a dozen feet away.

"Well, look who finally decided to show her stupid face," Xander called down. "Got the goods, Slayer?"

Buffy raised the Soulsword. It glinted in the darkened reaches of the courtyard, pulsing with amber light.

"Pretty," Willow said, the word coming out, *prrrrettttty*. . . . "But not all of it. Where's the rest?"

Buffy looked over to the Maiden, Mother, and Crone, who hugged themselves and looked about fearfully.

"Excellent," one of the two older figures behind Buffy's possessed pals said.

Buffy looked up at the portly professor type. "Props to Anya. She knows how to call 'em."

"Oh shucks, I do my best," Anya said, rolling her eyes, nodding and smiling and taking in the love.

"Uh—not now, pet," Spike said softly. "This is the Big Bad meets the Big Good part. Wouldn't want to miss that now, would we?"

"I dunno," Anya said. "Can't we just go to the slaughter-the-baddies part, then go home?"

"Not gonna be that easy," Dawn hissed, suddenly leaping for a high walkway, twenty feet up, where a hand caught hers and swung her up and nearly out of sight.

The place had been designed for acoustic perfection. Buffy could hear every word that passed between Dawn and her "rescuer."

"Boo. Whatchu doin', sweetness?"

"Tommy, how . . . ?"

"Simon sent a couple hundred rabble-rousers to get on those vamps. They couldn't get their own backs and watch us at the same time, so they turn around and we gone. Funny, really. There they are, now . . ."

Buffy looked at one of the closest monitors. It revealed an image of the vampires racing into the transformed mall, a flood of crazed humanity at their heels. These people had once been the sane and boring residents of Sunnydale: shopkeepers, barbers, real estate agents, moms and dads, and more. . . . Now they acted like rabid superhuman dogs answering the murderous call of their master.

"Well, that's headed this way, I have the feeling," Buffy said. She looked and heard running footsteps, and knew her sister was gone.

Of course. Simon was planning to push things to the point where Buffy might have to slay the women, and if she did, and Dawn saw it, that might weaken his hold on her. He had to get her away. . . .

Creep.

She looked up at the professor. "Simon, I presume?"

"Not precisely." He moved forward, spreading his hands open wide. "But you'll have to settle for me . . . at least, for now."

Oh, great. Simon's another one of those major-entrance guys, Buffy thought. *Shoulda figured . . .*

"Tell ya what," Buffy said. "I'll make a deal. You leave now, forget this whole thing, and I don't cram this sword right up your—"

Spike touched her shoulder. "Steady there, Slayer.

We're not exactly the ones holding the cards here, now are we?"

Buffy shrugged. "Aren't we?" She nodded at the trio. "So long as I don't reclaim the last piece of the sword, Simon's plan falls apart. And right now, I don't have the first reason to so much as give any of these women a teensy little love tap, let alone—"

"Good point," the professor called. "Willow? Release the inner selves of these three, will you?"

Just then, the vamp brigade, and the Sunnydale techno-zombie contingent, flooded into what had been the food court, engulfing Buffy and the rest in pure chaos. Spike and Anya were suddenly deep in the fray. Buffy, standing to one side of it all, couldn't hear the incantation Willow was speaking over the angry shouts and pitched fighting as the cornered vamps made their stand and the Sunnydale-ites went after anything that moved, but she didn't have to either. She could already see the effect it was having on the women.

The three women all began to shudder and writhe. Low moans and grunts came from their hunched forms. The Maiden reared back, her arms and legs dwindling and becoming scaly. Terrible black claws stretched out from her fingers and toes, and great wings with ash-gray feathers burst from her back, ripping apart her clothing. Her hair thinned and grew wiry. With a sickening series of snaps and popping, her neck stretched and narrowed. Loose folds of skin sagged from it. Needle-sharp fangs, nearly a foot long, extended from her mouth as her lips withered and pulled back. Blazing red eyes swept the crowd that surrounded them. The others transformed the same way, though each retained some subtle aspect that set one apart from the other.

In seconds, Maiden, Mother, and Crone were gone. In their place were three demonic harpies, slavering and hungry. Buffy cursed Simon under her breath. If he hadn't changed them . . .

The three sprang into the crowd and began slashing with fangs and talons. Buffy rushed toward them, brandishing the sword. The Sunnydalers might be Simon's techno-zombie slaves, but it wasn't like they had a choice in the matter. She kind of knew how they felt.

The Crone turned to meet her charge, stabbing at Buffy's eyes with her clawed fingers. Buffy ducked, dragging the sword along the creature's side as she slid past. The Crone shrieked with pain, her voice an unnerving cross between a woman's shriek and a bird's cry. Spinning, Buffy took off her head with a smooth stroke.

The headless body lurched and lashed out blindly. For a moment, Buffy thought it was still alive. Then it twitched and dropped.

A furious cry rang out behind her. Buffy dove to one side as the Maiden flew through the space where she'd just been standing, its fangs snapping. Rolling to her feet, Buffy lunged while the second creature was still off-balance from having missed its prey. The sword sank deep into its heart. With a gurgling squawk, the thing collapsed.

Dragging her weapon free, Buffy turned to face the last of the monsters. The Mother hovered in the air

not far away, tattered gray wings buffeting the Slayer
with gusts of fetid air and swirling dust with each
stroke. Buffy tried to shield her eyes. Taking advantage
of her momentary distraction, the Mother struck.
Razor-sharp talons slashed the forearm Buffy had
raised to block the dust. Ignoring her injury, the Slayer
grabbed the withered wrist and hauled. The Mother
slammed into her, the creature's fangs snapping shut
just inches from Buffy's face. Over the Mother's
shoulder Buffy could see the jagged tip of the
Soulsword, coated with dark blood. The red glow grad-
ually dwindled in the demon's eyes. Buffy pushed it
away, off the sword.

This time, there was no slow melting and melding.
A whirling maelstrom of prismatic light erupted from
the three corpses and engulfed the sword. Then it disappeared, leaving Buffy blinking, eyes watering. She
could feel their essences bonding with the blade, transforming into the final piece. She couldn't help remembering the three of them in the supermarket, frightened
and unsure.

Her eyes locked on Simon—*to hell with this Professor Sands business, he was who he was*—her anger
boiled up and over. "You want this, Simon?" hissed the
Slayer. "Come and get it!"

Sands sighed. "Gwen?"

The woman Xander had known as Rebekah
stripped off her business jacket and leaped into
action. Xander's face registered a twinge of surprise . . . then his features went dull and slack.

Gwen landed before Buffy, smiling broadly. "I'm

not just the best there is at what I do," Gwen said, shrugging off the Rebekah persona at long last. "I'm the best there is. Period."

"See about that." Buffy unleashed a punishing roundhouse kick to the side of Gwen's head. The other woman barely flinched as pain shot through Buffy's foot and leg. It was like kicking a wall. Scratch that—she'd kicked a lot of walls, and they usually crumbled.

Gwen wasn't crumbly. In fact, she was harder, tougher, and seemingly stronger than Dawn by about tenfold—and Dawn had kicked her butt.

Gwen's lips stretched into a wide smile. She was enjoying this. Buffy dropped back, ready to counter any move Simon's sidekick might throw at her. Gwen's hands dropped to her sides. Her fingers twitched and bulged. A change was sweeping up from her hands, along her forearms. Her skin expanded, reshaped, and took on a metallic sheen. She raised her hands, pointing them at the Slayer. Buffy's eyes widened as she realized that Gwen's fingertips were now hollow muzzles. With a rattling chatter, projectiles spat from the twin five-barreled firearms.

Buffy dove for cover behind the vibrating construct that had been a cell phone kiosk. Bullets panged off its surface and ricocheted. A series of diminishing retorts echoed as the slugs disappeared into the distance.

Please don't let them hit an innocent. Please, please . . . , Buffy thought, desperately scrambling to find some way of taking control of this situation.

She took a peek from behind her cover and saw

Gwen's eyes narrow. For a long moment, the women stood still, sizing up the sitch. Then her mouth opened wide, and her eyes began to glow. Light welled up within her, exploding in a trio of searing, brilliant beams. They lanced across to strike Buffy's shelter, which immediately began to glow and melt. Buffy hunched tighter behind her cover.

Hey, here's a nice break from the everyday, she thought. *A techno-witch spitting lasers. Yep, definitely a whole new kind of problem.*

Looking around frantically for some weapon to use against her, Buffy noticed something weird about the bottom of the construct she was crouched behind. The transformation hadn't secured it to the floor! The kiosk wheels had changed into convoluted assemblies of metal and wire, but it wasn't interconnected with the surface it was resting on.

Swiftly, Buffy rolled onto her back, bringing her knees up to her chest. Her legs uncoiled with blinding speed, slamming into the unit and sending the semi-molten object flying directly at Gwen.

Sneering, the other woman batted it away, her arms now back to normal. Well, as close to normal as she got anymore. Gwen laughed wickedly. "Is that the best you can do? Even if I still sweat, I wouldn't be breaking one."

Buffy rocked back on her shoulders and leaped to her feet in a smooth, swift motion. The technozombies and the vamps were fighting, but their action was being kept far from Buffy and Gwen.

Simon just *loved* to control things. . . .

Eyeing the other woman grimly, she retorted, "Big talk from the Gun Bunny. Maybe I should have brought a bazooka, just to even the odds."

Gwen sneered. "What, you think I need weapons?"

Buffy shrugged. "Just calling it like I see it, Robocopout."

With an indignant snort, Gwen rushed her, throwing expert punches with both hands. Buffy backpedaled, blocking furiously, never quite able to bring the sword around to her advantage. Each impact sent a shock of pain down her arms. Buffy tried a leg sweep, hoping to drop her opponent and gain a little time. Gwen jumped lightly above it and lashed out with a punishing kick to the Slayer's chest. Buffy was pretty sure she felt a rib crack. Maybe two. She sailed back toward a wall and, with a desperate twist, she managed to flip backward in midair, striking with her feet instead of her head. Still, she dropped painfully to the floor. The impact left her breathless. As she struggled to rise, she watched Gwen, trying to anticipate her next move. The other woman paused for a moment, considering.

"Screw this," said Gwen. "I have nothing to prove to you." Her right arm convulsed, reshaping into some new sort of gun. As she brought it to bear, Buffy kicked off from the wall with all her might, rocketing herself along the floor toward Gwen as the woman began to fire. A wave of heat scorched Buffy's back as she slid away from the attack.

Gwen tried to compensate for Buffy's velocity and trajectory, searing a furrow along the floor as she arced her weapon-arm downward, trying to blast the Slayer. Laughing, she realized that Buffy's path was going to miss her by a couple feet. "Not too good with geometry, are you Buffy?"

As the Slayer slipped by on Gwen's right side, the other woman twisted slightly to keep her target in sight. Then, still holding the sword, Buffy slammed one hand into the floor, stopping her slide, and let go with a ferocious kick with her right leg. Her foot caught Gwen's weapon-hand at the wrist. The angle of her arm prevented the woman from exerting much resistance to the force of the kick. Gwen's forearm pivoted up from her elbow, still blasting as it came. Her eyes went wide with realization, too late, that the weapon was about to carve a nasty arc right through the center of her body.

The wall behind her blossomed into a white-hot sun as the beam superheated its surface. Wisps of smoke and steam curled in the air around it and from the ragged wound that made up at least a quarter of the woman's torso. Gwen's body collapsed to the floor in a tangle of loose limbs.

"Geometry? Actually, I do okay, Brainiac," said Buffy.

"NO!"

Buffy looked up to see Xander shocked from his lethargy. "She was my friend, the only person I could trust!" he screamed.

"Xander, she was using you, making you think things that weren't true," Buffy said. Her friend wasn't listening. He and Willow both stepped to the edge of the platform.

Buffy had wondered what Simon would throw at her next. Now she had a pretty good idea. . . .

The vampires attacked.

Tressa kicked one of the Simonized humans, an Asian man in a tuxedo, in the face. He'd just landed a flying spin kick on her, and one of her scarlet lenses had popped loose, lost somewhere in the violent mob. Now she had one hazel eye and one red. It must look awful. Tressa was ticked.

She followed the kick with a flurry of blows to the stomach, each one robbing the penguin of just a little more air. Instinct took over. She grabbed him by the front of his frilly shirt and dragged him close. Her jaws opened wide, fangs glittering. A hand closed on the back of her jacket, dragging her away from the victim. From his blood. She lashed out with a wicked right at whoever had kept her from her prey. An iron grip closed on her wrist.

She turned to glare at Spike. "What the hell are you doing?"

He backhanded her, knocking her to the ground. Then he gave her a fang-filled smile. "Two things, luv. One, if you drink, you die. You filled us in on that tasty little tidbit about fatal indigestion, right? Two, if you drink, you die. See, you promised not to kill or bite these folks until things are back to Sunnydale normal. Break your promise and I break. You. Clear?"

Tressa sprang to her feet. "I'm not afraid of you." She spat at Spike's feet. "Slayer's pet."

Without a word, Spike turned, grabbed two of Simon's converts, and slammed them together. Their heads made a hollow thunk, and they fell to the ground, dazed. Then he backhanded another, throwing the woman several yards away. He shrugged. "Maybe you should be."

A loud cry of "Yeeee Haww" rang out nearby. Billy Bob had jumped to the level above so he could dive down into a crowd of converts, knocking several to the ground. He was swinging his big fists wildly around him, pounding the zombitized Sunnydalers with glee.

Spike thrust his chin toward the cowboy vamp and said to Tressa, "More like that." Then he pounced on a massive convert, obviously a steroid-popping weight lifter before Simon ever came along, that was pounding on the dark-haired vamp named Phillipe. Spike nailed the zombie with a knee to the kidney. The man grunted and turned away from the Canadian bloodsucker.

Spike ducked the ironpumper's grasping hands and kicked him in the chest. "Hey Frenchie," he called to the Canadian. "I didn't sign up for baby-sittin'."

From behind, Phillipe smashed the bodybuilder in the head with a two-handed blow. The man staggered and sank to his knees. Over him, the Canadian vamp locked his dark eyes on Spike's pale ones. "When zis is over," he said quietly, "we will hunt you down. Zen ze

Spike will know the stake, n'est-ce pas? Or perhaps a nice sunbath?"

Spike rolled his eyes and gave a dismissive wave. "Save it, mate. Heard it all before and from better than you."

Just then, Billy Bob crashed into the teetering weight lifter. It took a second for Spike to realize he was thrown, rather than tackling the man by choice. A tall redhead wearing nothing but lingerie was headed directly toward the cowboy, murder in her eyes. Spike intercepted her, raining punches and kicks on her until Billy Bob could get to his feet. While the woman was preoccupied with Spike, Billy Bob grabbed her by an arm and a leg and gave her an airplane ride to the back of the crowd.

Spike gave him a quick nod. "Y'know, I'm beginnin' to think your crowd doesn't like me much."

Billy Bob snarled. "That's 'cause we don't. Only reason you ain't dust is 'cause of this here truce. After that—"

"Yeah, yeah, yeah," Spike interrupted. "Pepe Le Pew already gave me the pep talk." His eyes widened as Billy Bob rushed him, swinging a big fist toward his head. Spike ducked to one side, barely avoiding the blow.

The cowboy's punch crashed into the jaw of a convert that had been ready to brain Spike with a chunk of concrete.

Spike glanced from his erstwhile attacker to the vamp. "How'd you know I was gonna duck?"

Billy Bob shrugged and gave an evil grin. "Either way would have worked."

• • •

When the proprietors of the Sunnydale Mall had installed the escalators, they took an MC Escher approach, zigzagging the various levels so that it was possible to travel all the way up, from level one to level three, with just a few simple turns, transitioning from one stairway to the next.

Xander, fully Simonized as he was, had taken this design approach and run with it. He had transformed the mall into a complex web with automated walkways crisscrossing and going in every direction. It was a confusing maze for those who weren't in the know, the sort of technophobic fogies that always gave Tommy such a hard time. He was the future, and they didn't want to get out of his way.

Tommy seemed to know the new layout as intimately as his favorite Slim Shady lyric. He knew every tempo change, every rhyme scheme—it was his world.

Dawn found it thrilling, racing up and down the high-tech pathways with no one to get in their way. No bad-taste consumers, no overweight security guards, and best of all, no Slayer and her square-edged cronies. She sat on the handrail, dangerously perched over the edge, the ground three stories below her, whizzing by. Tommy's hands were on her hips, hers were on his shoulders. His lips were on hers and, with the air rushing through her hair, it felt like they were flying in each other's arms.

Luna and Big J were hanging back about twenty feet. They were always nearby, but Dawn didn't mind.

It was like they were standing guard. None of them could be too careful.

"I wish this could go on forever," Dawn said, between kisses.

Tommy bit her bottom lip, and then flashed her his pearly whites in that way that still made her melt. She didn't think it would ever stop turning her insides into strawberry jelly.

"It can," Tommy said, "and we'd have you to thank. It's all good, all because of you. You did exactly what I needed you to do, you did it all perfect, so that we could get our best rewards."

Dawn pulled back a little. She looked at Tommy— *really* looked at him, looked beyond his cute smile. She looked at how he was looking at her. His eyes were full of greed. For the first time, she wondered if she was little more than a tool for Tommy, just another *Key*.

No, that was crazy. That was Buffy talking.

But what if it was true? What if Simon had wanted her, and he'd promised Tommy the world if he could get her? What if they were all being played, and she had fallen for it?

"Tommy, why do you like me?" she asked.

"Come on, Boo," Tommy laughed. "You're wicked cute, and you got everything it takes to be the queen to my king."

Dawn pushed him away playfully. "Everything to be your queen? Or everything to make *you* king?"

"No difference, Boo. 'S'all good . . ."

She looked into his eyes again, this time coralling the power inside of her in a way that was entirely o her own choosing. She felt an inner resistance, like a thin wall separating her from Simon and his control was tearing, and then she was looking into his eyes, seeing things very, very clearly . . .

Images formed in his pupils. It was like watching TiVo. She saw Willow cast a spell that turned those innocent women into crazed demons Buffy had no choice but to slay, and saw that Simon had used them just as Glory had tried to use her. He wanted his sword, and he got the blasted thing.

Everyone—everything—was just a means to an end. All his promises were lies.

"I can't believe I was so blind."

"Baby, why you talkin' like that?" Tommy said. "'S wrong, Boo?"

People might call this the splash-of-cold-water-in-the-face moment, but Dawn saw it more as a tidal wave of reality. All the events of the past couple of days were flowing through her mind, knocking over the illusions and leaving only the bare truth in their wake. There was Tommy ditching her outside the electronics store when she didn't want to rob it, Tommy not wanting to tell her his big secrets until she did what he desired, freaking out when she asked questions, all of it.

Tommy in control.

"You manipulated me," she said. "You used me to get in good with Simon. You bastard."

Tommy shot a look to his paladins. Big J and Luna took a few steps closer, their bodies tensed up. They were ready to do whatever Tommy wanted. They were his puppets, too.

The smile was gone. Tommy's jaw was locked, his brow furrowed. "You never know when to keep quiet, do you?" he said. His voice was rough with anger. "Are you stupid?"

"Apparently, I am."

Tommy softened. "Oh, Boo . . . let's not fight. I didn't mean that. You just made me mad, accusing me of those things. You know you're my special kid."

"I might be stupid, Tommy, but I'm not as dumb as you are. You actually think Simon will deliver on his promises. I know enough to see when I'm being used. You don't."

The anger came swiftly. Dawn had seen it before, seen Tommy snap, and she only had the second as his arm cut through the air to see it this time. He hit her across the face with the back of his hand. The force toppled her backward over the side.

There was an instant where she saw the rush, saw Tommy fly away from her, but it was overtaken by the impact of solid ground. She'd fallen three stories, putting a dent into the mall floor. It hurt, but her ego was hurt worse.

There were three loud thuds as Tommy, Luna, and Big J landed all around her, creating their own divots in the floor. Tommy stepped over her, put his foot on her chest. "Where do you think you're going, eh?" he taunted. "You need to stay put, girly-girl. Simon isn't done with you yet."

The metaphor-made-flesh of Tommy putting his foot on her heart hadn't escaped Dawn. It almost was like its presence had stopped the thing from pumping blood, and it pumped bitterness and bile instead. "You said you loved me." She released the words through gritted teeth.

Tommy threw his head back in laughter. "Love? That's your bad, kid. Anyone with a brain knows love ain't real. Power is the only thing that matters."

He put all his weight on his one foot, was standing on her. He lifted his other leg, and Dawn saw the bottom of his shoe coming at her face. Her hand moved on reflex, grabbed his ankle. A quick twist, and she took Tommy off her and slammed him into the floor.

Dawn pulled herself up out of the crater she'd created, ready to pounce on Tommy, but before she could, Luna and Big J were on her. Each of them grabbed an arm, but their grips weren't solid, they were too cocky. Dawn easily twisted her arms out, grabbed them each by the shirt. She was practically on autopilot now, her instincts taking over. She lifted both of her ex-friends off the ground and slammed them together. Their skulls collided. It sounded like when she hit the puck in air hockey.

She tossed both of them aside. Her muscles burned—not because she'd overextended herself, but because she could feel her strength growing.

"You're right, Tommy," she said. "Power is important."

Tommy got to his feet, lunged at her. Dawn easily dodged him, got him into a headlock.

"It's just too bad I have more of it than you."

Dawn delivered a powerfully satisfying quick jab to the bridge of his nose. She was pretty sure it broke under her knuckles, and she heard him gargle on a little of his own blood. Dawn flipped Tommy over, slamming him on his back onto the floor by Luna and Big J. All of them were out of commission.

"If you'll excuse me," Dawn said, "I need to go help my sister."

She raced off, listening for the screams of the crazies to guide her back to the courtyard where High Noon—even though it was the middle of the night—was in full swing. She reached the melee just as Willow and Xander were about to close on Buffy.

"Get Simon!" Dawn called, leaping high into the air and landing hard between Buffy and her former pals.

"Dawnie?" Buffy asked, clearly not sure if her little sis was really back.

"For once, will you just do what I tell you?" Dawn shot back. "And remind me *never* to use this much makeup again? Goth is one thing, but, *yow*—"

Buffy smiled. "You got it, sis."

She launched herself to the platform, where Professor Sands—Simon—was waiting.

Dawn looked back to Willow and Xander, who were about to follow the Slayer. "You guys have to stop! I don't want to hurt you!"

Xander gave her an understanding smile. "It's okay, Dawnie. I don't think you need to worry about that." Casually, he crouched down and touched the floor. He glanced at where Dawn was standing, furrowing his brow as he estimated distances, and then nodded briefly. From the point where he touched, stretching toward Dawn, the floor blackened and reflected diamond-bright flecks of light. As it reached the floor beneath her, Dawn felt her feet begin to slide. Suddenly, it was like trying to keep your balance on ice, except worse. Her arms gestured wildly as she tried to stay upright.

Xander looked toward Willow and gave her a satisfied smile. "Teflon," he said.

Dawn managed to stay on her feet, but there was no way she could move toward them without taking a dive. "Okay, fine. Maybe I can't get to you," she said defiantly, "but you can't get to me, either!"

Willow gestured, waves of bluish light rippling from her hand. Dawn felt herself lifted off the ground like a giant hand had grabbed her. She drifted over to Willow, struggling against the massive, invisible fingers that encircled her chest and waist.

Still hanging a foot or so off the ground, she drifted to a stop just a couple feet from where Willow was standing. The Wiccan shook her head sadly. "Tsk, tsk, sweetie. You didn't really think a slippery floor would keep me from you, did you?"

Dawn frowned. "No, not really." Then she gave a quick smile, very pleased with herself. "But I just realized something!"

Willow cocked her head to one side, amused. "Oh? What's that?"

"This spell is only holding me above the waist." Dawn's right leg shot upward in a ferocious front kick, catching Willow in the face. The witch stumbled backward. Her concentration wavered, and Dawn dropped to the floor. "Big whoops, huh?"

She heard Xander chuckle behind her. "Not bad, munchkin," he said, reaching out to grab one of the thick tendrils of conduit nearby. "Let's try something a little different." Yanking hard, he ripped free a five-foot section of cable from the wall. He lifted one end to eye level and paused briefly, concentrating. The conduit changed. Xander swung the newly wrought bar of metal a couple of times to get the feel for its balance. Then he charged.

Dawn ducked as the bar whistled overhead. She threw a punch at Xander's stomach, twisting her body to put her weight into it. Surprised, he grunted and fell back a step. She followed it up with another, this time catching him across the jaw. Then she threw a vicious side kick. From behind her, she heard Willow call out, "Contego!"

Her foot slammed into an immovable something just an inch from Xander. The force of her kick threw her back from him.

Willow was there to catch her. Spinning the girl to face her, Willow dealt Dawn a backhand blow that sent her reeling.

As she regained her balance, a heavy blow slammed her from the side. She staggered a few steps. Looking up, she saw Xander, a playful grin on his face, menacing her with the metal bar. Willow was walking toward them too. The witch made a clenching gesture with one hand and said, "Excrucio!"

Waves of pain wracked Dawn. She'd never felt anything this bad before. Xander took advantage of her agony to add to it. He swung the bar like a baseball bat, catching her across the stomach and doubling her over.

Struggling to breathe, Dawn clutched at the bar. Shoving Xander away, she tore the weapon from his hand. Then she kicked out, hard, and knocked him to the ground. She wasn't thinking, just functioning on rage and survival instinct. Nearby, Willow raised her hand and began to speak. Dawn spun 360 degrees, the bar whistling in a wide arc around her and struck Willow in the side before she could complete her spell.

A hand closed on Dawn's ankle, squeezing it like a vise. Xander touched her shoe with the other hand, turning the sole from rubber to glue. He neglected to take Dawn's augmented strength into account. She ripped her foot free of the shoot and bashed his hand with the metal bar, forcing him to let go. Willow, one hand held to her side, moved cautiously toward Dawn.

"That's enough," she gasped. A quick flick of her fingers sent the bar flying from Dawn's hand.

Dawn backed away as Willow and Xander came after her. Beyond them, she caught a glimpse of Buffy. It strengthened her resolve. She lunged forward, driving a shoulder into Xander's gut and kicking Willow in the stomach. All she had to do was keep them distracted so they couldn't help Simon against Buffy. She could do that. She had to.

Buffy couldn't *believe* what a hard time the nutty professor here was giving her. All he had to do was stand still so she could lop his fool head off, but he was fighting as hard and with as many tricks as Gwen. Maybe more. It was like he knew all her moves, like he'd been fighting her himself all this time—and, considering the way he seemed to be able to look out through the eyes of others, to see, hear, and control the actions of those he had infected, maybe that was true in a way.

It had all come down to the sword. Buffy had been beaten and bloodied by the professor, and now it seemed she needed a new trick, she had to do something unexpected or else she wouldn't survive this encounter. His arm changed to a heavy steel scythe that he brought down across the edge of her face, the tips biting into her cheek before slicing off a few locks of her hair.

"Oh, not the 'do,'" she quipped. "For that, you're gonna pay!"

"I'm waiting," Simon said. "Why don't you—"

Without a moment's forethought, Buffy spun, kicking his scythe arm away, and brought the Soulsword down on the top of the professor's grinning skull, slicing through him as if he were nothing but a thick, crackling cloud of energy.

Uh-oh . . .

A blinding light filled the room, bringing all the fighting to a screeching halt. All heads turned—and Professor Sands's claim that he was not Simon, that the Big Bad had yet to truly appear, finally made sense.

Before their eyes, the long dead husk that had been Professor Sands fell away, a crude collection of dried skin, cracked teeth, charred bone, scraps of clothing, and Simon took form, a shimmering construct of perfectly ordered energy, a god born from chaos to create order. . . .

"Thank you," Simon whispered, his eyes sparkling with primordial equations. "At last I am free of that fool."

Buffy raised an eyebrow. Simon was a digital Adonis!

"Well, that's a little cuter, anyway," Anya said from the small ring the vampires had formed, back to back, to stave off the attacking Sunnydale superhumans.

"Wait, wait, wait," Buffy said. "Hold up. I thought this whole thing was about power. You needed the Soulsword complete, and in that spot down there you had Xander build. Then, it'd be, 'hey, look at me, I'm transforming the whole world in my image' time."

"No."

"No?"

"All that will come, but there is no hurry, and no shortage of power. Your world is in pain. It wants to be reborn, wants to be remade, and my thralls, your former friends, are all I truly need for that."

Buffy shook her head. "Then . . ."

"This was all about freedom. My being in control, no longer bound to the wills and whims of he whose quest resulted in my ultimate perfect being."

"Think a lot a' yourself, don'tcha there?"

"I have reason to."

Buffy shrugged. "Gotta tell ya, pal, I've done this dance with a lot scarier than you, and it always ends the same—"

"Antwerp," Simon said.

The word rocketed through Buffy's skull like an ice pick doused in flames. She staggered as dozens, no, *hundreds* of voices exploded in her head, each one insisting, with brain-splitting buzz-saw urgency that the Soulsword felt too heavy for her to even carry, let alone lift and use against the digital apparition before her. Then her nerve endings were in rebellion, and Buffy felt as if she were falling into an abyss, one every bit as terrifying and endless as the one that had carried her to her death two years earlier. Yet—she was still in her own body; it was her mind, her conscious awareness, her ability to take control and perform even the simplest of tasks that was slipping down deep into a well from which there might be no return.

"Let me," Simon said, taking the weapon from the dazed Slayer. Buffy felt his touch, crackling like lightning against her numb skin, and found she couldn't move a muscle to stop him, couldn't even blink unless he willed it.

She had been possessed, just like the others. . . .

Below, Xander grasped Dawn's arm as she moved to help her sister, transforming her clothes—what little there was of them—into solid steel. Dawn struggled, the metal starting to bend, and he willed the material that comprised the very floor to rise up and wrap itself around her in shining metal belts, forming an unbreakable sarcophagus around her body.

"It's better this way, Dawnie. You'll see."

"She slipped free," Willow said sluggishly, not

sounding the least bit like herself. There were no funny little Willowisms, no spark at all in her eyes, and that made Xander wonder if this is how he would be before too long, if this was the perfect bliss Rebekah—no, Gwen, had described. A line from a country music song—the music of pain—echoed in his mind: *When you ain't got nothin', you ain't got nothin' to lose . . .*

Willow's head wobbled a bit from side-to-side and her hair fell partially over her face. She did nothing to move it away, and the effect was disturbing, making it look a little like her head was on backward. She muttered, "How could she slip free?"

"Because I still have a brain in my head, you little witch," Dawn snarled. "One with free will and stuff? Try it out."

"No thanks," Willow said in a singsong. "Happier this way."

Xander thought about that. Was she?

Was he?

He looked at all he had created and wondered if he had truly accomplished anything at all . . .

Dawn still struggled, though it was useless; all she could move was her neck and head, he had incapacitated her from the collarbones down. She said, "Will, Xander, listen to me . . . you're not in control. None of you are—*that's* the whole *point.* You've just given up. I did it, too. It's hard to be the one making choices. It's hard because you screw up, then you have to deal with the messes."

"Don't like messes," Willow whispered.

"But the screwups and the messes are yours,"

Dawn said. "You're not some cog in the machine. Life's unpredictable. Fine, bad things happen all the time, and worse can happen at any moment. But good things happen, too, some you can make happen, but only if you have control. You want control. Take it back—from him."

Xander looked up and saw Buffy standing still before Simon as he examined the Soulsword with what might have been a crackling smile of satisfaction and appreciation.

"Rebekah's . . . dead," Xander said, his brow creasing. "And she wasn't even Rebekah, she was some *thing* Simon made, some frontline soldier. He's been manipulating us all along, turning us against Buffy, pulling us apart—"

"No," Willow whispered, her voice faint.

"That's right," Dawn chimed in. "Xander, for the love of God, you saved the world once. Do it again."

He touched his face, where his scars should have been. "But you took them from me. The only reminders . . . how do you still remember?"

"I'm still here," Dawn said. "Xander, every time I see something new, something amazing, every time I feel anything at all, I remember what you did."

Willow stiffened. "Saved the world . . . from me."

"Not you," Dawn said, "a part of you, one you can control without that soulless SOB up there. Willow, please!"

The witch shuddered. "Antwerp," she said. "Antwerp!"

Xander felt nothing; the word had no effect on

him. Gazing into Willow's steadily sharpening eyes, he saw that it was the same for her.

"He's so into the sword he's forgotten about us," Dawn said. "Simon, guys. This could be our only chance!"

Xander felt the power he and Willow shared, and knew that he might never know its like again if he betrayed the one who had forced his way into his life, become his master . . .

Good.

With the flick of his hand, he released Dawn, the metal bindings transformed into water, the steel that had been her clothing returning to its original form.

He looked to Willow, whose eyes were growing dark. She was coming back to herself and then some.

She was unleashing Dark Willow.

Buffy felt the first few bolts of mystical energy pass right through her harmlessly—and watched with satisfaction as they plowed into Simon like munitions fire, causing his glowing form to shriek and stretch and reform around the wounds, the Soulsword falling from his grasp. And just like that, she was free, in motion, scooping up the weapon. Looking down, she saw Willow standing aside from the others, hands open, eyes black, green and black rivers of magickal fire shooting from her hands.

"You say you want a revolution," Buffy quipped, "I think ya got one!"

Buffy sliced at Simon's form, but the sword passed through him harmlessly. There was no soul in this machine, nothing for the weapon to cleave away.

Suddenly, the platform was tipping, and they were falling to the gaping masses below. Buffy landed on her feet, the Soulsword in hand, while Simon's ever warping body, looking a lot like William Hurt at the end of *Altered States,* static and pain—or so it looked to her—hit the ground and lost its form completely for a second or two. Then, liquid metal Terminator style, it pulled itself together, crackling with a crimson glow.

"Does this mean Simon's mad?" Buffy said in a condescending voice, as if she was seven and back in an elementary schoolyard, her first bully bruised and senseless at her feet. Boy, she *loved* taking down bullies . . .

Simon screamed, and the world—or, at least, everyone in Sunnydale—screamed with him. Pain lanced through Buffy's skull, driving her to her knees, causing her head to spin, her flesh to heat up as if it was about to explode from the inside. . . .

And she started to sweat.

"Water!" Dawn yelled from somewhere that had to be a couple miles off. "It got into us through water, and that's the only way it can get out again."

Struggling to her feet, Buffy looked around and saw everyone who'd been infected by the virus out cold except for Dawnie, Xander, and Willow, who were also covered in sweat. Anya, who'd never shown the first sign of infection, was next to Spike and the other vamps. They were backing away, unsure of what to make of this new development.

So was Simon, from the look of him. Willow's assault had left *him* weakened, battered, charred, and *transformed*, and that had clearly surprised and alarmed the otherwise smug techno-god.

"You can't reject me," Simon said. "Not—not unless . . ."

He looked up sharply, and, without warning, sprang at Buffy, his touch searing her shoulder and face as one hand closed over her features, and the other burning hand streaked down to rip the sword from her grasp.

"Weak," he said, forcing her to the ground. "Without a soul, nothing to bind me to the natural world . . . host . . . need a new host . . ."

Planting one foot on Buffy's chest, he pinned her in place, then raised the sword over his head, speaking the first words of what had to be a major league bad mojo incantation.

"Aw, crap!" Buffy hollered. "Will someone please give me something I can hit!"

"I can hit that," Willow said, stepping forward. "Transfer of essence spell, Simon? Problem is, takes quite some time to recite, and no one's getting your back."

Bolts of black lightning ripped from her hands, striking Simon squarely, shredding his perfect form once more and sending him screaming back and away from the Slayer.

It had grown hotter now, and Buffy was so covered in sweat, she could barely see from all the moisture rolling into her eyes and down her face. Her clothes stuck to her. It was like being back in the desert, only at high noon!

Then—it stopped, and she felt a coldness seeping into her, felt Simon's touch, his all powerful control, beginning to exert itself once more. Stumbling to her feet, Dawn by her side, helping her, Xander still at Willow's side, Buffy looked at Simon, who was holding the Soulsword before him, absorbing Willow's blasts, converting them into some kind of energy that was making him strong again.

"Uh, Will? I think we're feeding a fever here," Buffy said.

Only a few yards away, Simon began to laugh. "You had your chance. You could have—"

Suddenly, Dawn bolted from Buffy's side, leaping right at the shining man. "You want a host? Try me on for size!"

"Dawn, no!" Buffy cried, but her warning came too late. Her sister reached for the sword, one hand closing over Simon's, the other grasping the blade itself, and her eyes rolled back into her head, her body violently shuddering as a vortex and reddish-amber light moved between her and Simon, their shapes blurring, becoming one . . .

"You were the one I had in mind all along," Simon said triumphantly. "I had thought to reconvert you into pure power, to use you to unlock the dimensions once more and spread my control through all that is known . . . but this, this is better. You are more than a god yourself, child. More than you could ever imagine—and I will be, too!"

"Don't think so, Sparky," Xander said, falling to one knee, touching his palm to the ground. "Will, I don't know if Dawnie understood what she was getting into or if she was just pissed, but I'm seeing a shot here. How about you?"

The witch nodded. She changed tactics, forming a whirlwind of bright blue-white energy around the merging figures of Dawn and Simon.

"What are you doing?" Buffy hollered. "You'll kill her!"

"No," Willow said, her eyes flickering from normal to pitch black and back again. "Simon needs to be plugged into the natural world, into the source of magic and science, like a computer program in a mainframe, or a tree growing out of the earth. All of us, we're part of that world. The Key—Dawnie— isn't."

Buffy rushed forward and saw Dawn and Simon grappling within the vortex. Her fears of what might happen to her sister were swept away as she saw Dawn haul the Soulsword from Simon's grasp—and run him through with it. His head fell back, his howls lost in the whirlwind that allowed Buffy only tiny glimpses of her sister, who no longer looked like a child, who was strong, a woman, a warrior . . . and the thing that had tried to come between them.

"Dawn can exist, cut off like this," Xander said. "Simon . . . I don't think he'll be so lucky."

Suddenly, the whirlwind faded, just as Simon's crackling, crimson form sparked into nothingness—or so it seemed. The blade of the Soulsword itself, now grasped in Dawn's hand, had taken on the colors of Simon's very essence.

Rushing forward, Buffy kicked the sword out of Dawn's hand, and shattered it. A crimson light exploded before her, and she heard a scream in the back of her brain, Simon's death cry, that was terrible—yet, oh, so right—as everything around them changed.

Light shimmered briefly along the walls. It was almost like washing away a watercolor and finding an oil painting underneath. The strange machines and devices dissolved, flowing into old shapes; kiosks and clothing and mannequins resumed their normal forms and places. Tables and benches formed from the bizarre constructs they had become.

The wave swept through the mall, leaving nothing of Simon's mechanized nightmare. The only sound was the subliminal buzz of the fluorescent lights, so very different from the constant underlying drone that issued from the technological *thing* the mall had been.

In moments, everyone Simon had infected and held under his sway began to return to normal. Buffy and the Scoobs weren't the only ones covered in sweat. Everyone was sweating out the nanites, the dying machines scrambling to leave their now hostile hosts through the pores of their skin.

It was like *The War of the Worlds,* the big nasty aliens scrambling out of their protected pods, looking for someplace safe, but there wasn't any. Without Simon, they had nowhere to go, no purpose to serve. Soon, they would be nothing but a memory.

The formerly possessed people of Sunnydale rose and wandered around, attempting to reorient themselves.

"Look at this," Billy Bob said, nodding toward the groaning, awakening, and disoriented people of Sunnydale, "free dinner, compliments of the—"

"Oh, come on," Buffy interrupted. "You don't really think I'm gonna let you harm one hair on one head, do you?"

"I'd listen to her, mates," Spike said, drawing his own stake. "Because if she misses a couple of you, she's got plenty of us to get her back."

Billy Bob look to his friends and growled.

"Well, boys?" Buffy asked. "What's it gonna be? I'm tired, but I'm not that tired. If you wanna dance, we'll dance . . ."

The vampires murmuring in frustration, Billy Bob finally led them away. "Hugo had the right idea from the start. Greener, bloodier pastures, somewhere else. Anywhere else. Why hang around here and deal with the Slayer when there's a whole world out there she can't touch?"

"Uh-huh," Buffy said, having a feeling that she would see each of these vamps again, probably one at a time, at the end of her stake. They were drawn to Sunnydale, held fast by the Hellmouth.

Or was there another reason?

"I think it's kind of like why all those bad guys stay close to Gotham and Metropolis instead of moving to Florida or Beverly Hills," Xander said, clutching his shoulder where the tattoo had been. "For us, it's guys like Simon who're the Big Bad . . . for them, it's the Buffster. Take her down, or even take her on, and not get staked, and you've got bragging rights forever."

Spike shrugged. "Kid has a point." Then he frowned, rubbing at his throbbing temples. "Can feel the morning coming, gotta toodles, it's been real and it's been fun, but . . . no, hell, it's been a blast!"

He spun and raced off, clearly anxious for the comfort of his private madness, his basement sanctuary beneath Sunnydale High.

Xander, Willow, and Dawn turned to Buffy, their need for forgiveness clear in their eyes.

"God, Buffy," Xander said, his voice choked with emotion. "I don't know what to say. I can't even say I tried to fight it, not until the end . . . everything just seemed to make so much sense until then."

Willow and Dawn looked equally penitent.

"No big," Buffy said. "I felt it, too, and it took me down in two seconds flat. It just reached in and it knew where we were most vulnerable, it knew, on some level, we wanted to surrender control, to not have to face up to our acts. But it didn't know that was just a part of each of us, and when it came down to it, maybe it could get us one at a time, but together . . ."

Dawn eased into Buffy's waiting arms, the sisters embracing as the first stray beams of golden morning light broke on the horizon and filtered through a high window in the food court.

"Together," Dawn said, trembling, but managing not to sob.

Willow and Xander took each other's hands, nodding and smiling. Anya came up behind them, resting her head on Xander's shoulder, stroking Willow's back with the other.

Buffy looked at her friend and smiled. "It's just one of those things, guys. One of the things that makes us all human. And so's this."

They walked away, together again.

A family.

ABOUT THE AUTHORS

Scott Ciencin is a *New York Times* best-selling author of more than 50 books from Random House, Simon & Schuster, and many more. He has written Buffy the Vampire Slayer: *Sweet Sixteen* and cowritten Angel: *Vengeance* with Dan Jolley and the Angel short story, "It Could Happen to You," with his wife Denise. He has worked on the *Jurassic Park, Star Wars, Transformers,* and *Dinotopia* franchises, written for Marvel and DC Comics, and is the author of the popular Vampire Odyssey series and the Dinoverse series (which has recently been optioned as a feature film). He is also the writer of the acclaimed CrossGen Entertainment comic book series DemonWars. He lives in Ft. Myers, Florida, with his beloved wife, Denise.

Denise Ciencin has a Master's degree in Community Counseling and has worked with at risk teenagers, displaced homemakers, the developmentally disabled and many other populations in crisis. She was listed in the 2001 edition of *Who's Who in America.* She has also written in the field of neurology and neurosurgery, and worked with her husband on the majority of his fiction output, providing research, co-plotting and much more. She is the creative consultant of the acclaimed CrossGen Entertainment comic book series *DemonWars. Mortal Fear* is her first novel.